SUNSHINE ON A RAINY DAY

Bryony Fraser has written several books, none of which have been turned into Oscar-winning films, and makes a bolognese that would make the Pope weep.

She lives with her husband and children in a house which may or may not have a snail problem.

SUNSHINE on a RAINY DAY

Bryony Fraser

avon

AVON

A division of HarperCollins*Publishers*
1 London Bridge Street,
London, SE1 9GF

www.harpercollins.co.uk

A Paperback Original 2016

2

First published in Great Britain by
HarperCollins*Publishers* 2016

A catalogue record for this book is
available from the British Library

ISBN-13: 978-0-00-747708-1

Typeset in Sabon by Palimpsest Book Production Ltd, Falkirk, Stirlingshire

Printed and bound in Great Britain by
Clays Ltd, St Ives plc

Acknowledgements

As ever, to J, M, F and P, my magical gaggle of geese. To my breakfast crew, in particular Emma and Leonie, two of the funniest, smartest women I know. To all the childminders in my life, both professional and non-, you are amazing and wonderful and you keep humanity ticking over. Thanks to Rachael, for your firm tone and comfy typing chair. Thank you to my dear ma, for support, kindness, humour, and also for giving me the gift of life or whatever. Thank you all.

Thanks to Leonie, again, for answering all my hair questions; and to Paul Roberts, for answering all my legal questions. My many errors will be despite their wisdom and efforts. Thank you to the kind people of Twitter who answered my multiple – and apparently occasionally alarming – divorce queries.

Enormous thanks to the excellent Helen Huthwaite, for her editorial eye, great understanding and frankly infinite patience. I owe that woman a medal of some sort. Thanks too to the rest of the Avon team, and to Emma Rogers for this beautiful book jacket. Oh, is that my music? Are you playing me out? Fine.

The writing of this book was sponsored by those enormous

Cadbury's bars with jelly beans in, very strong salt & vinegar crisps, bright pink Lidl donuts, gallons of coffee and, when I needed to face the outside world, lashings of MAC's Ruby Woo lipstick. Goodnight.

*This book is dedicated to all the great dames
I know and love.
And also to burritos.*

'They say marriages are made in Heaven.
But so is thunder and lightning.'
— Clint Eastwood

The End

'We're getting a divorce.'

There's a moment, just a single heartbeat of a moment, where no one says anything. Then Dad puts his arm around Mum, and my sister Kat starts laughing, and Liz is standing up, cheering, and Jack's best man, Iffy, is raising his pint to us, and everyone else is chattering like am-dram extras. My other sisters tell off Kat for laughing, and Mum throws her hands up, and at the back of the room someone drops their glass, and Jack and I just look at one another.

Thinking about it again, maybe our anniversary party wasn't the best place to announce it.

ONE

Now

I stirred my rum and Coke with one perfectly manicured finger and took a large gulp. I hadn't smoked since my teens, but I'd have pushed a vicar through a stained-glass window for just a couple of puffs.

'You alright, love?' Dad sat opposite me, nursing his own rum. I blinked at him.

'Besides the obvious?' I said, gesturing with my glass at my outfit, our location.

'We've got plenty of time, Zoe. Have a drink. Take a deep breath. Decide what you want to do.'

That was what I needed to hear, ever since this morning, when I'd woken up in my old bedroom. Or when I was booking marquees. Or when Jack first asked me.

I sighed and stared out of the window. 'Did you and Mum never fancy this?'

Dad shifted in his chair a little. 'Did it ever bother you and your sisters that we weren't married?'

'No! God, no. It was quite cool, actually. But I'm just wondering, now. . . Why did you two never fancy it?' I turned

3

my engagement ring round and round on my finger, gold band. . . sapphire stone. . . gold band. . . sapphire stone. . .

'Things were different. And it just didn't suit us, back then. But we weren't who you and Jack are.'

'That's what I'm worried about.'

'The thing is, love. . . sometimes you just have to do what you think is right.' He took a sip. 'Even if it might seem like the hardest thing in the world.'

I looked at Dad's pale, smiling face, then knocked back the rest of my drink, stood up, and pushed my veil forwards over my face. 'Let's do this, Dad. Let's get me down that aisle.'

We stepped out of the Queen's Head into the cold, thin January sunlight, where the wedding car was waiting for us, driver Al in the front with a *Daily Express* and a bag of salt and vinegar. As he saw us coming out, he started up the engine; Dad tucked me into the back seat, passing me the second-hand Chanel clutch he and Mum had surprised me with last night, as if it were a vaguely radioactive but very precious baby, then sat down beside me, trying not to crumple my outfit.

'Fifteen minutes, Al,' Dad said. 'Do you think we can make it?'

'Nooo problem,' Al shouted over his shoulder, revving the engine and sweeping out into the traffic.

Fortunately, having huge wedding ribbons on your car seems to make other drivers a touch more charitable – there's no way we'd have made it in time otherwise – and we got to the register office to find Jack outside at the front, pacing with nerves at my delay, alongside his best man, Iffy, and my maid of honour, my oldest friend, Liz. My sisters were outside too: Esther watching Jack's pacing with crossed arms and Ava standing with her arms around Kat, who was painting her nails, both of them huddled together in a tiny splash of winter sun, breath hanging in the air. The rest of the wedding party waited inside as the wedding before ours began filing out. As the car drew to a halt, Jack bounded over, reaching in to help me out of the car before it had even come to a full stop.

As soon as I saw him, I thought, *Yeah. This'll be ok.* I watched Dad climb out behind me and give me a thumbs up, and thought again, harder, *This* will *be ok. I'm* sure *it will.*

Then Jack took my hand and smiled at me, and we headed inside.

'You may kiss the bride!'

There was a moment's silence while we leant into each other, then my sisters started whooping as one, and as we kissed the whole register office applauded, and it felt alright for a moment. We pulled away and Jack looked like he was glowing, happiness pouring out of his freckles, and I thought, *I wonder if I look like that?*

Then the registrar said a few more things, the music started up and we were back down the aisle, out into the sunshine and then. . . then we didn't know where we were supposed to go. The car wasn't there – Al wasn't due back for a good while yet. He was probably sitting back in the pub he'd picked me and Dad up from, enjoying a quiet drink before the happy couple spilt prosecco all over the back of his car. We milled about for a while, doubling back on ourselves to watch everyone trooping out, then we had to walk back in and out again so the photographer could get some shots of everyone throwing confetti at us on the stone steps.

My shoes hurt and my eyes felt heavy from the fake eyelashes I'd let myself be talked into, despite my choice of natural hair, plain white jumpsuit and simple faux fur. I was happy enough at this precise moment – all these people! Jack's face! – but I'd wanted us to just keep on walking when we got outside, just hit the road, no looking back until we'd had some time to talk about all of this. I squeezed Jack's hand and he squeezed back.

'Happy?' he said.

'I was about to ask you the same thing.'

We smiled at each other, but neither of us answered.

The photographer moved us around from car park to entrance steps to under the one tree in the vicinity not surrounded by cigarette butts and cider cans, in an attempt to get a satisfactory shot. I tried to avoid Dad's eye, until our driver finally turned up again. I dragged Jack into the car, and we sat back with a sigh, his arm around my shoulders, and we stayed in comfortable, quiet stillness until we reached our reception venue twenty minutes later. Al didn't attempt small talk either, just turned up the heaters in the back a little more.

As we pulled up the drive to our hired manor house, the first arrivals of our wedding party, Jack stroked my handbag with one finger. 'This looks fancy, Zo.'

'Gift from Mum and Dad last night. More Mum than Dad, I expect. In fact, probably more my sisters than either, but still. . .'

'You've always wanted one of those.' I shrugged, smiling, and Jack went on, 'And if everything else goes wrong in life, at least we know we can flog this and live like kings.'

I clutched it to my chest. 'You wouldn't. . .'

'Of course I wouldn't! I wouldn't dare, my dearest.' He picked it up, and looked at it more closely. 'It doesn't matter how expensive it was – you deserve something this gorgeous.'

Jack pulled me in for another kiss and I wondered if we could tell Al to go back down the drive. No one's seen us. We could still escape, just me and Jack. Then I remembered

Dad's words this morning – *sometimes you just have to do what you think is right* – and swallowed the feeling down.

'Looks great, doesn't it?' I said, in an attempt to distract myself from the thoughts running through my head, as the car stopped at the manor house. The marquee beside it, spread out over the small lawns and laid with hard flooring for the dancing later, was swagged with winter wreaths; huge thermal jugs of hot mulled wine waited for our guests under a smaller, flower-laden gazebo near the main entrance to the manor house. I could see through the doors that the photo-booth was set up in the entrance hall; the unseasonal ice cream van played its chimes softly by the outdoor heaters, accompanied by the gentle *pop pop* of the vintage popcorn stand in the marquee. I could hear our pianist already playing soft jazz inside the manor house, so the guests could hear her while they milled about with canapés and cocktails. It was a perfect wedding, copied dutifully from the wedding magazines and Pinterest boards everyone had sent me. Hadn't I done it right?

Jack got out of the car and held the door open for me, then suddenly swooped me up in his arms and half ran with me towards the hot wine.

'Quick! First toast. While everyone else is tagging along behind in the bus.' He held out a glass to me before taking one for himself. A passing waitress smiled at us both – the happy couple. 'It's going to get busy any minute, and we're probably not going to be able to talk until tomorrow. But I just wanted to say how amazing you look, how amazing this is, and how amazed I am that you're now my wife.'

'Don't blow your whole speech.'

'I mean it, Zoe. Sometimes I didn't. . . I didn't always know how we were going to end up, even though I always knew I wanted to be with you. And to look at us today, to look at all this. . .' He was welling up.

I chinked my glass against his. 'Happy wedding day.'

He smiled, and replied, 'Happy wedding day, wife.'

I drank my wine in one gulp, burning my throat.

The rest of the reception was a blur. I noticed that Liz, my maid of honour, was there without her boyfriend. She hadn't said that Adam couldn't come, but she didn't mention his notable absence, so neither did I, sensing it wasn't something she wanted to discuss. Instead she cooed over my bag, gasping as I explained that Mum and Dad had insisted the bride should have a special gift on her wedding day. Esther, my responsible, married eldest sister, who had our dad's smaller stature and our mum's gentle stubbornness, had been clapping her hands with glee when Dad handed me the box last night, having received a Céline bag (also second hand) when she'd got married four years ago – it had swiftly become her nappy bag when William was born a year later. Ava, taller and quieter, the next eldest, looked on with peaceful, happy excitement, while Kat, the youngest of us four by four years, bold and foot-stamping ever since Mum and Dad brought her home from the hospital, had stood with folded arms and bright purple pursed lips while I'd lifted the layers of tissue paper to find an old, impossibly soft, black Chanel 2.55 handbag.

'Now, it's not brand new,' Dad had said, apologetically.

We'd all laughed. 'Dad! It's beautiful. Thanks, Mum. Thanks, Dad.'

I hadn't expected it. My wedding to Jack seemed so different, somehow, to Esther and Ethan's, that I'd had no idea I'd get any kind of present. Their wedding had been all any of us had talked about for months – a happy event which had been a given since they'd got together – but ours just seemed to have arrived, surprising even me. I didn't think anyone would take it as seriously, somehow. And yet this bag! I'd slept with it on my bedside table, intending it to be the first thing I saw when I woke up that day, but in the end that honour had fallen to the breakfast tray Mum had brought up to me, with her coral necklace from her own wedding day on the side plate next to the boiled egg.

The wedding party bubbled on: speeches and toasts to us and to absent loved ones, tears, food and dancing, hugs and good wishes from some of Jack's employees at Henderson's, his shoe shop. All the while I was aware of Dad watching us, and Liz too, each wearing concerned faces when they thought no one was looking. My sisters were too busy to notice; flirting with the bar staff, even Esther, the Sensible One, hugging her toddler to one hip and ogling one of the hot barmen.

Mum hugged me whenever she walked past, kissing me and saying how wonderful this whole day was, how perfect, how sorry she was that Grandma wasn't alive to see it, but how much she would have loved it all – loved both me and Jack. Then she'd start to cry again, leaving Dad to come and steer her away and I would look at whoever I was with and laugh, loving my mum's easy emotions.

At one point I looked over to see Benni, my boss, on the dancefloor with Iffy, making wild jigging circles and calling out, 'Chidinma! Philip! Get on here!' as she tried to lure my parents into dancing too; Benni's wife Gina sat with Liz, watching them all and laughing fondly, enjoying a night off from her and Benni's twin boys. Later on, Benni and Iffy took the mic from the DJ to croon 'Total Eclipse of the Heart' at Jack and me. We joined in, far from embarrassed at their drunken serenade – it didn't seem too different to an average night out for us. Liz was unusually quiet without her plus one; she'd not mentioned anything to me recently about problems between them, but maybe she'd thought the run up to today wasn't the time. I wanted to return the countless favours of support and tact she'd given me over the recent months, but it felt like it would have to wait.

Jack and I met occasionally throughout the rest of the reception party. We hadn't wanted a first dance, so we mostly all danced together in a big group with our friends. I saw him at the bar; he kissed me while I was talking to his aunt. Then suddenly it was midnight, and our carriage awaited. I didn't want to go, didn't want to leave the moment of this party, didn't want to leave my sisters and our friends. I didn't want this party to be over, to face what days and months and years came next. I loved Jack, but I didn't want to start married life.

A cheering crowd lifted us both up and carried us to our wedding car, driver Al looking more hangdog than ever, his vintage Triumph covered in foam and balloons. Whistles, hollers and cheers followed us back up the drive.

'I'm sorry about your car,' I shouted forwards to him. 'About the foam and stuff.'

He waved his hand over his shoulder. 'Don't worry, love, it's all covered by the costs. Cleaning's part of the package – it happens every time.'

Jack gave me a look.

'What?'

'Nothing. Nothing. Doesn't matter.' He sighed. And I'd done everything I could to act the happy bride today. 'Did you have a good time, Zo?'

I smiled at him. 'When do I not have a good time at a party?'

'Good. Me too.'

At the hotel we were too tired to do much more than sign in, which Jack did with a flourish and a grin. When I looked at the sheet, he'd filled in *Mr and Mrs Bestwick* and I felt a different kind of exhaustion when he gave me a jokey wink. Up in our room, we lay on our bed, vases of flowers from friends and family all over the sideboard and dressing table, and I reached out and put my hand on the small of Jack's back. Then, with the lights still on, fully dressed, we both fell fast asleep.

The next morning we woke up to blinding light and sixty missed calls on my phone. We'd slept right through the bacon sandwich brunch for all our guests, and were being called by reception on the blaring landline to gently enquire whether we'd be checking out shortly or staying for another night. I was all for staying for another – hide away a bit longer, make the most of this massive bed and giant bathtub – but Jack reminded me that we'd blown our budget with even one night here. We'd debated for ages about whether to go home after the reception, back to the flat my parents had helped us buy, full of wedding presents that had already been delivered. But we'd thought we'd splash out because *that's what you do, right?* You lose your mind and do everything that's out of character and out of budget. And if for a moment you wonder if really that's the right decision – to get outfits that cost more than a white tiger, and the hotel room that you won't even notice because you were *so* tired and drunk and emotional you could have spent the night on a park bench and not noticed the difference – well, you just take a deep breath and repeat *But It's My Wedding*, and stamp your feet to really get into the role.

I stripped off my wedding jumpsuit and climbed into the shower, while Jack rang our families and packed up our stuff. By the time I'd got out, rubbed in some coconut oil and got into my favourite jeans, headscarf, soft sweater and Nikes, reception was calling again with a slightly less gentle enquiry. Jack said the Bacon Brunch had gone ahead without us at my parents' place, and everyone had had a great time. Both his dad and my parents were fine, understood completely, and everyone sent their love.

After finally managing to check out, wrapped in scarves and coats against the cold, we hit the Tube to discover that the only free seats were at either end of the row. Jack sat me down with the bags then turned to the man next to me.

'Sorry, mate, would you mind taking the seat at the end? We only got married yesterday, and I'd like to sit next to my wife.' He giggled a bit as he said the final word.

The man beamed at me, saying, 'Sure! Congratulations, guys!' in a sunny Australian accent, but I'd already covered my eyes with my hands and was trying not to set the carriage alight with my blushes. *It's fine*, I thought, *it's fine, he's just being romantic, he's just excited, it's fine, it's fine, it's fine.* One day I'm sure I'll get used to that word. *Wife*.

Everyone was watching us now, so I was too self-conscious to start up a conversation with Jack. We sat in a sleepy silence, holding hands, bags at our feet, watching everyone watching us. At Seven Sisters, we stepped out and heard someone call, 'Good luck, newlyweds!' and a few people in the carriage laughed. I squeezed Jack's hand, trying to swallow my nausea.

'Do you remember when we used to use actual words to talk to each other instead of hand actions?' he said. That got a laugh out of me, and he said, 'Thank god! I thought one of us might have had a stroke and forgotten English. Right. Lunch. Pub? Or home?'

We chatted about the various options, and it felt like normality again, the two of us planning meals and making plans. In the end, we picked up bits for lunch from the shop on the corner, and by the time we'd got to our front door I'd forgotten completely about what was waiting for us inside.

Boxes and boxes and boxes of *stuff*. Bedding, picture frames, coffee cups, lamps, a blender, an espresso machine, vases, cushions; piled up on our sofa, the floor, the kitchen counters, even balanced on the big hatch between kitchen and living room. Like the whole of the *Generation Game* conveyor belt had been carrying its load into our flat. Upstairs Jan, the neighbour above us in the top half of the house, had also left a bunch of flowers and a card for us at the door, and we added them to the pile like a tiny cherry on a huge, sprawling cake.

'I'd forgotten this lot was here. Do you remember asking for all this stuff?' I said.

'Not really. That day was a bit of a blur. Remind me why we unpacked it all already?' Jack was scratching his beard, wide eyed at everything filling our living room.

'This cushion, though. I don't even remember seeing it, let alone wanting it.' I picked up a needlepoint cushion with a white terrier picked out in murky shades of beige and brown.

'Or this vase.' Jack held up another vase. 'Or that one.' We worked for a few minutes, going through the gifts and lining everything up on the kitchen hatch and along the coffee table. We stared around us. Eventually, I said, 'Hang on, why would we want. . . seven vases?'

We looked through everything around us, at the plaid garden kneeler and the brass rabbit ornament.

'This isn't ours,' we said at the same time. The giddiness and bustle of the upcoming wedding had meant we'd opened and unpacked every box without really noticing what was in there; it was only the coffee maker which looked familiar from our own list.

'Mmm. Can we keep the espresso machine, though? Didn't we want one of those?' Jack looked at me pleadingly.

'Hell yes. We'll claim it as compensation for our missing gifts.'

While Jack made us a barrel of coffee each, I started on

the sandwiches: bacon, avocado and feta, slathered with hot pepper chutney. My sore head and tiredness got the better of my manners, and I'd almost finished mine by the time Jack brought the coffees to the sofa.

'That coffee machine was literally harder to set up than an actual spaceship.'

'Literally.'

'Having flown many, I'm confident in that comparison.' We peered into our mugs, staring at the black speckles scattered through the frothed milk. 'I might not have entirely mastered it quite yet.'

'Tea?'

'Tea.'

I swallowed my last bite of sandwich, headed into the kitchen and boiled the kettle. Hungover-peckish, I opened the fridge.

'Oh my god!'

Jack leant in through the hatch. 'What? What's wrong?'

'Look!'

Inside the fridge was the whole top half of our wedding cake, in all its creamy, buttery, sugary glory – one of my sisters must have dropped it off this morning, before we'd got home. Jack gulped down the sandwich he was holding, pulled out the cake, and said, 'Right, you keep doing the teas, and I'll get the forks. Do we need plates?'

I shook my head at him with mock horror. 'Plates? Please, who are we, the Queen?' Within five minutes we were back on the sofa, giant mugs of tea in our hands, forking wodges of cake from the platter. As we lazily watched *The Antiques Roadshow*, I cuddled up under Jack's arm.

This was better. This was the married life Jack had promised me.

He started laughing.

'What?'

His eyes creased up with how funny this genius thought was, and soon he was barely able to get the words out.

'I bet you're thinking. . . how if this is married life. . . it really suits you!'

'That's it? That's your searing insight of the day? How much I like lying on the sofa, eating cake and watching TV with you? Well done for having registered the basic facts of my life preferences.'

'Is this how you always saw yourself when you were grown up?'

'Unlike every other normal child, I didn't spend my youth fantasising about the chosen decor and potential TV habits of my adult self. I was too busy getting skinned knees and crushing on the local lifeguard.'

'I hope you'll give me his name so I can send him a note letting him know he lost his chance.'

'Romance, thy name is Jack. I think he was gay, anyway.'

'Wow, he really did miss his chance.'

'Listen, much as all this talk of the homosexual lifeguards of my childhood is turning me on, shouldn't we be consummating our marriage or something?'

'Is that an invitation?'

I responded by stripping off as quickly as possible, despite my sore, sugar-rushing head.

'Do you remember when we used to worry about sophisticated chat-up lines?'

'Jack, I said "I do". What more do you need?' I started trying to pull his trainers off.

'You're such a femme fatale.'

'I'll give you femme fatale.'

'Ooh, will you?' Jack's face lit up.

'If you mean will I put on red lipstick, then yes, I'm willing to do that. If you mean literally anything else, then no, unless you do it too.'

15

'I knew married life was going to change you.'

I stopped trying to pull his other trainer off.

'Yeah, you've got me. Now, are you going to get this kit off or am I going to have to go and visit my local pool for any heterosexual leftovers from my teenage years?'

Jack pulled his top off. 'You had me at heterosexual leftovers.'

We couldn't afford a honeymoon. Dad had said, Dad-like, that *he'd* never even been out of the country until he was in his thirties, which made Mum narrow her eyes at him until he'd offered us another cup of tea and a biscuit. Friends and family sent hampers and vouchers, and the three days after the wedding were spent mostly wrapped around each other in our flat, occasionally moving upright to get more smoked salmon or chocolate eclairs or boar pâté down us, or to tighten the curtains against the cold January winds. But just as I started worrying I might be coming down with either gout or scurvy, the honeymoon was over, and we were due back at work the next day.

It was a cold Monday morning as Jack handed over my packed lunch, kissing me goodbye outside our front door. 'Back to school. Have a good day, wife.' I was still uncomfortable with that. I'd swallow it down, though, just like that second tier of wedding cake.

'Have a good day, dearest husband of mine.'

We both made mock-vomiting faces, kissed again, then went in our separate directions: me a bus ride away to Walker High School, the secondary where I'd been teaching Science for the last four years, and Jack to the shoe shop he owns and designs for, all slick white spaces and open brickwork and handmade shoes strewn artfully around.

When I got into the Science office, I immediately set eyes on a tray of bubbling prosecco laid out on a table piled high with cards and gifts, with balloons sellotaped to each corner. No one was about. I walked around to the small kitchenette, where everyone was clustered around something on the other side of the room.

'Happy New Year. Is it someone's birthday?' I asked, making everyone scream in surprise. Our lab assistant, Miks, yelped and knocked the cake they'd all been huddled around off the counter. We all stared at the mush of icing and crumbs on the floor, the candles still somehow burning as they lay at odd angles from the side of the pile.

'You're early! You're never early, darling!' wailed Benni. 'These guys just wanted to do something to mark your wedding—'

'Since not all of us made the exclusive guest list,' Miks interjected, eyes rolling cartoonishly.

'And *I* said, Oh, don't worry, Zoe's never early, we've got plenty of time, and now. . .'

We all stared at the pile on the floor again.

'I solemnly swear never to be early to work again.'

'Better,' said Benni. 'Darling, you know I find it immensely unnerving when you get all Motivated Teacher. Or is this Jack's magical influence? Has marriage finally uncovered your work ethic?'

'If my work ethic involves eating wedding cake from unlikely places – *not like that*, Miks – then you might just be right. If you mean am I likely to be willing to stay until 9 p.m. to attend a four-hour school performance of *Annie* for you, then no, I'm afraid my marriage certificate has not yet altered the fact that I still prefer home to school. Just. Much as you're the best boss in the world, Benni.'

Benni, head of Science, smiled at me, then gave me a hug. 'Don't tell the Head about the prosecco. Anyway, I've given them a blow-by-blow of the actual wedding, so everyone can pretend they were actually there. I told them about the ceremony, your outfit, how drunk the priest got, how you punched a barman, how that fire spread so fast—'

'I'm sorry you guys couldn't all be there,' I laughed.

'*You didn't invite us!*' called Miks.

'But that's it now. We eat this cake, we open these gifts – thank you, by the way – and then all of life is as before. Ok?'

A look passed between Benni, Miks and the dozen other Science teachers and technicians.

'What? What's happened?'

'Nothing's happened,' soothed Benni. 'But, darling, we'd all just like to take a moment to remind you what a great sport you are.'

'Oh god.'

She led me back around to my space in the Science office, where the computer screen, keyboard, back and top of my desk were papered with 'Mrs Bestwick' signs, in a hundred different fonts and colours. I wanted to cry and set the desk alight immediately, but I threw my hands up and shrieked, laughing and shaking my fist at them. I left most of it there for the rest of the day.

I managed to escape comment throughout the day, but in my Year 11 class after lunch, my most promising and least delivering student put her hand up and said, 'Miss Lewis! Miss Lewis! I heard you got married, Miss.' At least my students didn't think it was funny to call me by Jack's surname, even if he did.

There was a buzz around the classroom: teachers aren't supposed to have lives, eat meals and go shopping, let alone get married, which is so inextricably linked with sex. The thought of your teacher *doing it* with someone is enough to start a riot.

'I did, Michaela.'

'Why, Miss?'

Of all the questions, this was the last one I was expecting. I'd expected a barrage of *Did I take a helicopter? Did I go in a carriage? Did I have a bridezilla meltdown? Was there a fight?* But this. . .

'That's enough, Michaela. This is a Physics lesson, not a Facebook status update.' The class hissed its approval.

'Ooh, you got *burnt* by Miss. . .'

And that was the only mention I got all day. I felt like I had somehow got away with something.

By six o'clock, everyone had gone except me and Benni. She came over and perched at the edge of my desk, fingering the tattered 'Mrs Bestwick' print-outs.

'You did well.'

'Did I leave them up too long?' I asked, indicating the celebratory remnants strewed around my desk. 'Should I have taken them off sooner?'

'No, that would have been too obvious. If I had medals to give, you'd be next in line, darling. After my mother, obviously, and possibly after my poor sons, but you'd certainly be on the shortlist.'

'If I open my mouth can you tell me if I've any teeth left at all, or just stumps?'

'It's fine. People just like to make assumptions, particularly after something as black and white as a wedding. Give it another week and they'll all be expecting the patter of tiny feet.'

'And "oh my god, your babies would be beautiful". . .'

'I know, I know, we had the same. But with added, "And which one of you would be the mum?"' She took my hand. 'And yes, I know you haven't changed your name. It was just Miks's little joke. Ok?'

'Yes, boss.'

'Now, are you coming for a Monday night cocktail or do you need to ask your hubby for permission?'

'You might have been my "mentor" – your words, not mine, I might add – since I started teaching, but—'

'If you don't know I'm joking then I'm going to have to put you up for a very long and boring disciplinary procedure.'

'Drinks are on you then.'

'Drinks are on me, darling.'

It was half ten before Benni and I had finished at the bar – departmental stuff had come up that required intense discussions over many glasses of melon daiquiri – and my entry into the flat was noisier than I'd intended. *Smash!* The front door. *Crash!* A low bookcase falling over. *Crunch!* The pile of recycling I was going to lie on for juuust a second.

'Shhh,' I recommended.

'Zo, is that you?' Jack called from the sofa.

If I stay quiet, he won't know it's me, I thought.

'Zo, if that's not you, it's a woefully clumsy burglar and I'll need to actually get up and do something about it.'

Shhh, I thought again.

Suddenly, Jack was standing over me.

'Come on, you, let's get you to bed.'

'Bossy,' I muttered, as he pulled me up and half walked, half carried me to bed. He removed my clothes, but as he tried to tuck me in I wrapped my arms around him, suddenly amorous.

'Stay with me,' I groaned.

'I'll get you a pint of water, then I'm coming to bed, ok?'

'I don't want a pint of water, I want you.'

'You'll want a pint of water when you wake up in three hours' time, Zo.'

'Yes, but I want you *now*,' I said, closing my eyes to give them a rest.

When I woke up again at 2 a.m., my mouth tasted like the sole of my shoe, and Jack was snoring next to me. There was a time, even a month ago, when he would have been with me tonight. He'd have been out, I'd have been out, we'd have eventually met up on our routes and we'd only just be getting in now. There might even have been dancing, Monday night be damned.

I wanted to wake him up and ask him why that hadn't happened tonight, but when I rolled over into a sitting position I realised I wanted to die instead, and any heart to hearts would just have to wait until I was able to sit up without vomiting, or had actually died, whichever came first. In my Magic 8-Ball brain, I thought about work tomorrow and came up with 'OUTLOOK NOT SO GOOD'. I'd email Benni and see if she'd mind telling the Head I'd passed on.

At 7 a.m., Jack was shaking me, shouting and shining a torch into my eyes like a friendly interrogator. I groaned and pulled the pillow over my head, but he kept on. Eventually his words translated, and I heard, 'Zo, wake up, you're going to be late. I've made you a coffee and toast. Do you want me to turn the shower on?'

'What the ever-loving fuck is this?' I groaned again, trying to turn away without having to move my body. 'What are you doing?'

Jack lifted the pillow off. 'Zo, time to get up. You've only been back a day. You can't call in sick.'

'I was out with Benni, she'll be the same.'

'It doesn't matter. Come on, once you're up you'll feel much better.'

I pulled the pillow over my head again. Jack pulled it off again, and tried to lift me up.

'Jack, just *piss off*, alright?'

There was a shocked moment of silence, then Jack lowered me down and put both his hands up. 'Fine. Fine. I'm off to work, you do what you want.' I caterpillared under the duvet and heard him pack up and slam the front door. I'd made one discovery already that morning: if there was ever a hangover tip to make you feel even worse, it was being a total bastard to your boyfriend. *Husband.*

I knew he was right though, and after a minute or two of checking my limbs were still attached, I crawled on all fours to the bathroom, threw up for a while, then got into the shower. I found a coffee and banana under the mirror when I got out again, once the water was running completely cold.

In the kitchen, Jack's toast for me was also cold in the toaster. I mashed the banana on top with a little cinnamon, and sat chewing thoughtfully until the shakes had subsided. This was a bad one. I'd already sent a text to Benni to warn her of the state I was in (I'd just got a *Ugh. Me too* in response), but I needed something more than just a text for Jack. Looking at the scattered remains of my breakfast, I realised that this was why I loved him – his thoughtfulness, his commitment, his kindness. But this morning I had a killer hangover and I just wanted to lie in bed and suffer. Why couldn't he just leave me be, if only for five more minutes?

I'd overreacted, but I couldn't bear being treated like a wayward child by someone insisting on what was best for me.

Staggering through the school gates as the bell rang, I was sure we could fix it.

TWO

Seven years earlier

Zoe sat at the bar and picked at her nail polish, something both Ava and her mum told her not to do whenever they caught her. She flaked off big chunks of deep blue onto the napkin on the copper-topped bar, then folded the napkin over to keep them from scattering. She took another swig of her salt-rimmed margarita and checked the clock on the wall. He wasn't coming.

She'd had to be convinced about this date in the first place, by the Chemistry course-mate who had set her up with this guy at a recent party – yes, he was good-looking, but she hadn't got a good vibe from him. Not at all. When they'd been introduced, he'd given her the kind of smile that made her feel like a mirror, that he was just looking at her to get a tab on how great he looked that day. And when he'd nodded a casual *Yeah, sure* to her course-mate's suggestion that he and Zoe should get a drink some time, she'd wanted to back away from the whole thing, hitting undo.

She might only be twenty-two, but she knew enough to listen to her gut on things like this. Glancing round the empty bar, she realised she'd just learned that the hard way. But she hadn't been on a date in ages, and if nothing else, she was reasonably sure he'd have put out at the end of the night. She sighed, and drained the final dregs from the glass.

The barman took the glass and the folded paper napkin, and wiped down the counter. 'Another?'

Zoe realised she felt slightly giddy from her margarita.

'What do you recommend?' She folded her chipped finger-nails inside her fists and rested them on the bar.

'Maybe a better date, from the look of things? Otherwise, I make a mean Bloody Mary.'

She speared three olives in the little dish by the napkins, and ate them, one by one.

'I feel pretty bloody. Go on then. Please.'

He didn't talk while he was making her drink, but once he'd served it he stayed at her end of the bar and chatted to her, in between serving other people. It was a quiet Tuesday in October, and there weren't that many people to serve, so they were mostly talking. He was a student too, doing a design degree. He was into shoes, he said, planning to make a break from behind this bar at some point to actually start his own shoe shop, shoes that he'd designed and created himself. She asked him if he'd make his escape tonight. He said he was now considering hanging around for a better offer. She said she was considering making one.

The next morning, Zoe woke up to a strange and empty bed. Fair enough. She'd only had one more drink after the Bloody Mary and could remember everything well enough to know she'd be disappointed that this was only a one-night thing, but it was a pity he hadn't even hung around long enough for a little small talk, perhaps a brief replay of last night. She stretched, got up, dressed – debated leaving a note, but thought there was little point. She found her handbag and shoes – one under the bed, one balanced on the dripping tap in the corner sink – attempted to shape her hair into something presentable, and headed out, pulling the door until it locked, heading down the corridor that looked just like every college hall corridor in the country, and out into the street. Her bus arrived almost immediately and she headed back to her student house to take a long bath and have a good long think about what she'd done. In fact, what they'd both done.

Five minutes later, there was a soft knock-knocking at the bedroom she'd so recently vacated. A key in the door, and the barman opened it from outside, juggling two coffees and two bags of pastries.

'I didn't know what you wanted, so I got one of—'

He stopped, saw the empty bed, the vanished shoes and bag.

'Bugger.'

Two weeks later, Zoe stood waiting outside a workshop at the design college with a tote bag over one arm. After a quarter of an hour, the doors opened and the students streamed out.

'Hey!' she called. Half the class looked around. 'Barman!'

He joined the half of the class who were looking, and smiled. 'It's Jack, actually,' he called back.

She nodded. 'Jack. Ok. Bit out there, but I can work with it.'

He walked over, stood in front of her. 'Zoe.'

'You remembered.'

'I did.' He smiled a little more. 'I remembered where you were at uni, too, and your course, and I was actually going to come and find you there, but I thought how would I actually find you—'

'There are literally three black students on my whole course.'

'And I didn't know if it would be a bit weird, me just pitching up at your lectures—'

'In front of my whole class? Like *this*?'

'Yeah – oh, no, I mean – this is different. It's charming when you do it. But it's a bit weird if this barman you just had a one-night stand with turns up, even if he's brought flowers—'

'You were going to buy me flowers?'

'Yeah, of course. I mean, I had such a great time with you. And then you'd bolted, and I didn't really know how to find you.'

'Again. Literally three black students on my whole course.'

'But here you are!'

'Ruining our romantic reunion.'

Jack laughed. 'A little bit. And I don't even have your flowers.'

Zoe opened her tote bag. 'But I have shoes. Can you fix them, please?'

He took the bag and offered his arm. 'But first. A drink?'

That second date was as good as their first, if that bar conversation could be counted as their first. For their second date, they made an effort: Jack wore a new jacket, Zoe wore the heels Jack had fixed for her, and the pair of them left their film early. They never made it to their restaurant booking, but later found one of the few obliging pizza delivery places still willing to deliver to university halls.

The third date was with Jack's parents.

On the morning after their pizza-in-bed date, Jack had waved Zoe off at the bus stop and headed back to his room to get ready for his day. Zoe, rummaging in her bag on the top deck of the bus, found that she'd picked up his student ID by mistake. She looked at her watch. Dammit, she didn't have time to return it now, but she'd swing by and drop it off later.

By the time she was free, it was early evening. She knew she could get buzzed in by anyone, and she'd just slip it under his door if he wasn't about. Outside his room, however, she could hear muffled voices. She knocked. Jack opened the door in nothing but a towel and face mask, and he stared at her for a moment before he gave a small scream.

'What are you doing here?'

She held out his ID. 'Sorry. I picked this up this morning. Good to see you too, Jack.' Zoe raised an eyebrow.

'Who's that, Jack?' A woman's voice came from behind the door.

Zoe crossed her arms in front of her and took a deep breath.

'Jack?' The same voice, more insistent.

Jack had jammed his foot on the inside of the door, and it was shaking with the effort of the person behind it trying to open it wider. 'Look, can you just – stop being so silly – can you—'

Zoe switched to her other hip and re-crossed her arms. The door was finally yanked open.

A middle-aged couple stood in Jack's room, the man stretched out on Jack's bed reading the *Telegraph*, the woman, slight and well-dressed, with glossy brown hair, her hand still on the inside door handle.

'Well, Jack,' the woman said. 'Aren't you going to introduce us?'

THREE

Now

When Jack got back that night, the flat was filled with the smells of jollof rice, his favourite of my mum's dishes and one of the few I managed to get even close to Mum's quality. I'd lit candles, drawn the curtains (you only make that mistake once – thanks to one amorous night when we forgot to close them, our blushing neighbours opposite now ran like rats whenever they saw us) and poured the wine. As he dropped his bag and coat, he said, 'Well, someone should have hangovers more often, if this is the result.' I laughed, then he added, 'I thought we were married already – do we still have to keep trying to seduce each other?'

I didn't laugh, although I knew it was a joke; it seemed too close to what I'd been worrying about in the small hours this morning. Why couldn't we keep seducing each other? What was the alternative – that we'd come back each evening to find our other half in an egg-stained fleecy dressing gown watching *EastEnders* and picking the hardened bits of a Pot Noodle out of the bottom of the cup?

Jack saw my face and came over. 'I'm sorry,' he said, and kissed me.

I sighed. 'No, I'm sorry. I was doing this to apologise for this morning, and now you're apologising to me.'

'Ok, we're both sorry. Although not as sorry as you looked this morning—'

'Thank you.'

'But we're both sorry.'

'I'm sorry for being so vile this morning.'

'And I'm sorry for the ill-judged joke. This smells and looks amazing.'

'And for trying to lift me out of bed?'

'Excuse me?'

'And you're sorry for trying to physically lift me out of bed this morning, even though I didn't want you to?'

'Zo, you were going to miss a whole day!'

'Of course I wasn't! I made it to school.'

'Eventually. I didn't know that though, did I?'

'You didn't ask. You can just take it as read from now on that you're free to treat me as an adult, able to make my own decisions about my own life, ok?'

'I know that you're capable, I just don't know if you always do.'

'I'm twenty-nine, Jack, I managed an awfully long time without you telling me what to do.'

My last comment hung in the air between us.

'I'm sorry. Again. I'm still hungover, and you know it makes me a bastard. Let's just stop. Let's have this nice meal, and. . . who knows, maybe I'll get lucky.'

'Maybe you will.' Jack brought our glasses over, still misted with cold, and cheers-ed.

When I arrived home the next day, our post was waiting on the table; Jack must have picked it up. Junk mail, junk mail, junk mail – and then one that was addressed to 'Mr and Mrs Bestwick'. Jesus Christ, the ink wasn't even dry on our marriage certificate yet. How the hell had – what was this, an insurance company – managed to get our names? Was this it, now? The choice to keep my name – which, let's not forget, is an absolutely fucking absurd thing to even make a choice about – didn't even matter, because everyone would just assume I was Jack's chattel, to be named and catalogued along with his other possessions. This was why I'd always felt so uncomfortable with the idea of marriage. There wasn't anything wrong with it, per se, it's just that all the assumptions and faff that came with it, including the name-changing rigmarole, wasn't something I'd ever seen myself having to put up with. And yet here I was.

I tore it in half with an *ugh* of despair. Jack came around the corner, carrying two cups of tea with a plate of salted-honey toast on top. 'Bad day at school?'

'No! Good day. I love my work. And I should clearly enjoy it while society still permits married women to actually hold down jobs that men could be doing.'

'I'm sensing. . . this isn't about your day at work.'

I held out the two pieces of the letter. 'Awww,' Jack said in a mock-touched voice. 'That's nice. How did they know?' He looked at me, saw I wasn't smiling, then said, 'No, that is creepy. I get your *ugh* now.' He screwed his face up. 'How did they know?'

I relaxed slightly, realising that this wasn't Jack's fault. 'I'm feeling slightly. . . disappeared when that happens.'

Jack put on a soft, exaggeratedly soothing voice. 'Does Hulk want to smash the patriarchy?' I nodded. 'Does Hulk want to come and smash the patriarchy on the sofa with some tea and toast?' I nodded again. 'Does Hulk want to do that on the sofa while a man cooks and cleans tonight as a token gesture of patriarchy-smashing?' I nodded again, smiling and giving him a kiss on the nose as I took the plate and a mug and lay full length on the sofa.

Taking a bite of the toast, I said, 'How's your week going?'

'Fine. Good. Nice and busy today, which is unusual for this time of year.'

I could hear cupboards being opened and closed as Jack got things out to make dinner.

'Jonjo thought it was funny to tease me about not being allowed out anymore, when I said I wanted to get back here tonight after closing up.'

I pulled a face. 'Jonjo's a dick.'

Jack stopped, and looked at me through the kitchen hatch, mouth agape. 'Oh my god! That's exactly what I said to him.'

'We're like two peas in a pod.'

Jack laughed. 'Well anyway, besides the small matter of me abusing my employees, everything's been fine. January sales still going well.'

'We're still going through the cake and prosecco I got on Monday.'

'You teachers. Always living the high life.'

'And I didn't have to swear at any colleagues.'

'Enough, enough. Alcohol and cake, and not forcing you to mistreat co-workers? They'll be giving you the vote next.'

I threw my toast crust at him, which landed perfectly in his hair. Jack reached up, deadpan, and slowly drew it down and popped it in his mouth in one bite. 'That's some good toast, though I say so myself.'

'You've got to have some skills if you want women to keep you guys around.'

'Not women. Just woman. You'll do me, thanks.' Jack gave me a panto wink.

I found an old *New Yorker* stuffed down the side of the sofa and read a piece about Malala Yousafzai, while the

31

smells of Jack's cooking filled the flat. Maybe married life wasn't the absolute worst thing in the world after all.

After a quiet weekend, I headed to the bar. It was crowded for so early in the week, but I found a table before Liz had arrived. She brought drinks over and hugged me.

'So, how is life as a married woman?' The question from her was tender, rather than wry. We clinked glasses.

'Fine.' She looked at me. 'It is fine, really. Do you want to talk about Adam?'

She'd been seeing him on and off for a few years; they'd repeatedly talked about living together, but she'd always backed off. Going by his absence at our wedding, she must have backed off pretty far this time. She shrugged. 'I dunno. Seems like a bit of a downer.'

I laughed. 'Given the downers you've had from me, Liz? Please. What happened?'

She shrugged again, a bit brisker. 'No, not tonight. Is that ok? I just. . . I want to think about something else.' She stopped. 'You know, I've always wanted something like you and Jack have. Is that weird?'

'Us?' I yelped. 'Liz, you know better than anyone how I've been feeling—'

'Yeah, but that's just *you*. It's not the two of you. You two have a better relationship than most people I know. And me and Adam, I just kept thinking, what if there's something better, just around the corner, and I. . . No. Listen. I really don't want to start on this tonight. Please. Save me from myself. Tell me about your school. Your sisters. International military policy. Anything.'

'Well, Kat's got a new job, which everyone's delighted about. I still don't really get what it is though. Some ad agency thing. We're all going to Mum and Dad's on Sunday to have a big meal – toast Kat, toast us, that kind of thing.'

'That's great news about Kat. How will you cope with the toasting to you too, though?'

I laughed. 'You've met Kat, haven't you? I don't imagine Jack and I will get much of a look in there.'

'Which suits you fine, I imagine.'

'Exactly.' I took a sip of my drink. 'This job of hers might turn out to be the best thing that's happened to me recently. Between Esther's toddler, whatever spirit-lifting social-work case Ava's currently on and the Job of the Century from Kat, I don't think I have to worry about the focus being on us at all.'

Liz and I clinked glasses again.

By our second week of marriage, things felt completely steady again between me and Jack, enough that we spent the evening semi-ironically filling out a questionnaire Jack had been sent by his stepmum: *What's Your Newlywed Score?* We had to answer things like 'Where do you see yourself in ten years' time?' and 'What's your happiest childhood memory?' – topics which neither of us had the courage to point out are maybe things you should discuss before the wedding, rather than after, but whatever. We opened a fancy bottle of Châteauneuf-du-Pape, a leftover from the wedding, and sat curled up together on the sofa.

Jack started. 'Ok, what would you save in a fire?'

'Besides you, of course?'

'Thank god. I think you get some bonus points for that.'

I thought for a moment. 'My picture of Grandma. Easy.' It was the first thing I'd put up when we'd moved into this flat: a colour photo of my grandma from when she was in her thirties, back in Nigeria, in a pair of black slacks and an emerald green sweater, laughing over her shoulder at someone just beside the photographer. Although I wouldn't be born until a few decades after that photo was taken, it was how I remembered her: smiling, beautiful, with the same dark bronze skin my mum, sisters and I had all inherited, and the same long arms. I remembered them wrapped around me when I was little, when she'd tell me stories and teach me about life, chuckling through her soft accent and keeping me safe from everything in the world.

I'd had the photo mounted in a frame to match her sweater, and the feeling of her looking over us as we'd moved into that little flat had felt like a blessing she could no longer give in person. She'd died when I was eleven, and I still thought of her almost every day.

'Right!' I shook myself. 'My turn. What's your dream job?'

'Honestly? Probably this one. I love the shop. It took me a long time to get it all together, to get Henderson's to where we are now. So. . . this. You?'

'Same. I love my job. I don't know if I'll do it forever, but it's certainly the thing that gives me the most pleasure.'

Jack coughed.

'Except you, of course?'

'Better.'

I offered him the list to take his turn. 'Right. Where would you like to live in the world, if not here?'

'Berlin!' I said, without hesitation.

'Of course. Your favourite.'

'Would you? Live there?'

'Yeah.' Jack thought for a moment. 'Yeah, I definitely would, although I can't imagine how that'll ever come about – I can't imagine how I'd ever leave the shop. But of all the places in the world, besides London, Berlin is probably where I'd most like to go.'

'Maybe when we're old, then?'

'Deal.'

We carried on with the list for another hour or so, and it was a strangely enjoyable time. We talked about children (we both want a couple, but not for a few years), films (the

34

fact that he picked neither *The Godfather* nor *The Shawshank Redemption* reminded me how much I loved him), religion (him: lapsed Catholic; me: pretty agnostic, despite Mum's best efforts), food (him: my mum's rice; me: beef wellington followed by chocolate mousse) and houses (we both dream of a magic house with a garden and a big bright kitchen and large windows, and which never raises any concerns about leaky guttering or cracking plaster or subsidence. Like I said, magic). The whole questionnaire forced us into enough of that emotional intimacy stuff that by the time we went to bed, let's just say I didn't have to undress myself.

On Saturday, I could hear Jack clattering about in the living room, moving all the wedding gift boxes around.

'Zo, what are we going to do with all this stuff? We don't want any of it.'

'Except the coffee machine.'

'Yes, except the coffee machine.' I could hear it humming away in the background as I joined him, and we looked at the endless repacked boxes of someone else's wedding presents.

'What if we return all this stuff and find out no one's bought us anything?' I was beginning to regret the pact we'd made not to look at what gifts had been picked off our wedding list.

'Zo, I'm reasonably sure that at least one of your sisters will have got us something. And Iffy. So that's two. Liz?'

'Fine. So will you call the place and have them come and collect it?' I pleaded, batting my eyelashes at him.

Jack winked at me, and a few minutes later I could hear him speaking in his most charming tones to someone in customer services, explaining the confusion about the boxes and how, in all the mix-up, the coffee machine had been opened and used before we'd realised the mistake.

'Oh, really? Really? Wow, that's awfully kind. Are you

sure? Wow, that's really, really kind of you. Thanks so much. Yes, tomorrow would be absolutely fine, we'll make sure at least one of us is in. Yup, thanks so much. Ok. Bye.' He hung up, and did a tiny dance.

'Well?'

'They said we should keep the coffee machine as an apology from them for their error, and they'd make sure all the other gifts and a new machine made it to the other couple.'

'*Sweeeeeeet.*'

'I know. What can I say – the gods were smiling on us for our wedding day.'

I looked at the boxes again. 'But who is this other couple? How can they have so much need for tweed sofa cushions and garden kneelers and – oh my god. Do you think they're old?'

'Uh-oh. Have an older couple married? Ugh, maybe they're *doing it*. That's *gross*. I'll call the police – quick, pass me your phone.'

'No. It's nice. It's nice that an older couple might be still so. . .'

'What?'

'I don't know, marrying when you need a garden kneeler. Optimistic?'

'Maybe they're not an older couple. Maybe they're Tories.'

'Nah, I don't have the energy for the sabotage of the boxes that particular truth would warrant. Let's just imagine they're a happy couple of indeterminate age who enjoy gardening and rabbits and tweed.'

'And coffee.'

'Well, not while we've got their espresso machine, they don't.'

Jack handed me another perfect cup of coffee (by now he'd mastered the art of the coffee machine), and headed off to dress for the shop while I stared at the chaos around us.

* * *

I tried as hard as I could, blinded with rage as I was, but I couldn't rip an entire catalogue in half. It was simply too thick.

'What are you doing?'

I looked up, sweating slightly, from where I was half crouched by the table beside the door. I thrust the catalogue at Jack, who had just come in with the Saturday papers.

'Yes, good, a babywear catalogue.' He paused, and blinked at me. 'Wait. What have you got this for?'

'That's what I want to know!' I realised I was shouting, and tried to pull my volume down a notch. 'I don't know why it's here! Why is it in our flat? Why has it got my name on it?'

'Did you order it?'

'*No, I didn't fucking order it!* Do you not think if I'd ordered it this mystery might have been solved a bit quicker? I didn't order it, I don't want it, and I *definitely* don't know why it's in my fucking flat!'

'Zo. Zoe!' I looked at Jack. 'It's just a catalogue. It's ok.'

'It's not ok! This never happened before we got married! Ever! But suddenly, somewhere, someone's ticked some "married" box against my name and I'm Mrs Bestwick all of a sudden, who's into babies and. . . wicker wine bottle holders and washable floral sofa covers and genuine porcelain models of royal babies—' I realised Jack was trying not to laugh.

'You didn't really get a catalogue of porcelain royal babies, did you?'

I bit my smile back too. 'No. But I bet it's on its way.'

Jack pulled me into a hug. 'That's grim. I'm sorry they're doing this.'

'But it doesn't happen to you, does it? You haven't been getting any mail for Mr Lewis, have you? You're not suddenly getting letters about joining your local Shed Club, are you?'

'Not. . . exactly.'

'Not exactly?'

'It's the ads on my computer. I used to get. . . holidays. And fashion brands. And. . . I don't know, cars and shit. Now I get terrifying ads about leaving your family without a will, and life insurance, and health insurance, and mortgage deals. I know it's not the same, but someone's ticked a box against my name somewhere too.'

'That son of a bitch.'

'I know. And one day, we'll hunt them down—'

'Tell me more.'

'And we'll force them—'

'Yes.'

'To *read all the spam and junk mail they've sent to us*.'

I gasped.

'I know, I know, strong words. But these people will never learn otherwise.'

I put my head on his shoulder. 'This bit of twenty-first-century life is weird enough – unsolicited messages from companies who presume to know us best. But when it's a name I don't use and stuff that's got nothing to do with where we are in our lives. . .'

'I know. It's weird.' He kissed the top of my head. 'Come on, let's go and do something fun and fancy-free which we can look back on nostalgically when we're old and decrepit.'

'Like interacting in person with other humans? Seeing family?'

'You got it, kid. Your mum's expecting us within the hour. Shall we do it?'

We grabbed our stuff and starting heading out the door.

'Hang on – one question. You did actually do all that wills and health insurance stuff though, didn't you?'

Jack looked at me. 'God yeah. Clicked right on through and tapped my bank details in straight away. I might not be a boring middle-aged husband and father yet, Zo, but I'm no idiot. You need to fill in your stuff, by the way.'

I grabbed my bag. 'Cool. Please will you leave me everything except your cigar collection?'

'Those are very valuable cigars!'

'They *were* very valuable cigars. I suspect that after keeping them in a box in a bag at the bottom of our old flat's damp wardrobe, they're now the world's most expensive fire-lighters.'

'Hmmm, fine. But you have to make sure your section of our will is *super* detailed. If I'm dealing with the grief of losing you, I don't think I can handle your sisters falling out over who gets your Chanel handbag on top of that.'

I laughed, although our laughter felt sad. I couldn't be without Jack, even in a hypothetical future. I kissed him again, and he wrapped his arms around me, breathing in deeply.

'Come on,' he said at last. 'All that face-to-face family fun isn't going to enjoy itself.'

'I love you,' I said. And I knew that whatever was to come, I did.

At Mum and Dad's, we were the last to arrive. Esther's husband, Ethan, had three-year-old William in the lounge, sticking flat plastic jewels onto a congratulations card for Kat. Ethan waved and grinned at us, which made William turn around and race over, grabbing Jack by the legs before trying to shimmy up him, eventually holding his hands up to be carried. I smiled as Jack and William babbled to each other, thinking of that baby catalogue I had no intention of needing in the near future, and left Ethan to continue care-fully sticking decorations onto his son's smudgy, wonky card.

In the kitchen, Mum, Dad, Kat, Ava and Esther were all gathered around the kitchen table, chopping vegetables, stirring bowls, pouring mugs of tea, snatching tastes of things and arguing amicably.

'Jack! Zoe! You're here at last, my darlings. Now we can all celebrate!' Mum came over and kissed us both, hugging us and handing us steaming cups of tea from a tray.

'Er, excuse me, haven't we just celebrated those two at their wedding? Didn't we in fact spend a whole day celebrating them? They got gifts and everything. I believe it's now—' Kat pointed to herself. 'Kat Time.'

I moved around the table to hug her. 'Congratulations, Kat. I am all in for some celebratory Kat Time: we brought wine. . .'

Kat grabbed it in one hand and hugged me back with her free arm.

'And flowers for the prima donna, and flowers for you too, Mum. Thanks for having us all!'

'Oh, darling, it is family! It is my pleasure to have you all here, and see your happy faces. Maybe one day you will know that feeling for yourself. . .'

I looked at Jack who very deliberately didn't look at me, just stood with his hand frozen halfway to the crisp bowl, his nostrils flaring in panic. I laughed again at his exaggerated terror and he unfroze, smiling back at me conspiratorially.

'Mum!' said Esther. 'Leave the poor girl alone. She's only been married five minutes.'

'Oh, you young girls, you think you know everything better than your mother. It is always the same-same with you!'

'Come on, love.' Dad pulled Mum into a one-armed hug. 'Let's leave these youngsters to tidy up in here, since they know so much better. Your grandson's in the other room, and I don't think he's realised how little we know yet.' He turned and winked at us all over his shoulder as he led Mum out. Then he put on a stern tone, adding to us, 'You better do a good job in here, or you'll have me to answer to.' As Mum made her way into the front room, he whispered, 'Oh, and your mum's done some lovely ginger snaps, in the tin in the cupboard. Don't tell her I told you, though.'

Kat and I raced to the cupboard to get the tin out first; she beat me to it, but she needed two hands to open it, so I got the first biscuit. 'Aha!' I muttered triumphantly, only to see her stuff four biscuits into her mouth at once in retaliation. I shook my head at her. 'I hope you're not going to behave like that at your new job.'

'What is it anyway, if I'm allowed to ask?' Ava said, dipping a biscuit into her tea with her enviable quiet grace. Ava, the second oldest of us, was a social worker, but far too kind to ever assume everyone else's jobs weren't just as important as hers.

'It's a digital marketing agency, and I'll be in planning and management. It's unbelievably boring to describe, and I can't believe I made it through the interview without gagging at some of the buzzwords I had to use—'

'How bad was it?' I asked.

'I had to strategise the outcrop of dissolving mindsets in a twenty-second-century digital mob.'

Jack bit his fist, looking comically panicked.

'Exactly. But the money's good, and I do actually like the work, just not having to talk about it. I suppose I'll get immune to that soon enough, at which point you'll just have to stop speaking to me.'

Esther took another biscuit. 'Are you nervous?'

Kat chuckled. 'Have we met? They're the ones who ought to be nervous. I am going to *boss* it. But you guys can see for yourselves – it's their annual family day next month, where all the employees can bring in their partners or kids or parents or whatever. I guess you twenty-second-century digital mob will have to do.'

41

'When is it?' Esther said, fishing out her phone. We all checked our calendars: Jack and I had a date with Iffy and his girlfriend that we couldn't get out of, but Esther and Ava promised to report back everything about the company.

'And let me know what her boss is like. If he's smoking, etc.,' I said. Jack coughed politely at my elbow. 'I meant for Ava!' I insisted, pointing to her. 'I meant for *her*.' Kat snorted at me, and Jack gave me a kiss on my hand, before releasing it to grab another biscuit himself.

Wednesday was an exhausting day at school – the revving up to reports time and parents' evenings had begun in earnest, with no consideration for how many hours we actually had in our days – and all I wanted to do was curl up on the sofa with Jack. I made myself a cup of tea and sat down, ready to finally exhale the day, but Jack doubled back to the sink.

'Zo, you do realise that I literally just finished doing the washing up, don't you?'

'Um. . . thanks?'

'You just dumped your teabag and teaspoon in here – it would have taken you five seconds to wash that spoon.'

'And it'll take me five seconds to wash it once I've actually sat down for five seconds too. It's not going anywhere.'

'I know it isn't! Unless *I* wash it up.' He looked exasperated.

'Jack, I really didn't leave it there for you to wash up. I'm knackered and I just want to sit down with you for a little while. I've been looking forward to this all day.' I sighed.

'I know you don't mean anything by it. That's the problem.'

'Jack! Please don't be a dick about it?'

Jack rubbed his face with his hands. 'I'm pretty sure if you'd just spent an hour on a boring chore you'd be delighted to hear me calling you a dick.'

'I didn't call you a dick! And I thought you liked washing up.'

Jack almost laughed. 'I don't like washing up! This isn't the hugest flat in the entire world, and I like living in a clean and tidy house, so I make sure there's not dirty laundry and dirty plates and dirty cutlery piled up everywhere! It's hardly a disorder. So no, I don't like washing up. I just understand that it needs to be done, and that, unlike some people, I don't have a magical fairy who comes and does it all while I sit on the sofa and reflect on my day.'

'Please, I'm sorry,' I said, feeling sick at how this argument was rolling out of my reach. 'Didn't we say we wouldn't still bicker about chores once we were married?' I didn't want to get into a lifetime habit of debating my teabags being dumped in the sink.

'No one's waved a wand to make housework go away, Zo. It still needs to be done. It just depends on how much you're willing to pay attention to that. Because I hate living in a pigsty.'

'Our flat is always tidy! It's never a pigsty!'

'Because I never let it get that bad!'

'We can't keep arguing about this for the rest of our lives!' I yelled.

Neither of us said anything, letting my last comment echo around us.

'Right,' Jack said, washing up my spoon. 'I'm actually pretty tired so I'm going to go to bed now. Are you coming?'

'I . . . I need a bit of time to unwind. I've only just got in.'

I ended up washing my hair and watching four hours of American sitcoms until my eyes were itching and my mouth was dry.

Another magnificent evening, Zoe. Really well played.

* * *

When I got into school the next morning, Benni was hovering around my desk.

'Hello, darling. I was just scribbling you a note – it's that fun time of year, updating all our details for the council's records!'

'Oh no, and I didn't even get you a card.'

'All you need to do is log in with your work email and make sure everything's up to date. Yay! Thanks, darling. And. . . pub after work? Gina's taking the boys to the theatre. Or—'

'Don't.' I narrowed my eyes at her.

'I was going to say have you got too much on here, but clearly there's something else going on. Pub it is,' she announced before hurrying off.

I decided to get Benni's request out of the way before I got sucked into the school day. It was simple enough: just as Benni had said, I just had to make sure all my personal and health details were up to date. Name – yes, goddammit, Zoe *Lewis* – date of birth, National Insurance number, blah blah blah. Oh. 'Cohabiting' now needed to become 'Married', so I unchecked the cohabiting box, and ticked the married box. Suddenly, half the options on screen were greyed out, and other options popped up below them. What the hell? The whole section on hobbies and interests had become unclickable, but another section had popped up asking how many dependants lived with me. Had I somehow slipped back to 1954? I unclicked 'Married' and the boxes ungreyed. Click again, greyed. Married life: children, dinner parties full of painful pointed subtext, the closing in on your inevitable death. Unmarried? You're probably just into scuba diving, mountain climbing and retaining your will to live. I clicked, unclicked. Clicked. Unclicked. Clicked. Unclicked. All the while watching my options fade in and out.

After a while I realised Benni had come back and was watching over my shoulder.

'Is someone having an existential crisis?' I raised a horror-filled face to her as she shook her head in sympathy. 'You should try telling these things that you're a female and so is your wife.'

I laughed a little. 'It isn't just me, is it?'

She bent forwards and looked closer at the screen, clicking and unclicking as I had. She laughed too. 'Bloody hell, that is a bit on the nose, isn't it? I reckon some bitter programmer's having a small dig. It'll probably be all over social media in the next half hour. Now, in the meantime, just tell them you're not dead yet and we'll leave it at that, ok?'

She watched me send off my details – including a checked 'Married' box – and led me into her office for some actual curriculum talk. We had a new exam board and a whole range of different topics to cover in our upcoming parents' evenings. For the next forty-five minutes, I managed to focus on what she was saying, making notes, and asking questions. But in another part of my brain, I was still simmering, perhaps more than I would have done if I'd not found out the night before that I hadn't been invited to someone's weekend away in Ibiza because they'd assumed I wouldn't go as a newlywed. *Sorry!!!* she'd texted, *I thought you'd want to be with new hubby at the mo ;).*

I just. . . I didn't understand. It was a choice, wasn't it? I might know a few people who'd changed their names to match their husband's when they'd got married, but I didn't know a single person who'd become a full-blown housebound Stepford Wife. I still dressed the same, I still did the same job. I even had the same friends – or so I thought. It seemed that assumptions would just be made no matter what I said or did, all because I'd signed that piece of paper agreeing to marry Jack.

After the meeting with Benni, I tried to focus for the rest of the day, working through lunch to get my head around the curriculum I'd be explaining to some of our more difficult parents, and to keep myself distracted. By seven thirty, I was starving, and very, very ready to leave.

'Right!' said Benni, as I stood in her office doorway. She slammed her laptop shut. 'Let's all go and right some wrongs.'

I didn't stay long – Benni and I only managed to right three wrongs each (if you count 'wrongs' as 'delicious and very strong cocktails') – and left her, along with Miks, his girlfriend from the English department, and a large bottle of wine, so I could get back to have dinner with Jack, having not seen him much for a few days due to our criss-crossing work schedules.

At just after eight, I had my head, slightly dizzily, in the fridge when Jack came out of the shower.

'What do you fancy?' I called through to him.

'Don't worry about me, I'm out tonight, remember?'

I didn't remember. 'Whereabouts?'

'Don't know yet. Just out with friends.' Immediately, my hackles were up.

'Why didn't you tell me?' I knew I shouldn't pick a fight, but I needed a way to vent my disappointment at an evening spent apart yet again.

'I did. Last week. I didn't realise I needed written permission. I'm just out with Iffy and people.'

'People? And Iffy who you saw yesterday?'

'Yeah, people. And yeah, Iffy. I know I saw him yesterday, but it's a group of us and we've had tonight in the diary for ages.'

Hearing myself, I couldn't help but think of what Jack might be saying about us when they did hang out.

'So do these *people* have names?' I realised I was slurring slightly.

'Well, this is a delightful conversation.' Jack cocked his eyebrow. 'What's up with you, Zo?'

I crossed my arms. 'I just didn't know you were going out, and suddenly there are these people that you absolutely have to see. I left my departmental drinks early to see you.' The alcohol in my system was making me sound much angrier than I'd ever have felt sober.

'I'm happy to cancel, although given the way this conversation is going, I can't begin to imagine why we'd want to spend the evening together instead.'

I thought of all the things I could do tonight if Jack wasn't about: have a long bath, watch a trashy film, call Ava for a chat, take an early night with Jilly Cooper flopping open at all the right pages. Lie really still and wait for the room to stop spinning. In all honesty, I didn't care that he was going out. And yet, something – utterly unreasonably – still rankled.

'Fine. Go. Have a nice time.' I gave him a brief kiss on the cheek and a tight smile, and before I knew it he was gone.

I was shaking. I was so angry at myself. I didn't care – I'd never cared – if he was seeing friends.

But I was also angry at his tone, and the creeping realisation that if I'd asked him to stay with me, he'd have had to tell his friends a lie, and they wouldn't believe the lie, and how they'd tease him for months about his wife being in charge now. Then, if I insisted on him staying with me again, they'd eventually stop teasing, and stop calling. Ugh. I didn't want to star as the worst kind of clichéd spouse. I couldn't stop seeing it from his angle too: his partner, suddenly turning the flame-throwers on him. But then I flipped back again: if I was feeling this bad, why was he going out? And yet, why was I feeling this bad if he hadn't done anything wrong? Then back again: I felt bad because I'd been a weasel to him. This was my problem, not his.

Back and forth, back and forth I went, the whole evening, sitting in front of unsatisfying TV, not doing anything I'd planned, losing my evening, losing my mind, feeling my pub-buzz sour. I scuttled to bed when I heard his key in the main door, throwing my clothes off and hunkering under the duvet as he opened our front door. I pretended to be asleep when he came in, wrapped up in fleecy pyjamas, not up to facing what I, or he, or we, had done, with one tiny, toxic argument.

FOUR

Seven years earlier

There was only so much refusing they could do before someone got offended, so within half an hour, Zoe and Jack – minus Jack's face mask ('The air round here is so polluting, don't you find?' asked Jack's mother, Linda; slim, groomed, tortoise-shell glasses pushed into her shiny chestnut hair) – were in a taxi with Jack's parents. Linda had taken Zoe's arm from the moment Jack had introduced her and hadn't let go since. Graham, his father, said very little, pale and quiet in a pale, quiet shirt and corduroy trousers, merely smiling at her and giving her a muttered hello. Once they'd been seated at the restaurant Zoe realised that was probably the highlight of his interactions for today. Linda chose his food for him, reminding him that *tomato soup never agrees with you this time of night, does it, Graham?* and *Maybe you should just stick to the garlic bread, Graham*, and, *Graham, I think you'd best have the lamb, after your trouble with the chicken last time*. Zoe, on a student budget, skipped the starters and chose the cheapest thing from the mains, a three-bean salad. Jack chose the same.

'So then,' said Linda, settling her glasses on her face and

tilting her head to one side. 'When were you going to tell us about your new girlfriend, Jack?'

'Oh, I'm—'

'It's quite—'

'Do you go to the same college as Jack, dear?'

'No, I'm way over the other side of town – I'm doing Chemistry.'

'Ooh! A scientist! Well, that is posh. Isn't that posh, Graham? Zoe's going to be a scientist!'

'Well, I hope I will. It's a long way to go yet. If I do my Masters I've got another couple of years left.'

'So Jack will have left before you've even finished?'

'Mum, we've only just—'

'Yeah. Yeah, I suppose he will. I hadn't thought about that. We really only met just—'

'My cousin's son is a scientist.'

'Mum, Stuart works in Boots.'

'No, well, he started in Science, but decided he wanted to be more hands-on.'

'He didn't "start in Science", Mum. He did a Science GCSE, which he failed.'

'Oh, so now you know all your second cousins' academic careers, do you? You can't ever remember to send your Auntie Chrissie a Christmas card, and yet you can remember all her children's grades?'

'Mum, I'm sure he's a really great. . . retail guy. But that's not the same as what Zoe's doing.' He looked at Zoe, who was smiling at him with something like sympathy in her eyes.

'Well, you know best, Jack, obviously.'

The starters arrived – garlic bread for Graham, crab terrine for Linda – and Zoe and Jack worked their way in silence through the complimentary bread basket while his parents ate, Graham in small mouthfuls, Linda spreading a single piece of toast with the crab terrine before sniffing it, wrinkling up her nose and putting it back on the plate.

'Is it alright, Mum?'

She wrinkled her nose again, her mouth a disgusted moue. 'I don't think that crab's any good, you know.'

'Well, do you want to tell the waiter?'

'Oh no, it's fine.'

'It's not fine – if your crab's off we should tell them. Get you another one.'

'No no, if that one's spoiled, they're probably all off.'

'Let's get you something else then. Do you want me to tell the waiter?'

'Jack, just leave it, I'm fine. I don't need a starter. Once they bring me something else your mains will be arriving anyway.'

Jack took in a huge breath, slowly breathing out through his nose while Zoe squeezed his thigh under the table. He put his hand on hers and squeezed it too, his breathing becoming easier.

The waiter came over, went to take the plates away, but saw Linda's was still full.

'Are you – is this still going?'

'No no! It's fine, I just don't want to spoil my appetite for my main course!'

The waiter looked baffled. 'Was everything alright?'

'Yes! Lovely! Thank you!'

Jack dropped his head down, closing his eyes. When the waiter had taken the two plates away, he said, 'Could you not have told him, Mum?'

'Well. I don't know. Maybe the crab wasn't spoiled. It just smelled a bit—'

'Don't say fishy.'

'Well it did!'

'Mum.'

'*You* didn't have to eat it, Jack. You wouldn't have been the one with food poisoning.'

'I didn't eat it because you didn't offer it to me. If I'd thought you were basing your rejection of your seafood dish on it "smelling fishy" I would have made more of an effort to try it myself.' Zoe squeezed his thigh again and Jack took a quick drink. 'Sorry, Mum. It was your food.'

Linda blinked at him. 'Thank you, Jack,' she said, surprised. 'I'm sure I'll say something if there's anything wrong with the main.'

Zoe gave Jack a tiny nudge, and he snorted into his glass of water. She smiled at Graham, who smiled absently back at her then returned to rearranging his napkin on his lap.

After a few moments, Zoe dabbed at her mouth with her own napkin, and said, 'So do you get to see Jack much then?' Under the bright restaurant lights, she was beginning to feel sweaty, as the aftereffects of the drinks she and Jack had shared with the pizza last night finally kicked in. She was also sweating with the realisation that she barely knew Jack from a broom in the corner, and she was wondering just how deep they were digging by sitting here and letting his parents think they was something stable and long term, when he was still listed in her phone as 'Hot Barman'.

'Well, you know how it is, Zoe, it's a long way to travel when we're *all* the way out east—'

'In. . . Asia?'

Linda looked baffled. 'No, dear, in Norwich. It's quite a way for us to come to visit Jack here at university, and Graham doesn't really like the journey. Do you, Graham?' She looked over at her husband, who was staring into his glass, rattling the ice cubes. She gave a tiny sigh. 'And where-abouts are your parents? Are they. . . Do they live in this country?' Despite having spoken with her for the last hour,

Linda's voice suddenly became fractionally louder and over-pronounced for this final part of the question.

Zoe beamed at her. 'Yes, they're up in Leytonstone. North-east London.'

'Right. Right.' Linda looked confused again, unsure how to navigate a question which surely had been misunder-stood. 'Well, speaking of your Auntie Chrissie, her dentist told her that his sister has just been imprisoned in Saudi Arabia.' She looked at Zoe, questioningly. 'Not like. . . your. . . people —'

'Mum, look, the mains are here!'

Zoe met Graham's eye and wondered if he'd heard a word, he looked so disengaged; when his lamb was put in front of him he just gave the waiter a grateful smile and tucked in, eyes down.

Zoe looked at the bowl in front of her – brown beans mixed in with some green unknowables and some sad lettuce leaves – looked at Jack's identical portion, then up at Jack. They both laughed.

'Anything wrong, you two?' Linda asked, a forkful of salmon *en croute* halfway to her mouth.

'No, Mum,' Jack said, scooping up some mystery salad. 'Everything's just fine.' He nudged Zoe's knee with his own under the table, and Zoe felt his body relax a little beside hers.

'I suppose it's nice to have a degree where you know what you'll do with it afterwards,' Linda said.

'I should hope so – I'll have spent long enough on it. Although sometimes people do change their minds and go into engineering, manufacture, even completely different subjects.' Zoe nudged her three-bean salad around the dish. 'I suppose sometimes you need to try things before you know if they're right for you or not.'

'I know, I know, I say this to Jack all the time! I mean

his friend Iffy's doing medicine, so he'll be fine, but Jack! He can do this little art course, though God knows what it's costing us—'

'Mum, I pay for the course myself.'

'But eventually the time will come when he has to decide how he's going to make his living. If he wants to settle down and have a wife and a family, he needs to think about how he's going to support them all, and stop lying around living this student lifestyle, waiting for hand-outs from the state—'

'What are you talking about, Mum? I don't get any state benefits.'

'Not for want of trying, I'll bet,' she chuckled ruefully.

'I. . . don't. . .' Jack looked at Zoe, wide eyed. She tried not to laugh.

'I mean it though, Jack, you have to think about life after college. Don't you think, Graham?' Jack's father was pushing his vegetables around his plate with great concentration.

'I literally think about it every day, Mum. My whole course is geared around making us skilled and employable in our chosen fields.'

'No, I mean, this is a nice hobby, maybe something you can take up again when you're retired. But really now – shoe-making? Everything's made in China, now, isn't it? What are you going to do, ship some of their little elves over for your workshop?'

Her laughter was interrupted by Graham abruptly getting up and mumbling something about finding the toilets. Linda was obviously put out by having what felt like one of her favourite jokes interrupted.

Zoe sat a little closer to the table. 'Do you get to go away much? On holiday, I mean? I think I quite fancy visiting China one day.'

'Oh no, love, Graham couldn't stomach somewhere like

China. The food would just go straight through him. No, when we go away we tend to stick to what we like – a narrow boat around the Broads in April and a Greek island in September.'

Zoe could just picture them: Graham shadowing Linda silently as she, with bumbag and sunglasses on a neck strap, spoke loudly about pickpockets and Proper Cups of Tea as she crushed millennia-old religious sites under her comfortable walking sandals.

'That sounds lovely. I've always wanted to go to Greece. What's it like?'

'Well. . .' She thought for a moment. 'The key is finding the right places to eat, I think. Once we've found a nice café with English owners, I can relax and enjoy my holiday. No offence, but I'm not sure I'd trust those Greeks to wash the dishes properly, if you know what I mean.' She looked at Zoe meaningfully.

'Thanks Mum, we'll get on with digging out your hidden subtext.' He looked at Zoe. 'Would you really like to go to Greece?'

'Yeah, I think so. I don't know if there's anywhere I wouldn't like to go, to be fair. As long as it wasn't on a Foreign Office blacklist, obviously.'

'No erupting volcanoes then.'

'Or actual war zones.'

'Or will.i.am gigs?'

'Oh, I don't know,' Zoe giggled. 'It's something for the Christmas newsletter, isn't it?'

Linda perked up suddenly. 'Oh, does your family do one of those too? Well, that *is* integration, isn't it? I absolutely love doing them – I start drafting it in September, although Jack and Graham both rib me terribly. But I always say to them, if I don't do it, it wouldn't get done.'

'And wouldn't that be a shame,' Jack said.

'See what I mean, Zoe? People *like* it, Jack, even if you don't. They want to know what's happening with their friends' children and spouses.'

'Only so they can feel better about their own lives.'

Linda tutted at Zoe. 'They never want to know about dinner parties and Christmas cards until there are no women around to organise it all for them.'

'Mum, maybe we just don't care about those things in the exact same way you do.'

'Of course you don't, Jack. But maybe you will. Maybe you'll care when you're seventy-two and haven't seen another human being for a month because your wife has died and your children don't call and you've never bothered to write a Christmas card or invite someone over for a coffee. Maybe you'll understand then how important "those things" actually are to living in a society.'

There was a silence as Zoe looked more carefully at Linda, who was panting slightly with her strength of feeling.

Jack picked his napkin up from the floor. 'That escalated quickly. I was only talking about those show-off Christmas letters, Mum. I didn't mean we should all die alone.'

Linda picked at some imaginary fluff on one jumper sleeve. 'Well. Maybe you don't understand that the line between the two isn't as black and white as you think. Maybe you don't know everything quite yet, Jack.'

Zoe gently touched Linda's hand on the table. Linda jumped. Zoe said, 'We're all the same, aren't we, students? Think we know everything because we've been to a few lectures. My mum despairs of me.'

Linda smiled at her, a warm smile, the first Zoe had seen that evening, and put her hand on top of Zoe's. 'Oh, I don't know. I think there's hope for a few of you yet.'

Just then, Graham shambled back from the toilets and slid into his chair.

Linda pushed her plate back and gestured to a waiter. 'Right. Pudding, anyone?'

'Alright. Yes, I wasn't expecting to meet your parents, but no, it wasn't actually as disastrous as it could have been. I mean, I didn't have my chosen Meet the Parents Outfit on—'

'You have a specific outfit?'

'Flowery skirt: not too short or I look like I'm the cheating type, not too long or it looks like they'll never have grand-kids. Soft jumper: wow, look how approachable I am, low key and fluffy. Wedge heels: yes, I'm into aesthetics, but not in a way that would ever get in the way of my relationship with your son.'

Jack had his mouth open. 'Wow, that's. . . that's awful. And brilliant. And *awful*.'

'I know. But I just managed in this,' Zoe said, gesturing at her jeans, t-shirt, leather jacket and battered trainers. 'This is like the *anti*-Meet the Parents Outfit.'

'And you still won them over.'

'Did I?' she said, with a disingenuous eyelash flutter. 'Little old me?'

Jack pulled her close. 'I don't know how you did it, but yes, you did.'

'Your mum's not so bad. I don't think it can be easy, living with your dad like that.'

'Like what?'

'He never talks! Ever! Does he? Or was it just me? I feel like the poor woman has to keep speaking just to fill that void between them.'

Jack stepped away. 'Really? You think there's a void between them?'

Zoe took his hand, laughing. 'I don't know. I've met them once, for one fairly odd dinner. You know them better than I do.'

'I'd honestly never thought about it that way before.' He looked up at her. 'That maybe my dad might be hard to live with. I always thought it was my mum who was the difficult one.'

She kissed him. 'Either way, we all survived the dinner, didn't we? It might have been unexpected, but it wasn't the apocalypse it could have been. Was it?'

'My dad, when they left, actually said to me "She's nice."'

'Wow, high praise.'

'I don't think you understand. That's like Raymond Blanc saying your bouillabaisse is "quite tasty".'

'Because he's such a connoisseur of women?'

'No! It's like Simon Cowell saying you've got a good voice.'

'Because your dad's made a career out of judging your girlfriends?'

'No!' Jack was laughing. 'It just. . . it means he really means it. That when he says it, someone who never says much about anything, you must really have made an impression.'

'A good one?'

'Yes. He said you were *nice*, for god's sake. Approval doesn't come much higher than that.'

'Well. I'll make sure to put your father's approval of me on my CV.'

'And my mum's.'

'And your mum's? Bloody hell, I did do well.'

'You did indeed. But if there's any chance you might be staying over again, please can we stop talking about my parents?'

'Deal. Although now of course you've got to meet mine.'

They were both laughing, but there was a fraction of a second where both their laughs froze. *Are we definitely doing this?* thought Zoe. *Is this it, now?*

58

She gave Jack a kiss at the side of his mouth, and pulled out of his arms. 'I'd love to stay another night, but I've got an early start in the morning. Thanks, though. I had a nice time.'

Jack offered a wonky smile, aware too of the oddness they'd accelerated into this evening. 'Call me?'

'I will,' she said. 'I'll call you tomorrow, maybe.'

'If I'm lucky.'

She opened his door. 'Exactly.'

After she'd pulled the door closed behind her, Jack sat down. For the first time in his life, he could see his future ahead of him. And it looked pretty good.

On the bus home, Zoe looked at Hot Barman's number on her phone. What was happening here? Yes, she liked him, yes, they seemed to have a nice time together, and yes, he actually seemed like a decent human being, but they'd known each other less than two weeks and she was talking about introducing him to her family? If nothing else, her sisters would eat him alive.

She smiled at the thought: that poor boy facing her three sisters. *And* her parents.

This was all too fast. She hadn't ever felt like this with anyone else, this urge to be with them all the time, every day. She'd had the opposite – someone claiming all *her* time – and she didn't want to do that to Jack. Tonight she'd had to make herself leave, despite every fibre in her body wanting to stay with him again. But she also knew that this was probably just lust, and she didn't fancy getting burnt that way. She wouldn't get hurt again. She was careful now. In a moment of certainty, frustrated by her urge to call him, she deleted his number from her phone: she would *have* to get over him now.

Still, it had been interesting to meet his mum and dad.

She believed that everyone eventually grew into their parents in some form or another, and couldn't help wondering what any future wife of Jack would have to look forward to: an unstoppable flow of empty small talk, or an impenetrable wall of silence as he slowly became a ghost haunting their lives. She shuddered.

It was one of the reasons she'd always dreaded the idea of marriage: you were bound to someone forever, no matter how completely different a person they became over the *decades* spent living with them. Her own parents had got round it by never marrying, but living in blissful sin, as they'd say to their four daughters (who thought nothing of their parents' sin, but who'd wince and howl at the thought of their bliss).

Zoe quite liked it now, the bloody-mindedness of their refusal to marry in the seventies, and sticking with someone for years and years when no legal documents said you had to. It was touching in a way. But it had meant that for as long as she could remember – ever since she'd asked Mum if she could see her wedding dress, and Mum had sat her down and explained that she and Dad had never wanted to get married like everyone else – Zoe had learned that marriage wasn't something that was for everyone. And while her head had taught her that lesson growing up, nowadays, her heart felt the same way.

FIVE

Now

Since I'd got back to work after our wedding, school had been frantic. Yet another education rejig was on the cards, which meant our latest student reports had to be rewritten, handed to the pupils, then re-rewritten with their feedback taken into consideration – I'd been in school until ten every night that week. I was looking forward to Friday night in front of the TV, inhaling burritos under a blanket with Jack. When I saw him on Friday morning, I asked him if he fancied the burritos, or something else – my treat, I'd pick it up on the way home.

'Zo, it's the Henderson party tonight. At the shop? God, we really need to get a calendar up in here.'

Oh no. I loved Jack's shop, loved hanging out there with him, looking at his gorgeous shoes and wondering if I could get Dad into any of them. But his staff were another matter. Paisley, Agatha, Jonjo, Gabben, Mint: Mint was the worst, always trying to touch my hair and saying how amazing my skin was. Nooope, no, thank you. I did everything I could to support Jack in his career, but a Henderson party after the week I'd had? To make matters worse, I had a

61

sneaking suspicion that Jessica would be there too. Jessica, the Chief Financial Officer of Gillett – the company which had bought Henderson a few years ago – seemed constantly to watch Jack like he was the last cheeseburger on the grill and she hadn't eaten in days.

'I'm so sorry – please can I skip this one? It's been such late nights all this week.'

Jack looked disappointed. 'Are you sure you can't come? Even for a little while?'

'What about if I say I'll try?'

'That's a no then.'

I stepped into him and tried to wrap his arms around me. 'I said I'll try.'

He stepped away. 'And I know that that means you won't be there.'

'I don't know what else you want me to do!'

'You could try actually turning up?'

'Jack!' I stepped back too, acres of dangerous space opening between us. 'I've had the week from hell. I'm cross-eyed with tiredness. I just want to hang out with you, not your staff with their *names* and their *agendas* and their *conversation*.'

'I'm sorry I'm asking you to hang out with people who have names, Zoe. I'll be careful to only introduce you to abstract concepts from now on.' He turned away, heading out of the kitchen.

'I'll see you later?' I called after him.

He opened the front door. 'I won't hold my breath.'

I'd fallen asleep by the time Jack got back that night. After a tense weekend with him, both of us stepping around each other to nip any potential argument in the bud, Benni's cheerful smile was a welcome sight on Monday morning. Miks, however, gave her a suspicious look. 'That never bodes well, does it?' he muttered.

Benni arrived at my desk. 'Ah, Zoe, that lab order form you were waiting for has come in. If you'd just like to follow me to my office.'

Miks lowered his head onto his arms, and in muffled tones, said, 'You're so unconvincing. It's actually depressing.'

Once I'd closed Benni's door, I said, 'Is Miks alright?'

'He's fine, darling, but I think he and his girlfriend are splitting up. It's fine, though, he'll be fine.'

'Mmm. If you say so. What's this order form I'm meant to ask for?'

'Darling.' She frowned at me. 'Now, how much did you mean it when you said marriage wouldn't change you?'

'This is a really worrying conversation, Benni. A hundred per cent?'

'I'm glad you said that.' She smiled at me and pushed her computer around so I could see the screen. 'Check out the Physics teacher who'll be visiting us from our sister school in Manchester. Part time, but still. . .'

On the 'Our Staff' page of our Manchester school's website was the most handsome Physics teacher I had ever laid eyes on. I loved Jack completely, from his wonky toenails to the tip of his sandy beard, but my god: this guy looked like he'd been created in a lab. A lab I would definitely like to experiment in, if things were different. If I was single. He was a young Idris Elba genetically spliced with a sexy librarian.

'I know, right?' Benni smiled at me.

I realised I was fanning myself. 'He is. . . very refreshing,' I said, nodding at the screen, my eyes drawn back to him. 'Not your usual type, though. And I'm a married woman, might I add.'

'He might not be my preferred gender, but I'm not *blind*. It's always nice to browse the gallery, even if you aren't in the market for a painting.'

'You *perv*.' I looked at him again. 'How did you discover him?'

'I didn't – the Head told me about him. He's on some kind of fast-track course, to extend his teaching skills. Part of some new initiative. They want to reshuffle all the core subjects and staff around a bit, have some of the Maths, English and Science teachers swap schools.' She waved her hand, unconcerned about the details. 'And. . .' Benni was almost singing now. 'Guess who'll be sitting in on some of your lessons?'

I coughed a little. 'I am a. . .' I swallowed and looked at the screen again. 'A happily. . . married woman?'

'In which case none of us have anything to worry about, do we?' Her smile had turned slightly wicked, but it melted away. 'Oh, Zo, darling, I'm only joking. I know you'd never look at another man while you're with Jack.'

'Which, lest we forget those vows, is for the rest of our lives.'

'Yes, yes, but it doesn't hurt to look, does it?'

I looked at the screen one more time before I left the office, and thought, *Just looking. Just looking.*

Coming through the door from the supermarket early evening on Saturday, I saw Jack lying on the sofa, pizza box on his stomach.

'Hey! What's this?'

'Don't worry – there's another one in the kitchen for you.'

'No, Jack, we're going out with Liz tonight.'

'Oh god, really? Please can you invent an illness for me, I really don't fancy it.'

'Just one of the many blessings marriage conveys. We're stuck with each other's friends, I'm afraid. Just jump in the shower and you'll be fine, come on.'

'No, I'm serious, Zo. Please can you just tell her I couldn't make it tonight? I've already eaten, anyway.' He gestured at the half-empty pizza box.

I gaped at him. 'Jack, we haven't all been out together since the wedding. Can't we please just try and look semi-convincing that we can bear to still be in each other's company?'

'I know we're married, but we don't have to live in each other's pockets. You don't want to be one of *those* couples, do you?'

'Which I'm *sure* you'd be saying if the boot was on the other foot. We just had lunch with Iffy, didn't we? If we were meeting one of your friends, I'd never flake out on a plan.'

'Like the Henderson's party?' Jack sighed. 'We saw her at the wedding; that was only a few weeks ago. I'm sure she can't miss me that much. You go and have a nice time without me.'

'It's not about whether Liz misses you, it's about whether *I* do.'

'Zoe, this is one evening!'

'Maybe it's *not*,' I shouted, then took a deep breath. I dropped my bag on the table, put my keys in the bowl, and held my head in my hands. 'I don't understand what you want, Jack.'

'I don't understand either,' he said, looking baffled. 'I thought I was just asking for an evening to myself.'

We both waited, feeling winded. I thought of all our recent arguments, the tension. I thought of our wedding day.

'I think. . . I think this was a mistake,' I said.

'You think. . . what was a mistake? This fight?'

'Jack,' I said. 'All of this.' He looked at me, his mouth dropping a little.

'Are you kidding me?'

'No. Is it really that much of a surprise? Have you never thought that?'

'What, in the *month* since we've been married?'

'Yes!'

'For fuck's sake, Zo, everyone feels like that.' He lifted his hands, then dropped them in exasperation. 'What the hell are you talking about?'

'No, everyone feels like that at some point in their married life, but not in the first four weeks,' I said. 'Not on their honeymoon. Not on the way to the register office.'

Jack gaped at me again, then stood up, stormed into the bedroom and slammed the door closed. There'd been a lot of that recently. Soon Upstairs Jan would be as pleased to see us as those voyeurs opposite.

I met Liz at the bar, where she and her new squeeze Henry were waiting, drinks in hand. Liz had mentioned him for the first time when we'd confirmed plans that afternoon, but she'd also said I wasn't to ask anything until I'd met him. I could see why – Henry sported his sunglasses on the top of his head, just in case I hadn't got the message clearly enough from his chinos and pink shirt. What wasn't clear was why she was with him in the first place. Liz hugged me, then he leant in, as if for a kiss, despite the fact I'd never met him before in my life and didn't particularly fancy pressing my face against his. Before he could make contact, I pretended to look in my bag for my phone; by the time I looked up again he'd leant back, his face slightly mottled with indignation.

'Ooh, I'd forgotten about this!' Liz said, getting back off her chair to stroke my Chanel handbag. She explained to Henry, 'Zoe's parents gave it to her for her wedding.'

'In fashion, are they?' Henry said with a smirk. Liz flinched slightly, then her face settled again.

'Every woman wants a Chanel, don't they?' She smiled at me. 'God, it really is gorgeous.'

'You'll be giving her ideas, Zoe,' Henry said, picking his teeth with a cocktail stick as he looked around the bar.

'Is Jack on his way?' Liz asked.

I was so repelled by Liz's date for the night that I'd briefly forgotten that I didn't have one at all. 'No, he can't make it. He sends his apologies, but he's a bit under the weather. Too much work on at the moment.'

'Sounds like bullshit,' Henry smirked again. 'Just didn't fancy a night out with his wife's cronies, I bet.'

The truth of this made me blush. Thank god the bar was too dark for Henry to tell. But Liz understood, and took my hand. 'Do you still want to eat, or shall we reschedule?'

'I'm here now! Let's have a nice time.' My eyes landed on Henry. 'Or we can at least try the food,' I said brightly, swallowing my dislike of our company.

A tall, slim waitress took us to our table, where the fourth place was whipped away like a rebuke. Henry looked the waitress up and down, then said he just needed to visit the little boys' room, we'd have to excuse him, and followed her away.

'Please, *please* tell me the sex is amazing, at least,' I said to Liz as soon as he was out of earshot.

Her mouth turned down at the corners. 'I had a theory that if I dated the worst man I could find, it might make me less fussy about only-slightly-flawed men.'

'He really is the worst. In that way, you've done pretty well.'

'Think about it, Zo. I broke up with Adam because he put on slippers the second he came in the house.'

'Is that really why? That's. . . that's a fairly reasonable habit.'

'No, I mean he used to take his slippers with him. To other people's houses. The first time he met my mum, he took his slippers out of his bag before he'd taken his coat off.'

'We've all got peccadilloes. Rather that than the toxic wasteland of this guy.'

'I know! I know that *now*! But I broke up with him over it! And before that, do you remember Phil? I dumped Phil because he ate with his mouth open.'

'No, that's gross. I'm with you there.'

'He'd just had dental surgery! He only had to do that for a week, and I dumped him for it.'

'Mmm. Did he know that was the reason?'

'I told him it was some other feelings stuff, but I knew he could see me flinching every time he ate. It was like going out with a massive bull.'

'Oh yeah?' I gave a heavy wink.

'Poor Phil. He was really nice. And Adam was really, *really* nice.' She sighed. It seemed like we both missed Adam, although she was the one who'd been with him for the last three years. 'Anyway, I read this article in a women's mag, about how once you date someone who's totally wrong for you, it's not actually a bad thing, because it can help you sort out in your mind what it is you actually want from a relationship. Particularly in your twenties, it can be hard to know what's just sexual attraction, what's just a reflection of how you want the world to think of you, and what you actually need.'

I nodded slowly, chewing on a breadstick.

'I mean, you're lucky – you found your better half. You knew what you wanted. But how do I know what works for me?'

I took a sip of my water. 'Did Adam make you happy?'

'So happy!' she smiled. 'But I decided one day that I couldn't bear the thought of going to someone's house in our thirties, or forties, or fifties, and Adam bringing out his woolly slippers. How humiliating it would be. I didn't really think about how kind he was, or how funny, or how much my mum liked him, or my friends. Or me.'

'He *was* pretty good.'

'Exactly. I just thought, at the time, that any imagined embarrassment over slippers was more important than how happy we were together, right then.'

'And now you've got Henry.'

'Yes! And he makes me so unhappy, almost all the time. He's going to be the perfect cure. And here he is.'

'What's that?' Henry said, pulling out his chair and sitting so wide-legged I wondered if he was about to start playing a cello for our entertainment.

'Liz was just saying how perfect you are,' I smiled.

Henry snorted. 'Bloody hell! I turn my back for two minutes and you've got her making wedding plans. Sorry, you've got the wrong guy.'

Liz patted his knee and smiled back at me. 'No, I think I've got exactly the right one.'

We stayed for only two courses – Henry didn't want dessert, although I think he'd actually got some ideas in his head about how lucky he was going to get with Liz that night, after all that talk of the *right one*. Liz gave me a hug and asked me to send her love to Jack, that she hoped he felt better. I said, 'Thanks, I will,' and wished her luck with her theory. I left feeling utterly miserable, and sat miserably on the Tube home, before walking miserably up our street and into the flat. I thought all the way home about the crack in our relationship that I'd crowbarred wide open this evening. I wasn't sure yet whether it was about to let in a tidal wave of pain or some sweet fresh air. And I didn't know either, really, how much I'd meant what I'd said, but I'd take my lead from Jack. If he was ready to talk about it, it's probably best that we did.

Jack was still on the sofa.

'Feeling any better?' I tried to sound sympathetic.

'Oh hey, Zo!' He sat up and smiled at me. 'How was it?'

'Fine. Liz sends her love,' I said flatly.

'Nice one. She alright?'

'She's got a prick of a new boyfriend.'

'How bad?'

'He wore his sunglasses on his head all night.'

Jack bit his fist.

'She's got a theory about being more tolerant of partners once you've gone out with someone terrible.'

'Is that about Adam?'

I sat on the coffee table. 'Liz reckons we're lucky, having found each other already.'

'And did you say, "Yeah, it's lucky how my husband's really making me know how important being sociable is, for my next husband"?' I blinked at how accurate that was. Jack laughed, seeing my face. 'Oh my god, I was joking!' He pulled me off the table and onto the sofa, lying me down alongside him. 'Look. I saved you some pizza.' Inside the box were two slices of jalapeño pizza, which he fed to me while we watched the end of a terrible film, everyone firing guns and exploding.

He kissed my hair. 'Did you mean what you said earlier?'

'No. Sorry.' I buried myself against him. 'Hormones or something. I didn't mean it at all.'

'Phew,' he said, kissing my hair again. 'I'm sorry too. I love you, Zo.'

Maybe I had made a mistake with what I said earlier. I just needed to relax. I pulled his arms a little tighter.

As we relaxed into the sofa, there was a buzz from the front door.

Outside, Esther and Ava were waiting for me, looking worried.

'What's wrong? Is it Mum? Dad? Kat? What's happened?'

Esther said, 'Is Jack home?'

'Yeah, we're just watching a film. This is a bit late for you two to be out, isn't it? What's going on?'

Ava linked her arm with mine. 'Nothing. Don't panic. It's ok.'

I brought them both into the flat and put on the kettle; Jack waved through the hatch, but saw from their faces they weren't here for small talk.

'Right, kettle's boiling, you're inside. *What's* going on?'

Esther leant against the kitchen counter. 'It's nothing disastrous. But you know we had that thing at Kat's work this afternoon? The family day for her ad agency?'

Ava chipped in: 'It was nice, Zo, the company looks like it's a good fit for her.'

'Only. . .' Esther looked at her, then at me. 'Only we met Kat's boss. The guy who's just bought the whole company.'

'And?' I said, feeling baffled.

Ava stepped closer to me. 'And it was Chuck, Zo.'

SIX

For the next week, Zoe didn't hear from Jack. Her studies kept her busy; there were family birthdays; a night out with her sisters.

But she didn't for a single moment stop thinking about him. Family mealtimes reminded her of dinner with his parents. She picked at her food, until she could see her mum and dad regarding her, and each other, with meaningful looks. Every university lecture was spent wondering if she'd find him outside afterwards – just as she'd waited for him – but he was never there. The night out with her sisters ended early when a guy had approached their table, asking Zoe if he could buy her a drink, and she had stared at him mutely, calculating all the ways in which he wasn't as good as Jack. Eventually Kat had stuck her in a cab and sent it back to Mum and Dad's. On that taxi ride home, she was glad she'd deleted him from her phone to stop herself from tumbling headfirst into something she didn't understand – she couldn't call even if she'd wanted to. Which she did. And which was, she thought, even more of a reason not to call. If she was this obsessed with him already, it was a warning bell to stay well away, to protect him from that kind of suffocation.

Until Tuesday morning, when she got a text from an unrecognised number, saying, simply, *Call me please*. Only, she recognised it. Her stomach dropped through the floor. What the hell had happened? A death? An STD? Oh Jesus, did he have a girlfriend he'd forgotten to mention?

It rang once, before Jack's voice said with plain delight, 'Hey!'

'What? What is it? What's wrong?'

'What do you mean what's wrong? You called me.'

'You said I had to call you. What's happened?'

There was a pause. 'Oh god. No, I didn't—'

'You didn't mean to send that message to me. Ok, fine, no problem.' Zoe swallowed hard.

'No! No, I very much did mean to send it to you – I just didn't think – I hadn't thought how it sounded. I'm really sorry. I didn't – it's not an emergency. I just. . . I was just asking please if you might call me again.'

It was Zoe's turn to pause. 'Oh. Right.' She felt herself blushing. 'Why?'

Jack didn't pause at all now. 'Because I missed you. I wanted to talk to you again. Maybe even to see you again?' There was a silence. 'Unless. . . Have I judged this all wrong? God, I'm so sorry, Zoe, I thought we'd both had a good time. Sorry. Sorry. I won't. . . I won't call you again. Sorry. I just wanted to say that I'd had a really nice time with you. So. . . thank you. Ok. Bye.'

'Wait!' The call was still connected. 'Jack?'

'Hello.'

'I did have a nice time. With you. A really nice time.'

'But. . .'

'But? I don't think there is a but. And that's the but.'

'I. . . Ok. So do you fancy a drink? It's fine either way, I don't want to—'

'Yes.' Zoe let out a relieved sigh, and felt her shoulders drop three inches, feeling a hundred pounds lighter. It felt like time to stop protecting herself. 'Please. Yes. I would like a drink, thank you.' She was smiling again. 'I'd really like that a lot.'

'Good.' She could hear the smile in his voice too.

She hugged the phone a little. 'Good.'

They met at a bar around the corner from his work, where he knew the staff. They greeted him with high fives and hugs, and Jack introduced Zoe to them all.

'And this, Zoe, this is one of the most talented people you'll ever meet,' he said, nodding at an older woman with cropped grey hair. 'Nic, this is Zoe. Zoe, Nic.' They smiled at each other. Jack added in a stage whisper, 'She literally makes the best cocktails I've ever had. It's actual witchcraft. And I mean that in the best possible way.' Zoe looked curious, and Nic nodded slowly.

'It's true. For them, slugs and toads and frogspawn. But for you. . . a vodka martini?'

'Oh my god, yes. Please.'

She nodded at Jack. 'I'll let you off the cauldron sauce for once. Same for you?' He nodded back, with a huge grin. 'Go on, you two, take a booth. We'll bring them over.'

They took a small booth in the corner, where no one would be passing by. It was cosy, but not so cosy that Zoe couldn't put a little distance between her and Jack as they sat down. His face flickered with disappointment for just a moment. 'Are we. . . is everything ok?'

Zoe picked up a cocktail stick from the miniature barrel in the middle of the table and chewed on it briefly. 'It's all ok. I suppose that I missed you too.' Jack's grin returned. 'But I don't get what's happening here.'

'It's a cocktail bar. They'll bring us drinks and we give them money,' Jack explained.

'Seriously. What is *this*? Why did I miss you so much? Why did I think about you all day every day? What even is this? Who *are* you?'

'You thought about me every day?' Jack's grin crept even wider across his face.

'I don't understand what's happening. I'm serious.' They stared at each other, saying nothing.

Nic herself arrived with their drinks, and added two bowls of olives to their table. 'Compliments of the manager,' she said, before slipping away with the infinite discretion of an experienced bar worker.

Jack reached for an olive but knocked over the barrel of toothpicks in his haste. 'Jesus Christ, I'm nervous,' he muttered. After hurriedly putting them back in their pot, he glanced up at Zoe, turning his glass round and round in his hands. 'Hold on, can we go back a bit, to these feelings you're having. These are. . . good feelings? Bad feelings?'

'Good. They're good feelings. But I don't know anything about you, I've known you less than a month and I don't understand how this works.'

'Zoe,' he said gently. 'I'm not going to talk you into having a relationship with me.'

'I know. I don't want you to.' She sipped her drink. 'Oh my god, this is amazing.'

'I told you.'

'Seriously. How does she do that?'

'I wish I knew – she won't tell me.'

Zoe took another sip. 'Jesus. And no, you don't have to talk me into anything. I definitely don't want you to.' She took a deep breath. 'But I just. . . I want it on record that

75

I am freaked out by this. Even if it seems wonderful, I don't know what to do with it. And that's even more terrifying. That I might. . . break it, or something.'

'Then how about we start again? Let's have this as a proper, formal date – you ask questions about me, I ask questions about you, we drink more cocktails, I reveal the most embarrassing misadventures from my schooldays, you reveal how completely perfect you are—'

'Don't,' she interrupted. 'I like the rest of it, but let's not pretend either of us is perfect. Those kinds of discoveries are the stuff I'm afraid of. Realising too late that the person you're with isn't the person you've held them up to be. So let's realise it now.'

'Fine. Absolutely. You are a typical flawed human, who may just, after lots of questions and conversations and misunderstandings and cocktails, turn out to be perfect for me.' Jack smiled at her again. 'And vice versa.'

Zoe shrugged and took another sip. 'Ok. Why not. Let's start at the beginning. Surname?'

Jack smiled at her.

They went to their separate beds that night, and after their next date at the weekend. That date saw them talking over dinner about school and family. Jack did have some excellent misadventures to recount, many of them involving his oldest friend, Iffy, whom Jack had promised to introduce to Zoe as soon as she was ready. Zoe promised Jack could meet her sisters as soon as she thought *he* was ready. They discussed work plans, ambitions, favourite books, favourite drinks, loathed film stars, good shoes, emergency hangover breakfasts, pets they'd never had, songs that made them cry, TV that made them laugh. They never seemed to run out of breath, even when the maître d' had to interrupt them to serve them their bill, as the restaurant was closing. Another great date.

At the end of their next formal date – dinner and a movie again – Zoe went back to Jack's room and remembered another reason she liked him so much.

And after that, they were very rarely apart.

SEVEN

Now

February was starting like February always does – grey, damp, and miserable, like a shampooed Blue Persian cat. We had no plans to look forward to, and no money to undertake any plans with, anyway.

I was lying on the sofa, painting my toenails a sympathetic sludgy grey colour. Belatedly, I was realising it made my feet look dead. As I heard the *clunk-pfffshh* of the washing machine going on, I called out to Jack, 'Did you put it on thirty?'

'Why does it have to be on thirty?' Jack yelled back.

I bit back a scream, forced a smile and tried to keep my tone as light as possible. 'Do you remember, my yellow top can't be washed above thirty.'

Jack came and sat next to me, narrowly avoiding my freshly painted toenails. 'Don't worry, there wasn't any of your stuff in that load anyway.'

I gave him a sideways look. 'Are you sure? Because when I put my top in the laundry basket last night there were only about six other things in there. Unless you've been secretly soiling your clothes in your sleep.'

He screwed up his nose. 'Pleasant image. No, I always just leave your clothes out of my washes – I don't want to mess them up.'

'Jack!' I took a deep breath, lowered my voice. 'I appreciate you don't want to wreck my clothes. And I really appreciate that you're trying to be thoughtful and do the right thing. But, as we've discussed more than once – probably a few hundred times in fact – if you're putting a wash on, and it's not even full, and we live together, AND WE JUST AGREED TO BE MARRIED FOR THE REST OF OUR LIVES—' I took another deep breath. 'Then, darling, please can you just look at the label, like I do when I wash anything, ever, of yours, and avoid boil-washing it? And just put my clothes in. . . with yours. I'm sure they won't get germs from each other.'

He picked up my bottle of nail polish. 'I dunno. Doesn't it just seem easier if you do your own washing?'

'And my own cooking? And cleaning? And next time we go to a restaurant, shall we divvy up the bill according to who had what?'

'Hang on – I do the cooking, ninety per cent of the time.'

'It's hardly ninety per cent! As if I only cook a meal every ten days!'

'Neither porridge nor bringing something from your parents' house counts.'

'Oh. Well, that's not even the point. Please Jack, I am asking you – and I am happy to put this in writing if that's what you need – *please* will you please put some of my washing in when you do some of yours. Please.'

He stroked the nail polish brush along his thumbnail, turning it the same sludgy grey colour as my toes. 'Can't I just do most of the cooking and you do that stuff yourself?'

'No no no, don't say "that stuff". Things like "that stuff" are just millimetres away from other things like "women's stuff", and you *know* there will be *none* of that dismissive That's Not For Men talk in *this* house.'

'You sound like your mum.'

'Good!'

Jack looked at me with a glimmer in his eye, and kissed my nose. My anger began to subside. I just wanted us to be happy again. 'Now go and make me one of these ninety per cent meals, please.'

When he came back an hour later with squash and feta empanadas, my bad mood had dissolved almost entirely.

'Zo! Zoe!'

I'd fallen asleep with a cup of tea in front of an old western, where the cowboys were generally making life a hell of a lot worse for the Native Americans. For a moment, I couldn't work out where I was. Was someone invading my settlement?

'Zoe! Please can I just show you something?'

I stumbled into the kitchen, hoping it was another batch of empanadas.

'Look.' Jack was pointing at the sink. I leant forwards. 'What's this?'

'A teabag? Did you really wake me up for that?' I felt Jack's forehead. 'Are you ill? Did you really not recognise it? Well, now that we've sorted this taxonomical mystery out, I'm heading back to the sofa. Sweet dreams, cowboy.'

'Hold on, hold on. One more question.'

'Is it "how great does this other thing I've cooked taste"?'

'No. Please can you show me where the bin is?'

With exaggerated slow motion, I turned around, bent down and pulled out the bin drawer. 'Ta-da! Now, if there're no further conundrums to address, I really must be getting back to ruining tonight's sleep.'

'Since you're clearly a little sleep-addled, I'm going to

show you the conclusion of this wonderful interchange I've been enjoying so much.'

Uh-oh. This was serious talk.

'Watch!' Jack lifted the teabag from the sink, pinching it between two fingers. 'Wait!' He held up the forefinger of his other hand. 'Marvel!' He leant over the open bin and released the teabag into it. 'Ta-da!'

'Jack. You can just ask me to put teabags in the bin, you know. Pantomime season is over.'

'Can I, though? Can I just ask you, and you'll never leave it in the sink again?'

'I'm sorry I always forget. I just can't understand why it bothers you so much, though – a teabag is literally the smallest thing you can put in the sink without it going down the plughole. And I put them in the bin at the end of the day.'

'No, you don't! I do!'

'Only because you get there first. I'd never leave it in there overnight!'

'Yes, because *that* would be ludicrous and gross.'

I rubbed my face. 'Nnnggg – how can it bother you this much? Jesus Christ! It is only a single teabag—'

'It's never just a single teabag—'

'And it is in the sink. Not on the side. Not on the floor. Not placed delicately in the centre of your pillow. It's in the sink.'

'It's massively unpleasant. It bothers me. Please can you do this favour for me?'

'Like you do my laundry?'

'You know it's not the same thing.' There was a silence, while we shifted gears.

I launched first.

'You're damn right it's not the same thing—'

'I have to use this kitchen too, in fact I use it more—'

81

'And if you really want, I can show you where we keep the washing powder—'

'And I ask you for one favour when you use this space we share—'

'Except, oh no, you already know where it is, because you've just used it for your own, exclusive, Jack-only wash—'

'And it's something so small, that takes no effort, and no time—'

'As if just doing something for me when you're *already doing that exact same thing* for yourself already—'

'But your way of doing things is the only way it could ever be done—'

'Because it's the *right way*! It's a teabag! It's wet! Wet stuff goes in the sink!'

'Now you definitely sound like your mum.'

'Stop saying that like it's a fucking insult! We are talking. About. A TEABAG.'

'It's rubbish and it belongs in the bin! *What* are you keeping it for?'

'Finally. A perfect summary of how I feel about this marriage.'

Jack looked winded. I was shaking.

'Just. . . Can you please not fucking leave your teabags in the sink. It's fucking gross.' In despair, he threw down the handful of cutlery he was holding, fresh from the drying rack, and turned to leave the kitchen. But the cutlery, bunched together, didn't land square on the counter – one fork flipped up, bounced by a heavy knife handle, and I watched it travel up and through the hatch, in horrible, inevitable slow motion, until it hit, with a crunch, a framed photo. My grandma's.

'What the. . .' I followed Jack out of the kitchen, and over to the smashed frame, trying not to step on the broken glass. 'Jack! JACK!' He was right next to me, when I turned round, looking down at the mess on the floor. 'Are you kidding me?'

'What?' He looked baffled. 'Did I just do that?'

'Jack! That was the fork you just threw!'

'*I* didn't smash it.'

'Wait – is that supposed to imply that *I* smashed it?'

'No—'

'You just threw that cutlery down, and it—' I looked down at the picture, torn and punctured by the broken glass it had landed against. 'It *destroyed* a picture I love *so* much—'

'Zo, I'm sorry, but that was just a terrible accident—'

'Look at it, Jack! It's ruined!' Surprising myself, I started to cry. 'But it's my fault you got angry enough to break it?'

Jack looked almost as surprised as me. 'But— I didn't—' I felt bone tired. 'I'm sure we can fix it. Zo?' I crammed my trainers over my slipper socks and picked up my handbag while Jack stood there with his mouth open, staring at me like he had concussion. I opened the front door and shouted, 'I'M GOING TO AVA'S – SEE YOU LATER,' slamming the door closed before my words even reached his ears.

Ava lived a bus ride away, a bus on which I watched a teenage couple in front of me kiss passionately. I got an unfortunate eyeful of him licking her ear with a hygienic thoroughness of which even Jack would have approved, before her phone bleeped and they descended into wicked bickering, culminating in her demanding that the driver let her off between stops as she *couldn't bear to be on a bus with this stupid little prick for moment longer and couldn't be held responsible for my behaviour otherwise.* The driver let her off. At the next stop, he met my eye in the mirror and chuckled. I smiled back at him, but thought, *I don't know why I'm smiling – I just had a worse argument with my husband. Yet again.*

The word 'husband' closed up my throat. This seemed exactly as life with a husband would be, I thought grimly.

Spending your weekends arguing about household chores. Just like I always dreamed. Marital bliss, sandwiched between *It's Your Bloody Turn* and *I Already Did It This Week*. I may have agreed to marry Jack, but I didn't promise to start behaving like a Stepford Wife in his perfect home – particularly not if he thought it was acceptable to do separate washes for the rest of our lives.

By the time I'd walked the three streets from the bus stop to Ava's flat, I was hurt and furious all over again. Unexpectedly, it was Kat who opened the door, immediately taking in the look on my face. 'The oppressive patriarchal regime of marriage treating you well, then?' I grunted in reply, and showed her the bottle of wine I'd picked up from the shop at the end of the road.

'Your ticket has been validated, come on through,' she said, opening the door wider and pulling me inside.

I gave her a hug. 'How's your new job, by the way?' I peered closely at her, and she pulled back.

'Fine, thanks. Why are you being weird?'

'Is it ok? Your colleagues ok? Your boss?'

'Yes, thanks. Is this how teachers talk to each other? Because it really is *very* weird.'

She seemed fine, for now, but that didn't mean I wasn't going to keep my eye on her. Not with Chuck in her office, not with him as her boss. 'Good. I'm glad.' I headed further into the flat while she took the wine away to open. 'What are you doing here, anyway?' I called after her.

'Nice to see you too, dear sister. Guessing by your demeanour, the same as you – I've come for the wisdom of our elders,' she said from the kitchen.

'Careful,' said Ava, coming in and pulling me into a hug. 'Wanting me to give you a pedicure is not seeking the wisdom of your elders.' She switched to a whisper: 'Kat seems fine. She's not said anything about Chuck, or work. She seems ok, Zo, honestly. Anyway,' she said at normal volume, 'it looks like Zoe might need it more.'

'What?' Kat wailed. I poked my tongue out at her when Ava gave me another hug. Once she'd found wine glasses, brought me a blanket and tipped a giant bag of crisps into her fruit bowl – after removing a lone, shrivelled tangerine – I not only felt calmer, but brave enough to talk about the situation.

'Go on. I can see it in your face. What have you done?' said Kat, pouring the wine.

'Thanks a lot.'

'Kat!' Ava threw a cushion at her.

'That reminds me, I saw Liz the other day. Her new boyfriend is the *worst*. And I say that as a direct quote from her.' I sighed, hard.

'Hey. Did Jack do something?' Kat asked. 'Don't tell me the bubble has burst already?'

'I think it burst a long time ago. Or maybe there wasn't even a bubble in the first place. Do you think that's possible? Seriously – do you think we got married, and maybe. . .'

'You shouldn't have?'

Ava threw another cushion. 'Kat, I'm serious,' she growled.

'No! Bloody hell, Kat. No!' I frowned at her. I only wanted them to tell me how ridiculous Jack was in this argument. Or I was. I didn't want to discover they felt our whole relationship was a mistake. 'No! We just had a fight. And it was shitty.'

'I'm sorry, Zo.'

Ava slipped away and came back a few moments later with a huge square bowl of gently steaming water. I pulled off my trainers, then my socks, and sank my feet into the water. Rain started up, drumming against the darkening windows. Kat turned on low lamps around the room and I closed my eyes and let out a deep sigh. 'Well *that* sounds serious,' Ava said in a soft voice.

I opened my eyes again, feeling increasingly calm. 'I don't know. I don't think it is. Everyone fights when they first marry, don't they? Either that or they never have a cross word for seventy years, but I don't think Jack and I were ever going to fall into that category. It's just. . . shittier than I thought it would be.'

'What happened?'

'It was stupid, really.' I shrugged, and leant back against the sofa. 'Jack refuses to do any of my laundry and I always leave teabags in the sink.'

'Oh Christ, like Mum? Urgh,' Kat moaned. Even Ava was pulling a face.

'Don't you start! They're wet, aren't they? The sink is where wet stuff goes.'

'Or the drying rack. Why don't you just drape them over the plates and cups there?'

'It's not a legal offence, for god's sake! It's a teabag. And why have I spent my afternoon saying that?'

Ava intervened. 'I have to say, that laundry thing definitely isn't ok, though.'

'*Thank* you.'

'Does he do his own laundry?' Kat asked.

'Of course he does! He's not a monster. But he ran a half load today, rather than risk ever damaging any of my clothes.'

Ava took one of my feet out of the bowl and dried it on a towel in her lap. 'Isn't that quite thoughtful?'

'Did he call you and tell you to say that?' I said. Admittedly, I'd like to see the man who tried to *make* Ava say anything. 'Fine. Yes, it's officially thoughtful, but it's day-to-day bullshit. I'm not going to live with someone for who knows how many decades and still be doing separate laundry loads. What if we have kids? Whose responsibility will that fall under? It's insane that he can treat me like some German flatmate who he'll share meals and sofas with, but wouldn't *dare* be so inappropriate as to wash their *delicates*. Oh, it's so hard to stay as angry as I'd like when you're giving me a pedicure.'

'Should I stop? You can get really angry and throw things at Kat. I find it immensely soothing.'

I gave a beatific smile to Kat, and said, 'No, I think enough damage has already been done to her poor brain. We should leave her the few faculties she has left. Like wine pouring.'

Kat took the hint and topped up our glasses, giving herself twice as much as me and Ava.

'He smashed my photo of Grandma, too,' I added.

As soon as the words were out of my mouth I realised my mistake. I saw their horrified faces and suddenly saw Jack through their eyes. 'No, I mean – it was an *accident—*'

'That's what they all say,' hissed Kat.

'No, I mean it – he chucked some cutlery down on the worktop and a fork pinged up through the hatch and knocked the glass out.'

'Oh.' Kat looked deflated.

'Zo!' Ava said, with gentle rebuke.

'I know. I phrased that wrongly. But on top of our arguments already. . . I know it was an accident, and it could have happened at any time, but it just felt like a sign.'

'A sign of what?' Kat was picking her nails, looking at the polish bottles lined up.

I sighed. 'Maybe that Grandma wouldn't approve. Of what we were doing.'

'Arguing all the time?'

I closed my eyes and didn't reply.

Ava lifted my other foot from the water onto the towel, removed my nail polish and rubbed my feet, covering them in thick, rich shea butter, before wrapping them up again in soft muslin cloths. While I kept my eyes closed, she and Kat talked softly about the best nail colours, hand creams, dinner at Mum and Dad's, Kat's new job. I listened to them, smiling, content in my nest on the sofa. This is what I wondered if marriage would feel like in a perfect world: warm, comfy, safe. It's how I used to feel with Jack, before we said *I do*, but it didn't feel like that anymore. It wasn't just today's fight, either. It was a growing unease, a discomfort that I'd been stamping down ever since Jack proposed, which had threatened to erupt on our wedding day but which I'd managed to trap in a box and mostly ignore since then. It hadn't gone away, though. I was just as suffocated by the thought of our lifelong marriage as I had been on the night Jack first asked me. I loved him so much, and was so desperate to do the right thing, that it had seemed my only option was to say yes and to agree to marry him, even though the suffocation when he'd hugged me and started phoning our families was overwhelming. Instead I'd just ignored it. And now that suffocation was matched by my souring temper, and my inability to just *be* with Jack, to have our easiness back.

In my more optimistic moments, I'd thought the day-to-day disagreements that are a part of any normal relationship might be ironed out by marriage; that this was the advantage to getting hitched, that all these silly quarrels would just become history. I'd reassured myself the whole time: if I made this choice freely, the reward would be freedom from the constant fear that every disagreement would end with our relationship ending too.

Either that, or you divorced.

I opened my eyes.

It was the first time I'd thought of that word, and it made me feel sick to my stomach. But it also – just a little, just a flicker, just a tiny speck of a flash of a fragment – made me feel free.

I drained my wine glass. 'Don't take this the wrong way,' I started, 'and *absolutely* don't say anything to Mum. But do either of you know anyone who's divorced?' Kat's jaw dropped. 'I mean it. Don't you dare tell Mum I asked that.'

Ava peeled open one of the muslin wraps around my feet. 'Is that what you're thinking about? After this fight?'

'I'm not thinking about it. And it's not this fight. I was just wondering, that's all.'

'We know loads of people Mum and Dad's age,' Kat said tentatively. 'Most of my friends' parents were divorcing during GCSEs and I felt really jealous because I could never get out of any extra revision sessions like them.'

'Yeah, bloody Mum and Dad's secure relationship. Ugh,' I tried to laugh.

'I know, right? But no, none of my friends are even married yet. Ave?'

She thought for a moment. 'Two couples I know. One set got divorced last year, the others are just getting started. The first ones tried counselling but it just didn't take. I think they realised almost instantly that they didn't really like each other that much, but it turned out they couldn't get divorced for a year. He moved out two weeks after the wedding and they only saw each other again to do the paperwork.'

'How come they couldn't get divorced for a year?' I asked. It was sharper than I'd intended and I felt Kat's eyes on me.

'No one can. It's the law in the UK, apparently – no one can even begin to divorce until a year after their marriage started. Don't know the logic behind that. Maybe that's why we've never rivalled Vegas for wedding chapel adventures.'

I hadn't been seriously considering divorce – I'd really, really only just been idly wondering – but now that I knew it wasn't even one of my options, I felt even more thoroughly smothered than before. A year. What if things got worse? It had only been just under a month so far, and that left. . . still almost a year. A voice in my mind that sounded a lot like Ava tried to tell me that I should calm down, see how things went, nothing was set in stone one way or another, I would be ok. But all I could think was that I couldn't even get a divorce if this all turned out to be a terrible mistake. I was stuck.

Again.

But worse.

I couldn't get into the marriage to make it work, and I couldn't get out. I'd walked into the trap.

'I'm stuck,' I said softly.

Ava took my foot in her hands, and began rubbing in the rest of the butter. 'You're not stuck, Zo. This is scary, and you don't seem happy right now, but you love Jack and Jack loves you. Try to think about that. And Kat—'

Kat looked up from her buzzing phone.

'Don't even think about telling *anyone* about this conversation. Or the only physical contact we will ever have again will be me throwing you out of my house by the ear.'

'Yes, yes,' said Kat, 'I know that counts when it comes from you. I wouldn't dare. I am sorry though, Zo. Bullshit as marriage probably is, I don't want someone I actually care about to be one of its casualties.'

For even Kat to say that. . . Did she see something I didn't? Was it terminal already?

Any calming influence of Ava's gentle hands dissipated entirely once I got back home in the early evening. Jack was watching TV in a darkened living room, eating some delicious-smelling pasta. I stood behind him and forced myself to put a conciliatory hand on his shoulder. 'That smells nice. Any left?'

He didn't look up. 'I didn't know when you'd be back,' he said blandly. 'Sorry.'

I closed my eyes for a second, and said in as neutral a tone as possible, 'Ok, I'm pretty tired, so I'm going to go straight to bed. Sleep tight.'

I didn't open my eyes when he came to bed, hours later, but my mind was churning, rolling over hot lumps of anxiety, regret, anger, hopelessness and fear. The perfect cocktail for a good night's sleep.

Some time around 3 a.m., I remembered Benni's comment about the reshuffle of staff between our school and our sister school in Manchester, and by the time I woke up, I was convinced it was the perfect solution: a fresh start. Whatever that meant for our marriage.

The next day, in the Science office, Benni was surprised.

'Darling, are you sure? We'd miss you far too much down here, you know. I'd miss you too much. Oh god, and I'd have to find your replacement for your classes. What can I offer you? Gold? Diamonds? Plus, you'd have to find new friends, new shops, new bars.' She pouted.

'Are you trying to talk me out of this? Because those last things sound like amazing reasons for signing up right now. And Manchester isn't the moon, it's only a train ride away.'

'I know, I know. If that's really what you want. What does Jack say?'

I hesitated. 'Not much. I'm sure he'll be ok with it. And I think it's best for both of us at the moment, really.'

Benni looked at me, baffled. 'He wouldn't be going?'

'Maybe not. Not now, anyway. We'll see how it goes.'

She nodded, turning away. 'Well, that's very modern of you. Marriage split between two cities. Why not.' She banged her hands down on her desk, calling her thoughts to order. 'Right. I'll talk to the Head about this – we've got a meeting after school on Friday – and I'll let you know asap. You know this is a permanent swap, don't you? And it's starting next term – that's only a couple of months away. Is that ok? They want to get everyone sorted and settled before the year starts up again in September.' She sighed. 'All these bloody changes they're making so fast, no one knows if they're coming or going.'

I gave her a wry smile; I knew which I'd prefer. 'Fine. Perfect. Thank you.'

She patted me on the shoulder and headed off to her office, leaving me to indulge in a few daydreams about a solo Manchester flat, Jack visiting, me showing him around, settled in this conflict-free home. Ava and Esther would have to keep an eye on Kat while I was gone – it was bad enough as it was, me worrying I might bump into Chuck round every corner in London. I mean, yes, I'm sure I would miss Jack from time to time, but we'd see each other at weekends, sometimes, and school holidays. It might be hard first thing in the morning, when I'd normally see him. Or bedtime, when we'd talk for ages in bed. Or at mealtimes. Or when he'd be making me laugh. Or when he'd surprise me after school for a quick coffee. Or when I'd have a crappy day at work and he'd make me feel better. Or when I'd have a brilliant day and I could make him feel better. Fine. I'd miss him. And fine, there was a tiny voice in my head reminding me that none of this was the logical action of a rational person. But I wanted to save whatever good there had been between us. And if it meant cutting off my right hand to stop this gangrene spreading. . . What else was I supposed to do?

The next morning, Jack was in the kitchen drinking coffee. I flicked the kettle on to start my tea. 'I've had an idea,' I said, pulling out a mug and keeping my face hidden in the cupboard, choosing a teabag. Jack didn't say anything. 'The school's looking for people to go up to Manchester at the moment. I was thinking of putting myself forward for it.'

I heard Jack gulping down his coffee behind me, before starting to wash up the mug. 'How long would you need to be away for?' He carefully placed it onto the drying rack. 'A couple of days?' He looked at me. 'A couple of *weeks*?'

'I'd be gone. . . at least a year. Maybe two. I don't know.' I wasn't ready to admit it was for good. 'Depends how they liked me up there.'

'Zo, you know I couldn't leave the shop.' The kettle clicked as it reached a loud boil, and I took it off the stand, not pouring yet, just holding it, finally turning to face him.

Jack made eye contact for the first time, as realisation dawned. 'Oh. You weren't planning for me to leave the shop.'

'I would never expect you to. I wouldn't ask that of you.'

'But you're going to the other end of the country.'

'It's hardly the other end of the country! It's only a couple of hours on the train. I just thought. . . it might give us a bit of space to sort things out. We both want this marriage to work, don't we? I just worry that we're already starting to lose. . . you know. The good stuff. And maybe living apart, even for a little while, might help us both to clear our heads, and enjoy being together when we are together. We'll both still be doing what we love. . . Will you think about it, at least?'

'There are no closer schools?'

'Of course there are! But this is an exchange with our sister school – I know the senior staff, I know the management, I know how they work, I know they like me, and I like them. This feels like it could be a great opportunity for me! Get me out of the same school I've been at for years, try something different!'

Jack didn't say anything for a moment. 'When would you be off?'

'I haven't even discussed it with Benni yet,' I lied. 'I don't know. I wanted to talk to you about it first.'

'That's noble.' Jack's sarcasm had given me my out from this conversation, and I quickly poured the hot water from the steaming kettle, trying to disengage myself from another potential row. I turned back to say something else, to change the subject to something less fractious, but Jack had grabbed his coat and bag for work, shutting the front door behind him with a bang.

EIGHT

Six years earlier

Whether they were merging friendship groups, meeting each other's families or even talking about marriage and kids, conversation between them from the very start had always been easy and honest. Life wasn't how it was in their parents' generation, where it was a wedding, then children, then retirement. You could do things in any order now, or not at all, if that's what took your fancy. In one of their many discussions, Zoe told Jack that she did want kids, eventually, and did want to work abroad, and she wanted to follow in her parents' footsteps and not marry at all.

'Fine by me,' Jack smiled.

'Aren't men supposed to say that, though?'

'I don't know. I think most of my mates want to get married. Lots of them are quite happy to admit that they hope to meet someone who they'll settle down with forever.'

'Whereas you're happy to enjoy the life of an ageless playboy.'

'It's not commitment I'm avoiding. Commitment I'm fine with. Give me kids and mortgages and a shared dog or parking space or whatever.'

'Those things aren't equivalent,' Zoe said pointedly.

'Well. Whatever. I just don't really get marriage. My parents have done it. Some of my friends have, some of them haven't. Sometimes it's worked out, sometimes it hasn't. I'm not that fussed either way. I don't think it necessarily makes anything better, and if it doesn't do that, what's the point? It's just papering over cracks, isn't it?'

'Oh, heartwarming.'

Jack shrugged. 'I'd get married if you wanted. I just don't really care one way or another.'

'Stop, stop.' Zoe wiped her eyes. 'That's just too beautiful. It's. . . it's poetry.' She gave a dramatic sob.

'How about you then? Not fussed about marriage because you're ragingly anti, or just romantically apathetic, like me?'

Zoe narrowed her eyes. 'When I'm raging, you'll know about it, my friend. I suppose apathetic. No, somewhere between apathetic and anti. Maritally atheistic.' She thought for a moment. 'It's not for me, although I don't want to ban anyone else from doing it. It's just not ever been something I've believed in.' She stopped, looked down. 'I think it would feel a bit. . . suffocating. And old-fashioned.'

'Am I seeing a little bit of raging coming out? Just a little?'

Zoe sighed. 'And. . . I was engaged before.'

Jack stared at her. 'Wait,' he said, *what?*'

Zoe leant back in bed. 'I was really young. Sixteen. Seventeen by the end of it. And I was a young sixteen, if you know what I mean. And this guy – this prick, if you want a slightly more three-dimensional picture – he picked me out at a sixth-form college party, and he seemed so mature, and so great, and so clever, and funny, and he decided to become my boyfriend.'

'You sound like you had no say in it.'

'I didn't, Jack. That's my point. I was sixteen – I didn't fucking know what I was doing. We were together for over a year, so it seemed like this was forever, as stuff does at that age. I didn't have anything to compare it to – I'd not even had a boyfriend before then, or at least nothing longer than a few days. And this. . . *man* comes along, telling me how fantastic I am, how brilliant, how grown up, how different I was. And how could I resist?'

'Hang on – how old *was* he?'

Zoe thought about it for a moment, then looked at Jack, shocked. 'Your age. Your age, *now*. He was mid-twenties and going out with a sixteen year old.'

Jack looked queasy.

'Yeah. Exactly. His name was Chuck.' She sighed again. 'I haven't said that name for a long time. Then he thought we should be together properly, that we should be engaged, that. . . I needed to commit to the relationship, or I didn't love him enough.'

'Zoe.'

'Well,' she said tightly, leaning back from Jack's hands and looking away from him again, remembering, just needing to say it all and not have Jack's comfort stop her. 'The happy ending is that none of that mattered anyway, because I completely fucked up my A Levels and didn't get into any of my chosen courses anyway. It was pretty much thanks to him I fucked up every single paper I sat.'

'But. . . I didn't know this.'

Zoe gave him a look. 'That's the point,' she said more softly. 'No one did. He was good at that. Ava and Esther saw us out once, so I had to admit that I had a boyfriend, but they didn't know what he was like. He wanted us to stay secret, so the relationship was just about us – no one else could be involved in something so special. No one could know. So he never met my parents, never spoke to my sisters, never hung out with my friends. In the end, I barely did either.'

'Fucking hell.'

'Yup. In the end, I told Liz, who said she'd been watching me since I first met him and knew he was up to no good. She wanted me to tell someone, someone at college or my parents or anyone at all really, but I still wanted to protect him. I thought I must have done something wrong to drive him away. To make him not want me anymore, for him to treat me the way he did. All I could think of during my exams was what I could have done to make him so upset. This was the man I was supposed to marry, remember. I was going to spend the rest of my life with him, but I was such an awful person that I couldn't even keep him when I was already at his beck and call.'

'Zo. You had such a narrow escape.'

She laughed. 'I know. I realise that now. But I didn't for years – and, the thing is, it's kind of put me off marriage. Plus all that wearing white and changing your name and having your father hand you over, signing your life over to someone. It's gross.'

'But you can get married without all that stuff. Wear black and keep your name and have no one hand you over. And not everyone is like your incredibly gross ex.'

She blinked at him for a moment. 'Yeah. I suppose. But it doesn't really change the nature of the whole institution. That's it's just the government's way of keeping tabs on who owns who.'

'Now who's the romantic poet?' Jack tried to laugh.

'It is, though! I can go to a wedding and cheer and throw confetti with the best of them, but I can't say a little bit of me doesn't die inside. Just a tiny bit. And it might come back to life later on, after a few drinks and once I've hit the dancefloor, but it doesn't change my feelings. I just don't get marriage. I don't want to. I've had my little nibble at the edges of it, and it just didn't sit particularly well in my guts.'

'Alright, alright. I'll throw away the floor-length black dress I've bought you and bin the Haribo ring.'

'No, I'll take the Haribo. You can keep the frock, though.'

Jack pulled Zoe into a strong hug. 'I'm sorry, Zo. I'm sorry you had to go through that.'

Zoe kissed him, already feeling better. Lighter. Freer. Jack understood now.

NINE

Now

Things were quiet in the flat for the next few days, both of us waiting for confirmation of our new lives together. Or rather, our new lives apart. I'd managed to whip myself up into an almost constant cocktail of the familiar fear, regret and anxiety, when Benni came barrelling over one Monday morning, just as I arrived in the Science office, and headed straight to my workspace.

'Looks like it's a no,' she said.

'Good morning to you too. What's a no?'

'Check your email, darling.'

In my inbox was a staff-wide message from senior management explaining that for various reasons, no further school transfers would take place between the two schools. Shit.

'Zoe, I'm so sorry—'

'It's not your fault. It was only an idea, anyway.'

'If it's any consolation, at least our new Physics teacher got in under the wire?' She had her hand on my shoulder again, so different from the confident pat just a few days before. I knew she felt awful about it, too. She understood that I wouldn't have asked if it wasn't important to me. 'There'll be other opportunities, I'm sure, darling.'

'I know.' I tried to smile at her. 'It just would have been really handy right now.'

In the afternoon, I noticed an unread email from Liz, titled 'New theory', just as I saw the new Physics teacher heading my way. Forgetting about my cancelled move for the first time today, I stumbled to open the email, desperate to look like I was doing something other than just swooning and waiting for him to arrive at my cubby. My eyes raced over Liz's words, reading and re-reading to distract myself from my blush.

> *Going out with a terrible person makes EVERYTHING better, not just other possible partners. I actually smiled at birdsong this morning. But what if I end up marrying Henry because he makes every single other thing in the world more beautiful by comparison?*
>
> *This theory has potential hidden dangers, I'm finding. How are you? How's things with Jack? See you tonight.*
>
> *L xxx*

Interesting. Liz knew me well enough to know that Jack's absence at our meal out a couple of weeks ago – and my pathetic effort at explaining it away – would be a 'thing', although even she might not have guessed that things were so bad. Or that I'd tried to move to the other end of the country. I realised I'd been avoiding her, not willing to talk about this yet. Maybe the current status between me and Jack would mean I could get my smiling-at-birdsong magic just from small talk with the new Physics teacher in the sandwich-smelling Science office.

'Oh hey, Ms Lewis, is it?'

I tried to compose my face into one which didn't scream

'I've looked at every holiday picture you've ever posted on Facebook' and turned around. 'Hi. Zoe, please. And is it George?'

He blushed. 'Yes, hello. Wow, everyone's really friendly here.' His gentle Mancunian accent was delicious. I smiled at him and he blushed deeper. 'I thought I'd only be down to do this bit of the training,' he said, gesturing at the folder under his arm, 'but it looks like I'll be staying around a little longer. Anyway. . .' He fumbled with his armful of files. 'I just wanted to say hi.'

I thought idly about how I'd have felt arriving in the Manchester school on my own and discovering I'd missed the chance to have George as my colleague. Then I remembered I was still here, in London, making Jack unhappy, and felt completely squashed once again.

'And are you settling in alright here at Walker High?'

'Yeah, yeah, it's grand. I mean – I miss Manchester, but London's great. It's just. . .' He blushed again, apparently his main reaction when I made small talk. 'I was talking to Benni and she said you might be able to show me around a bit?'

I swivelled in my chair, craning towards Benni's office. A blurry figure jerked back from the safety glass when it saw me looking.

I looked back at George and began blushing too. 'I'd really like that, George, only. . . I'm a bit busy at the moment. . . I'm just trying to sort some stuff you see—'

'Fine, fine. Fine, no problem. Don't worry about it. Maybe a coffee some time instead? I mean, here at school if you're really busy?'

I wanted to laugh, our blazing faces matching one another. 'That'd be really nice, thanks. And don't worry,' I added, on second thought, 'I'm sure I'll manage to find some time to leave the school grounds for it. The coffee here is legendary only for its usefulness in our Chemistry experiments.'

We swapped numbers, agreeing to arrange a coffee date soon, and George headed off, just as I caught Miks's eye. 'That. Was. Painful,' he said.

'Tell me about it,' I muttered, and shook my fist only half jokingly in the direction of Benni's office.

Kat had asked me to come and meet her for drinks that evening, but I told her I'd arranged to see Liz, so she said to bring her along too, as it was just a big gang of them from work. Liz was happy to meet me there – 'Perfect: corporate credit cards o'clock' were her actual words – but things had been so hectic that I'd somehow not thought that Kat's boss might also be with them. Kat's boss. My terrible ex, who had broken my heart and wrecked my exam chances in sixth form. A small fact Kat knew nothing about.

Kat greeted me with a hug and danced me over to her colleagues when I arrived, then to the bar where she ordered me a tequila shot and a martini.

'Never one for half measures, our Zoe,' came a voice behind me as I hovered at the bar.

I heard those familiar Californian honey tones and turned around and saw him there. Chuck: his face older, a little looser, his hair salt-and-peppered around the hairline, his body tight, unruffled as ever. I felt a hard knot form in my gut. Here he was, after all these years.

'Chuck.'

Kat grinned at us. 'You two know each other!'

'No, Kat, just a lucky guess,' I said, trying to smile at her, trying not to taste the bile in my mouth.

'I guess I knew Zoe when you would have been just a little thing,' he said, and I thought, *I was just a little thing too, you son of a bitch*. 'Who would have guessed you two were sisters?'

'Kat, would you mind just checking if Liz is here yet, please? I'm worried she won't find the bar.' I felt Kat's questioning eyes on me, but she did as I asked – for possibly the first time ever – and I turned to face Chuck again.

'You look great, Zo. I can't believe you're here! I never expected to see you again.' He smiled, easily. 'I knew Kat was bringing her sister tonight, and I have to admit,' he said, leaning in, 'I kind of hoped it would be you.'

I wasn't sure if I could trust myself to speak. I felt sick. But before I could get any words out of my mouth, he kept talking. He always did like to speak over me.

'Listen, Zo, it's really great to see you – I mean, I never got to say goodbye, properly. We were young, and neither of us behaved as well as we might have done—'

I felt my mouth fall open.

'And I've always really regretted not being able to just, you know, clear everything up between us. But I wanted to say. . .' He turned to pick up my tequila shot. 'Water under the bridge? Peace between us? We're both adults, and it would be good for my spirit – for both of our spirits – if we can make this ok between us. Ok?' He clinked the shot glass against my martini glass. 'Cheers?'

I lifted the martini to my lips, taking a sip I couldn't taste. 'Cheers,' I said between clenched teeth. In answer, he knocked back the shot, slamming the empty glass back down on the bar.

'Oh, that feels good. Doesn't it feel good? Oh *man*!' He held out his arms and stepped closer, wrapping them around me. 'Doesn't that feel better?' he murmured in my ear, holding me to him before I had a chance to get away. I didn't know if I had the strength to push him off me.

'What the fuck is this shit?' I heard someone say, and took the opportunity to gratefully wriggle away, feeling dizzy. Liz was standing beside me, staring at Chuck.

Kat was looking between us all. '*Liz*,' she said. 'This is my *boss*, Chuck.'

104

'Oh, I'm fully aware of Upchuck, thanks. And he's your *boss*? How did you swindle that then, laddo?' she asked, eyeballing him.

Chuck smiled at Liz, and put an arm back around my shoulders. 'Zoe and I were having a great chat, but I think I'd better check the rest of my team are having a good time, too. Excuse me, Liz, Kat.' He nodded at me. 'Zoe.'

We watched him strut to the other end of the bar, where the rest of the staff greeted him with whoops and cheers.

'Fucking hell, you two. What was that?' Kat looked furious.

'Liz's ex,' I said, before she had a chance to say anything. 'Sixth-form college.'

'He seems a bit old to have done A Levels with you lot?' Kat said.

Liz looked at me. 'Oh no, he wasn't at college with us. He'd just be in a lot of places we were, picking off vulnerable women. Our pubs, our bars, our parties, he'd be there.'

Kat was watching Chuck again now. 'And that's where you met him, Liz?'

Liz lifted her eyebrows at me, questioning. 'Yeah? Yeah, something like that.'

Kat seemed to make a decision, and snapped her attention back to us. 'Right. Good. Now that the agency Amex is behind the bar, let's work our way through this cocktail list.'

I stayed for two more drinks, at Kat's insistence, and those drinks made me feel slightly – *slightly* – better. Maybe I didn't have anything to worry about, I reassured myself on the way home. It had been over a decade and we'd all made mistakes. It was clear that Chuck wanted the whole thing between us to be, as he'd said, water under the bridge; we'd both been young and stupid, although I'd been ten whole years younger than him. It was fine, he was Kat's boss, there was nothing to worry about there, they were just co-workers and it was fine, it was fine, I was fine, Kat was fine, Chuck was fine, Jack, fast asleep and snoring, was fiiiiiiine – it was all going to be fine.

All I needed was to lie down for one second on the nice cool kitchen floor, then I could clear my head and work out just how fine everything really was.

The next day, after long hours spent in classrooms with the volume dialled up to eleven and with nasty sweats breaking out all over my body, I arrived home clutching a hot box of comfort pizza, liberally scattered with jalapeños. I drizzled honey over the pizza, sat down in front of the TV, and started eating.

Jack came out of the bathroom, wrapped in a towel. I was torn between relief at seeing him and a strange new awkwardness at his semi-nakedness so soon after our discussion of my possible move. That stupid, pointless discussion.

'Hey,' I said, wanting to make the first move.

'Hey.'

Jack sat down, keeping a good two feet of distance between us. 'I'm sorry about last week,' he said. 'I've been thinking about it, lots, and I think you're right. I didn't love the idea – at first – but maybe it is what we need. We can let this place, and I'll find a studio or something, nearer to work, maybe. Anyway.' He coughed. 'I just wanted to say that I think you were right. I'll support your move, if that's what you want.'

I chewed my pizza, now tasting like wet cardboard in my mouth.

'What do you think?' he prompted.

'It's not happening,' I mumbled.

He reached for a slice. 'Because of how I was when you told me?'

'No.' I swallowed. 'For "strategic reasons" they've decided to cancel any intra-school moves.'

106

'Oh.'

'Yup.' I picked up another slice, folded it in half, then in quarters, and pushed the whole thing into my mouth.

'No transfers then?'

I gave him a thumbs up, cheeks bulging.

'You're staying here.'

I gave him a double thumbs up.

'That's. . . that's good. That's fine.' He spoke with careful ambivalence.

I opened a two-litre bottle of cherry Coke to stall for a moment, and glugged a third of it down. Sober, in the cold light of day, I no longer felt so reassured about trusting Chuck as Kat's boss, but didn't think I could talk to Jack about it right now. When my mouth was clear, I said, 'You sound like I feel.'

'What does that mean?'

'Well, you don't sound delighted that I'm staying, and if we're really honest about it, I wanted to go *just* as much as you wanted me to,' I said drily.

'Hang on – I was in the wrong for not wanting you to go the other day, and now I'm in the wrong for wanting you to go?'

'Thanks very much for that.'

'No – not – not *wanting you to go* – I just want to support you. In what *you* want to do. I thought that would be the right thing.'

'No, you didn't. You realised how nice it would be if we weren't fucking arguing every single day of our lives,' I snapped. 'But don't worry, because I feel the same.'

'Oh god! Well, wouldn't it be nice? It would be fantastic to come home after a hard day at work and not be told off for something I've done in the privacy of my own home.' Jack slouched against the back of the sofa, towel flapping open.

'*Not* done! You *haven't* done my laundry! Don't make it sound like I'm persecuting you for your personal proclivities! I just want you to occasionally act like I'm not some troublesome elderly housemate!'

'It's JUST. LAUNDRY.'

'It's not just laundry! It's the philosophy behind it!'

Jack tried to laugh. 'The philosophy of laundry?'

'It's the feeling that you don't consider me. You never really think about what I want, Jack. Fine, you upsize meals you'd otherwise make for yourself, but you don't actually consider me. You finish the toothpaste and neither get more nor tell me it's finished. You use up my shampoo and my face wash, the same. You'll put my almond oil on your beard. You'll use my wrapping paper, my birthday card stash, my stamps—'

'Stamps, Zo, come on—'

'And I came to the shop once and you had my vase in the window!'

'You weren't using it! It's a compliment to your good taste. And we're married now. We're meant to share stuff.'

'You're happy to have me as your stationery and beauty product cupboard, but I ask you to just *fill a load in the washing machine*, with my socks and t-shirts and dresses, and suddenly I'm asking you to give up a kidney? I *know* these are just little things you take, but you're happy to share only when I'm doing the sharing. I ask you to actually do stuff for me, and I'm being ridiculous, somehow!'

Jack scratched his beard. 'You're not perfect either, you know.'

'I know I'm not!' For a flash of a second, I thought, *I don't care about shampoo and birthday cards. What is this really about, think, think, find the words before it's too late.* But nothing came. 'I'm not perfect, Jack, but this combination of our imperfections just. . .'

'What? It's what?'

'I don't think it's working.' My mouth was speaking but I had no control over it. I picked up another slice of pizza, but this time just picked at it in the long silence that hung over us, pulling off the jalapeños, scraping off the cheese, then rolling the whole thing up into a dough ball and dropping it back in the box.

Jack watched the pizza box. 'So what does that mean?'

'I don't know. I don't like feeling like this, Jack, but what am I supposed to do? Just pretend that I don't?'

'Yes!' Jack cried. 'No one's life is perfect! Everyone struggles sometimes! But you can't just run away the second you don't feel ecstatically happy!'

'But we were happy before! What's so wrong with wanting that? Instead of. . . this! We were happy! *You* were the one who wanted to get married.' I screwed my face up, and sighed. 'Jack. I think if I can't go to Manchester, maybe it's a sign that we need to think about some time apart. Maybe even. . .' I watched Jack brace himself as my mouth kept talking, utterly unresponsive to any screaming commands my brain might be making to try and shut this line down. 'Divorce.'

Clang. The seven-tonne word was now in our home, invited by me, and it sat on top of us, slowly squeezing the life from our bodies.

Jack finally spoke. 'Oh my god, I thought you'd been joking about feeling that way at the wedding. Are you serious? It's been two months, Zo! I thought we'd been through all this. You can't just throw that word around when you've had a shitty day.'

I felt in surer waters now. I'd had variations on this conversation with myself every day of those two months, and now we were talking about it, I felt more certain than ever. The relief I already felt was palpable.

'It's just not for us, Jack. Marriage. It's not worked. And I think it's better, for both of us, if we can walk away from this in one piece, not letting it drag on for decades. You're still young enough to find someone else.'

'What the fuck, Zo?' Too late, I realised I'd gone too far.

'Sorry, I don't mean that. Shit.' I took a deep breath. 'I just mean. . . Can we both just think about this, for a couple of days? If it's easier, I'll go and stay at Ava's. Give you some space to consider it all.'

'Do I have a choice?'

'I'll stay if you want.' I didn't know if I meant that or not, but Jack just turned back to the pizza box.

'No, you go. It's fine. I guess I'll see you in a few days then.'

I packed a bag as quickly as I could, throwing in toiletries and a couple of outfits, then headed back through the lounge to the front door. I didn't know how to say goodbye to Jack now, what strange limbo I'd put us in by uttering the D-word.

'Zoe.' Jack was still on the sofa, next to the box of my shredded, deconstructed takeaway. 'I'm sorry about your pizza.'

I tried to smile. 'Right. See you later, then?'

I started to go, but Jack said again, 'Zoe.' When I turned back, he looked grey, sitting hunched in only a fraying, too-short towel. 'What's happened? Seriously, what's happened here?'

I wanted to wrap my arms around him and say it would all be ok, and sit curled up with him again, one blanket warming us both, but I couldn't. Something was stopping me.

'I don't know. But I'll see you in a few days.' I pulled my bag over my shoulder, and left without looking at him again.

TEN

Six years earlier

'Are you sure you want to do this?'

'I'm sure.'

'And you remember the safe word?'

'Yellow bus.'

'And the second you use it, we stop the whole thing. Ok?'

'Ok.'

'I really like you, and I don't want you to do this if you're not ready.'

'We've talked about this.'

'I know. But it's really important we only do this when you're totally and completely ready. We've only been together a year.'

'I'm ready! I'm ready.'

She kissed Jack. 'Ok. Thanks again for this.'

Zoe reached up and pressed the doorbell. Before the bell had even stopped ringing, the door was yanked open and Zoe's three sisters stood in the doorway, screaming and hugging Jack and Zoe and pulling them both inside.

Magically their coats were off, their shoes taken, and they

were propelled into the kitchen, where Zoe's mum and dad were waiting with heroic patience and, frankly, saintly casualness, Dad stirring the gravy, Mum wiping some imaginary spill from the counter top, the radio off for the first time in Zoe's entire recollection. Only when Zoe said 'Hellooo' did they turn, with exaggerated surprise and hug both Zoe and Jack.

'My darlings! When did you get here?' asked Zoe's mum, although Zoe knew the silence of the kitchen was because her mum would have been worrying about missing the doorbell.

'Just now, Mum – look, my face is still cold from outside.'

Her mum pressed her hands against Zoe's cheeks. 'Zoe! You will make yourself ill if you let yourself get so cold. You *must* wear a coat in this weather.'

Zoe was laughing. 'Mum! I was wearing a coat but Ava just took it. And I'm not going to start wearing a balaclava, despite your best efforts to convince us they were cool when we were little.'

Her dad laughed too. 'Well, it's lovely to see you both. Lovely to meet you at long last, Jack.'

Her mum nodded her delighted agreement.

'Mrs Lewis. Mr Lewis. It's really kind of you to have me here.'

'No, no!' Zoe's mum cried. 'I am Chidinma, and this is Philip.'

Jack smiled, pleased, but too shy to say their names yet.

'Let's get you something to warm you up, at least.' Zoe's dad flicked on the kettle, which boiled almost immediately – it had probably been boiled repeatedly for the last hour.

Five minutes later, they all sat around the big kitchen table, warming their hands on mugs of tea. 'So, Jack,' began Zoe's mum, 'Zoe says you are going to make shoes?'

'Yes, I—' Jack's voice came out slightly strangled, and he choked and coughed. Zoe's mum and two of her sisters were up, banging him on the back, offering him a glass of water while he held up his hands in surrender. Eventually he was deemed to be likely to live, and everyone sat down again. Jack took a careful sip of his tea. 'Yes, I'm hoping to go into shoe design. I'd like to design and make them, and maybe – eventually – even have my own shop one day.'

'A shoe shop?' Esther asked politely.

Zoe narrowed her eyes at her. 'No, a fruit and veg shop.'

Esther tipped her head to one side, and opened her mouth, but Zoe's dad jumped in.

'And would that be in London? Are your family around here?'

'They're actually in Norfolk, but yes, I think I'd like to start in London.'

'Start in London?' Kat questioned.

'Yeah, I think—'

'What, you don't think London can support another shop? Might be better to start out in the fashion frontline of Norwich?' Zoe asked Kat, with narrowed eyes.

'Actually—' Jack started.

'Zoe, I was just asking.' Kat smiled sarcastically. 'I don't know if you've heard, but there *are* other cities in the UK.'

'*Girls,*' their mum added warningly.

Jack tried again: 'Norwich is actually—'

'No, Mum, I'm fascinated to see what insights into the design world my little sister can offer. Sorry, just remind me again, Kat, you're doing your A Levels in. . . Biology, Chemistry, Maths and Further Maths, is that right? Sorry, just checking before we continue this discussion about retail and fashion. Sorry. Carry on, little sis, do fill us in.'

'Zo, she is allowed to ask questions,' Esther insisted.

'Not if it's an interrogation, she isn't.'

'Maybe let's all leave this topic,' Kat said, rolling her eyes.

113

'Guys, chill! I think it's pretty cool. I've never met someone who opened a shop in town before,' Ava said, smiling at Jack.

Zoe leant over the table and squeezed Ava's hand. 'You've always been my favourite sister.'

Esther and Kat yelled their disapproval of this, and by the time their mum had remembered the wire rack of cooling ginger biscuits that she'd made for the gathering, peace – or what stood for peace in a family of six – was restored.

Over lunch – a huge chicken pie that Zoe's mum deemed 'the kind of thing that a young man would want to eat' – the family talked over Jack as they asked him about his course, his parents and his interests. By pudding, he didn't need further questioning, and the conversation reverted to the usual familiar tracks: relatives, plans for the house, what the girls ought to be doing with their lives.

'My darlings, you know I love you all so much, but it's only Zoe who has a path she can follow to a good job, you know?'

'Mum!' However old this conversation was, none of the sisters would let her get away with it.

'Mum, I've not even finished my degree yet. I'm just lucky it's the kind of thing that leads naturally to a job. If I'm lucky. If I manage to last the whole course. If jobs still even exist by the time I graduate.'

'What? Are you going to *leave*?!' Zoe's mum almost wailed.

'No! I hope not. I'm not planning to.'

'Mum, I'm doing four of the hardest possible A Levels right now,' Kat called. Esther threw a napkin at her head in disgust.

'And my job isn't exactly playgroup, Mum. I'm deputy manager of my whole sales region,' Esther reminded everyone.

'Yes yes, but is it a *real* job?'

114

'Love, come on now, they're all doing very well. Ava's doing very well with her social work – we're proud of them all,' Zoe's dad interjected, putting an arm around his wife.

She looked pleased as she thought about this. 'Yes, you are right. We have four most excellent girls.'

'Women,' muttered Zoe, as Kat shrugged and followed Esther's example, throwing her own napkin at Zoe's head this time.

Zoe and Jack had cinema tickets for a late afternoon showing, so they headed off shortly after, with many thanks from Jack and many Tupperware containers from Zoe's mum. In the kitchen, she gave Zoe a long hug too, saying, 'Jack is a good boy.'

'I'm amazed you could tell, from the amount he was allowed to speak.'

'You can always tell a good boy, Zoe. I knew with your father the moment I saw him.'

'I know, I know. The second you saw each other, you knew you'd be together forever.'

Her mum hummed a little, as if she was going to say something, but was interrupted as Kat burst in, saying, 'You and your *boyfriend* are going to miss your film.' Zoe didn't rise to her sister's bait because, overall, the whole meal had been so much more painless than she had been expecting.

At the door, Zoe's dad was giving Jack a hug goodbye, as were all her sisters. Her mum came from behind her and gave Jack a long hug, so long that Jack's hands kept falling away then coming back up when he realised the hug wasn't over yet. Eventually, he looked at Zoe in something approaching alarm.

'Mum,' Zoe said.

'Alright, alright,' she said, releasing Jack and stepping back to Zoe's dad, who put an arm over her shoulders. 'Thank you for coming, you two – now you go and enjoy your evening, yes?'

Zoe gave her a hug that was almost as long, thanked her and Dad again, hugged her sisters, before finally heading out with Jack.

She looked at him as they headed down the garden path away from the house, arms linked. 'How are you feeling?'

His voice actually cracked as he replied. 'Yellow bus?'

She laughed. 'That bad?'

He cleared his throat. 'It really wasn't. And I'm hoping your mum's hug meant I made a good impression.'

'Either that or she was just saying goodbye forever,' Zoe said, raising her eyebrows in horror at Jack, who looked suitably alarmed. 'Just kidding. I guess now you know where I get my – actually, where I get *everything* from. My conversational skills—'

'Direct.'

'Very diplomatic, Jack. My eating habits—'

'Tactical.'

'And now you see why I've had to be. You don't grow up with three sisters and not learn the early bird catches the biggest portion.'

Jack laughed.

'But I think you made a good impression on everyone. After a year of my careful training.' She nudged him as they walked. 'Pretty impressive.'

Jack stopped walking and turned to face her.

'What?'

He sounded slightly surprised. 'I love you.'

She blinked. 'Ok.' She turned him and started walking.

Jack stopped again and stared at her.

Zoe laughed. 'Oh my god, I love you too! Is that what you want?'

'*Do* you?' He sounded even more surprised.

116

'Yes. I do.' She shrugged, and Jack suddenly realised where Kat had picked up her shrug from. 'And. . . seeing you with my family, not freaking out, and what my mum said—'

'Ooh, what did she say, what did she say?'

'I might tell you, one day. In the meantime, you'll just have to survive on knowing that yes, I love you too.'

He kissed her. 'Good.' He let out a wild laugh, half whoop, half cheer, and picked her up, twirling her around.

'Good,' she returned. And kissed him back.

ELEVEN

Now

'Back already?'

Three days later, as dusk fell, I found a carefree-looking Jack in our kitchen, sitting on the side with his feet up on the counter opposite, drinking a coffee and reading that day's paper.

'Sorry, were you hoping I was gone for good?' I winced, hearing the words as they came out of my mouth. I hadn't meant for it to start off like that. 'Sorry. I mean. . . Yes. I'm back.'

'How was your stay? If I'm allowed to ask.'

'Ava was trying to fatten me up a bit, since I wouldn't go and stay with Mum and Dad.'

'Why wouldn't you?'

I flicked the kettle on. It was late, and I needed something calming before bed. 'I haven't quite broken it to them that their newlywed daughter wants a divorce.' Jack flinched. 'And I definitely didn't want them to find out by discovering their daughter wasn't living at the flat they'd bought.'

'They only paid the deposit, Zo.' I ignored him. 'So does that mean you're back?'

'I'm back. Living here, anyway. It's my flat too and I can't stay with Ava forever.' I tried to soften my tone. 'But we're not. . . I think I meant what I said. Have you thought about it?'

Jack jumped down from the worktop and walked through to the lounge. He pretended to busy himself with something in front of the window, then turned around, gasping.

'Of course I've thought about it! Are you serious?' He almost growled. 'My new wife walked out after asking for a divorce, and—' He couldn't go on; he looked shell-shocked, hearing himself say the facts out loud. 'What is going *on*?'

'Well. . .' I took a deep breath; I needed to stop him, to talk practicalities. I didn't want another argument. 'We need to sort some stuff out.'

He shook his head again, stunned. 'Like what?'

I'd spent the last few days thinking about this. If I couldn't move cities to give us some space, I could at least move rooms. The thought of any space at all between us right now was all that had kept me going. 'For a start, where we're going to sleep. We can't both sleep in that bed anymore, Jack. It's really weird.'

There was a moment's pause, when we both looked at each other and did the same mental calculation. Then we both bolted – Jack over the back of the sofa, me from the kitchen door, meeting in the bedroom doorway and briefly tussling to get through first. Then we were on the bed, pulling the covers, trying to get control. Eventually I managed to get enough purchase on the duvet cover that I could roll over and over, cocooning myself and pulling it entirely off Jack. Jack looked at me, then snatched up all the pillows. We were both panting.

'This is ridiculous,' Jack said.

'Speak for yourself,' I replied, head poking out from the depths of the duvet, arms pinned down within the rolls of bedding like a giant sausage roll.

'We can't live like this,' Jack went on. 'We can't scrap for the bed every night.'

'Toss a coin? It's as fair a way as any.'

'Every night? What if one of us is out when the other person wants to go to bed?'

'Then they just get dibs. It's the other person's fault for being out late.'

Jack narrowed his eyes at me. 'This isn't at all related to me generally having later hours than you, is it?'

I tried to shrug. 'Let the coin fall as it may.'

'If you say so. Looks like you're having the bed tonight, though.'

'And we start the coin-toss tomorrow. Deal?'

'I suppose. Good night.' Jack headed out.

'Night.' I wiggled in my duvet. 'Jack? *Jack*?' He turned around, unable to hide his hopeful look. 'Please can you get me out of this? I think I'm stuck.'

Over the next few days, none of it seemed real – it felt as if we were playing at this break-up, somehow. The next night I was home at 6 p.m. sharp, and when Jack still wasn't back at nine, I crawled into bed and fell fast asleep. I definitely didn't hear his key in the lock and hurriedly shut my eyes as he came in the door, so all was fair in love and bed-war.

On Thursday, I was held up at work; they needed extra staff at a Year 8 parents' evening. By the time I got back at eight, Jack was already thoroughly asleep in my bed. He didn't even wake when I banged a saucepan in the doorway.

Tuesday evening saw me wrapped up and dozing under the duvet when Jack got back at six thirty. I heard him sighing in the bedroom doorway, so I muttered, 'Hard day at work,' in explanation, and drifted back to sleep.

On Sunday, Jack didn't get out of bed all day. Every time I went in, he was on his back, mouth open.

'If I was a better person, I'd check you were still alive,' I said. I thought I saw him smile slightly as I went to make another night's bed up on the sofa.

'Right! That's it!' Jack shouted the next Tuesday.

'Whuuu. . . what's happening?' I mumbled, having rushed home from school when the bell went to make sure I beat him back to the flat.

'It's five o'clock – unless you are very ill, there is no *way* that you are legitimately asleep in bed.'

'Mmm. . . where am I? What day is it?'

'Oh, stop it.'

'Fine. I did get home first, though.'

'We need a new plan. This isn't working.'

'It would if you weren't always home late. Or asleep.'

Jack scoffed, waving at my pyjamas. 'Says Rip Van Winkle over there. I think we need a rota.'

'A rota for bed custody?'

'If you want. A week at a time.'

We shook on it. Then I huddled back under the duvet and said, 'I suppose you can have the first week. I've had a good run of early nights to keep me going for a while.'

Jack looked surprised. 'Right. Thanks. Ok. I'll draw it up.'

The next evening, I finally resolved to deliver some more bad news. Dad opened the door, the comforting smell of Mum's cooking spilling into their porch. 'Hello love, come on in, don't let the heat out.'

He took my coat and I kicked my shoes off, padding into the kitchen with a slight nervousness, looking for Mum.

'Hello, my lovely Zoe! How are you! Where is that husband of yours?' She peered behind me, trying to see if Jack was talking to Dad. But when Dad followed me into the kitchen alone, a little confusion brushed over her face. 'He surely is not going to miss my dinner, is he?'

'Mum, Dad, I have to tell you something,' I blurted out.

Oh god, I hadn't thought the possible connotations of this nervous announcement through at all. Mum's face was lighting up with impossible hopefulness at what she thought I might be about to tell them, while Dad was watching me a little closer and not smiling.

'No, Mum. . . it's about me and Jack.' Her smile became a little less sure.

'Is he alright? Has he been hurt? Is he ill?'

'Love, let her speak,' Dad said, moving round to stand next to her. He knew.

'Mum, I think that. . . Jack and I are. . . getting. . . a divorce.' It never got any easier, saying the word out loud.

'No no no no no. That is madness. The two of you have only been married this little-little time.' She waved her hands, trying to ward off what I was saying.

'Love,' Dad said, and put an arm around her.

'Please, Mum.' I leant back against the counter, too weak to stand up properly. 'Jack and I have talked about this, and we agree it's for the best.'

We'd talked about it, at least. And we both knew it had to happen. I wasn't sure if we agreed on anything anymore.

'But my darling. . . it has been such a short time.' Mum put her head on Dad's shoulder. 'What does your poor Jack say about all this?'

Dad put his arm around her. 'Is he ok, love?'

'He's fine!' I rubbed my face. 'No, he's not fine. He's terrible, I'm terrible, and neither of us knows what we're doing. I feel like I've let everyone down. I don't know how to function anymore. I feel like I'm losing my mind. I should never have done any of this.'

Mum seemed to come to. She rushed over to me and

pulled me into a hug, a huge embrace that made me feel like a kid again. Then she pulled away for a moment. 'Did he hurt you?'

'No!'

'Has he been kissing with other women?'

'No! God, no.'

She relaxed, and pulled me in again. 'Ok. Then we will just have to make sure that you are both ok. We do not need to worry about punishment for him.'

I looked at Dad over Mum's shoulder; he gave a rueful grin, holding his hands up.

Mum held me at arm's length again. 'And where is it that you are going to live now?' She looked pale, still, shocked, but she was trying to show me that I was her priority.

'In our flat. It's my home, Mum.'

'Love, you're always welcome here, you know. I know it's harder for Jack to go anywhere, but we're right here, and you can have your old room back whenever you like,' Dad said gently. 'However this stuff with Jack goes.'

'Of course she knows this! But I do not think it would be a good idea for you to come back here. A thirty-year-old woman living back with her parents?'

I looked at Mum, surprised.

'My lovely girl, I am not such an old fool as you think. I know this would not be good for you, not at all. But where is Jack going?'

'I'm not thirty yet, Mum. And he's staying in the flat too. We've drawn up a rota for the bed – the other one gets the sofa.'

'Oh, love. . .'

'It's ok, Dad, honestly! The sofa's pretty comfy when I have to have it.'

The two of them looked at one another.

'It's fine, really.'

'So. . .' Mum spoke slowly. 'The two of you will keep living together, until. . .'

'Well, it's kind of funny – Ava told me that actually you can't divorce until a year after your marriage starts.'

'Heh. A year. Heheh.' Mum laughed humourlessly.

'No, ok, not funny, but. . . I hadn't realised. It's true, I checked, so it looks like we'll just have to keep living together until the year is up. We can't afford to pay rent somewhere on top of the mortgage, so. . .'

Dad took my hand. 'You two know what you're doing, I suppose.'

I hoped my face didn't show doubtful panic.

'Just remember that you can come here, whenever you want. Don't mind your mother – we all know it'll just be until you can sort yourselves out.' I opened my mouth indignantly, but Dad went on, 'I mean, your accommodation. Until you can both sort out your accommodation situation.'

'Thanks, Dad.'

Mum nodded in agreement next to him. 'What happened, my Zoe?'

I shook my head and pressed my lips together. 'I'm sorry. I'm not ready yet. I will though, I'll tell you everything once I can.' She brushed her hand down my cheek. I swallowed a sob. 'Thanks, both of you. And I'm sorry.'

'Zoe!' Mum looked cross. 'What could you be sorry about?'

'For. . . leading everyone on. For having that big wedding only for it to end like this.'

She looked fierce. 'You do *not* need to be sorry. You have done nothing wrong here. I do not want to hear you say again that you are sorry to us for something that happened in *your* relationship. Do you understand me?' It was my turn to nod. 'Alright then, my lovely girl. You do not owe us anything when it comes to your marriage. It is between you and your husband.'

I squirmed at the word. 'I just wish we'd never got married. We should have done things like you two.'

Mum looked at Dad, who bustled me out of the kitchen and tucked me up on the sofa. He brought me tea and cake, and asked whether there was anything else they could do.

'Nothing. Thanks. I'm just. . .' I yawned.

'Oh, love, you must be tired. Remember, you can stay here in a proper bed any time you like.'

'Thanks, Dad. For being so cool with everything.'

He gave me a wink and went back into the kitchen, where I could hear vague whispers I tried to ignore.

When I asked Benni for the number of a divorce lawyer she was utterly shocked at my request.

'Who do you want this for?' she said, looking panicked. I looked at my hands, suddenly noticing I still had my wedding rings on. 'You?' she yelped. 'And Jack?' When I nodded, she looked ashen. 'Alright, darling, no problem.' She sat down abruptly on her desk. 'I thought all that stuff about Manchester was a bit odd. Oh, darling. Gina's going to be crushed: my poor wife has been raving about your wedding to everyone.' She *tsk*-ed, sounding like Mum. 'Sorry, that's none of your concern.' Then she started scrolling through her phone. 'Right, this is a friend of a friend who helped us with parenting rights and stuff. Nell Anderson. She's a fantastic family lawyer. I trust her to get you everything.'

'No. . .' I took the number she'd scribbled on a scrap of paper. 'I don't want everything. I'm not out to get Jack. I just think marriage was a bad idea for me.'

'Oh, Zoe. . . I'd only suggested to George that you take him out as a friend – I didn't mean to compromise you and Jack.'

I laughed abruptly. 'No! God, no. It's nothing to do with that.' I dropped my eyes.

'But darling, it's only been a few *months*.'

'Two. And you really do sound like my mum. But when you know, Benni, you know. And I know this just isn't right for us.'

I managed to get an appointment with Nell the divorce lawyer after school the next day, thanks to a cancellation. Her office was grey and plain, with family photos turned tactfully away from the clients, who were visiting her to formally dismantle their own.

'So,' she said, in a practised kindly voice, 'why don't you tell me what your situation is?'

I told her about the wedding, and how we were living now; how I wanted to get divorced the moment the legal year was up. Her face gave nothing away. I thought about the hundreds of stories she must have heard already, and whether it had changed how she felt about marriage.

'Well, we've got a couple of options.' She looked down at her pad, where she'd made a few notes. 'One of you can move out of the flat and you can be formally separated. Then, within two years of your formal separation, your divorce can be granted.'

'*Two* years? Is there no way of doing it any quicker?' I swallowed. 'And neither one of us is able to move out of the flat at the moment.'

'Ok. In which case, you've got another option: adultery.' I put my face in my hands. 'As long as one of you is willing to be accused of adultery, the divorce can go through much faster. But you'll still need to show that you've lived apart within six months of finding out, so I'd recommend making the formal accusation once one of you is in a situation to move out.' She looked down at her pad, and then up again. 'Is it going to be contested?'

I took my hands from my face. 'No. At least, I hadn't

thought so. But I don't know what this adultery angle will do to him.'

She smiled gently. 'You can take away these leaflets, just to give you a very rough idea of what we're talking about here. No one else needs to be named in the proceedings, no one else needs to know about it – it's just the accusation in the petition that we need. Do you understand?'

I couldn't speak. I was trying to breathe, but the air was coming in more and more jagged waves, crushing my chest as I tried to tell myself to stay calm. Suddenly Nell was sitting beside me, offering a box of tissues. She spoke again.

'Divorce is always a difficult situation, Zoe, and in the cases I've dealt with, sometimes it can be even harder when there's no one to blame – when it seems like it should have worked, but it didn't. And I know that talking about adultery, when it's someone you've loved very much, is a very hard, very brutal way of ending things. The UK laws on divorce are crazy, if you ask me, and force people into very tough situations. But, if divorce is what you both want, I'll do everything I can to make it as easy as possible for both of you.'

I know she was trying to be kind, but *adultery*? She said I should take some time to think about what I wanted to do. She gave me some print-outs, and said I could call her any time I wanted, even if it was just to go over my options again.

As I dangled from the Tube handles on my way home, I replayed our conversation in my head and felt like a slowly deflating balloon.

Jack was there when I got back. 'So,' he said flatly, 'how did it go?' He was on his laptop at the coffee table, and didn't look up at me.

'It was fine,' I said in an emotionless tone. 'She was nice.

She said. . . that to get the quickest divorce, one of us would have to petition on the grounds of adultery.'

Jack looked up then. 'What?'

I flopped down on the armchair. 'She said that's the easiest way, if we don't want to wait at least two years after a formal separation.'

'And *have* you committed adultery?' Jack asked, staring at me.

I couldn't speak.

'Well, isn't that what she said?' he persisted.

'No! Jack! Jesus Christ!'

He folded his arms.

'What? Have you?'

'No! For fuck's sake, Zoe. Of course not.' He looked sickened, like he didn't recognise me at all. Yet in the middle of this awful, nightmarish conversation, I was at least glad of his indignation and his denial, in some buried spot in my subconscious.

'Right. Well then. So do we. . . toss a coin, or something?'

Jack looked at me, stunned. 'No, Zoe. I am not going to toss a coin with you over who gets to be named as the adulterer in our divorce papers. If you want this to go ahead, there's only so much cooperation I'm willing to give you, I'm afraid.'

School was my main distraction, split between the upcoming exams and watching new teacher George around the Science office and much of the Technology building. It was like a Mexican wave when he walked past – heads just followed him.

On a drizzly Thursday morning, distracted by thoughts of class 10C, it took me a moment before I realised he was heading for me again.

'Hey, Zoe! I don't know if you remember, I'm George, from the Manchester school?'

128

I smiled, wondering how many hits his page on the school website had racked up. 'Oh, hi, George. How are you doing?'

'Yeah, yeah, good. It's just, we're all headed out after school, just for a few drinks round the corner, and wondered if you fancied it?'

I hesitated. 'Are we. . . all going?'

'I'm in, sounds great,' Miks piped up from his cubby.

I tried to ignore George's nerves, his interest. 'I'm sorry, George – I'm shattered at the moment. And I've got tonnes of marking tonight. But we will find time one day, I promise.' I might be dismantling my marriage, but I didn't want it to actually explode in my face. Despite George's magical face, I was nowhere near ready to actually start seeing someone else, even if it was only in a harmless group.

Jack and I still shared the same bed, for god's sake.

We just slept in it on alternating weeks.

TWELVE

Five years earlier

They were lying in Zoe's bed together one Sunday morning, relaxing away from the blissful grown-up world of post-university first jobs. Jack had already gone out and returned with papers and breakfast burritos, Zoe taking the burden on herself to stay in bed and keep it warm for him. They swapped burritos halfway, reading the supplements and lying against each other, occasionally kissing as one of them came to the end of an article, trying to keep the noise down for the benefit of Zoe's silent Finnish housemate. Zoe offered Jack a piece on a new parade of shops opening in North London.

'Any good for a potential shop?'

Jack skimmed over the article, taking another bite of burrito. 'I don't know, Zo. The few designs I've had out have sold well, and the orders have been going up, but. . . it still seems too soon. I don't want to rush into committing to something like that if a year later I'm just going to be economically and professionally hollowed out.'

'I've literally never been so turned on. I think it's your go-getting spirit that does it.'

Jack laughed. 'I have to admit that the place does look good. I just don't want to fuck up something that's so important. We're talking about something I want to do for the rest of my life. I want to get it right.'

'Well. Speaking of doing something right,' Zoe gulped, 'how about, in the meantime, we commit to not taking the bus every time we want to see each other?'

'Meaning. . .?'

'If you don't fancy opening a shop right now, how about you come and put all your stuff with my stuff? Well, maybe not in this flat, which really only fits us both if we're lying down. But in the same flat. Without a. . . *roommate*,' she mouthed. 'Like. . . we live together.'

Jack threw his newspaper over his shoulder and pulled the blanket over them both. 'Really?'

'Yes.'

'You and me?'

'Yes.'

'Living together?'

'By jove, I think he's got it.'

'Yeah, alright then.'

Zoe gave a whoop and kissed him. Then he kissed her, in a way that made her think she could probably wait for them to start house hunting for at least a few hours.

THIRTEEN

Now

I got home from school feeling exhausted. I'd completed my marking, but still had lesson plans to do for the next day. Even so, I'd just got an invitation to William's third birthday party, with subsequent promises from Esther and Kat about the food Mum had promised to make. I was smiling merely at the thought of it.

Jack was in the kitchen, dressed up for a night out, sternly slicing up a massive ham before he left. My glow lessened a little as I saw him carefully knifing each piece into a large Tupperware box. No ham for Zo. Fair enough.

'You not eating either?' I called.

He looked over his shoulder. 'No, I'm out tonight. This is for the rest of the week.' He looked at me again, then turned around completely to face me. 'You look well. You look really well.'

'Thanks. No need for such a surprised tone.'

He shrugged. 'You just look really. . . happy, I guess.' He sounded hurt at the word he'd come up with.

I shrugged back. 'Maybe I am,' I said, thinking of the feast awaiting me at Esther's house in a few weeks.

'What are you smiling at?' Jack asked.

'I didn't know I was.' I reached up to touch my mouth.

'You were,' Jack said, frowning. 'You look happy, and you were smiling.'

'I promise not to do it again.'

'Have you. . . met someone?'

'No! Not. . .'

'Not what?' he demanded. 'Not anyone I'd know? Not anything serious? Not that you'd want to talk about with me?'

I folded my arms. 'Sorry, how is this any of your business? Even if there was anything to tell. Which there isn't.'

'Fine.' He turned back to his ham. 'Fine, it's nothing to do with me, even if we are legally married. Forgive me for wanting to know if my wife was seeing someone.'

'Fine.' I took off my coat and dumped my keys. 'Where are you off to tonight? Is this. . . for your birthday tomorrow?'

Jack gave a snort.

'You don't have to tell me. I was just trying to be polite.'

He finished carving, clicked the lid on the box and put it in the fridge, then washed his hands, dried them, and got to me, standing in the doorway. 'Excuse me.' I stood aside, watching as Jack pulled on his coat and picked up his wallet and keys. 'Don't wait up.'

'Happy birthday!' I called out, but it sounded too sarcastic. Fortunately, he'd already slammed the door.

Despite Jack's hostile departure, I somehow slept that night for the first time in weeks. I didn't even hear him get home.

At seven thirty, I was eating breakfast at the counter when he stumbled into the kitchen, trying to make the coffee machine work.

133

'Happy birthday,' I greeted him. 'Looking for a hot cup of hangover?'

'Glad someone finds this funny,' he mumbled.

'Sorry. Sorry. Do you want some coffee?'

'Coffee's perfect, thanks. Any chance I could get a fucking DECREE NISI WITH THAT?' he reared round and bellowed at me.

'Oh, we're going down the Al Pacino route this morning, are we? That sounds like fun. In the meantime, I'll be in the shower and leaving for my day of actual sanity in the outside world. I invite you to join me there.' I thought for a second. 'Well, not in the shower. That's not a birthday invitation. I meant in the world. Without me.'

He suddenly looked extra drunk. 'Shoulda jus' stayed wherewas. Wass fuckin' point.' Then he staggered into the living room and collapsed sideways on the sofa. I watched him for a while, as I finished my breakfast, then I tucked his legs up, turned him sideways and went for my shower. When I came back out and found that he still hadn't moved, I covered him with a blanket and got dressed. Before I left, I put a mug of birthday black coffee and some birthday buttered toast on the coffee table in front of him, and gave him a kiss on the top of his head. I didn't mean anything by it. It was just a birthday kiss, like a distant aunt gives a child; just a meaningless habit that I could innocently, momentarily get away with while he was in this state.

As I walked out of the door, closing it quietly so I didn't wake him, I said to myself over and over, it's just a habit. I didn't mean anything by it. A habit that came from years together, years of being in love, of being in a relationship that led to marriage. If I thought about it anymore, let myself dwell on the smell of his hair in my nose, I'd realise that my heart was about to break. That we were over. That our relationship was done.

This was the first of his birthdays without me since we'd been together. I didn't even know what he'd done last night, where he'd been and who he'd been there with. I wasn't sharing today with him, making a big deal of it in the way I knew he loved – just as he knew how much I loathed my birthdays. I didn't have a gift for him, nor a card, and I definitely couldn't opt for the birthday shortcuts I'd used in the past, which mainly involved various levels of nakedness. I was out of his life. That's what I'd wanted, wasn't it?

I was struck by the thought that divorce meant a new start for both of us: a new place to live, packing up all our stuff, and moving it to a whole new building, new street, new neighbourhood. New city? New. . . country? Would Jack move abroad? Would I? Is that what I needed?

But buried somewhere beneath everything else, I realised that I still felt hopeful. After the end of something, there was another beginning. Heartbroken and hopeful, optimistic and overwhelmed. The future seemed bright, possibly, eventually, if I could actually shift my weight from the reality of *just get through this minute* to *let's make plans for tomorrow*. It was the best thing to do; I just didn't know if I could do it. And I didn't know if I could do it alone.

On the Tube, I went for a seat at the same time as another woman. We both stopped and looked at each other, and she laughed a little and said, 'Go ahead, I need the exercise,' and motioned to the seat. I swallowed, and thanked her, and when I took it I noticed she was looking at me oddly. The other people opposite were looking at me too, giving me little 'don't really want to get involved' glances, like I might actually talk to them or something. Eventually, the woman leant down to me and said, 'Are you ok?' When I touched my face, it was wet – my eyes, my cheeks, tears dripping off my chin and spattering my top.

'I'm. . . crying?' I don't know which of us was more

shocked, but it was my stop, and I couldn't stay to talk through my disastrous non-marriage.

Yes, I told myself, I've just got to push through all this. Something that feels this horrible has got to be the right decision. Nothing voluntary feels this bad without having some greater good, does it?

Liz was waiting for me at the restaurant, looking *very* un-Liz, with huge blown-out hair and shiny beige nails. I hugged her, wide eyed.

'What's. . . happened?'

'Henry likes his woman to be well groomed.' She laughed. 'It's deranged. I am having so much fun going out with someone I dislike so intensely. Even the sex has got better – it's added a real frisson.'

I curled my lip.

'I don't understand it either, Zo. It's the weirdest dating I've ever done, but I'm so happy that he makes our time together so miserable. And our time apart so great, too, of course.' She shrugged happily. 'It's like I'm roleplaying his girlfriend. I fucking love it.'

'But you don't even look like you.'

'I know! It's like I'm in costume!' She pulled her hair into a shaggy ponytail, and looked at least half like herself again. 'Better?'

'Better. Thank you.'

We ordered, and took long gulps of our long cocktails.

'And how are you? What's happening now with Jack?'

'I asked him for a divorce.'

Her mouth hung open. After almost a minute of me slowly nodding at her, she shook her head. 'Right. Ok. I've accepted that now. Wait.' She raised her hand. 'No. I haven't. I won't process this for a really long time, but I want to support you right now. Is it ok if I freak out later?'

136

'Permission granted. Can I get the same permission from you?'

Liz squeezed my hand. 'Jesus, that came out of nowhere. Was he shagging someone else?'

'No. I don't think so, anyway. I just. . . don't think it was working.'

'After *two* months?'

'It was after one month I first mentioned it to him.'

'Shit! That answers that one then. Sorry. I didn't mean to sound so sceptical. I'm just surprised, I suppose.'

'Not as surprised as Jack.'

She laughed, then covered her mouth with her beige finger-tips. 'Am I alright to laugh at that? Is any of this funny yet?'

'Not really.' I put my head down on the table, and shocked us both by starting to cry again. 'I feel like I'm doing this all the time,' I sniffed, 'and I can't work out why, or how to stop.'

'Is a divorce actually what you want? Do you want to stay with Jack?'

'Yes. No! We can't stay married anymore. It's just. . . it's so *awwwfuuu-uuull*,' I wailed, and started crying even louder. 'The way we're just on top of each other the whole time – and not in a good way. We can't be in a room without arguing, if someone wants something off, the other one wants it on. . . It's just miserable. *Miserable*. Everything that was good about our relationship has just. . . vanished.' I sobbed harder. A moment later our waitress came, and without a word delivered two more drinks to us, unordered.

'She gets it,' Liz said, and slid the end of the straw into my mouth. 'And I think the nachos are on their way. It's ok, I've heard about this, loads of people have starter marriages.'

'What's a starter marriage?' I sobbed.

'Where you have a first, kind of practice, marriage. To work out what you want from a husband or wife. Loads of

137

people are doing it now. Then you marry who you *really* want.'

'But I don't want anyone else! I want Jack! It's just so horrible between us, and I'm terrified that we've lost what we had. *Forever*. And there's this guy at work – I don't want to be with him, not at all, but he's so good-looking, and – I just don't want me and Jack to be together if I do ever start wanting someone else. What if I ever start thinking about being unfaithful?' I sighed, hiccupping. 'I don't want to put Jack in a position where I ever think about cheating on him, just because being told by a piece of paper that you'll never want anyone else *ever* again is some kind of stupid red rag. Being cheated on. . . people don't get over that.'

'And do you want to cheat on him?'

'No! God, no. But what if I do, one day? What kind of person does that make me?'

'Oh, Zo. This is all just so hypothetical. You're not that person, we both know that. You of all people would never do that.' Liz brushed my hair from my face, so she could see me properly. 'So what are you going to do?'

I lifted my head from the table. 'Apparently we can't get divorced until we've been married at least a year. But neither of us can afford to pay a separate rent on top of our mort-gage.'

'And in the meantime?'

'What do you mean?'

'You can't really both live in the flat, can you? You're getting divorced. That's a pretty unequivocal statement about how you feel about the relationship, isn't it? You must really want to get out of there. And what if one of you does meet someone else?'

I put my head down again, and cried until our waitress brought nachos with extra sour cream and guac.

* * *

138

I psyched myself up on the way home, but Jack was already asleep. The next morning, I cornered him in the kitchen.

'Jack, we need to sort this out.'

'Sort what out?'

'Living arrangements. We can't live on sofa rotas for the next year of our lives.'

Jack made a show of looking at his watch. 'Well, the good news is, it's more like nine months, eight days annnd. . . about sixteen hours.'

'I'm serious. We need to talk about what we're going to do with this flat.'

'What do you mean "do with it"? I think I'm quite busy living in it, right now. What are you talking about?'

'We can't both live here, Jack.'

'Have you lost your mind? Have you *seen* how much rent is these days?'

'We can sell this place—'

'The value of this flat might have gone up, but we still wouldn't get anything with half each.' He threw his arms up. 'Sorry, can we just slow this conversation down for a minute – how the hell am I debating with you what homes we could find with half the sale proceeds of this flat? This is my *home*, Zoe. It's *your* home too. And it's been *our* home for three years. It's not just. . . some investment!'

'I know! I'm fully aware that it's my home! I remember painting every square inch of it when we moved in!'

'And I remember sanding every single surface down. And plastering the bathroom. You weren't the only one who contributed, Zo.'

'*I* plastered the bathroom. You did the kitchen.' For a moment I thought of us, two years ago, in overalls, radio blasting, bacon sandwiches from the greasy spoon, playing at being grown-ups. It never felt like that anymore. Adulthood was creeping up on us like mildew, along with all the disappointment and disillusionment that seemed to go with it.

'Yeah, that's right. We've both put a lot of work into this place.'

'And we'll get more for it, because of that,' I persisted.

Jack looked crushed. 'I didn't mean that.' His voice dropped. 'We put a lot into making this our home, Zo.'

I spoke gently back. 'I know. But things change. And we have to be realistic.'

His face hardened. 'Sorry. But I'm not going anywhere. I can't afford it, and I don't want to. You'll just have to wait until your year is up.'

'Jack—'

'Don't worry.' He looked at his watch. 'Only nine months, eight days and fifteen hours to go now. It'll fly by.'

FOURTEEN

Four years earlier

At the bar, Jack was waiting impatiently with two drinks. He took a slug of his aged artisan rum and winced slightly – what was the point in £18 cocktails if Zoe wasn't there with him? She was never this late usually. And what was the point in living together if they couldn't come to a party *together*? A woman heading for the bar bumped into his hip – he drew away, saying, 'Sorry,' giving her an apologetic glance.

At which point he had two thoughts that were almost, but not quite, simultaneous: that this woman might just be the most beautiful woman he'd ever seen, let alone bumped hips with; and that this woman was Zoe.

She was laughing. 'Hello, roomie.'

'Whoah. You look nice.'

She laughed even harder. 'It's the surprise in your voice which really makes me value that compliment.'

'No, I mean. . . you. . .'

'It's fine, it's fine. God, a woman puts on a little bit of lipstick and a pair of earrings and suddenly it's like a

Hollywood makeover scene. It is literally just some lipstick, you know.'

'And your hair looks different.'

'Fine, and I've combed my hair out. Hence my ever-so-slight delay.' She looked pleased. 'Thank you for noticing.'

'Well whatever magic your womanly wiles are enchanting me with, it's really, really nice to see you.'

Zoe smiled at him. 'You too. It's really nice to see you. I've missed you since this morning.' She took a sip from his rum glass, and winced too. 'What *is* this?'

'I know. I paid almost twenty quid for that.'

'Is it artisanal?'

'You know it is, baby.' He pursed his lips sexily and took a sip himself, before spitting it back into the glass. 'God, that really is utterly vile.'

'What did you get me?'

'Gin and tonic.'

She took a sip. 'Oh yeah, that is much better. Here, halves on the gin?'

'Let's leave the rum for an unsuspecting stranger.'

'Don't you think we have a responsibility to warn them?'

Jack shrugged. 'You never know. There might be someone out there who loves the taste and scent of wet soil and hot dog fur.'

Zoe retched.

'Anyway. Let's go and wish Iffy a happy birthday at least.'

'Hold on. There's something. . .' Zoe looked thoughtful. 'I'm forgetting something. . .'

'Peanuts? Crisps? Because they probably only have sundried organic beetroot here.'

'No. . . it's. . . oh yeah. That's what it is.' And she pulled Jack into a huge embrace, kissing and kissing and kissing him, and he kissed her back until Iffy came over to greet Zoe, and asked if Jack would now be willing to join in the celebrations. He was getting complaints, he said, and it was his birthday, so really, shouldn't they actually be kissing him? And he pointed to his cheeks where they both dutifully kissed him too, then he danced with them onto the dancefloor, holding their hands, where they stayed until the bar closed and it was somehow morning.

'Mum, I know, I know. . . Well, what can we bring? No, let us bring something. Mum, this is supposed to be a party for you and Dad. Can't I do something for it? Drinks or food or a cake or something? Mum. Mum. Mum. Mum, I know it's your anniversary, but no one will think less of you if your son brings the cake. You don't have to bake for – how many people are you expecting? *Seventy*? Mum, no one expects you to make a cake for seventy people yourself, particularly not if you won't even let me help with the food or drinks. Well, what's Dad doing for the party? No. . . No, I suppose not. Listen, there's a cake maker just around the corner from us, I'll ask him if he's got space that weekend, ok? And I can send you a picture of some of his other cakes, and you can just tell me what you want doing, alright?'

Jack sighed and Zoe could only wonder at the sudden feeling in her gut that he would be a great father one day. 'Yes Mum, of course I'll let you know how much it costs. Alright? Good. Thank you. No, Mum, it's my pleasure. Alright. Talk to you soon.'

'Party planning going well, then?'

'Oh, Zo. A thirtieth-anniversary party seems like the least fun of all the parties.'

'I hate to break this to you, but we don't have a cake maker around the corner. Do we?'

'No, and I won't ever tell her how much a real cake maker charges in these parts either, but I'm sure I can find one that will meet her exacting standards.'

143

'You're a good son.'

'Now I just need to hear that from both parents and I can save myself thousands in future therapy bills.'

Zoe rubbed his hair. 'Are you really dreading it?'

'I'm not *dreading* it. I suppose it's quite nice that they're still together after all this time. I'm just. . .'

'Surprised they are?'

Jack looked surprised himself. 'No. Why. Are you?' He didn't wait for an answer. 'No, just. . . It's never that much fun hanging out with the pair of them, is it? I don't know if I can bear to watch Dad being steamrollered by Mum for another evening, particularly in front of all their friends.'

Zoe sat beside him on the sofa, and swung her legs up into his lap. 'I'll be with you. We can supervise everyone's behaviour, make sure both your parents are having a nice time—'

'Are you suggesting we're the chaperones?'

'Yes! Exactly. Pulling snogging couples out from the bushes, that kind of thing.'

'Checking the punch isn't spiked.'

'Or spiking it ourselves.'

'I don't imagine Dad's friends will require any additional spiking.'

'Alright then. And if we have no other job besides getting a cake from our fictional cake-making friend, we can make sure both your mum and your dad have a great time at the party. With or without each other. Ok?'

Jack held her face in his hands, and kissed her mouth, softly. 'I do love you, you know.'

She beamed at him, and kissed the end of his nose. 'I know.'

FIFTEEN

Now

Esther was in her kitchen, spooning ice cream into plastic bowls for the birthday boy and his guests while I attempted to decant various dips into other bowls at the same time as describing the latest developments with Jack. Mum and Dad were heroically trying to entertain a gaggle of three year olds in Esther's garden – I didn't want them to hear this conversation, even though the process of family osmosis would mean they'd know most of it anyway, somehow.

'And tell me again why you can't move out?'

I'd explained the difficulty of the situation, how until we could legally separate our lives for good, neither of us felt we could afford to move out, so we were stuck with each other for the rest of the year. Esther gave William his spoon and looked at me, one eyebrow raised.

'So you are absolutely stuck there? With Jack? For eight more months?'

I raised the spoon up in frustration. 'I know! That's divorce, I guess.'

She folded her arms. 'So there's absolutely no escape for you?'

'Have you *seen* how much rent is these days?' I insisted, realising too late I was echoing Jack.

'Zo, all of us live a bus ride away from you. Ave probably lives closer to your school than you do. If you really wanted—'

'I can't live with you guys for eight months, Es. It's not fair on any of you.'

'And you're sure you're not trying to find an excuse to stay with Jack?'

'I just asked him for a divorce! I don't think I could be accused of that.'

'What about Mum and Dad? They wouldn't mind you going home.'

I folded my arms too. 'Yeah, that's what I need. To be the almost thirty-year-old divorcing her husband and moving back in with her parents. My god, even *Mum* said that was a bad idea.'

Esther came over and put an arm around me. 'Alright, alright. Sorry. It's not an ideal situation—'

I snorted.

'—and I'm sure you'll do the best you can with it.'

'It's going to be fine, I'm sure. As long as we can remain pleasant and mature with each other, I don't see why it has to be that hard.'

Esther squeezed me. 'Ok. If you say so. Now keep being a helpful waitress and I might let you take some leftovers home.'

'You have got to be kidding me.'

'What's the problem?'

I was standing over Jack as he lay reading in bed, late one Saturday evening. I'd been out all day with Liz, and was now pulsating with rage, clutching a wadded mass of snot-green cotton.

'What. Is. This?'

146

'Bedding. Don't you remember? We got it from my old boss for our wedding. If you can bear to recall such a hideous occasion. I put it in the washing machine. Sorry it isn't quite dry yet.'

'It wasn't *green* when I left this morning.'

'Ah, see, there's always that risk when I do the laundry. Haven't I always tried to warn you? Still, at least it was only sheets. At least it wasn't your wedding outfit or anything,' he called cheerily to me. 'Although I expect that'll be in a bonfire any minute.'

I stomped back to the sofa and wrapped myself in a blanket. *So that's how you want it, is it, Jack? Ok. But you're going to regret it.*

The next weekend, I was tucked up on the sofa, reading the papers and enjoying the fresh cup of tea I'd just made – carefully squeezing out the teabag then placing it exactly in the centre of the empty sink – when I heard Jack's key in the lock. The sofa's back was to the door, so he couldn't see me, but I hunkered down lower just in case, hoping I could make myself entirely invisible. But with him, I could hear a woman, one who seemed very giggly and eager to look around Jack's flat. *He's brought another woman back here?* I thought. Well, at least I'd have my adultery grounds. Jesus Christ.

I waited until Jack was about to show her the bedroom before I piped up from my hidden position on the sofa. 'Hi, guys. I'm Jack's wife. Did he tell you about the time he accidentally called out his grandmother's name during sex? I'm sorry, I didn't catch your name.'

Jack was biting his lip. 'This is Jenny. She's Iffy's new girlfriend. Iffy had recommended that she come to see our flat because she's doing hers up. But thanks for making her feel *super* welcome – I know Iffy will be really grateful.'

147

Jenny looked like she was really hoping there might be a freak earthquake any minute, and I waved silently at her while sinking slowly back into my hiding place on the sofa.

A few days later, seriously premenstrual and in desperate need of some dark chocolate, I remembered my luxe emergency stash in the back of the cupboard. Mmm. It wasn't behind the pasta, or the rice, or hiding behind the spices or stock cubes or the jars of mystery chutney. I was beginning to panic.

'Jack! Have you seen that bar of chocolate that was in the back of the cupboard?'

'Oh yeah, I had that after a run the other day.'

'Iffy gave me that!'

'I think you'll find Iffy gave *me* that.'

I crossed my arms.

He held his hands up. 'Fine, sorry, my mistake.'

'You don't even like chocolate!'

'I needed an energy boost. It was a really long run.'

'You could have eaten literally anything else.'

'Whoops. If it's any consolation, it wasn't even very nice.'

I resolved to harness my hormonal fury for revenge.

Two days later, Jack managed to seriously pull a muscle on another run, and was advised to rub some vile-smelling ointment into his thigh each morning before his shower. I'm not saying I definitely squeezed a whole tube of hair removal cream into his ointment tube, then squished it all around to mix it – but I'm also not saying I definitely didn't.

This morning, there was a satisfying amount of screaming coming from the bathroom.

The week after, all my chargers went awol for the whole week. I was reduced to calling my sisters on the *landline*.

* * *

'So who's next then?' Kat stirred her drink with her straw and smiled innocently at me.

We were at the opening of a new bar and I'd made the effort to dress up, on Kat's orders. We'd got two seats at a high table in one corner, but the bar was already rammed.

'What do you mean, who's next?'

'Come on, Zo. Look around you! We all love Jack, but it's probably time you got back on the horse, isn't it? Before it dries up entirely.' She banged her handbag somewhere between my thighs.

I choked. 'I *really* don't think it's the right time for me to start dating.'

'You're missing out. Every day you're alive is a day you're never going to get back.'

'Is that supposed to be a pep talk?'

'I'm serious. All these opportunities, and you're just ignoring them all. You're divorcing, we get it, and what's the best remedy for heartache?'

'A medically induced coma?'

Kat rolled her eyes. 'What about that guy over there? In blue. The one in the hat.'

'He's wearing a hat. *Indoors*. Nope.'

'Well, that knocks about eighty per cent of our options tonight.'

'Good!' I took a swig. 'Only twenty per cent left for me to reject.'

'You shouldn't be so fussy, sis. You're not getting any younger.'

'I'm twenty-nine, Kat. Also, this is not the nineteenth century.'

'What about him? In the red trousers?' She looked at me, laughing. 'Ok, fair enough. The bartender?'

'Stop, stop. This is insane. We're still living together, Kat!'

149

'You're going to be living together for ages, according to you. What are you going to do, become a nun?'

I tried not to think about George's face. And his arms. 'My wedding bouquet's probably still blooming, for god's sake.'

'Alright,' Kat shrugged. 'I'm just saying, maybe Jack's going to get the wrong idea if you don't start seeing someone else.'

'And if I do, he might get an even worse wrong idea. That I was seeing someone else all along?'

'Fine. Maybe not tonight. But I think – for both of your sakes – you need to seriously consider getting back out there.'

'Kat, this is a horrible discussion that I'm ending now. Anyway,' I said, watching her out of the corner of my eye, 'I'd much rather hear about your new job. Since that night at the bar with your team, I've not heard a thing. How are you finding it?'

Kat turned away. 'It's fine. Bit awkward to discover your boss is your sister's best friend's ex, but it's fine.'

I looked down at my drink, remembering my lie to her at the bar that night.

'He's not mentioned it, so neither have I. It's *fine*.'

'But what about the rest of the job? How're the colleagues?' I took a sip of my drink, keeping my eyes down. 'How's. . . Chuck?'

'You're being weird again, Zo. Did you have a crush on him back in your teens or something? He's a bit. . . creepy, isn't he? Ugh, please don't make me think about you fancying him.' She shivered dramatically.

'Creepy? But. . . it's ok, isn't it? What do you do? What's your job? What do you have to do every day?'

'It's a job! It's just a job, dude.' She was eyeballing me like she was trying to burn a hole in my forehead. 'Stop

150

grilling me. It's a job. I go there, I do work, I come home again. Just. . . stop.'

With both work and relationships declared off topic, we finished our drinks quickly and headed to our separate homes. I texted Esther: *Is it just me or is something up with Kat? Any news on Chuck? I think we need to keep our eyes peeled xxx*

If I couldn't even look after Kat, what hope did I have?

The end of term saw two departures from our Science department, so we headed out for curry and karaoke; it ended in kebabs, something I realised when I woke up in bed fully dressed and face-first in a greasy tray.

Various images were filtering through: singing, arm in arm with Miks and the deputy head; the night bus; selfies at the kebab shop with a group of teenage girls – oh god, please don't let them have been my students; lying on grass, somewhere. Upstairs Jan calling my name? Was that a dream?

Where was my phone? Christ, where was my *bag*?

I found the phone down the side of the bedside table, mayonnaise smeared up the back. But my beautiful Chanel bag was nowhere to be found.

I'd had it in the evening.

I'd had it on the bus.

I must have had it coming in, because I'd clipped the house keys inside so I wouldn't lose them.

And only one other person had been in the house since then.

I scoured the bedroom and bathroom, then stormed through the rest of the flat as best I could while suffering under a clumping, sharp-hooved hangover. Not in the kitchen. Not in the lounge. Nowhere.

'Where is it?' I growled.

'Where's what?'

151

Jack was eating breakfast, hunched over a casserole dish of Cheerios, eating them with a giant yellow plastic ladle. He looked up at me, then his eye was caught by something on my hand. Or rather, not on my hand.

'Right. You've taken your rings off, then,' he said quietly.

I put my hands behind my back, vibrating with rage.

'Don't change the subject, Jack. You *know*.'

He slurped dramatically.

'I *don't* know.'

'Jack, where's my bag?'

He slurped again. Then he slowly lowered the ladle into the soupy cereal and beamed at me wickedly.

I narrowed my eyes at him. His eyes flicked for a moment to the back door, then we both rushed towards it, him beating me there by a fraction of a second. He stood in front of me, blocking the way.

'Zoe.' He looked suddenly guilty. My heart pounded. And then I saw it, through the window of the back door.

Stranded.

Stained.

Soaking.

My handbag. With a howl of horror, I pushed Jack out of the way and slid the door open, rushing over to my beautiful bag. The leather was dappled with rain, where it wasn't streaked with mud. I let out a sob, and picked it up by one handle, at which point a squirrel, who must have thought she'd really lucked out with new digs, leapt from the warmth of the bag and launched herself at my face.

I screamed.

The squirrel screamed.

I could hear Jack doing something in the doorway, before I became aware of him putting one hand on my breastbone and pulling the squirrel off with the other.

The squirrel scampered away.

152

Jack was biting on both his lips, desperately trying to keep a straight face.

'What the HELL did you do that for?'

He looked stunned.

'Did you want the squirrel on your head?'

'You know that's not what I'm talking about. Why would you put my bag out in the rain? Jack, it's my one nice thing that I own. Why would you do that?'

'Why would *I* do that?'

'For fuck's sake, I know you think it's just a handbag. Haha, Zoe's parents spent all their money on something to carry her lipstick in. I *know* you think it's stupid, but it was the only really special thing I owned, and you thought it would be funny to just chuck it into the garden and wreck it—'

'Whoah, hold on a minute—'

'What, you didn't think it was stupid to spend that much on a bag? You didn't make fun of it?'

'Zo, I might have said—'

'No. You did. And now it's ruined. I hope you're pleased with yourself.'

'Hang on a minute—'

'No! I will not hang on a minute! You doing something so petty, so spiteful, has lost you the right to demand a single *second* of my time, Jack. I never thought you were perfect, but I thought you were above this. Chucking my bag in the garden? Thank god we're getting a divorce, is all I can say.'

Jack's face hardened.

'I feel exactly the same.'

He stomped back into the house, tipped the rest of his breakfast back in one, grabbed his stuff and left, shutting the door behind him as gently as he could, considering we were in the middle of yet another fight.

153

I wasn't sure how we'd got here again. We'd both agreed to split up – technically, this was an amicable divorce – yet we couldn't even be in the same room as one another, and to top it all, I now had a wrecked handbag. I couldn't work out where I was going wrong.

SIXTEEN

Four years earlier

They'd only been in their new flat for six months, and Zoe's heart would still flutter when she arrived home each night. But when she came in after work one evening, her heart's fluttering turned to pounding when she saw Jack on the sofa, his head in his hands.

'Tough day at work? Jack?'

He didn't move. Zoe sat down beside him, and he twisted slightly away from her. She put her head against his back. 'Jack? What's happened?'

After a minute, he said in a choked voice, 'Mum's left my dad.'

Zoe didn't know what to say, mainly because in that moment she didn't know who she should be cheering for. Who was the villain here? She put an arm around Jack, saying, 'I'm so sorry. I'm really sorry, Jack.'

He twisted to put both his arms around her, crushing her to him, and she realised he was trying to keep from crying. She leant into him, rubbing his lower back and letting him squeeze her.

After a while he pulled back from her, rubbing his face with both hands.

'What happened?'

'Dad called. He said he'd found a letter from her saying that she couldn't stay any longer, that she should have left a long time ago. The anniversary party's off, obviously.' He laughed bitterly. 'He didn't really want to discuss it. Understandably.'

'Have you heard from her?'

'She called me too. She wanted me to know that she *loved me very much*, and that it wasn't anything to do with me. Like I was just a kid, or something.' He rubbed his face again and hiccupped.

'She said she loved you?' Zoe suddenly realised how serious Linda must be about leaving.

Jack paused for a moment. 'Yeah. I don't know if she's ever said that to me as an adult before. Maybe not even when I was little. I don't know. Anyway, what's she calling me for? I don't care if she loves me. I care if she loves Dad. Why would she leave him? Why would she do that?' He hiccupped again. 'I thought they were happy enough. Not perfect, but no one's relationship is perfect, is it? Do you think I should try and see her? Why would she do this?'

She kept rubbing his back, and spoke as gently as she could. 'I don't know, Jack. They've been married a long time. Maybe she just wants to live on her own for a bit.'

'So you think it's just a temporary thing?'

'I don't know. Maybe not.'

'Why would she leave him?'

'I don't know, Jack. I don't know your mum.'

'Well clearly none of us do.'

She put her head on his shoulder again. 'People have to make the decision that's right for them, Jack. Maybe she just wasn't happy. Maybe she was lonely. We don't know what was happening in their marriage.'

'Why wouldn't she be happy?'

Zoe sat up and looked into Jack's face, seeing all the hurt and betrayal and shock in it. She knew that if this were anyone else's parents, Jack would see the absurdity of these questions. But if she imagined it was her parents splitting up, her mum who had upped and walked out, leaving only a note for her dad. . . She could well understand those feelings, that pain, that wish to lash out and punish someone who loved her, who she loved, who she'd trusted to stay in a happy bubble with her dad. She shook herself.

'I don't know, Jack. The only people who have those answers are your mum and maybe your dad. If you want to ask them that stuff, they can tell you. But I can't, and you'll drive yourself round the bend trying to second-guess them.'

He flopped back further on the sofa, legs spread, arms by his side, and stared ahead out him out of the window. He sighed. 'I just don't get it, Zo. You should have heard Dad's voice. I've never. . . He just sounded like a wreck. I'm so worried for him. Men that age, they don't bounce back from things like this. All on his own in that big, cold house. While she swans off to god knows where.'

'Do you know where she's gone?'

'No. And I don't care.'

'Jack.' She spoke gently, putting her hand on his.

He shook it off. 'Why should I care? She chose to leave. Neither Dad nor I have any responsibility for her now. She can just live with the consequences of her actions for once.'

Zoe couldn't imagine a time where Linda hadn't been living with the consequences of her actions. She thought that thirty years of living with your consequences sitting silently every morning at the breakfast table might be more than most people could stand. But she also knew that she couldn't share those thoughts with Jack, not at the moment. Maybe one day he'd see it for himself, but right now wasn't the time to bring it up.

'Jack? Do you really not care where she's gone?'

'I don't know. She's probably gone to my aunt's house or something. I don't think she's sleeping on the street, if that's what you're accusing me of.'

'Jack, I'm not accusing you of anything. Do you want me to call her? Do you want us to go to your dad's this weekend?'

He shrugged. 'No. Don't call her. She doesn't deserve us worrying about her. We can't be running after her when she's the one who's done this to Dad.'

Zoe breathed slowly. 'So shall we go and see him this weekend? Or sooner? One evening after work? I reckon I can head off early one day if you want to drive over there.'

'No. He says he doesn't want us worrying. That he might come over here if he needs the company.' He sighed again, a soft hiccup in the middle. 'Honestly, Zo, you should have heard him. He just couldn't talk. . . at all.'

Zoe didn't dwell on any thoughts of Graham's inability to talk about anything, ever. She lay back against Jack and put an arm across his stomach. 'I'm sorry, Jack. This is just a horrible situation for everyone.'

Jack tipped his head against hers, seemed to soften a little. 'Well,' he said softly, 'it's her fault. And we won't ever forget it.'

Zoe hoped she wasn't included in that *we*. She didn't feel like Linda had committed the worst crime in the world. Hell, Zoe didn't even know if she wouldn't have done the same thing.

SEVENTEEN

Now

I was still mourning my lost bag (I'd had Esther come over and carry it off in a black bin bag, to be disposed of humanely – I couldn't face how ravaged it was, nor the thought of finding it full of baby squirrels) as I sat hunched over my desk, pounding my keyboard with Jack-shaped rage.

The night before he'd been standing at the fridge, peering into it moodily. I watched him while I banged down a mug, boiled the kettle, slammed bread in the toaster and murderously chopped up an orange.

'Any plans tonight?' I eventually asked. 'Any more of my stuff you want to wreck?'

'Oh. Yeah. Tonnes of it. I've written a "To Destroy" list on my phone with some reminders to go off whenever you're not home.' He closed the fridge and turned around. 'By the way, I meant to leave you a note, if I didn't see you. I'm off to New York for a while.'

'How long is a while?' I didn't sound as casual as I'd wanted.

Jack gave a bitter smile. 'Only a week or so. Don't get your hopes up, it's not a *permanent* move. I'm heading off on Tuesday – it's the Gillett people, they want me to see some stuff there.'

'Oh.' I understood. Jack's bosses were paying him to fly to New York and hang out with the CFO, Jessica, who I'd bet my Chanel ex-handbag would be on that same trip. 'Have a great time.' I turned away, picked up my food.

'Yup,' Jack said.

'Cool.' I carried my breakfast to the sofa, keeping my head down. 'Hope it's *productive*.'

At my cubby in the Science office, I tried not to grind my teeth as I thought about the fun he'd be having, whisked away to New York on some kind of work jolly with the Gillett bigwigs. I didn't even know when he was due back.

I was suddenly aware of someone standing over my desk. George. I hadn't seen him since he'd sort-of asked me out, and although I hadn't been *avoiding* him as such, his where-abouts in the office had certainly had an effect on where I chose to eat my lunch. Or whether I took a break duty. Or how long I spent looking for something under my desk.

But here he was, smiling that smile and proffering some books.

'Zoe, hey! I hope this is ok, but. . . I've just got a couple of books that I thought you might like? I was clearing out from my move, and thought. . . I don't know, if you don't want them, that's fine. . .'

Damn it. That smile.

'Thanks! They look great.' All I could see was Benni watching us from her office door, pretending to talk to Miks – who was also watching us out of the corner of his eye. As if it was *totally* normal to just bring in unrequested books you *thought* your colleague might *happen* to like, on a *whim*. I turned back to George, telling myself, whatever I did, not to look at his forearms. 'Is there anything else?'

He actually blushed.

'Yeah, actually – I was wondering if you felt like that drink, too? That we'd talked about. Maybe tonight? I know you said you didn't fancy it before, but I just wondered if anything had changed.'

Damn it again. And it's not like I had anything to go home for; in fact, Jack was off in New York on his own romantic break. Thinking of what Kat would advise me, I decided to take the plunge.

'Sure. I've got to run a few errands after school, but do you want to just email me the place and I'll meet you there? At seven-ish?'

He gave me that smile again, and I gave him a thumbs up like a gameshow winner. But I'd agreed to it – Kat would be delighted, having worn me down – and I'd have to actually turn up; I could hardly stand up someone in my own school. Benni was watching me strangely, so heaven knows what faces I was pulling as I imagined all this. I winked at her. She smiled at me, and Miks leant in and gave me a sarcastic thumbs up. Oh well. How bad could the whole thing be?

I decided to leave my marking for tomorrow, instead hurrying out of school to meet Esther for a coffee.

'I can't stay long, I'm afraid.'

'Good to see you too, dearest sister. I can't stay long either, I've got to get William to bed – but what's your excuse?'

I laughed. 'Kat's finally worn me down. I'm going on a date.'

Esther's eyes opened wide. 'Whoah. Jesus. That soon? And is he worth it?'

'He looks it.' We both laughed. 'But I've got no idea if he actually will be.'

Esther looked at me, suddenly serious. 'Zoe. Are you sure you're ready?'

I stirred milk into my coffee. 'I don't know. Kat says I should just get on with it.'

'You do remember that Kat's the one who set fire to her bedroom carpet trying to dry her nail polish with a hair dryer. I don't think we should worry too much about what she has to say about your love life.'

'I know. But maybe she's right. Maybe it's the best way to get over all this. Plus, Jack's off on some jet-setting trip at the moment, with a woman from his work—'

'Ah.' Esther nodded. 'Right. Got it.'

'What?' I asked. 'It's unrelated. Sort of.'

'Doesn't matter. And listen,' she said, leaning forward over the table, her voice dropping, 'I wanted to talk to you about Kat, anyway. I think you're right about her. I don't know what's going on, but she's acting oddly: won't talk to any of us about her work and freaks out if I mention Chuck. I think maybe we ought to pay her office a little visit.'

'Under what guise? We all bring boiler suits and clipboards and pretend to be checking the electrics?'

'We're just going to meet our sister after work. Nothing sinister.'

'You make it sound sinister.'

'Have it your own way. But think about it. I'd like to see her there. She won't tell us anything of her own will, so we'll just have to drag it out of her. Anyway, come on – drink up. You've got a date to get ready for.'

I dawdled in the café after Esther left. Then it was suddenly ten to seven and I knew I'd have to hurry to get to the bar on time – it was better this way, I thought, so I didn't dwell on the whole thing too much. By the time I arrived I was sweaty, hair frizzing and my shirt sticking to my back. Just beautiful. But George greeted me with the same huge smile and fussed around me, taking my bag, getting me a seat, ordering me an ice-cold gin gimlet, asking me about my day,

162

listening to my answers. It felt like getting into a deep, relaxing bath in a rich stranger's home – I knew it wasn't completely right, but I wasn't about to give up the pleasure of it.

After only an hour, though, the overwhelming sense that the homeowner was about to return was crippling. I was almost squirming in my seat.

'George, look, I'm sorry, I—'

He smiled. 'It's ok, Zoe. I know that you're going through some stuff at the moment.'

'Yeah, it's. . .' I screwed up my face. 'I thought this would be ok, but. . . I don't think it is yet. I'm sorry.'

He pushed the remains of my second gimlet towards me. 'Come on, let's finish up.' He looked at my face. 'It's ok, really!'

I knocked back the last of my gin, and held out my hand. 'Friends?'

'Friends,' he said, shaking it.

My sole consolation, as I rode the Tube home, was that I'd proven Kat wrong: it was way too soon for me to start dating again. And proving Kat wrong was comfort enough.

When I got back to the flat, everything was calm and dark. Thank god, I could just climb into bed in the peace and quiet and get tucked up before I really became miserable about the date.

I kicked off my shoes, headed through the bedroom to the bathroom, dropped my clothes in the laundry and climbed into bed in just my pants, thinking again just how much I loved this particular spot. Good mattress, good sheets, good duvet, goodnight. I was just falling asleep, drifting off on a cloud of gin and resolutions, when I felt a heavy hand creep across my stomach and pull me across the bed.

My murmured 'What the—' became a full-throated scream by the time I'd leapt out of bed, and was only magnified by a pasty figure on the other side of the bed doing exactly the same thing. It took several seconds to realise that the figure was Jack, looking just as terrified as me.

'WHAT ARE YOU DOING?' I roared.

'WHAT AM I DOING? WHAT THE HELL ARE *YOU* DOING?' he roared back at me, shaking.

'I THOUGHT THERE WAS A MURDERER IN MY BED!'

'LIKEWISE!' We both looked at each other, semi-naked.

'Fine, I thought you were a sexy murderer,' Jack said, half smiling. 'I was asleep. I thought you'd —' His voice cracked a bit. 'I thought you'd come back to me.'

I tried to ignore what he'd said, just snatching a blanket around me and backing towards the door.

'What are you *doing* here?'

'The meetings were moved. We're flying out the day after tomorrow now.' Jack's sigh sounded just how I felt and a part of me wanted to hug him, to get back into bed and let him pull me across to him, to fall asleep curled up together.

But that wasn't what we'd agreed. It wasn't the path we were on now.

'This was just a mistake. Sorry.' I left our bedroom and shuffled in the blanket to the sofa, where last night's pillows were still piled up. I didn't even remember falling asleep.

At school the next day, I had emails from Kat every ten minutes, asking about last night's date, until I finally caved in and called her at break time.

'Well? How was it? Are you in love? Is he perfect?' she said, before I'd even said hello.

'It was great. Until it wasn't.'

'Did he try to put it—'

'No! God, Kat. No. It just. . . I wasn't ready.'

'You wouldn't give him a—'

'Stop it!'

'I've got tonnes of these, I can go all day.'

'Stop it.'

'That's what he said. Sorry. Carry on.'

'It was really nice. He's a really nice person. But we've agreed to be friends.'

'What a waste.'

'It's *not* a waste. He *is* a really nice person. And I *would* like him as a friend.'

'A friend with benefits, maybe.'

'No, no benefits. I'm not ready for benefits. I did tell you that.'

'Fine. But I'm just going to email you over a picture of me to show him in case he's looking for something with a little more—'

I hung up and sat back at my desk, hoping the school's email filter would catch whatever she sent over.

I got home just after seven. I'd been so busy with Year 11's Bunsen burner experiments that I hadn't even considered the wall of awkwardness that would be waiting for me back at the flat. In fact, I'd spent the bus ride home trying to get Iffy on the phone – it had been months since I'd seen him – but eventually I'd just got a text back from him saying, *Sorry, hard to talk at the moment, shifts at the hospital crazy. Maybe soon x*

Sure. *Maybe soon.* I knew what that meant from Iffy. I knew that this was his tactful way of keeping me at arm's length.

At home, Jack was cleaning the kitchen with his usual zen-like thoroughness, something I used to love watching. Now, there was nowhere to hide – the sofa directly faced the huge hatch onto our little galley kitchen, and it seemed pretty clear that the bedroom was off-limits until my bed shift came around again.

165

I sat on the sofa with the TV on and tried to be invisible, but eventually Jack came to a stop and, without looking at me, said, 'So you were out late last night.'

'Yeah, sorry again about that. I didn't mean to wake you.'

'By scaring the shit out of me.'

'I honestly didn't think you'd be there. That was hardly my fault.'

There was a silence.

'Well, was it a good night?'

There was an even longer silence. It stretched out, then swelled up until it filled the room, and I had serious concerns that I would no longer be able to breathe.

Then I squeaked, 'Yeah. It was fine, thanks.' I could feel my face changing from soft copper to glowing garnet and I worried my whole head might explode.

Jack came out of the kitchen and stood between me and the TV. 'You can just tell me, you know.'

'Tell you what?' Then I thought of Jessica, and their work trip abroad that he was about to enjoy. Deep breath. '*Fine*. I was out with someone from school. It's not anything serious. But it was a guy. And. . . well, that's it. You now know as much as I do.' Apart from me telling that guy that I wasn't ready to go any further, that is. But Jack didn't need to know that.

'Name?'

'Sorry?'

'I don't know his name. I'm assuming you do.'

I flicked through the channels, hoping maybe Jack would get distracted and just forget his question. He stood in front of me, unmoving. 'George.'

'*George*.'

I stopped. 'How can you say the guy's name sarcastically? What's the point of that?'

'I didn't do anything. Anyway, it's no skin off my nose.

The sooner you meet someone else, the sooner you can be out of this flat.'

Ouch. But I wondered what else I deserved. I'd started this ball rolling. It was my fault if I stood in front of it and got crushed.

I heard the bedroom door slam, and wondered if our room exits were making the plaster crumble in Upstairs Jan's flat too. Well. What fun. And *well* worth the single date that wasn't even going anywhere anyway.

I spent the rest of the night on the sofa, watching garbage on TV and trying not to think about Jack or dating or Kat's NSFW selfies, and Jack didn't come out again all evening. Great.

EIGHTEEN

Three years earlier

At Christmas, it was clear that between his distant father and his absent mother, Jack had nowhere to go for the day itself. As soon as Zoe realised, she begged him to come to her parents' for the festivities. If she made it sound as though he was doing her a favour, he would come. When she asked her parents the next day, out of Jack's earshot, they were so delighted; they'd wanted to ask since his parents' split last year, or even since they'd first met him three years before. 'Lovely,' her mum said. 'Great stuff,' her dad said.

That year the presents were more thoughtful than Zoe had managed in years: a set of soft fine-knit wool socks for her dad, wrapped around a smart leather nail-file kit; a pair of earrings for her mum, picked by Jack to match a necklace he'd complimented her on previously, and a pair of baby-soft sheep-skin slippers; lipsticks, books, keyrings, sunglasses and candles for her sisters and brother-in-law and the centre of attention, William the new baby in the house (although he had fewer lipsticks and candles, and more books and hats). Jack and Zoe shopped for them together, although Jack chose many of the gifts himself. When Zoe picked something out, Jack, with his eye for colour and feel for texture, suggested something even better – not always more expensive, but more special, better matched to each recipient. He wrapped the gifts himself, too, in tissue paper and thick purple ribbons, having already sent his annual hardback historical thriller to his dad and nothing to his mother. Zoe brought them both mugs of hot toddy while he wrapped everything and turned up the carols on the radio.

Even as the family had grown larger, with new members added, Christmas Eve was always spent under the family roof. There was a Christmas Eve spread, with a whole salmon, and baked yam and cheese, followed by mince pies made by each of the sisters with the initial of the baker on every individual pie. Then the whole family bundled up in their warmest clothes to knock on neighbours' doors, where now-adults who had been once-children would join Kat, Ava, Esther and Zoe in the streets, rolling their eyes good naturedly at one another, as they stood together to sing Christmas songs for their parents and grandparents. Jack stood with Ethan and baby William, and wondered how he'd got so lucky. Zoe, trying to make Kat laugh as they strained for the descant, looked at Jack and marvelled at her own luck.

On Christmas Day, William's stocking had split open on one side, due to each adult sneaking down in the night to squeeze in more items. While Zoe's mum got her sewing box out to mend it, Zoe watched as Jack took William from her. He sat down on an armchair and played peekaboo, pulling faces and entrancing baby William.

'My son is available for hire, you know. Good rates for family members,' Esther had said when she saw how well they got on together. Jack had laughed, and asked if she needed him back, but she backed away, saying, 'No no, as long as he's not crying, you can keep him, please.'

Zoe had the overwhelming feeling again that Jack would

be a wonderful father, whenever it might be, and maybe she'd like to be the one to witness it first-hand. At that moment, Jack had looked up at her, as if he could hear her thoughts, and they'd both laughed as they caught one another's eye.

After that, Jack spent every Christmas with the Lewis family: his father was often away on festive cruises, remarkably, and his mother wasn't around either. Every year, Zoe's dad would make the same joke, that Ethan and Jack had become like the children they'd never had, and Zoe or her sisters would say *Don't you mean sons you never had?* and their dad would give a guilty chuckle and say, with exaggerated care, *Ah, yes, sons, of course*. And every time Zoe and Jack would smile at each other. A perfect Christmas, every year. And every year, it was all they ever wanted.

NINETEEN

Now

I'd given Esther the impression I didn't want to go to Kat's office, that I didn't want to get involved with Chuck again. But the more I thought about it, the more sense it made: Kat wouldn't answer any questions about work, and was being awfully vague when she did mention it. I'd go without Esther, straight after school, while she and Ava were still at work. Just one sister, visiting another, checking out the lay of the land. No big deal. I took a bus over there after school and hung around outside for a while before I plucked up the courage to go in.

The receptionist looked up at me with a plastic smile. 'Can I help you?'

'Yeah, hi. Zoe Lewis, to see Kat Lewis?'

'Sure. Take a seat.' She picked up the phone and muttered into it, and I had the strong sense it wasn't Kat she was calling. Sure enough, it was Chuck that came through the frosted glass doors, strutting towards me and sitting too close on the leather sofa.

'Zoe! It's such a pleasure to see you! Who knew we'd keep meeting like this! It must be fate.'

I found it hard to look at him. 'Is Kat around?'

'She'll be somewhere round here. She works hard. Like a *dog*, you know?' I felt my face burn. 'But let's get you a coffee! Miranda, can you get Zoe here a coffee, please?'

'I'm fine, thanks. I'm just here for my sister.'

'Sure, sure.' He leant even closer, his voice growing quiet. 'The thing is, Zoe, your sister is my concern now. Do you understand? I've got plans for her, and if you care about her future, I'd recommend keeping your mouth shut about anything you think you remember about you and me.'

'What I *think* I remember?'

'Yeah. Whatever impression you got back then, you were just a kid with a crush and I can't take any responsibility for how you felt.' He gave me a pained-looking smile. 'It's just not fair to put that on me. You do understand, don't you?' He leant back again, clapping his hands together. 'Your sister, on the other hand! There's a woman who's going places! As long as we all look out for her,' he said, putting his hand on my knee, 'I really think she could go far.'

I stood up. I could feel Miranda's eyes on me from her perspex reception desk. 'Leave her alone,' I said, as calmly as I could with my heart pounding in my throat.

Chuck stood up, smiling at me. 'I can't, Zoe – I'm her boss. And she's a grown woman. So I'd *really* recommend keeping your nose out of our business. Both work,' he smiled wider, '*and* personal.' He looked back over his shoulder at Miranda. 'Miss Lewis is just leaving.' He took my arm, and led me, dazed, to the door. 'I mean it, Zoe. I'm strongly recommending that you keep your nose out. And let's keep this conversation between us, yeah?' He smiled at me – a warm, sunny California breeze of a smile. 'Great! Good to see you, Zo.'

I was out in the street, the door closed in my face. I didn't know what was worse: that Kat didn't know I'd been coming, so wouldn't think to look for me out here, or if she'd happened to see the whole thing.

That's that, then, I thought, heading to my bus stop.

But I didn't mean it.

'Iffy!' I squealed excitedly down the phone. It was two days after my disastrous trip to Kat's office and I was still trying to work out my next move. But fate was finally offering me something: it looked like my persistence in trying to get hold of Iffy was finally paying off.

'Hey, you. Long time no speak.'

'Iffy, are you avoiding me?' There was a moment's silence on the line and I could picture his face: thoughtful, patient, trying to find just the right way of phrasing this.

'Zoe, my darling, you know I'd never avoid you. You're too fantastic not to have in my life. But right now my boy Jack is having a fairly shitty time – you're probably aware, since I believe you two are still roomies. And he hasn't got a great many people to make sure that he's taking care of himself. If you know what I mean.'

Of course I did. I had Liz and Benni and my sisters – although maybe not Kat at the moment, not while I couldn't talk to her about Chuck – and Mum and Dad, and colleagues. All of them watching, texting and calling, many of them visiting and making me food, or taking me out and sitting with me, wiping my tears and making sure, between them, that I was still a functioning human being, on the outside at least.

Jack had Graham – silent, absent Graham, always busy with his new life that didn't seem to involve Jack at all – and he had Iffy. He was the boss to almost everyone he socialised with. I realised how short-sighted I'd been. How could I have begrudged for a moment the time that Iffy would dedicate

173

to him, that maybe it wouldn't be right for him to be meeting me for drinks and soothing my frayed nerves, when he was solely responsible for the care and support of my husband. Ex-husband. Almost ex-husband. Oh god.

'Sorry, Iff. But do you think, one day, we might have a drink again?'

'I look forward to it immensely, Zo. And who knows? In this grand new glorious future of happy friendships, maybe Jack could even tag along too?'

I didn't know which thought was more weird: that Jack and I could ever be just friends, or that there was a vein of sarcasm that revealed Iffy was angry with me. I thanked him, and apologised again, and said I hoped we'd talk soon, but as we hung up I couldn't imagine when that might be. I realised that no friendship was so strong that a break-up couldn't produce a fracture that would carry all the way through, with no regard for all the nights out you'd had, all the conversations, the sharing, and the love between you. The rules were clear: Jack and I broke up, so Iffy and I had to throw away almost a decade of knowing each other.

TWENTY

Three years earlier

'Here?'

 'Lower.'

 'Herc?'

 'Mmm. . . tiny bit lower.'

 'There?'

 'Nearly – nearly – hold on. . . tiny bit. . . a little more. . .'

 'There?'

 'YES!'

Zoe picked up the pencil and drew a tiny cross on the wall. She grabbed a hammer and a small nail, and tapped the nail gently into the cross. Both the nail and the hammer went straight through the wall. 'Oh my god, this place is the worst.'

 'You hit it too hard.'

Zoe let go of the hammer, leaving it stuck in the wall halfway up the handle. 'I really don't think that was my freakish strength. And anyway, last week you hung your coat on the pegs by the door and the whole rack came off.'

 'Fine. There may be a slight problem with damp in the walls here.'

'Which our scumbag landlord refuses to do anything about. Or even acknowledge.'

'Yes. But what's our alternative?' Jack asked.

'What, just never ever touch the walls? I'm genuinely worried that I'll close the front door one day and the whole thing will just fall forwards on me.'

'What else can we do?'

'Well. Rentals are generally holes. We'll have to pay to re-plaster that hole for starters—'

'Or we can just do it ourselves?'

'And meanwhile, we still don't have a picture on the wall. Or a coat rack.'

'So?'

'Why don't we buy somewhere?'

Jack grinned. 'Together?'

'I might be doing ok at work but I'm not Beyoncé. Yes, together!' She sat next to him. 'What do you think?'

'Can we afford it?'

'I think so. We need to look at the actual figures, but we've both been saving. And my parents have a chunk of money for each of my sisters and me, for weddings or deposits or whatever we think is the best way to blow the only big slice of cash we're likely to see in our lives. That'll help.'

'Oh my god, you're an heiress? If you'd mentioned that before, it would have made this whole "getting together" stuff *way* easier.'

'Yes, that's right, I'm an heiress. I'm sooooooo rich we can probably get any one-bedroom flat in zone three that our hearts desire.'

'With outside space?'

'Well, certainly with windows that look outside,' Zoe offered.

'Oooooooh.'

'I know. Don't spread it around or our friends will all be wanting a piece.'

Jack stood up and pulled the hammer out of the wall. The plasterboard toppled out with it, landing on the thinning carpet and smattering into a hundred dusty segments. 'So we're really doing this?'

'Do you want to?'

'I really do. Can we paint the bathroom black? And get one of those massive hotel shower heads?' Jack was looking excited now.

'Whoah there, cowboy, I never said we could afford a *bathroom*.'

'Fair enough. Can we paint our toilet bucket black?'

'Sounds luxe. Let's do it,' Zoe agreed.

'Let's do it?'

'Let's do it.'

Jack looked at the huge hole and lifted up the picture frame from where it rested against the wall. As he pulled it up, the frame caught the edge of the fireplace, and the whole mantel above gave a soft cracking noise and slid down to the floor with faint *whoompf*. They stared at the wreckage.

'Shall we phone for some viewings this afternoon?'

'Let's not even wait that long,' Zoe said, grabbing her coat and throwing Jack his. 'At this rate, we're unlikely to have a flat to call from by then.'

They found plenty of terrible flats: new builds with paper-thin walls, basement flats with only the faintest memory of natural light, top-floor flats where neither of them could stand all the way upright. They contemplated fleeing abroad, to some European utopia of dirt-cheap, beautiful housing and a desperate hunger for Science teachers and shoe designers. But eventually they found one property: dark and airless, on the ground floor of a battered old terrace with a garden and a tenant on the floor above, a woman named Jan.

They'd both loved it. In a miracle of good luck, the flat was theirs within two months, and they set to scraping and cleaning windows, painting, sanding and putting up shelves, putting down floors, and refitting the kitchen when one of Zoe's dad's colleagues was getting rid of hers. They spent their days and their savings on paint and wallpaper, finding the perfect mirror, the right light fitting. White and wood and warmth.

It was a busy time. The plans that Jack had made to open a shop somewhere, someday, suddenly coalesced as the perfect location came on the market. Over the school Easter holidays, Jack took off some mid-week days from the shoe studio he was still working at and the two of them shuttled between the shop and the flat with brushes and trays, Polyfilla and picture frames, putting every hour and ounce of effort into making these two new homes beautiful. The shop, the flat, and Jack, and Zoe: all four shone with love.

As the days wore on, their new flat started to take shape. Still small, but light at last, even in London's thin winter sunlessness, the lounge now had an armchair from Zoe's mother and a huge sofa they'd decided would be their one big outlay. The walls were white or soft pink, and the en-suite bathroom was black – just as Jack had wanted – with plants filling the sill of its tiny window. It was cosy, beautiful, and so small it sometimes felt like they were actually treading on one another as they tried to get dressed in the mornings, but gradually they choreographed a routine that worked for them: one of them making coffee for them both, one getting dressed, then one making toast for breakfast while the other dressed. The evenings were easier, as often one of them was working late; either Zoe at school, preparing lessons and writing reports, or Jack at the shoe workshop where they let him produce his own designs on their equipment after closing time. By the time they were both home, with a takeaway or something Jack had rustled up, they could slump on the sofa with plates and the TV on, or in the summer, sit on rickety chairs in the garden under the tree. It felt like bliss.

They had dinner parties around their tiny table, enjoying with self-consciousness the fact that these were their first dinner parties in their first real home. Liz brought over her wonderful new boyfriend Adam, along with two folding chairs and a box of wine glasses. Benni, Zoe's colleague at her school, brought her wife, when they could get a babysitter for their twins. Iffy brought a succession of beautiful young men and women over several months. Everything was nights in, saving money, plus wonderful, long early nights, and meals with friends and plans for the future and holidays to look forward to.

Over the months, with Jack's consent, Zoe had stayed in touch with Linda. Jack didn't speak to her himself, he wasn't ready yet, but Zoe had seen something in Linda, had understood why she'd left, when Jack couldn't. At first it was just emails of a few lines, telling her they were looking for a flat, letting her know their new address, thanking her for the housewarming flowers she'd sent. She offered up little details of their lives, and received little details in return. Linda said she'd left the UK, wanting something warmer, and had found a little house in Spain near Bilbao. She was careful not to step on any toes: she wanted both Zoe and Jack to understand that she knew Jack wasn't ready, that she knew he held her responsible for the divorce, that Jack saw his distant father's further withdrawal from him as her fault. It was clear to Zoe that Linda was grateful there was a channel open between them. But in those emails, and then phone calls, Zoe and Linda grew closer, talking more openly – and with more humour – than Zoe would ever have guessed possible. Zoe would pass Linda's news back to Jack, and tell Linda the things Jack had agreed, with a one-shouldered shrug, that she could share.

But for Jack and Zoe, everything felt ahead of them. Zoe couldn't think too far into the future – it was dizzying to think of all the potential paths open to them, all the places they might live in years distantly ahead, all the work they might do in those places – but she felt like they were a blossoming tree, the two of them, just waiting to see what fruits might grow.

Not that she'd say that to anyone. Jack would wonder when she'd got so sentimental, while Kat would just curl her lip at such optimism. Mum would probably cry, which might be even worse. But it was there, anyway – the feeling that, despite everything that had happened, something good was ahead of them. And the nicest feeling of all was not knowing what exactly that good thing was going to be.

TWENTY-ONE

Now

Despite our non-starter date, I found that I was noticing George more and more at school. I realised I spent so much of my non-teaching time watching him move around the Science office that I never had time to think about whether I might ever want to be non-friends with him. He was great looking, definitely. And he was fun to be around, sure. But, but, but. . .

Maybe I should investigate Liz's theory for myself: forget about George and find my own Henry, have some deliciously disastrous dates and discover how bad it could really be, so that I would appreciate the good all the more when it came along. Maybe George was too good for me. Or maybe I was still too close to the last too-good-for-me man.

Maybe.

In the absence of anything good to distract me, one of my most dreaded days had finally arrived, with nothing I could do to stop it.

My birthday.

For every year I'd been with Jack, he'd booked cinema tickets, concert tickets, indoor-ski-slope lessons, less as birthday celebrations and more as diversions from the annual day I loathed. But today I'd be alone, fending off well-wishers and Fun Plans single-handedly.

I woke with a groan, hiding my head under my pillow. The day had fallen during half term, thank god, and I had plans to stay inside, watching TV and otherwise doing nothing remarkable at all. I wanted something to take me out of my head today, to keep me from dwelling on another passing year, another day in my collapsing life, but I'd have to settle for repeats and whatever sugar hits they had in stock at the corner shop.

Crawling out of bed at ten o'clock, I turned my phone on and put it straight onto mute without checking my messages, before showering and dressing in joggers and a sweater – what Jack always called my outdoor pyjamas. Craving some junk food, I went to see what was in our cupboards before I ventured outside, and found a tray set up in the kitchen. On it was a teapot, just waiting for some hot water, alongside a mug, milk, bowl of muesli, quartered orange, and with a cinnamon roll on the side. Then, in Jack's handwriting, an envelope. *For later*, it said. Divorce papers? An annulment? General hate mail?

Either way, 'later' was probably now, by now, wasn't it? I opened it up, chewing half of the sugary roll I'd somehow bitten off already. Inside was one ticket, to the BFI, for a marathon screening of the BBC version of *Pride and Prejudice* this afternoon. It ran from 1 p.m. until 7 p.m.

If I went to this, pretty much my whole day would be written off.

I smiled, and ate the other half of the cinnamon roll.

After a lunch of Pringles and tinned crab from the corner shop, I caught the Tube to Waterloo, smiling to myself all the way. This was an absolutely perfect thirtieth birthday. Utter anonymity away from all the confetti and bells everyone else would want for me. And only one person in the whole world knew where I was right now.

The next day, when it was deemed safe to talk about the topic, Liz took me for breakfast and wished me happy birthday in a stage whisper.

'And did you have the terrible, unremarkable day you always dreamed of?' she asked, sliding a small gift across the table to me, looking both ways as if she didn't want to get caught doing it.

I laughed. 'Thank you! It wasn't too bad, actually. I didn't get breakfast in bed, but I did find it in the kitchen, on a tray.' I opened the wrapping, and the box inside, to find a gold name necklace, Zoe in cursive script.

'Who'd done that?' Liz said, surprised.

'This is gorgeous! Thank you.' I put it on, and looked at her, bemused. 'Jack, of course.'

'He's still giving you birthday breakfasts?'

I sipped my coffee, straightened the name against my collarbone. 'I don't know. I guess so.'

'And are you. . . ok with that?'

'Yeah. Yeah. It's fine. Shouldn't I be?'

'Well. At least he didn't give you a present. That would have made things super weird.'

I put my coffee down with immense concentration.

'Oh my god, he gave you a present as *well*?'

'It was just a ticket.'

'To what? His bed?'

'No! Liz! It was just a *Pride and Prejudice* marathon at the BFI. You know. So I could hide out there for the day. On my own! It wasn't a big deal. It's not a diamond necklace or something. It's not that weird between us – we're finally

183

getting along, just about, and I'm not about to throw anything back in his face when he's just trying to be nice. We've still got months to go until it's all done. We might as well keep the peace.'

She held her hands up. 'Ok, ok, it's no big deal. It just seems all very amicable. . .' She sighed. 'I don't know. Seems like kind of a waste.'

We sipped our coffee in silence.

At home a few days later, Jack was making noodles on the hob when I came in. He peered over his shoulder, saying, 'Oh, hey, I've made way too much by mistake, there's loads more here than I expected – you can help yourself, if you're hungry.' He looked at me. 'You alright?'

I dumped my bag on the worktop. 'Yeah. I've been meaning to say, thanks for the birthday stuff. We just keep. . .' I mimed a kind of ships-passing-in-the-night motion with my hands.

He waved his hand in dismissal. 'Don't worry about it. It's fine. I had the ticket already.'

'Oh. Ok.' Liz's words had been playing on my mind, but maybe it really wasn't a big deal after all. I blew out a deep breath and ran the tap to fill two glasses of water for us. 'Just so you know, things with that guy aren't going any further.'

'Oh. Right. You alright about that?'

'Still yes.' He paused, bringing two bowls down from the cupboard. 'Sorry, yes. Fine. It was just awkward with him, something which barely compares to the awkwardness of this. Here, why don't I tell my husband about the progress with my new boyfriend?'

'Boyfriend? I thought you guys were just seeing how things went.'

'Well, I guess now we know.'

184

Jack put the bowls on the counter, tonged in the noodles and veg, and stuck chopsticks in each bowl. 'Ginger?'

I knew as well as he did how much he hated grating fresh ginger, ever since he lost the tips of two fingers while distracted with a mandolin, but this was the best he could do to show me he truly was trying to be nice. I took my bowl, and wondered whether the extra noodles really were a mistake. 'No, you're ok. Soy sauce'll be fine.'

We crunched and slurped the food in front of the TV, and every time I looked at him, he was smiling a little.

TWENTY-TWO

Two years earlier

The flight had been easy, despite Jack's increasing nerves. It wasn't the take-off or the landing he worried about, it wasn't even the bit in between which saw them cruising over Europe at 30,000 feet in a small tin can; it was the bit where Jack would have to face what was waiting for them at the other end.

They collected their luggage from the carousel, engaging in that subtle competition only the British can bring to the start of a holiday – eyeballing other competitors to see who'd got the prime luggage-grabbing location – before wheeling their bags towards the Arrivals door. The heat was intense; bleached white light flooded through the automatic doors ahead of them.

'Ready?'

Jack just looked at her.

'We can't stay in the Duty Free shop forever, Jack.'

In reply, he started wheeling his bag towards the doors and she hurried to catch up with him. They came into the Arrivals hall together, where he stopped dead and looked around.

'See? Not here. As if I expected anything else.'

'Excuse me.'

Jack turned around expectantly, but it was just a fellow passenger trying to get through. Zoe pulled Jack out of the way and looked around. At one end of the Arrivals hall, waiting behind the nylon cord, an older woman was smiling at them uncertainly. She had short-cropped grey hair, a plump, comfortable body, and golden, tanned skin. She raised a nervous hand in greeting.

'Oh my god.'

'What?'

'Jack. She's here. That's your *mum*.'

The woman walked over to them, and smiled in return to Zoe's wide smile. Jack held onto his suitcase handle with both hands, mouth slightly agape. Linda looked so different.

'Mum?'

'Hello, darling. I'm glad you could come.' Zoe looked at Jack and saw he still wasn't able to move, so she stepped forwards and put her arms around Linda. Linda hugged her back, and they stood together like that for a while. Zoe worried she and Linda might both start crying. It was so wonderful to see her in the flesh after all their talks. When she pulled away, she saw that Linda's eyes were wet too. Linda looked at Jack.

'Right. Have you got a car? Shall we go?' Jack said, turning away abruptly and starting to walk towards the exit. Linda's face crumpled a little. Zoe took her arm and smiled at her, saying nothing while Linda gave her a weak smile in return, squeezing her arm as they followed Jack out into the brilliant whiteness.

It was impossible to maintain any level of anger when surrounded by so much sunshine, so Jack had to resort to staying in a different room to his mother as much as possible for those first few days. When she brought in breakfast, he would walk outside to the shared pool and float face down in it before coming up for a gasping breath, then rolling back onto his stomach. When she and Zoe came outside to the pool with glasses of fresh lemonade for them all, he would head to Linda's guest room, saying the sun was getting a bit too strong for him. He had no chance to see how much happier she was, how much calmer. Only at the evening meal would he sit with his mother, but by then the pool and the sun had done their work and he was falling asleep at the table as Zoe and Linda made plans for the next day. Zoe couldn't say it aloud to either of them, but she thought Jack was being unkind, even childish. He had agreed to come after Zoe had begged him, had eventually agreed to see it as a holiday, albeit one where he'd have to face his mother. It had been two years since she'd left the family home, two years since he'd seen her.

On their third night he excused himself immediately after dessert, stumbling up to the guest room where he would, from experience of the previous two nights, fall asleep on the bed fully dressed.

'How's he doing?' Linda gently asked Zoe.

'He's alright, I think. It's hard to tell – he barely talks to me either. It's like the sun's sedated him.'

'I know he's angry with me, but I've never known him so quiet, Zoe. Even as a little boy he'd chatter away to me every day after school, even if he was just talking about who he'd played with in the playground, who he'd sat with for lunch. By the time he went to university he knew better than me about everything, but he'd still talk to me whenever he called, about his course, about you. But now. . .'

'It's horrid, I know. I think. . . it was just harder for him than anyone would have guessed. He's really been hit by it. I don't. . . I don't think he'd ever thought it might happen, if you know what I mean. It wasn't like you two used to. . . fight, or anything?' Zoe felt like she was on a terrible tightrope – she didn't want to be disloyal to Jack, to say out loud that she thought he'd behaved wrongly, but she didn't want Linda to feel like she was having to win both Jack and Zoe over at the same time.

Linda laughed a little. 'I'm sure that's what he thought. We never did fight. But it didn't mean we got along. You know what Graham's like,' she added, looking at Zoe, who tried to smile noncommittally.

'It was impossible, Zoe. If he agreed with me, if he disagreed with me, if he wanted something, if he didn't want something. . . it was just silence. All the time. Him moving from room to room, sitting behind his paper, looking like some lost orphan just waiting to be saved, and all the time I'd be trying to get something from him, anything, and I could feel myself talking more and more just to try and get a reaction from him. . .' She was almost crying now, and Zoe shuffled her chair closer and put an arm around her. 'Jack couldn't even begin to imagine what that was like. Feeling like the villain, him and his dad rolling their eyes at me.'

'I'm sorry, Linda.'

She wiped her eyes. 'Oh, my dear, it's not your fault. It's not Jack's fault, either. It's maybe not even Graham's fault.' She thought for a moment. 'We just were never right for each other. It might be my fault as well, for letting him behave that way, for staying with him for so long. But what was I supposed to do when Jack was little? Leave him with Graham? I doubt he would have chosen to come with me, and even if he did, I wasn't working – what was I going to raise him on?'

Linda got up and turned the kettle on, bringing cups and milk over to the counter. 'Oh I know, I know, I could

189

have managed somehow. People do, don't they? But it just seemed. . . easier. . . to stay like that. I thought he might change, or I might get used to it, then suddenly it was our anniversary approaching and I thought, if I died tomorrow, would I be glad I'd spent my life with Graham, feeling like a stupid babbling chatterbox every single day? Everyone laughing at the wife who never stopped talking? So I packed my bags. And that was it. This is *my* life we're talking about – not Graham's, and not Jack's. I know Jack's finding it hard to understand why I did what I did, but I think. . .' She paused. 'I'd like him to start understanding that.'

Zoe nodded, seeing the sadness that had run through Linda for so long, in one form or another. Looking for something to do, she started clearing the table. 'Were you. . . frightened?'

'Zoe, my dear, I was petrified. I thought I'd lose all my friends, my husband, my house. . . I knew Jack might be upset but I never once, not *once*, thought that I might actually lose him too.' She poured boiling water into the cups. 'I was so frightened that my life would change more than I could cope with, but I never thought the one person I actually cared about more than anything else would just. . . stop speaking to me.'

Linda bumped the kettle down on the counter top, and started crying.

'He's my little boy, Zoe. I don't know if you ever want children of your own, but I hope you never understand what this feels like, to cause your own child such pain that he can't even look at you. And I can't understand what I've done *wrong*. But whatever I've done, it must be truly awful for him to hate me this much.'

Zoe moved to the counter so she could put her arm around Linda again. She peered down at her rumpled, tear-streaked face and saw Jack in her, completely; saw how they carried their pain and saw how they cried it out when they hurt too much to ignore it any longer. Zoe put both arms around her, hugging her tightly.

'Linda, we're going to take care of him. Between you and me, we'll make sure that Jack's ok. Alright? We can look after him.'

Linda shook in her arms. 'Zoe, I'm so glad you're here. I'm so glad he's got you. I remind myself over and over that he's got you to talk to—'

'He's hardly talking.'

'But you're there for him. I see you together, even now, even here, and I see how different you two are to me and Graham. You *talk*. When we got married, I was so in love with him. He was such a handsome young man, Zoe.' Linda sat down at the table again and looked out of the window, her mind disappearing into her faded wedding memories. 'It was a beautiful wedding, too, all our friends, my parents. . . I dried my bouquet and kept it for years, in a little box on top of our wardrobe. I was so proud that day, looking at Graham as I walked up the aisle, how smart he looked, how beautiful I was in that dress, and I knew everything was going to be ok once we'd signed that wedding certificate. I was so happy, Zoe. I thought Graham was going to fix all my qualms about us being together. I really loved him.' She sighed, dry-eyed. 'But it just wasn't right between us. It wouldn't have been right between us in any country, at any time, with any dress or kitchen or car or children.'

Zoe brought their teas over. 'But you got Jack.'

Linda clasped the tea in both hands, warming herself. 'Exactly. He's been the best thing in my life for all these years, but it's time for Jack to start thinking about his own family, his own life. That's what having children means. Teaching them to leave you. And thinking about that made me realise that I owe it to myself to get on with living my own life. I can't expect to feel different if I do the same thing every day. If I want to see Jack happy in this brief life I have, I deserve to have some of that too. So I packed my bags. And here we are.'

Zoe sipped her hot tea. 'You raised a good son, Linda. He'll come around.'

Linda looked doubtful.

'He will, you know that. He's just. . . Something in him is reverting to being a kid again. But he'll be ok. We just need to give him a little time.'

Linda blew gently into her cup. 'I don't know,' she said, 'I just worry. Something seems to have shifted in him at the moment. I just don't want him to make any decisions right now that he might regret for the rest of his life.'

That night, Zoe sat on the edge of the double bed in the guest room, and kissed Jack's shoulder until he'd half woken, pulling her into a hug.

'Jack,' she whispered. 'Jack. Your mum. She's really sad, you know.'

'I thought you said she was happier out here,' he mumbled sleepily.

'She is. But she misses you. Please, please don't think I'm siding with her. . . but I don't think you're being completely fair to her.'

Jack woke up a little more, and opened his eyes. 'I hate to think what that would actually be like if you were siding with her.'

Zoe kissed him. 'She loves you. You're her child. Please – this is really hurting her. She would never have done something to hurt you, would she? Sometimes you just need to let someone live the life they want.' Jack closed his eyes and rolled over. 'Jack?'

He grunted, then reached back and pulled her in with him. There'd be no more talking that night.

The next morning, Jack said good morning to his mum, dropping a quick kiss on her head as he walked past to the fridge. Linda and Zoe were both speechless. It seemed the sun was warming Jack, thawing him gently. That day he made lunch for them all, and he and Linda went to the market in the afternoon to buy ingredients for dinner. The fourth day Zoe spent entirely by the pool, on her own, listening to the faint, constant hum of Jack and Linda talking softly to each other.

By the fifth day, Zoe didn't want to leave, and by the sixth, though he didn't say it, it was clear Jack felt the same. He and Linda had drifted into a comfortable quietness, but all three of them felt the peace that Linda had travelled out there to find.

At the airport, Jack's eyes filled when he said goodbye to his mother, and Linda and Zoe were just as bad. Linda wept, and Zoe dabbed at her face with the hem of her t-shirt, and they all laughed at themselves.

'I'll see you soon,' Linda said. 'You know where I am, now, right?' She kissed Jack again, her boy, and Zoe, who'd brought them closer than they'd ever been before, and they waved at her from the far side of security, and Zoe felt something new and green and hopeful grow between her and Jack. Something had been healed in him that neither of them had realised was damaged.

TWENTY-THREE

Now

Saturday morning, a few weeks after my birthday, and Jack and I were lying around the flat, reading the papers – just like the old days, except I was on the sofa and Jack was on the bed, as far apart as we could possibly be while both still being indoors. It was almost companionable.

Jack's phone bleeped. After a long silence, he shouted through the doorway, in a baffled tone, 'It's Iffy. He's having a house party tonight.'

'Not exactly an unforgivable crime,' I observed, after another long silence.

His phone bleeped again. 'Yeah, but he wants *you* to come.'

I narrowed my eyes, even though Jack was in the next room. 'Why?'

'That's what I said. He reckons you're his friend too and he wants you to come if he's throwing a party.'

His words faded into nothing. Today would be mostly silence, it seemed. Eventually, I said, 'And what do you think?'

Jack bucked the trend by replying almost instantly. 'I don't care. You do what you want.'

'Thanks very much.'

'You know what I mean. You go where you want. It's not up to me. It's Iffy that invited you.'

'By texting your phone.'

'He knows we still live together.'

I didn't push it, but of course Iffy was asking for Jack's tacit approval. If Jack didn't want me to go, he wouldn't have told me. I didn't know if I admired Iffy's tact, or felt exasperated at the need for Jack's nod of assent. We'd already established how close Iffy and I actually weren't now; it didn't help matters that Jack was the only one who'd got the invitation. I told him I'd think about it, and headed out to lunch with my sisters.

'So he actually invited you?'

'Yes, but he said it was Iffy who'd really asked.'

'Of course he would!' Kat stuffed a lobster roll in her mouth. I'd sworn to myself that I wouldn't ask about Chuck or her job today, despite the fact that I'd realised recently I was thinking about them both at least daily, with a growing feeling of nausea in my gut.

Esther dipped a rice ball in some wasabi. 'Do you want to go?'

'I haven't seen Iffy in ages. I'd really like to, but—'

'But do you want to go with Jack?' she asked.

'I haven't got any choice, have I?' My sisters looked among themselves. 'I haven't! If I want to see Iffy, I have to go with Jack. I don't think we can arrive and leave the party separately. We can't!' I insisted, seeing eyebrows raised.

Ava chewed thoughtfully, and said softly, 'And what if Jack wasn't going? Would you still want to go?'

'Yes, of course! I've missed Iffy. But it's an extra plus that Jack and I are actually getting on at the moment, and I'm not going to turn my nose up at that, am I? We did get married at the start of the year, after all. It'll be nice to have some neutral, amicable time together.'

'Neutral,' said Esther.

'*Amicable*,' said Kat.

Ava tried to hide her laughter.

'I should never tell you guys anything,' I muttered.

By seven o'clock, I'd made my mind up, cemented by a message from Iffy to my phone, at long last, saying, *You better come or the whole party will be a waste of time. You're welcome to ignore Jack all night long – just don't forget me when you disappear into the sunset with husband no. 2. See you at 8 with as many bottles as you can carry x*

Jack was already dressed, so as I jumped in the shower I told him I'd meet him there. I took my time; tried on a few outfits, did my hair and make-up, took off my jeans and favourite simple top and put on a party dress and some giant, heart-shaped earrings. Better. If I was going to go, I should go big.

I pulled open the bedroom door and headed to the hall to grab my shoes and coat, and found Jack sitting on the sofa, feet on the coffee table, book in hand. I let out a surprised yelp.

'If we're going to the same place, we might as well go together,' he said. Then, 'Wow. You look nice.'

He helped me on with my coat, then put on his own. We walked to the Tube and took seats next to each other. I idly wondered whether we looked like a happy couple to outside observers, or whether it seemed like we'd had a fight. Maybe we didn't look like a couple at all. We weren't talking. A passer-by might say we were simply strangers.

At Vauxhall, Iffy's stop, we got out and headed to a corner shop, picking out a bottle of wine and a spirit each.

I turned to Jack, laughing. 'If you see me about to drink

both of these, please stop me in any manner possible.' Jack smiled for a moment, and I realised it was the first time we'd spoken since we'd left the flat. Then I realised that he had no responsibility for me anymore, and I couldn't and shouldn't ask him to stop me doing anything. We walked on to Iffy's in a heavy silence again, bottles clunking in our thin plastic bags.

Iffy opened the door to us with a smile, a gold party hat perched on the top of his shiny scalp. 'My favourite couple!' he said, then saw both of us flinch. 'Pair, I mean! Two humans standing next to each other! Oh Jesus, just get in here. I've accidentally invited the most boring people from the hospital and I don't know how to get them to leave, so you've got to come in and be vivacious enough to defibrillate this party, but dull enough that they might leave early.'

'Can we split the work?' Jack said, giving Iffy a hug. 'Zo can be charming about GCSE students and I can bore them senseless with stock management systems.'

It was a compliment, but I was waiting for the punchline. It didn't come.

'Perfect,' said Iffy. 'Give me your booze, and come in out of that bitter May cold.'

Two hours after arriving, both Jack and I were many, many cocktails in. Subconsciously – at least on my part – we hadn't stayed in the same room all evening; I'd drift out from the lounge into the hall, only to hear Jack's voice and realise he'd just come into that space. But suddenly I found him at my elbow, as I was pouring myself another gin and bitter lemon.

'Could you find a spare one of those for a parched party-goer?'

I laughed, full of gin-fuelled merriment, and sloshed some into a second plastic cup.

A new voice behind us said, 'Are you two the divorcing pair who still live together?' I turned around to see Lottie, my least favourite of Iffy's friends. He'd gone to med school with her and somehow hadn't shaken her off in the last decade. He said she was good fun and meant no harm; I thought she used Iffy to get herself into gay bars so she could perv at men who, pretty much by definition, had declared they weren't into her right now, thanks.

Jack slung an arm round my neck and I felt his hesitation at where his hand should fall – gravity would put it almost on my breast, so he kept moving it until it came back around my chest to the shoulder closest to him. We stood facing Lottie, in an awkward headlock position.

'That's us,' Jack said, tightening his arm in his discomfort, 'the Happy Divorcées.'

I choked a little, and Jack lowered his arm, pulling me into a more familiar hug.

'Sure,' I said, bristling at Lottie's sneering expression. 'So busy having a great time that we forget to keep fighting.' Lottie pouted at me. Jack lowered his arm to my waist and pulled me tighter. I tried not to think about how good it felt.

'Riiiiiight,' said Lottie. She gave us a brittle smile. 'Good for you two, I guess.' Bored, she wandered off, but Jack didn't remove his arm, and I didn't pull away. She'd given us the opportunity it seemed we'd both been waiting for.

'This is good gin,' Jack said.

I didn't say anything; just let some enormous invisible weight fall from my shoulders that I'd been carrying for the last six months, and tipped my head back against his chest.

'Really good,' he said.

We stayed like that for another hour, chatting to people as they came into the kitchen, mixing more drinks, neither of us mentioning Jack's arm, or my face, which I could only imagine was like the cat who'd tumbled into a tank of cream. By midnight, everything had a vaguely rosy glow, and I was suggesting we get a taxi home, *god knows if we'd make a Tube now anyway*. Jack stumbled in the hallway as we hugged Iffy goodbye, and Iffy and I had to slightly carry him into the back of the taxi.

'He ok?' shouted the taxi driver. 'This guy ok in my car?'

'He's fine,' I said. 'Just take us home, please.'

I didn't have Iffy to help at the other end and despite the fact that Jack had kept my promise and not thrown up in the car, the taxi driver refused to help me with him. As a result it took some time to get Jack into the flat.

I wrapped one of his arms around my shoulder as we made it towards the main door; I propped him against the wall while I rooted around for my keys, feeling only fractionally less drunk than Jack. By the time I'd finally managed to open it, Jack had slid silently down into the front garden and was trying to pull some blue tarpaulin over himself as a blanket. It took me another ten minutes to pull him upright, get through our own front door too, and stagger into the living room. We landed, sweaty and panting, on the sofa, side by side and entirely horizontal. Jack at last seemed to come to.

'I had a nice time tonight,' he said clearly, as if we had taken a sober carriage ride home filled with polite conversation.

'Me too.'

'Do you think I can see you again, some time?'

'How about tomorrow morning, between the kettle and the toaster?'

'Are you propositioning me, Ms Lewis?'

I blinked at him. He leant forwards and kissed me. Suddenly, I was kissing him back too, and his hands were in my hair, and it was fireworks, and all I wanted was to throw out the bed rota and both of us to tumble into it together and not come out for a month. I'd forgotten what a fantastic kisser he was. His hand pushed into my hair, slid down my neck, and sat gently inside the back of my collar, stroking up and down, up and down. I pushed closer to him, lifting one leg over his thigh, touching my hand to his chest.

There was something holding me back, though: memories of these last few months, the bloodiness of getting this far, our terrible unhappiness. His New York trip. Some tiny whispered suggestion that this wasn't the best idea.

I pulled away, and saw Jack's dilated pupils and slight smile curdle to shock as he saw my own face.

'Jack—'

'It's fine. I get it. I'm too drunk.'

'No!'

'Oh thank god, I thought you were going to stop us kissing.' He leant forwards again.

'No, wait. I mean it isn't because you're drunk.'

'Good, because I'm definitely not, anyway.'

'This just isn't a good idea, is it? This isn't what we both wanted when we were sober, was it?'

And then he looked at me, with such a heartbreaking expression that I wondered if I didn't have the same expression on my face. I watched him put his head on the arm of the sofa and close his eyes, a painful wince on his face. I waited for him to speak again.

The terrible silence stretched out.

Jack let out a gentle snore.

I rolled my eyes, laid him down properly on the sofa and pulled his shoes off, put a blanket over him and placed a pint of water on the coffee table next to him.

It wasn't going to happen. Gin and parties and drunken

kisses? That wasn't fixing something. That was breaking it even more.

In the morning, Jack could barely stir himself from the sofa. I was woken by soft sounds from the TV – tinny squeaks and muffled voices, the sound turned down to the lowest volume. My mouth felt like it was coated with something from a bus engine, and my brain had been removed, shaken inside out, and stuffed back in by a child with knuckledusters on, but I was alive. And more to the point, I hadn't kissed my almost-ex-husband. Or rather, hadn't continued kissing. Even if I'd wanted to. Which I didn't. And I definitely also hadn't stayed up until 4 a.m. thinking about it. So. . . great.

Still in bed, I scrolled through various sites to see if there were any incriminating photos from last night anywhere. I was in the clear, but on Instagram I came across three photos of Kat's office night out, featuring Chuck and Kat looking very cosy indeed: his arm around her shoulder, his head tipped to touch her head, both of them dipping straws into something murky in a giant martini glass. I'd been planning to do something, anything, since he threw me out of their office. This revolting display only turned my resolve to pure iron. But until this hangover shifted, I had no hope of making any kind of plan.

I set down two cups of coffee and shifted Jack's feet off the sofa so there was room for me to sit down next to him. We drank them in silence, watching the TV together. By the time Iffy came round with bacon sandwiches for all of us, we still hadn't spoken. Once he'd finished his sandwich, licked his fingers and chugged down an entire can of Coke in one go, Iffy looked at us and narrowed his eyes.

'Jesus, was the party that bad?'

'The party was great. But you do remember trying to get

him into the taxi, don't you?' I said, gesturing to Jack but still not able to look at him.

'I remember the taxi. . . but. . . my spidey senses are telling me something else happened. Did you fight the taxi driver? Did you fight each other?'

At that moment, Jack became fascinated by *Hollyoaks* and I started picking my toes.

'Riiiiiight. I see. Well, you are *welcome* for the bacon sandwiches.'

We both mumbled our thank yous.

'And I will be on my way. Much as you guys are unbelievable fun right now, my night seems to have been even wilder than yours. So now that my salt and fat levels have been topped up, I'm going to hibernate until the internet is devoured by melting arctic glaciers and any incriminating photographs have been erased from human existence.'

'That bad?' I asked.

'I've got an ache in one leg and I'm genuinely too scared to look in case I got a tattoo last night.'

I took his hand. 'I'll be thinking of you. How the hell do you look so well, though?'

He smiled. 'Part of the job, isn't it? Can't be cruising the wards looking like death, can I?' Before I could stop him, he was back out the door, and the atmosphere was crushing once again. You'd think if you kept encountering something so heavy and difficult, your body would gradually strengthen and adjust, but the reality was the exact opposite. It just kept on being impossible in these situations, the air too thick to breathe, silence too dense to wade through. I can't remember the last time we'd been that drunk. Or the last time Jack had tried to kiss me. And I'd said no. I really regretted saying that.

The sensible part of me, the one saying I needed to get out into the fresh air right now with a bottle of water and a bag of fruit, was reminding me that no one ever benefits from drunken erroneous make-out sessions.

The other part of me, the one with my comfy cardigan on, and the sofa blanket – purchased for just such emergencies – wrapped around me absolutely perfectly, and the knowledge we had a full *Friday Night Lights* box-set we could power through for the rest of the day. . . That part of me didn't regret the kiss at all.

The trouble was, there was no separating those two parts. I was stuck with my regret, and would just have to try to smother it with my triumph at making one, single, solitary, good adult decision. I just wished, a bit, a little, it hadn't had to be this one.

I got up, rinsed out my coffee cup, picked up some water and an apple, and headed out the door. I was two streets away before I realised I still had my slippers on.

TWENTY-FOUR

Two years earlier

Jack was down on one knee.

He'd been fine a moment before. He'd been standing next to her on the bridge, they'd been talking; she'd only turned around for a moment to look at the lights on the Southbank and then when she looked back Jack had gone. Only he hadn't *gone* gone, he'd just somehow ended up on one knee on the woven metal planking of the bridge, the flat and level bridge, un-moved by earthquakes or blistering gusts of wind. Had he dropped something? But he was looking up, was looking at Zoe's face, and it didn't look like he was about to say, 'Shit, my Oyster card just fell in the Thames.'

Zoe put up a hand as if to ward him off.

'Zoe.'

She stepped back. She saw a few people had stopped a little way distant, and were watching them, smiling.

'It's been a hard year or so for us both. With my parents splitting up, and your workload, and selling Henderson's to Gillett, and hundreds of other things I've probably forgotten because I'm so nervous.' The bystanders chuckled softly. Jack spoke up a little. 'But I've also probably not even noticed those other difficulties, because you've been by my side.' Someone in the growing crowd *aaah*-ed. 'Every single day I wake up with you, I'm grateful for the day we met. I'm grateful for your kindness, for your sense of humour, for your good sense, your ambition for us both, for the way you get on with my mum. . .' The crowd chuckled again. 'I want to spend every single day with you for the rest of our lives. Zoe. . .' Jack pulled a small box from his coat pocket. 'Will you marry me?' The crowd cheered, but not fully, not yet.

Zoe thought, *What, every single day? Forever?* And what the living fuck was he doing down on one knee in front of this group of people who were probably videoing it before they put it on Facebook captioned 'look at this couple we saw in London' before the tabloids scraped it and Jack and Zoe would have to appear on their lifestyle page under a banner heading of 'The Cutest Thing You've Ever Seen on the Golden Jubilee Bridge' although really it wasn't that cute. It's not like he'd released doves or puppies or a golden helium balloon for every day they'd been together. And hadn't Jack not wanted to get married either? She was almost hyperventilating. Stop. *Stop.*

Then she heard the expectant silence as the bunch of fifteen or so strangers waited, and she saw Jack's happy, open, loving face, and she swallowed her rage and her disappointment and her confusion. She knew that she loved Jack back, and so she said, 'Yes!' and did the happy face that everyone was expecting, getting down too and kissing him as the crowd went wild.

Zoe suggested a drink at the bar of the BFI, since they were on the Southbank; she wanted to get away from everyone watching them.

They wound their way in and out of the crowds to the cinema, Zoe barely able to believe what had just happened. When they got to the bar, Jack ordered a bottle of champagne, telling the smiling woman behind the bar, 'We've just got engaged,' to which she said 'Congratulations!' as Zoe did that happy face again. Zoe picked up the champagne and two glasses as quickly as she could, and carried them off to a distant bench seat in one corner, Jack following her. She was foaming the fizz into the glasses and knocking one back before Jack had even taken his coat off and sat down beside her.

'Hey, wait for me!'

Zoe topped up her glass. 'Sorry. Sorry.'

Jack snuggled against her, his thigh pressing against hers. 'You ok?'

'Yeah! Yeah, I just. . . I wasn't expecting that.'

'I wanted to surprise you. I've been thinking about it a lot.'

'Apparently so.'

'Was it a bad surprise?'

Zoe took another swig of champagne, and said quickly, 'No.'

She thought again of his face, looking up at her, lit up with hope and all the neon of London. 'Of course it wasn't a bad surprise.' She picked up the champagne bottle, pretending to examine the label so she didn't have to look at Jack. 'I just thought. . . I thought we'd agreed not to get married.'

'We'd talked about it. But that was ages ago. I know we didn't want to get married *then* – we'd hardly been together long enough. But all the stuff we've been through. And seeing Mum, and Dad. . . You said yourself how different Mum says we are to them. Zo, you're the most important thing in my life. I enjoy every moment we're together.'

Yeah, Zoe couldn't help but think, she'd also enjoyed that documentary on the South American convent, but she wasn't about to go off and join it. Then she thought, *Or am I?*

'And these last few months, I look at you every day and think, I don't ever want to be with anyone else. Ever.' He leant in and put his hand gently against her cheek. 'I love you so much, Zo. You make my life better in every single way.'

She nearly cried then, partly because she felt the same, and partly because she felt the complete opposite. Jack made her life better every day; he made *her* better, and she loved him. But the thought that the correct response to that was to change everything, to stand up in front of a crowd and declare your love publicly and sign a document that may as well be written on rice paper for all the permanence it had when you looked at divorce rates, and swear you'll never ever *ever* want anyone else, or change your feelings, or choose a different path to the one you're on in your late twenties. . .

So she kissed him. They kissed for a long time, before Jack pulled away with a 'Mmmoh!' and reached into his coat pocket again, pulling out the little box. 'In all the excitement, I was worried I'd drop it. Do you want to open it?'

No, thought Zoe. *Nope nope nope nope nope.* 'You do it,' she said, putting her happy face on. Jack smiled at her. He popped open the box and lifted the lid to reveal a small gold ring with a sapphire stone. Just what Zoe would have picked if she was buying an unexpectedly expensive piece of jewellery for herself.

'Wow. That's. . . that's really nice.'

'Do you like it? It's the stone from Mum's old ring, but she made me promise to have the ring bit melted down and remade.'

'It's your mum's?' Zoe felt tearful again. Linda had given them this?

'Just the stone. I designed the ring. One of my friends from college actually made it. Susie? Do you remember her?

207

So I gave her the design, then she had her friend look at it too, and they made a couple of suggestions, and here we are. With Mum's stone. For you. Am I babbling? It feels like I am. Am I?'

Zoe took the ring from its deep blue velvet box and slipped it onto the top knuckle of her finger. 'It's. . . really lovely, Jack. It's beautiful. Thank you.'

Jack's shoulders dropped. 'Oh thank god. I can't tell you how terrified I've been that you wouldn't like it.'

'So what did your mum say? When you told her you were proposing?'

'No, she doesn't know. But when we went out there, when she said goodbye at the airport, she gave me this box. Told me about redoing the ring for you. I hadn't said anything, but she. . . she must have just known.' He smiled at her.

Zoe thought of Linda saying, *I see how different you two are to me and Graham*, and realised she must have been hoping even then that things would play out this way.

'Does it fit?'

Rather than pushing it down to the bottom of her finger, Zoe twirled it round and round the top knuckle. When she looked at Jack, she saw something like fear flicker in his face.

'I never thought you'd do something so public. I felt. . . it was a lot of pressure.'

Jack's voice was tight. 'So you didn't actually want to say yes?'

'Jack, I love you so much—'

'You just don't want to marry me.'

'No, I—' *don't want to marry you*, Zoe thought. *I don't want to marry anyone. I just want to live with you and keep having this great time and agree to forget this whole evening, and if we make it to however many thousands of years it is to our sapphire anniversary then I can have this remade yet*

208

again into an enormous knuckleduster and I'll sport it proudly. She took another swig. Her head was beginning to feel bubbly and her coat was too warm. She pulled it off and laid it next to Jack's. Two coats, side by side, comfy and matching and content. *Was* it a disaster if they got married? She might not want to, but she did want Jack. She knew that. Plus, the whole thing would make Mum, and Linda, so happy. Kat and Ava and Esther would be excited for her too, and Iffy would take them out to supper and talk about all the ways he'd make all their ideas better, and they'd have a great time with more champagne, and cocktail ideas that they'd have to try out there and then, and maybe all their unmarried friends – some of whom were actually engaged, now she thought about it – could just come along to a wedding for them now, instead of a sapphire anniversary party in however many years. . . And maybe she'd just get used to it; she wouldn't have to think about it every day, would she? It's not like she'd have to call Jack 'Husband' from then on, and ditch her job to make sure his meat-gravy-and-veg were on the table every night? Was it? Was it?

Stop, she thought again. *Stop*. She took another large swig, draining the glass. She was beginning to feel almost dizzy.

But look at Jack's face! She could do this. She had to do this. It was all going to be – Zoe swallowed – ok.

'Ok,' she said, aware of how Jack was looking at her. 'Ok, let's do this. Let's marry each other.' The words sounded strange. 'Is that the right answer?'

Jack blinked. 'Really?' he said. 'Are you sure?'

She swallowed again, and held her empty glass to her hot face. 'Yes! Of course!'

Jack whooped and bundled her into a huge hug, rocking her on their chair until they were kissing again. Then there was a bustle of movement, and a huge crowd poured out as one of the screenings finished. The bar was full, but Zoe and Jack slipped away with the crowds as they headed home.

Neither of them remembered much of the journey back, although they would remember some of the things they did once they got home for quite a while.

The next morning, Zoe awoke alone with a sore head, sitting up a little and shaking it, uncertain what it was she was trying to shake loose. With a crunching nausea, she remembered both how much they'd ended up drinking – Jack had thoughtfully placed two bottles of prosecco in the fridge for their return, both of which were now empty – and then, a beat or two later, why they were drinking in the first place. She remembered the bridge, the proposal, her acceptance.

Well, she thought, collapsing back on the pillow. That was that then. She'd accepted and she couldn't un-accept now. You accepted your fate – or your punishment – and it made you a better person, didn't it? If she just kept her eyes closed and swallowed her medicine, she could get on with living her life around all this stuff, couldn't she? She blew out hard, and tried not to taste her own mouth. She'd just keep her eyes closed, that's what she'd do. It was fine.

Just as she was nodding back off to sleep, having found a position where she could be lightly unaware of her tongue, her stomach and her head, Jack came bounding in puppyishly and dropped a tray of clinking glassware and crockery at her feet.

'Breakfast in bed, fiancée!' he called softly, giggling.

Zoe opened one eye. 'Please just give me some ibuprofen and then let me sleep for at least a week.'

'Croissants? Juice? Bacon sandwich?'

Zoe slowly slid one of Jack's pillows over from the other side of the bed, then placed it over her own head. Within half a minute, Jack could hear her softly snoring.

He took a bite of flaky pastry. 'Hmm. We'll continue this later, I think,' he said, half to himself. He was too happy to wonder about any hesitation on Zoe's part. He'd probably just surprised her, that was all.

TWENTY-FIVE

Now

Summer hit the city. Women filled the streets and the Tube in sandals and sundresses, and the parks bloomed with office picnickers. By the time I got home, eating a Twister from the corner shop, I was in high spirits, filled with the infectious optimism in the air, thinking about tennis games and summer lunches.

Jack seemed to be waiting for me when I got in.

'Hello! You look smart.'

He was in a dark blue suit, flecked with cream nubs, with groomed hair and new glasses.

'Twister,' he said in response. 'Nice.'

'I didn't know you were here – I would have brought one for you, too.' On a day like this, it was all too easy to fall into familiar habits with Jack. But with last month's kiss still seared onto my brain – and my lips – I didn't want him to think there was anything other than Official Platonic Civility between us.

He ruffled the back of his hair, leaving a tuft up at the top like Mr Majeika.

'Cool, yeah.' He'd stopped listening. My good mood popped.

'What's happened?'

'It's Jessica. At work?'

I knew what was coming, but I couldn't make it easy for him. Not after the kiss. I just looked at him.

'You remember her? The CFO at Gillett – I think you met her at the. . .'

My eyes widened.

'No, sorry, not the point. Anyway. So. . . I think we're seeing each other. Properly.'

Right. Suspicions confirmed then. Ouch. I shuffled towards him, and held up one hand, numbly. 'High five!' I shouted. Jack reached up to softly slap my hand and we stood for a moment, palm to palm, saying nothing. I let my hand drop. Jack coughed.

'So is this. . . ok? Are we ok?' he asked.

'Sure! Why wouldn't we be! It's fine! It's cool!' Jack looked like he was about to leave, picking up his bag, checking himself in the mirror, and I started to wonder whether he'd be out of the flat before I disintegrated into a thousand tiny shards of Zoe, scattered all over the floor. 'Have a good night!' I shouted, momentarily panicked that I would never be able to talk at normal volume again.

As soon as he was through our front door and I heard the outer door slam, I whispered, 'Fuck,' kicked my shoes under the sofa, crawled into bed, and fell fast asleep.

Kat had lured me into discussions about my love life on the promise of a free Saturday brunch.

'Come on,' said Kat. 'Things can't have been that bad with George. Why wouldn't you give him another chance at a proper date?'

'Are we seriously still talking about this? It was weeks

213

ago. And I told you. It wasn't bad. It was just. . .' I tried not to think about my kiss with Jack only a month ago.

'What. Impossibly sexual? You couldn't keep your hands to yourself?'

'No!'

'Don't lie to me. I've seen his photo.'

I gaped at her.

'What? It's a public page on the school website. I'm not letting someone date my sister without me vetting them. Why did you think I was so eager for you to pass my photo on if you were opting out? Anyway, what exactly was the problem then?'

'It just didn't feel. . . right. I hate to have to keep reminding you of this, but I was getting married this time six months ago. So despite his face—'

'And body.'

'And body,' I sighed, then collected my thoughts. 'I just didn't feel like it was the right thing to do.'

Kat curled her lip and sat back in her chair. 'The last thing you need, Zo, is a relationship that goes anywhere. You need a bit of fun, a slice of handsome to take your mind off all this shit.' She gestured behind her, presumably at my marriage.

'I don't want to lead anyone on, Kat. I feel like I did enough damage doing that with poor Jack.'

'You're not leading George on. He's just moved down here. He's a couple of years younger than you. Do you really think he's after The One? Listen: if he ever asks you again, just enjoy your time with him! Relax! Get your head back into dating, and you can decide later on how you feel about him. No one's asking you to *marry* him.'

I reached over and took the last of her pancakes, thinking about whether she was right. To be honest, I wasn't sure if she should be giving me advice – besides those awfully suspicious photos with Chuck, I hadn't seen her with anyone for years. On the other hand, she seemed more content than anyone else I knew: neither desperate for company nor smothered by anyone. Although that reminded me. . .

'Jack's got a new girlfriend.'

'Has he!' Kat screeched in grim delight. 'That frisky son of a bitch.'

'I'd suspected he was seeing her already. I just didn't expect finding out to feel this bad.'

She ran her finger through the maple syrup coating her plate. 'I rest my case. Time to jog on, dear Zo.'

Whether or not it was time for anyone to jog anywhere would have to wait – I had to find out about the pictures of her and Chuck. Somehow.

'Listen, Kat, tell me about your work. Your night out together looked good fun.'

'Not this again.'

'I'm serious! You're my little sister and I don't know what the hell you do at that office.'

'It's strategy, alright? Is that enough information? Zo, I'm not little anymore.'

I felt queasy, hearing the echo of Chuck's words in her defence. 'I know you're not. You're super grown up and capable and don't need your sisters worrying about you.'

'Sisters, plural? What the hell have you three been chatting about behind my back? And *what* are you worried about?'

'Kat, we're not doing anything behind your back. We just want to know that you're happy.' She gave an ironic snort. 'Does that mean you're *not* happy?' I probed as she looked away. 'Is it Chuck?'

She grabbed her bag from the table and stood up. 'It means, Zo, that you really need to trust me, alright? I'm not a little kid. Just let me look after myself.' And before I could stop her, she was gone.

* * *

215

I'd managed to avoid Jack for almost two weeks, since he'd told me about his new significant other. He was coming home late and leaving early, and I wondered if we could keep that up for the remaining five or so months. If only. I got home from school one Friday soaked from a flash summer rainstorm, shivering and dripping onto the carpet, shoes squelching. Jack's keys were on the hall table, so I wondered why there were no lights on, no music or TV. Then a two-headed beast rose up from the sofa, resolving itself into Jack trying to do up his flies, and a woman, Jessica, desperately struggling back into a blouse that had turned itself into silken fusilli.

'Zoe! Christ, what time is it?'

'Good to see you too, Jack.'

The woman spoke. 'I'm really sorry, we didn't know. . .'

It was nice to be on the moral high ground, for once. I reverted to my most formal British manners. 'It's fine. I'll. . . be in my bedroom. Nice to meet you.' I couldn't quite bring myself to say her name, even though none of this was her fault. This should have been in a year's time, Jack and I each happy with new partners, both of us impeccably dressed for a double date at a pub, all four of us able to laugh and talk together like the impossibly modern metropolitan millennials we undoubtedly were. Not like this. Not in my living room, not with them half dressed, not mere days after Jack had even told me of her existence, not with me dripping from my hair to my now wrecked brogues. This was not how Moving On was meant to look.

As I swaddled myself up in a towelled bathrobe and hair wrap in my room, I deflated further. Our kiss now seemed ancient history, to be discussed only by historians in heavy, dusty tomes – not our immediate, neon present. I took small consolation that I'd managed not to shout 'WE WERE KISSING RIGHT HERE LAST MONTH' directly into the new couple's happy faces.

I sat in front of the mirror. A bedraggled, blotchy face stared back at me, hair poking from her wrap, mascara down her cheeks, lipstick smudged at one corner, mouth turned down at the corners, pouting and pitiful. 'Oh, stop,' I whispered to my reflection, almost laughing at how pathetic I looked. I took a deep breath, closed my eyes, and let all the air out. I sat up straighter. I cleaned my face, toned, moisturised, fluffed out my hair, painted my nails and shaped my brows. Nothing in this situation was a disaster. *I'd* asked for this divorce. *I'd* wanted it. Him getting a girlfriend was – as any divorcée would tell you – probably the best thing that could have happened to me. He'd be agreeable, make the whole thing easy; he'd act like a grown-up.

But it didn't mean I had to do the same.

TWENTY-SIX

Two years earlier

On the train to Norwich, Jack glanced at his phone as he heard it beep. He read the message, his face screwing up in bafflement.

'Dad says there'll be *four* of us for lunch.'

'Who's the fourth?' Zoe flicked through a magazine and sipped her paper cup of coffee. And they said the age of luxury train travel was dead.

'He doesn't say. Captain fucking Mystery. Can I have a sip, please?'

'Of course. I got a large with extra whipped cream to give us energy for the day ahead.'

'Ooh, you're good. Thank god for you.' Jack pulled off the lid and took a big glug.

'Who could it be? A friend? A relative?'

'He doesn't have any friends, at least none that he'd invite to lunch with his son and his son's girlfriend. Sorry, fiancée.' Jack chuckled. 'I still love that. It makes me feel really old school.'

'You sure he wouldn't be planning any kind of engagement celebration?'

Jack pulled an incredulous face. 'He might, but then I'd be asking what that man had done with my real father. That kind of thing was always Mum's job. I don't think Dad would even know how to go about planning a party. Anyway, he did say it's only one extra person. Oh my god, but can you imagine though, if we turn up at this gastropub and Dad's filled a room with all his masonic drinking buddies?'

'Is your dad in the Masons?'

Jack laughed. 'No!' Then he looked thoughtful. 'Would he be allowed to tell us, even if he was?'

'I think you're thinking of Fight Club.'

'Maybe. No, it's just some Rotary organisation or something – middle-aged men drinking in pubs with the excuse that they're planning the same charity event they've done for the last two decades, that kind of thing. Grainy photos of them holding up three-digit cheques for a cancer charity to pad out the local paper.'

'Someone's very needlessly cynical this morning.'

'Sorry. I know. Sorry. They're all really nice guys, of course they are. I just don't know if I'd want to celebrate my engagement with them.'

'Jack. Listen. Name one person it could be. Focus.'

'Yes, right. One person. One person? I honestly don't feel like Dad knows "one person". Not that he could invite anywhere. He knows me, you, his ex-wife, his gang of drinking buddies. . .'

'Colleagues?'

'Same, not that he'd invite out.'

'I don't think we're going to guess this one. He clearly wants to be a bit Dark Horse about all of this, so we're just going to have to wait—' Zoe looked at her watch '—forty more minutes until we can solve the mystery, ok?' Jack was staring out of the window, frowning. This would be the most time either of them had spent with Graham in two years,

219

since Linda had left him; every other meeting had been a snatched coffee in a train station when Graham was on his way to somewhere else. He hadn't been prioritising time with his son since finding himself alone.

Zoe rummaged in her bag. 'Jack.' She waved a book at him. 'Crossword with me?'

Even though they'd agreed to meet Jack's dad – and now his surprise guest – at the pub, he was there waiting for them on the platform. Jack saw him from the train window and turned to Zoe with sudden light in his eyes. 'You don't think it's Mum, do you? That *must* be why he didn't tell us! That's the surprise!'

Zoe put her arm through his, gently saying, 'No, I don't think so. Linda would have told us she was coming, Jack. It must be someone else.'

Jack turned away from her, and watched his dad through the window again. 'Mmm,' he said. 'S'pose so.'

As they got off the train and approached Graham, he looked different too, in a similar way to how Linda had looked so different in that airport, but with some kind of undertone that Zoe couldn't quite put her finger on.

'Hello,' he said, waving at them both, fingers waggling. He clapped Jack briefly on the back, smiled and nodded at Zoe, and headed off towards the car park. Zoe and Jack looked at each other, Zoe amused, Jack incredulous, before hurrying after him.

'Dad?'

'Oh yes, yes, I know I said we'd meet you there, but we were passing anyway and I thought I might as well pick you up.'

'We?'

'Yes.' He stopped by his pristine car, and the passenger door opened. 'Jack, do you remember Christine? Used to work at your primary school?'

'Not really.'

Zoe put her arm back in Jack's.

'Well, she's joining us for lunch today.'

Christine stepped out, all cashmere waterfall cardigan and perfect neutral lipstick. Zoe could tell – her neatness, her adults-only knitwear, her brittle, practised smile – that Christine hated children, and could tell from Jack's reaction that he had known it for years. But they weren't children now.

'Hello, I'm Zoe.' She walked towards her, hand out, and Christine's smile became brighter, harder.

'Hello Zoe, I've heard *so* much about you.'

They both turned to Jack, who was completely speechless, but after a moment raised a hand in greeting. Christine's smile faltered, but she caught it and turned it back on. 'Hello, Jack! Lovely to see you again after all this time.'

They stood in silence for a while, four of them around the car, Jack looking shocked and Christine looking uncertain, Graham beaming at them all. Finally, Zoe said, 'What time is our reservation for?'

Then suddenly they were all action, Christine saying, 'Right, you young ones can have the back seat to yourselves,' while Graham started the engine before any of them were even inside, and Zoe was looking at Jack and his frozen face.

Once they were in, Graham turned the radio on. A Radio 2 jingle blared out, followed by the opening bars of 'Bohemian Rhapsody'.

'Oh, this is my favourite!' breathed Christine, clasping her hands together. Graham smiled at her and turned it up to an almost deafening volume, which she adjusted slightly downwards as he continued driving.

Zoe turned to Jack, who now looked outright horrified.

'Dad doesn't listen to *music*,' he hissed, the sound buried by Freddie Mercury's deafening falsetto.

'Why wouldn't you shake her hand?' Zoe whispered back.

'Zo, I didn't even know she still existed. Apart from some uncomfortable childhood memories where she terrified me through the hatch of the school office, I have literally no idea who she even is. I didn't know she was going to turn up at a lunch with my dad. Forgive me if I've forgotten the social niceties of meeting your dad's girlfriend – with absolutely no warning – only to find she was your childhood nightmare fuel.'

'That bad?'

'That bad. Seriously. I mean, she wasn't beating us up and putting us in the chokey, but in terms of people I imagined my dad hooking up with, Christine Churchill is somewhere between Angela Merkel and George Michael.'

'Alright. Alright. You did pretty well in that case. This is weird, isn't it?'

'This is *totally* weird, *thank* you. I actually feel like I'm in a dream. What next, my old lecturer turns up naked and the pub turns into a giant cake?'

'You're panicking.'

'Yes, I'm panicking. She was awful at school. Awful. *When* did this happen? *How* did this happen?'

Zoe looked in the rearview mirror, and saw both Jack's dad and Christine were distracted, singing along to the music. She turned towards Jack, putting both her hands on his shoulders. 'Hey,' she whispered. 'It's going to be ok. We just have to get through lunch, which will be fine: ordering food, eating food, we've done this before. Then we'll get back on the train and we can have full meltdowns, ok? This'll be, what? Three hours tops? We can do three hours of just biting our tongues and being insanely polite, ok? And then we can freak out and analyse the many thousands of ways in which this is completely weird. But later. Ok?'

'Ok.'

Zoe kissed him. 'I'm really proud of you.'

Jack looked pleased. 'Thanks.'

She turned forwards in her seat again, put her head on his shoulder, and smiled.

The pub, far from being the traditional, low-ceilinged, tiny-windowed, smoking fireplaces kind of place, was beautiful and bright. One whole glass wall looked out onto a babbling stream; their table was tucked in a corner against a huge mirror, carrying in the shimmering light from outside. Christine and Graham took the furthest seats, after a long, lingering kiss; Jack and Zoe sat with their backs to the room, but still able to watch everything behind them in the mirror's reflection.

Christine ordered them all a bottle of house white, which they sat sipping in silence for a moment after the waitress had half filled their glasses. Zoe watched Jack gazing at Graham, who looked at the liquid in his glass with something like surprise, as if unsure how it had got there, before taking a sip and smiling slightly. Zoe was busying herself with the menu when she saw in the mirror the reflection of Christine's hand resting on Graham's knee under the table, stroking it softly. Thankfully, Jack had now fixed his attention on the menu, in the kind of sightless way that reminded Zoe of how Graham had looked at his wine.

She leant over to him. 'What do you think you'll go for?'

He looked up, distantly, then looked at his dad and Christine. 'Something with cyanide?' he whispered.

She put her hand on his knee, then jerked it away in surprise, seeing in the mirror Christine's hand slide up Graham's thigh. Jack looked puzzled. Zoe tried to compose herself. 'Pâté? Then lamb? What do you reckon? Or go halves on the lamb and the steak for mains?'

Jack nodded. 'Sounds fine. I'm going to the toilet. Please will you order for me?'

Zoe took his hand as he got up, and mouthed, 'Please don't hang yourself.' Jack laughed, and bent back down to kiss her hand.

In the silence, Zoe took a nervous drink, and hoped the waitress would come back soon. Christine leant towards Zoe and said, in a stage whisper that cut across the room, 'Is Jack alright?'

'He's fine, just tired.' She explained that they'd had friends over for dinner the night before and he was just a little sleepy.

Christine wrinkled her nose. 'Had he forgotten he was seeing us today?'

Zoe tried to think of a polite way of saying *Us?* but just smiled and said, 'It was only a quiet meal with friends. Perhaps we're just getting old too.' She realised the weight of her insult as she watched Christine's mouth slowly pucker around the comment. Fortunately at that moment the waitress arrived, and although Jack was still absent, Zoe was able to persuade her to take their orders, rather than wait for him. 'He might not be out until dessert,' she whispered as the waitress took her menu. The waitress smiled knowingly back and Zoe thought there was some solidarity there – at least she could rely on the staff if she and Jack absolutely had to escape and needed a distracting plate crash or small kitchen explosion.

By the time the bread basket arrived, Jack had returned. 'Feeling a little better after last night?' Christine asked. Zoe opened her mouth to explain again that it was just a quiet but late dinner, and Jack looked at Zoe, wondering what she'd said. Graham interrupted them with his first comment since they'd sat down, saying, 'They do good bread here. Lovely stuff,' before laying the entire dish of butter on a single piece of warm sliced baguette and pushing the whole thing down his throat in two mouthfuls.

While Jack asked for another dish of butter – 'Actually,

better make it two, please?' – Zoe ate a whole slice herself, unbuttered. Last night's dinner felt like a long time ago, and all she'd had since then was their coffee from the station. She tore the bread in two, chewed one half, swallowed, and was chewing the second when she noticed Christine staring at her with something like horror. Zoe swatted at her face, patting it down for any smears or crumbs, then looked over Christine's shoulder into the mirror to see if there was something she'd missed.

Christine blinked at her. 'Well, you've certainly got a good appetite, haven't you? It's like watching some kind of medieval banquet from this side, isn't it, Graham?'

Jack's father nodded and smiled. 'Glad you're enjoying yourselves,' he said, before swallowing his own unbuttered slice in two unchewed mouthfuls again. Christine watched him with an oily smile on her face. 'We'll get you some more bread, Graham, before these two polish it off.'

Jack tipped the bread basket towards Christine, offering the still-warm slices, but she shook her head quickly and said, 'Oh dear, no, thank you, Jack, bread doesn't do any favours to a lady. By our age we have to be a bit more careful, don't we, Zoe?'

Zoe looked at Jack with a deadpan face; he made a slight choking noise as he tried not to laugh. Zoe picked up a second slice, took the new butter from the waitress's hand, thanking her, spread it thickly on the bread before biting into it and almost groaning with pleasure. 'You're right,' she said. 'Graham, this really is *very* good bread.' He nodded and smiled again, and Jack joined them in a new silence, filled with chewing and spreading and little noises of enjoyment and delicious gluttony.

The main course was a little better: Christine actually ate something, but Zoe's appetite was all but blasted to smithereens when something moving in the mirror caught her eye, and she saw the reflection of Christine's hand not just stroking Graham's thigh, but actively moving higher and higher up his leg throughout the entire course. When Jack asked if she was ok, Zoe muttered something about last night catching up with her.

After the bill had been paid – Christine had refused dessert, looking meaningfully at Zoe, and Graham said he was sure he had a Cornetto in the freezer at home, that'd do him – and they had stepped out into the pub carpark, Christine muttered something in Graham's ear.

He nodded, cleared his throat, then said without any preamble, 'Listen, Jack, Christine and I – we're actually married. Got it done quietly the other day. Just the legal stuff. Didn't want to bother you. But thought you two – you three – should probably meet.'

Jack looked stunned. It was the most his father had spoken for the whole meal – for much of recent history, in fact, as far as Jack and Zoe could tell. Christine leant in to give him and Zoe a hug, arching her body away from theirs as if physical contact would be the terrible icing on today's uneaten cake. She stood back with a face that suggested she'd never quite mastered spontaneous happiness, as Graham gave Zoe a peck on the cheek and Jack a firm handshake, two-handed, with real warmth.

'Thanks for coming, son. Thanks to both of you.' He nodded again. 'It's been really great that you could join us. And, er, congratulations on your own engagement.' He nodded at Zoe, this time. 'Welcome to the family.'

Christine took Graham's other arm. 'I'm sorry we can't give you a lift back, though. We've got plans for later.'

Zoe hitched her bag up on her shoulder and Jack released his dad's hand. 'No problem,' he said. 'We've got all that bread to work off, after all.'

They watched Graham and Christine head to their car,

Christine waiting for Graham to open the door for her as he walked around the car to his own side and got in, starting the engine and rubbing his hands in the cool of the car. Christine looked around, saw Zoe and Jack watching her, and climbed into the car in one sharp movement, slamming her door and turning her face away from them. Graham raised his hand once more to wave goodbye, before the car slowly crunched over the gravel and turned away into the road.

'That was. . .' Zoe couldn't find quite the right word.

'I know. Wasn't it just.'

'Did you have any idea?'

'That my terrifying primary school secretary had secretly *married* my dad? No, Zoe, I can honestly confess that I did not.'

'But has he ever said anything about seeing anyone?'

'Has he ever said anything about anything?'

'Good point.' She put an arm around Jack's waist. 'Married, though. Do you think your mum knows?'

'Oh god. Mum. I doubt it. Unless. . . Oh god, do you think that's the real reason they broke up? That she found out about her and Dad?'

'No. No, it can't be. It didn't feel like that, did it? He'd look more. . . embarrassed or something, wouldn't he?'

'Plus I haven't heard anything from the Norwich grapevine. It would have been all over the local gossip pages had he run off with someone from his son's school. Or at least all over the pubs at Christmas. No, this seems a bit. . . new.'

'Ah, young love.'

'Ugh.'

Zoe put on a mock therapist voice. 'Now now, Jack, your father is allowed to be happy too. Can you accept his happiness without it lessening your own?'

Jack slung an arm around her shoulder. 'As long as this

is just his rebound marriage. That's up to him. And as long as I don't have to actually ever spend any time with her in any kind of family situation, that'll be fine.'

'So you're not up for opening your stocking with her on Christmas morning?'

'Or holding her hand while I search for Easter eggs?'

'Or giving her a New Year's kiss at midnight?'

Jack put his hand to his mouth and swallowed. 'Oh god, seriously, that lamb's going to come up again.'

Zoe laughed, and tried not to think about exactly what Graham might be getting out of that apparently quite handsy relationship. 'Maybe your dad just needs to have a bit of fun.'

Jack looked at her. 'I'm sure he does. But if fun's what he's after, he might be dipping his bucket in the wrong well.'

'Don't worry! We'll probably only ever have to see her once a year. Twice, tops, I reckon.'

Jack hugged her and kissed the top of her head. 'I'm sure you're right. Come on, let's head back to some stinking, crowded, anti-social civilisation.'

TWENTY-SEVEN

Now

A week after I'd caught Jack and his new girlfriend on our sofa, our kitchen units were coated in more paperwork than an origami exhibition. It started with a rota I drew up the night after interrupting Jack and his girlfriend, because no one wanted to find their spouse *in flagrante*, even if they were in the process of splitting up with them already. I'd decided we needed formal arrangements for when we could have partners over. When I'd come home two evenings later just as Jessica was leaving, I had reprinted the rota with Jack's times circled in red. I woke the next morning to find Jack had created a rota for washing up.

I understood. He was after blood.

I countered with a bathroom rota. Jack parried with a TV rota. I launched a hot water rota.

This morning, I discovered Jack had labelled every single item in the fridge: Jack's, Jack's, Jack's, Jack's, Jack's, Jack's. A single jar of capers from an ambitious pasta recipe six months ago bore my name, plus a wilted paper bag of carrots that were fractionally softer than the overcooked linguine I'd served with the capers.

With a flourish, I wrote Jack a thank you note and stuck it to the mirror with a hearty dollop of his artisanal jalapeño-and-red-pepper-hummus. It wasn't big, it wasn't clever, but it was unbelievably satisfying.

That evening, Jack had emptied my capers jar to spell out *THANKS FOR THE NOTE* along the kitchen worktop. I gently squeezed out his pricey deli tube of chilli and ginger paste to write *YOU'RE WELCOME* underneath, underlined four times.

If we couldn't keep our good manners, what did we even have?

A few days later, Jack crashed into the flat in a chaotic whirlwind of boxes and leather samples, linings and thread spools. I looked at him over the top of my magazine. 'You're home then.'

He checked his cheerful face and sighed heavily. 'Sorry, I didn't realise I had to give written notice.'

I swallowed my own sigh, knowing that a comment about the noisy nature of his entrance would have garnered a smile in the old days, not a sigh. I tried again. 'Got a new project on?'

'Mmm. Something like that.'

I went back to my article, when something reminded me. 'Oh, the wedding list people called. They said our own stuff should be with us in the next four to six weeks.'

Jack laughed humourlessly. 'Just in time for us to mail it all back to our guests then.'

'Is that what we're going to do?'

He looked at me, with exaggerated horror. 'Is that *not* what you were planning?'

'I don't know. . . It hadn't crossed my mind. I wouldn't

even have called them – *they* called *me* today. I hadn't thought about it for ages.'

'But you'd taken for granted that you'd keep these gifts that, thanks to this company's incompetence, didn't even arrive during the actual marriage?'

'But sending them back to people. It's a bit. . . passive aggressive, isn't it? "Thank you so much for your lovely salad bowl but actually we've broken up now so you can keep it."'

'Who knew you could still surprise me after all this time?' Jack was smiling sarcastically at me.

'Jack,' I said pleadingly. He picked up all his stuff and carried it into the bedroom, closing the door with a horrible gentleness until I heard it click. 'Ugh,' I said to myself. 'Handled with your usual tact and charm, Zo. Keep up the good work.'

Jack called through the door. 'I can still hear you.'

I balled a fist in my mouth and screamed silently.

A couple of weeks later, I was sharing dim sum with Liz. Her hair was back to normal, and her nails were still beige, but only in scraps, chipped and chewed down to their usual stubby length.

'So am I to find a hat for your summer wedding?' I asked.

'I'm not saying my theory was wrong,' she said, pushing a cabbage parcel into her mouth, 'I'm just saying that the practice is only sustainable for six months, max.'

'You seemed to be having a pretty good time there, for a while.'

'I was! I loved it. He was so rude, so bossy, so dim – I just kept thinking what a contrast he was to my last few boyfriends. And we'd go to great restaurants, great bars, always fifty-fifty, because he "didn't want to invest in me until he was sure he'd get a return".'

'He did *not* say that.'

Liz nodded gleefully. 'He did! And it was fun, like I was stepping out of my life for a while. I was never going to stay with him—'

I stuck my lower lip out in mock disappointment.

'—but it was like a holiday from all that real dating.'

'Yeah, right, ugh, real feelings.'

'Actual connection, bleurgh.'

'Common interests, yuck. What finally finished things?'

'No great event. I just woke up one morning and felt like I'd had enough.'

'Enough to find someone better?'

'Mmm. Not sure. Just enough of him, for now. I'm not sure where that will take me. . . But maybe next time I won't give up on a relationship so quickly. New Dating Plan: as long as they aren't Henry, give 'em a chance.'

'Snappy.'

She bowed her head. 'You're welcome. How's *your* dating philosophy going?'

'Ugh. I've got enough to worry about with Kat and Chuck.'

'Jesus, is that prick still alive? I thought karma would have taken him out by now.' Liz squeezed my hand. 'I'm sorry. What does Kat say?'

'Nothing. She won't talk about work at all, which I think is what worries me most.' I toyed with my duck hearts and sighed. 'So there's that, and no, I'm not seeing anyone – Jack is, though.'

'Is he? Brutal. How do we feel about it?'

'Fine. I was the one who asked for a divorce, so I can't really complain.'

'I know you can't, but do you want to?'

I speared one of the little hearts on a chopstick. 'I don't know. Things are getting more and more difficult between us. I'm starting to wonder how we ever thought we'd get through a year of living together like this.'

'And neither of you can move out? Definitely?'

'We can't afford it. And Jack's so bloody-minded that he wouldn't, even if he could.'

Liz nodded sagely. 'Yes, he can be very bloody-minded, refusing to move out. Yes, that stubbornness. . . it's almost like it's familiar from somewhere, but I can't. . . quite. . . place it. . .'

I ignored her, continuing, 'We're not talking at the moment, me and Jack. And we're on rotas for everything like we're living in a youth hostel, plus I'm terrified I'll hear him and his new girlfriend at it one night.'

'Ugh.' Liz put her hand on mine. 'Would it help if I had her killed?'

I closed my eyes, and nodded. 'That would be awesome. You're a pal.'

Benni caught me in morning break on the last day of term, asking if I was prepared for today's meeting.

'What. . . what meeting? What prepared? What have I done?'

'You know it's your cool head that really impresses me, darling.'

I looked at her over my glasses. 'I'm in a fragile state. And I might be even more fragile if you're suddenly telling me that I'm meant to be preparing for a meeting you're announcing. . . what, five hours before? I've got all the excuses about why they haven't done as well in their A Levels and GCSEs as we'd hoped, but that is *all*. Summer's nearly here. Don't make me call my union and have them man the barricades over unfair working conditions.'

'Alright, Karl Marx, calm down. It's just a certain young Mancunian Physics teacher has been looking for you all morning. Maybe he's after some kind of meeting?' I opened my mouth, but she said, 'I'm saying nothing, there's nothing to see, nothing's going on. So shall we just carry on and pretend I never said anything?'

By the time George finally got to my cubby, I'd relaxed. And his face made me relax a little more.

'Hey, Zoe!' he smiled.

'Hey, George. Benni said you were looking for me?'

'Yeah.' He blushed a little, and focused on the textbooks on the corner of my space. 'I just wondered if anything had changed? If you'd fancy a drink again. Just you and me?'

I willed my face not to blush back in sympathy. 'I'm back to back with plans at the moment. . .'

George smiled, backing away.

'But I'll be free after the summer holidays.'

His face lit up again.

'Is that any good for you?'

'Great! Do you want to let me know where you fancy? You know your way around better than me. . .'

We agreed that I'd suggest a venue closer to the time. That gave me six weeks to make my peace with a real date. *If it's good enough for the gander*, I thought. What the hell was the point in holding back – I liked George. Or at least, all the parts of him I'd seen so far. Why would I turn that offer down again?

That evening I walked home smiling to myself, just a little, and wondering how I was going to tell Jack that I had my own romantic interest.

On Wednesday, Jack texted me to find out what time I was coming home, which I assumed meant he had Jessica over. In the end, I got back half an hour earlier than I'd planned – entirely not my fault, I swear – and when I put my key in the lock, Jack was right there. Before I even had a chance to step in the door, he said, 'Can you close your eyes a sec, please?' When I did he led me right into our bedroom, where

234

he said I could open them again, before leaving the room and shutting the door behind him, with no further explanation. Was Jessica dressing in our living room? What was she – they – doing that I couldn't see? Oh god, it didn't pay to dwell on that thought. I had the bed that week, so I was tempted just to brush my teeth in the en-suite and go straight to sleep, bypassing whatever he and Jessica were up to. On the other hand, it wouldn't hurt to give Jack a heads-up about George, if he was going to be bringing Jessica here more frequently. I called to Jack through the door, and tried not to think about what – or who – he might be doing in there.

'Listen! Jack! Sorry to yell, but I just have to say something.'

'Hang on a sec, Zo.'

'I just wanted to let you know – about that guy I was seeing.' Or not seeing at all, I thought, more accurately. There was a clanging in the kitchen. 'God, something smells good! That guy – so I'm seeing him again. Properly.'

Or at least properly in the sense of *finally saying yes after repeatedly turning him down*. That kind of properly. But hell, telling Jack this was a lot easier when I couldn't see or hear him. I hoped Jessica could hear too.

There was an even longer silence, with no more sounds from the kitchen, and no response from Jack. Were they going to have to eat in silence while I hid in here?

'Jack? Did you hear that?'

There was a beat. 'Sure, ok.'

'So. . . Is it ok if I just go to bed now?'

'Yeah. . . ok.'

'You alright in there?'

'Yeah. I'm just. . . clearing up. I had someone over and I just need to. . . tidy up.'

'Ok. Night.'

The kitchen went quiet for a long time, while I got ready for bed. As I climbed under the duvet and started drifting off, I thought about George – about what might happen after the holidays. Hoping for something simple, fresh, unspoiled. It was a good feeling.

I fell asleep quickly, for the first time in ages.

Around 3 a.m., some drunk partiers stumbling home down the street woke me up. I had a sudden craving for a slug of ice-cold milk, so did my own stumble to the kitchen, past a sleeping Jack on the sofa. I took out the milk and stood glugging it for a while, pleased no one was awake to catch me swigging out of the bottle. I emptied the whole thing, and opened the bin to throw it away; on top of the rubbish was a pile of food, a huge mound of it, a meal at least. I used the milk bottle to lift up the layers. It looked like a complete beef wellington, sliced up then tossed away, scattered with green beans, and with a huge slug of – I sniffed – chocolate mousse on top. An empty bottle of Châteauneuf-du-Pape sat at the top of the recycling side. My fuggy 3 a.m. mind couldn't work this out. Why was Jack making Jessica my favourite meal? And why had it all been thrown away?

Then something shifted in my brain.

He'd wanted me home at a specific time; he was doing something in here he didn't want me to see immediately; and he'd reacted pretty oddly when I'd told him about George.

No.

If Jessica *hadn't* been here, if the meal hadn't been for her, if the whole thing was something else altogether – something romantic, something I definitely couldn't think about, at 3 a.m. or 11 a.m. or 6 p.m. or ever – then I was going to have to go back to bed, fall asleep, and wake up pretending this had all just been a bad dream.

* * *

236

A few weeks later, when I was in full summer holidays mode, I sat with Esther in her back garden on one of her half days from work. In the August afternoon sun, I thought about how I'd be back to school again within a month, and I knew the momentum would carry me all the way to Christmas, to new flats and divorce filing.

'So you're trying again with him, then?' Esther said, from her prone position on William's Peppa Pig bath towel on the grass. Ava came out of the back door with a tray of tea for us all, on her own day off, her ears pricking up. 'George, from school,' Esther explained, and I saw Ava's shoulders drop slightly.

'It's just a date. And officially, we're still just friends.'

'Is that what you want?' Ava asked, handing out the teas.

'Either. I don't mind. I don't want to be alone forever. I know, I know,' I said, as Esther choked on her tea. 'I'm just following Liz's example: something unexciting, undramatic, something I don't have to deal with, that I might actually just *enjoy*.'

Esther and Ava looked at each other.

'I don't know what I'm supposed to do here! If I go to a party with Jack, you guys are rolling your eyes and pulling faces; if I see someone else then it's too soon and I need to be careful what I'm doing.'

'Are you happy?'

'I don't know. Are you? Am I supposed to be?'

'I miss Jack,' said Esther, as Ava gasped. 'What? You know you feel the same, Ave.'

'Zoe, we trust you,' Ava said, putting a hand on Esther's arm to calm her. 'We just don't want you to get hurt.'

I drank my tea. We'd arranged this afternoon off together a while ago, but there was another reason I'd wanted to see them both. 'Speaking of which – I really think we need to worry about Kat,' I said. Ava looked slightly apologetic.

'Zo, please,' she said. 'We understand that he's your ex

and you're not fond of him, but what precisely are we supposed to be worrying about here?'

'He's creepy, we know that, but. . . is there something else going on?' Esther asked.

'I tried to see her at her office a few months ago. I know, I should have spoken to you guys, but I was caught up in all this stuff with Jack, and I didn't know how to explain everything. To you two. Properly.' I checked we still all had tea left, then brought out a Tupperware of Mum's ginger biscuits from my bag. It was time to start talking.

'Chuck. . . isn't just an ex. Well, he is. But that's not why I don't like him.' Ava looked anxious as I spoke. 'He chose me as his girlfriend. I was sixteen, and he convinced me that we were supposed to be together. He was in his mid-twenties. Do you remember that time you saw us?'

Esther nodded and Ava's eyes just grew wider.

'He was furious with me. Wanted me to go straight home and find out whether you'd really seen him. He was *so angry* that I'd got my family involved in our relationship.'

'Did he hit you?' Esther's voice was shaking.

I almost laughed. 'No, hitting might leave marks. He'd punish me by not speaking to me – we'd go on a date, somewhere we wouldn't run into anyone we knew, but he wouldn't talk to me all night. He'd flirt with every other woman in there, and then at the end of the night, he'd say, "I hope you understand how lucky you are that I've forgiven you. I've got so many more options." And he'd do that. . . a lot.' I took a steadying breath. 'If I went out, he'd say I'd probably been flirting with other boys. Then I'd probably been sleeping with them. So it was best if maybe I didn't go to parties anymore. And maybe I shouldn't keep my Saturday job, either, if it meant I'd be flirting with other boys. Didn't I love only him? By this time, we'd got engaged.'

'What the fuck?' Esther yelled, shock screwing up her face.

'Oh, yeah, I wasn't allowed to tell you about that. I'd gone to his flat once and one of his friends was there, and Chuck introduced me as his fiancée. I didn't know what to say. When the friend left, Chuck said he'd been thinking about it, and he'd decided it was best if we really committed to the relationship. And wasn't that what I wanted too? He never actually proposed, not formally, but that meant I never had a chance to say no. Of course I loved him. How could I not love this charming, handsome man?'

'Zo. . .' Ava whispered, but I couldn't stop.

'And the fact that I kept talking about my schoolwork really bothered him: if I had so much work to do, why did I have to do it in the library? Why couldn't I work at his house, and we could spend some time together? Only, when I got there, it was either to clean his house – he was sick, he couldn't do it as well as me, no one cared about him – or to. . . you know. Sleep with him. The only time I was able to actually revise was when I got home in the evening.'

'Me and Ave kept saying how knackered you looked. We were really worried you were working too hard on your A Levels.'

'Is that why your grades weren't as good as you'd been predicted?'

I did laugh, then. 'Nope. I might have scraped through – I still went to class – but the night before my first exam, he texted me to come and meet him at our usual pub. I told Mum I was going to Liz's and sneaked off. Turns out,' I sighed, 'he just wanted me to meet his new girlfriend. He was sitting on a bar stool facing the door and she was straddling him. They were all over each other. When he saw me come in, he just grinned, and said, "Hey Zo." I ran out, ran all the way to Liz's, who called Mum and asked if I could stay at hers as I was already asleep, tired from all my work. Liz always hated him, always knew he was a shit. She knew better than to say anything to me, though: I'd always defend him, the second she even *looked* sceptical about me not coming to a party, not coming to the library, quitting my job, missing out on trips and holidays. I was with him for a year and a half, altogether.' I clapped my hands together. 'So. That was it. I spent the entire morning of the exams throwing up. I don't even remember writing anything. And that was pretty much my A Level hopes over.'

Ava was on the verge of tears and Esther looked murderous.

'He did that shit to *you*? To *our* little sister?' She gritted her teeth. 'Why didn't you tell any of us, Zo?'

'Because you would literally have killed him, Es. And I – I *thought* that I loved him.'

'Oh, Zo,' Ava said, her voice catching. 'And now he's after Kat.'

'I don't know. I don't know what he's doing. Maybe he *is* just her boss. He made it clear that I'm not welcome at the office, and that I shouldn't say anything to Kat, which he hardly needs to worry about since she won't talk to me about him either. She might be older than I was, but she reminds me so much of me when I knew him – always knowing better, never willing to listen to anyone else. I can't make her talk to me. And I didn't know if I should come to you and tell you two all this – but she won't talk to me, won't tell me anything. I'm so worried.'

'*We* might not know what he's up to, but I bet he fucking does.' Esther looked at her watch. 'Will and Ethan won't be home for a few hours yet. And when's the next time we're all going to be off together during the week?'

I gaped at her.

'You might not be welcome at their office. But I think maybe we should go and visit our little sister – together. She needs to know what's going on.'

*   *   *

240

My heart was pumping by the time we got there, not helped by Esther driving her Ford Fiesta into East London like we were in Le Mans. We parked with a handbrake crunch and strode into the office like a mile-high robot made of witches and fury.

Miranda was on reception. She gave me a pitying smile, recognising me immediately. 'Here to see Mr Johnson again?'

Esther leant over her desk. 'We're here to see our sister. Kat Lewis. We can wait. And no, we don't want any coffee.'

Ava smiled kindly at her. 'Thanks, though.' We took the same sofa I'd been sitting on before and waited for Kat.

'One guess who actually comes out though,' I murmured to my sisters.

Miranda picked up the phone and murmured into it. A moment later, the frosted glass door opened, but it wasn't Kat. It wasn't even Chuck. It was three security men, thick chunks of gristle wrestled into heavy-knit navy polyester jumpers, and they were coming our way.

'Sorry, ladies,' the shortest one said, not looking remotely sorry. 'I'm afraid the management has asked that you vacate the premises.'

Ava sat forwards, tucking her knees together and smiling at them, happy to correct their error. 'It's ok,' she said. 'We're just waiting for our sister, Kat Lewis? She works here. If you just give her a call, she can confirm we're ok to be here.'

'I'm sorry, ladies,' Gristle repeated, his autocue stuck. 'I'm afraid the management has asked that you vacate the premises.'

Esther stood up, the top of her head reaching Gristle's armpit. 'I'm sorry,' she said in a dangerous tone, 'we're here. To see. Our *sister*.'

'I bet you are, love,' said Gristle, and stepped forward again, so that his chest was nearly touching Esther's nose.

I stood up too, half turning my back on the security guards. 'Es. We need to go. Now. This isn't going to help anything.'

She turned to me, shaking with anger, and said, 'Let's go.' She helped Ava up and the guards stepped back. Esther and I walked through the exit and into the street, but Ava stopped and turned around to the watching guards.

'I know you're just doing your jobs,' she said, in her soft voice, 'but sometimes, you really need to a take a good long look at your life choices.'

I could see Main Gristle looked unperturbed at this, but the two guards behind him looked at each other, then down at the ground.

In the car, I was shaking almost as much as Esther. 'Do you see what I mean? That is not normal behaviour, is it?'

'What did he think we were going to do?' Ava said.

'That sick bastard is definitely up to something. And he's not going to get away with it,' Esther growled.

Ava reached forwards from the back seat and put her hand on my shoulder. 'Again,' she said. 'He won't get away with it again.'

I was beginning to realise that everything was slipping away from me, as I slouched at a child's tiny desk on a child's tiny seat at a new bar in East London. Photos were still popping up of Chuck and Kat at various office events and launch parties, and I'd not had a chance to speak to Kat alone – whenever I'd been at Mum and Dad's, she'd been out. Working. And she wouldn't answer my calls or my messages.

I looked at my surroundings then looked at Iffy. 'This is not where teachers want to drink in their holidays, by the way.'

'Listen, Zo.' Iffy was pouring me a glass of something bright yellow from the jug we'd panic-ordered. 'You know I love both you and Jack. And all I want is to see you both happy, either apart or—'

'Don't say it.'

'Together. But I can't help being glad that this ridiculous thing between Jack and that Jessica character is over.'

I sipped my drink, wondering whether my face was aflame as it felt. 'Right. They broke up,' I said as neutrally as I could. That was the first definite news I'd had of it.

'Oh my god, didn't he tell you?'

I looked at him. 'Tricky as it may be to believe, discussing our sex lives with one another is still kind of taboo at the moment.'

'So you do have a sex life?' Iffy looked at me, one lascivious eyebrow raised. I sighed, and Iffy looked disappointed. 'I feared as much. So no communication about this stuff at all?'

'We tell each other when we're seeing someone else. I guess it's a bit harder to say when we've stopped seeing them. So back in June, Jack told me that he was going to New York with Jessica.' Iffy gave me a look. 'Well, he said afterwards that they'd been. And I was *fine* with it.' He coughed. 'Kind of. But he hadn't mentioned this.'

'Well! How little you know after all, my dearest Zo. He wasn't supposed to be going to New York with her – she just turned up at the airport, saying that head office had said she needed to go along too. Jack didn't think anything of it—'

'Too trusting.'

'Exactly. But she was at all his meetings, they stayed in the same hotel. . . Hold on, don't do that face, nothing happened there, but they did a lot of hanging out, and eventually she said to him, "Well, shouldn't we do more of this when we get back to London?" Then he discovered that *you* were seeing someone, so when they got home, he *did* give her a call. They hung out for a while, but I went out with them once—'

'Judas.'

Iffy stopped. 'Do you want me to tell this story, or not?' I put my straw in my mouth, muting myself. 'Anyway, I went out with them to dinner and she was. . . Not. Fun. Poor Jack was so serious all night, kept checking she had enough water, was warm enough, that she was enjoying her food.'

'Sounds like he really liked her.'

'No! She made him so neurotic, and all Jack could do was dance around, trying to work out what he could do to make her happy. Like, he was so miserable, thinking it must be something *he* was doing wrong. It was so different when he met you, Zo.'

I sucked my straw again.

'So. That's the story. He broke things off a little while ago. She took it badly, is trying to make things awkward for him at Gillett, doesn't want to know him,' he rattled off, counting on his fingers. 'The end.'

A few weeks ago. . . That meant the binned meal had definitely not been for Jessica. I didn't want to tell Iffy about that, though – not yet. I didn't fully understand myself what I'd be telling him. I changed the subject, and Iffy didn't mention Jack again all night.

TWENTY-EIGHT

One year earlier

'But Dad, I don't know if I want to!'

I was sitting with him at our family kitchen table, sharing a pot of tea while Mum played with William in the living room.

'You don't want to be with him?'

'No! I definitely want to *be* with him. I don't know what I'd do without him. But this wedding stuff. . . all the planning. . . it's not something I'd ever have chosen. But it's making him so happy, and he's so clear about how he sees our future together.'

'But it's not how you see it?'

'It's exactly how I see it. Just without the marriage bit. But. . . with his mum leaving, it's become so important to him, to prove that we're different from her and his dad. That we can make it work.'

'So everything apart from marriage – plans, kids, jobs, you agree on all that?'

'Yup. Completely. But I don't know how to even discuss this with him. And it's the first time I've ever felt that way with him, to not be able to tell him something I'm feeling. And it feels so *huge*.'

'The path of love isn't always that clear, I'm afraid.'

'But you and Mum knew instantly, didn't you?'

Dad let out a little laugh. 'Not exactly, love. I know your mother likes to tell that story, but it's not really what happened. For a start, she wasn't interested in me at all when we first met. She fancied my best friend at the time, Larry Pearson. He took her to the pictures, tried to kiss her, and she threw a tub of popcorn over him. Wouldn't talk to me for weeks afterwards, as if I was to blame for his scoundrel ways.'

'*What*! I nearly had a different *dad*?'

'No, love. No. Whatever smudges your mother wants to make to our early days, *I* always knew that she and I would end up together. Although I don't think she did. Our first date was almost as bad as hers and Larry's.'

'Did she hit you with her handbag?'

'No,' he chuckled. 'We went to an Italian restaurant in Battersea and the waiter poured my spaghetti and meatballs all down the front of my bri-nylon suit. Had to eat the whole dinner with my napkin in my collar and your mother's napkin on my lap. Looked like I'd murdered someone when I walked her home.'

'But after that – you both knew after that?'

'Yes, love. But knowing something doesn't always mean you're right.'

'So you're saying I shouldn't marry Jack.'

'I wouldn't know anything about that, love, I'm just a silly old man who landed the most wonderful woman in the world. All I'm saying is – know what's important to you. Know what it is that makes you happy, then hold onto that for as long as you possibly can. And don't order spaghetti and meatballs when you're in your best clothes.'

'Thanks, Dad,' said Zoe, hugging him.

'S'alright. It's important for us of the older generation to pass on our wisdom.'

TWENTY-NINE

Now

I had back-to-school September blues as I lay wrapped in thick fleecy pyjamas, heavy socks and a plush dressing gown on the sofa, painting my fingernails with Ava's green polish and Kat's glittery nail pen, pinched last time we'd all been at Mum and Dad's. I was trying to ignore the marking that had already built up from the first week back, which lay sprawled across the coffee table in a tired slump. My phone and the doorbell went at the same time; Jack leapt out of the bedroom towards the door, saying, 'I'll get it, I think I know what this is.' I glanced at my phone, seeing a message from Esther: *No dice talking to Kat, so I've looked at her phone – she's meeting him tomorrow night at Blue Bar in Soho at 8. Me and A will meet you outside at 8.30 xxx*

I took a deep breath and tried to tuck my dressing gown around me with my feet, holding my wet nails up, as two delivery men came in, carrying in four, five, six, seven boxes, addressed to me and Jack.

Jack signed their clipboard and they left. I said, 'Did you know this was coming?'

'No, not all these.' He looked around at the boxes. 'They'd called and said it might be this week, but I wasn't expecting them today.'

I held my nails a little higher. 'Do you want to open them?'

'Do you?'

I indicated my nails. 'I can't,' I said, avoiding the real question.

Jack went to the kitchen and came back with the scissors, slicing open the top of the first box. 'Do you want me to. . .'

I didn't say anything, so he pulled out the first item. A metal milk jug, to go with the coffee machine we'd added to our list all those months ago. A huge, thick blanket; we'd chosen it thinking we'd share it in the evenings, on the sofa, watching films together and being content after our Perfect Wedding. Wine glasses, for all the dinners we'd share with each other, and with friends. Then a set of six espresso cups. In the second box, a lamp we'd debated. Next came a big wooden salad bowl and matching servers. In the third box, larger and flatter than the others, were four chairs and a little folding table for the garden, for our summers together. On and on, item after item, gift after gift, reminding us of the life we thought we'd have, all unwrapped in silence, lined up on the floor and piled up on the coffee table and the kitchen hatch, a shadow of the unpacking before our wedding. Everything we'd chosen but couldn't use now, because each gift was meant for Zoe-and-Jack, and Zoe-and-Jack didn't exist anymore. In the final box we found the coffee machine, the same one we'd wanted back then, the same one we'd kept when our own marriage hadn't yet fallen apart. The one we had kept from all those months ago was scratched and chipped now: this one was beautiful, unblemished.

We sat for a while and looked at all the things around us – shiny, new and whole.

'What are we going to do?' said Jack.

I looked at him.

'With this stuff, I mean?' He didn't look back at me.

'I don't want it.' I tried to soften my tone. 'I mean, I can see that it's not right for us to keep it.'

'So we send it back?'

'No. I don't know. That still seems. . . Sell it?' I picked up the espresso cups from the coffee table. 'Sorry. I don't mean that. That's a terrible idea. Yes send it all back, I suppose.'

'You've smudged your nails.'

Two of the fingers on my left hand had caught the edge of the table, and the delicate gold design had smudged into ridged lines across each of the nails. I stared at the cups. 'Doesn't matter.'

'Shall I just. . . take care of it?'

'Yeah. Is that ok?' I couldn't stop looking at the cups, thinking of who we were when we'd chosen them together. 'Thanks.'

'S'alright. So you don't mind—'

'No. Just. . . do what you think is best.'

'And there's nothing—'

'No. It's fine. Honestly. They're not. . . Just do whatever you like with them. Thanks.'

Jack reached to take the espresso cups from me, to pack them back in the box, but I put them down on the coffee table instead of putting them into his hand. He waited a moment, then picked them up gently to return them to their packaging, along with the jug and glasses and blanket, packed up for another couple who'd have dinner parties and film nights and hot milk together into their twilight years, snug and comfy and fond of these, their wedding gifts from the loved ones who had faith in their union.

Jack picked up a smaller box that had fallen under the armchair, and put it on the coffee table. 'This box doesn't seem to go with the others.' He stopped. 'Oh. This is what

I was expecting today.' He nudged it towards me with a slight shrug. 'I didn't know if you'd want to see it.'

I looked at it for a second, then felt myself sag a little. 'Hang on.' I got up and made us each a fresh cup of coffee while Jack kept packing up the gifts. I brought the coffees through, perched them carefully amongst the remaining gifts on the table, then sat down on the opposite sofa and opened the box. On the address label, along with both of our names, was the logo of our wedding photographer, gold-printed confetti and intertwined birds. I took a deep breath and lifted out the photo album, which had a close-up of Jack and me smiling at each other on the cover.

It was sixty-four pages of us dancing, laughing, beaming, looking lovingly at one another, hugging each other, mixed in with shots of our nearest and dearest. In not one photo did I look nervous or anxious or unsure. I was clearly having a whale of a time with Jack by my side, without a care in the world. I stopped at one picture: the two of us cracking up at something, his arm round the back of my chair, my hand on his knee, laughing into each other's faces, not aware of anyone else in the room.

Did I look that happy about anything now? Did anyone look that happy ten months after their wedding?

Jack came around the table to sit right next to me. Before I could stop myself, I'd twitched my leg away from where his pressed against it.

I looked at him, trying to undo the action. 'You knew this was coming too?'

He held his hand out for the book, not looking back at me. 'They emailed last week to say it had been dispatched. They apologised for the delay. With all the hold-ups on the wedding gifts I'd forgotten all about it.' He flicked through, stopping at the same picture I had. He let out a huge sigh.

'Good party, wasn't it?' I ventured.

'Yeah. It was.' He chuckled. 'Do you remember Liz dancing on the table?'

I laughed with him. 'Oh my god, yes. And did you see Iffy get up there too? Half the staff must have given him their numbers.'

'Or when the popcorn machine broke open, and William started rolling around in that fountain of popcorn?'

'And your stepmum got so drunk, but kept insisting she was only falling over because she had an ear infection, even when she was trying to breakdance with Iffy?' We were both laughing now.

'And when your sisters' speech was heckled by your aunt?'

'Yeah,' I laughed. 'And Mum said she couldn't tell her off because she looks so much like my grandma now that she was scared to. . .'

There was a moment when we were both still laughing, frozen, before both our thoughts congealed into memories of that broken photo frame, the picture of my grandma torn and smashed. The poison that had rotted the roots of this marriage before they could even find a hold.

I went to get up from the sofa, just as Jack said, 'Zo. . .' but when I turned back to him again, he was looking at the book.

'What? What, Jack?'

He kept his head down. 'Nothing. Sorry. Carry on.'

'No. Were you going to say something?'

He let out a puff of breath and his shoulders dropped. 'It just seems like a waste, doesn't it?'

'Of a good party?'

'No.' He laughed, bleakly. 'Kind of. It's just. . . a waste. It was *good* before we got married, wasn't it? So good. I just wish I'd known. That it could. . . get ruined.'

I took the book from him. 'I'm glad we did it.'

'The party?'

251

I laughed. 'No. All of it. I'm glad we did all of it. Even if some of this year has been. . .'

'Unbelievably shit?'

'Well.' We sat in silence.

'You don't regret it?'

I didn't know what to say: I didn't regret the wedding party, I didn't regret meeting Jack, I didn't regret loving him enough to agree to marry him. But did I regret our behaviour over this year? Did I regret watching the one relationship that mattered most to me in the whole world slowly turn to dust and become a toxic cloud? Did I miss our old relationship every single day and kick myself that I'd gone ahead with something I'd been so unsure about? Did I feel responsible? Yes.

'No, not unbelievably shit.' I nudged his shoulder with mine. 'It's been. . . interesting.'

Jack blinked, then his face changed, somehow. He wasn't upset, but there was something beneath the surface as he looked at me.

'Sorry, Zo, I've just remembered – I've got to go out. I'll clear the rest of this later. I'm sorry.' He grabbed his coat and almost ran out of the flat, without another word.

I was lost. We'd finally managed to have a conversation about our relationship without fighting, without hurting one another. We hadn't been entirely honest – at least I hadn't been – and getting our words out had seemed impossible at times, but we owed it to each other to end this relationship well. With kindness. The least I could do was to be civil to Jack: no more notes, no more sabotage. This pain I felt was natural, I told myself, it's how you feel when something you love dies. Just because it had become such a mess, it didn't mean I couldn't grieve for the relationship that had gone before.

It was a disaster, the two of us caught up in terrible carnage

252

just because we'd got on the boat marked 'Marriage'. I'd never wanted to get married, not once, never fantasised about weddings, but I had dreamed of meeting someone who made me feel the way Jack had. I'd never wanted to stay with someone for the rest of my life – until him. But I still hadn't wanted to get married. The second they handed me the marriage certificate I'd felt like it was burning my fingertips.

I wanted mortgages, kids, finding ourselves struggling for money but basically alright, caring for each other's parents when they got old and ill, caring for each *other* when we got old and ill. I wanted all the shittiness of a long-term relationship – boredom and complacency and routine. I just couldn't bear that damn ring on my finger, and the garbage that had come with it. It had ruined everything.

Before I knew it, I was lying on the sofa, clutching the photo album, and howling. I bawled so hard I gave myself hiccups, and burst a tiny blood vessel in one eye that I spotted when I peered in the mirror to check how miserable I looked. That mark might last longer than my whole marriage, I thought, with dramatic self-pity, setting myself off again. I kept going until I was completely dehydrated and felt much calmer. Then I made myself a cup of tea, and I went through the photo album again.

It was ok. Yes, we looked happy, but I'd be happy again. Jack would, too. We wouldn't be happy with each other, but that was the way of the world. I might hurt today, but it wouldn't last forever. After all, I'd probably die one day, wouldn't I?

I cried until I fell asleep on the sofa, and woke up in the morning with a pile of blankets over me. Maybe I wouldn't have felt this way if it hadn't been for Chuck; maybe I would. But I knew one thing: I wasn't about to let him wreck another Lewis woman's life.

*   *   *

I wrapped my scarf around me and turned up my coat collar as I left the school grounds. I had somewhere a little better to be, for once.

After last night's tears, I'd woken up this morning with a dull ache, but the early morning sun had bleached it away. And now, meeting George by the school gates as we'd arranged, I was happy just to walk with him, saying little, heading for a bar. The calm after the storm of a busy day.

It was easy. Maybe it was down to spending our days trying to charm moody teens into wanting to enjoy our company, but there were no awkward silences between us. And because neither of us was throwing stuff or swearing under our breath, a feature many of our classes couldn't claim, it was. . . relaxing.

As the evening wore on, one drink became two, which swiftly rolled onwards into a third and a fourth. We were sitting closer to each other now, and we were laughing about some of the kids we taught, comparing classes, comparing teachers. This was what I'd needed. I felt something like real affection stirring, mixing up with my four gin sours.

Later on, we walked through Covent Garden, buzzing from our drinks. I saw a bar I remembered from somewhere – I couldn't think where – and grabbed George's hand, pulling him towards it. He laughed. It was so easy! Just to hang out with someone! Someone with a face like an angel, but still, there was hope for me. There was a future out there, still rolled up and merely waiting to be unspooled.

'Honestly. There are some *seriously* great drinks in here,' I insisted.

'Your round this time?'

'My round,' I nodded, as he stepped forwards and held the door open for me. The inside looked familiar too, but I still couldn't put my finger on it. 'Listen,' I said, 'I'll get a booth, you order the drinks.' Handing him some crumpled notes, I raced off and plumped down at the most distant table, a curved seat in the corner that felt comfortable and romantic.

George came back shortly after. 'They're bringing the drinks over. So how do you know this place, then?'

I closed one eye to help my memory. 'I . . . don't know. . .' I said thoughtfully, then we both started giggling.

A waitress brought the drinks over. George reached for mine but managed to knock over the whole container of toothpicks in the middle of the table. He began apologising profusely, but I laughed and said to the waitress, 'Don't mind him, Jack's always clumsy with—'

I stopped myself, suddenly feeling completely sober, all the alcohol disappearing from my body in a finger-snap. I saw George's face, and I saw the waitress's face – not a waitress at all, but Nic, Jack's favourite bartender in the whole of London. We were in Jack's favourite bar, the location of our first formal date. With experienced understanding, Nic swept the toothpicks onto her tray and slid the bill under the empty holder, giving me a short nod and heading back towards the bar.

'George, I—'

'It's ok.'

'Really, I'm—'

'It's ok, Zoe.'

'It's not ok!' I put my face in my hands.

'It's not ideal, no,' I heard him say softly, as he pulled my hands from my face. That happy future was dissolving, burning up in its spool even as I held it in my hands. There wouldn't be a happy ending for me. Everything I touched was still going to be poisoned.

George spoke again. 'But I'm the one who asked you out again when you said you'd wanted to be friends. I think you're a good person, Zoe Lewis, and maybe we will be friends one day. I'd like that.'

I looked at him and tried to smile back, swallowing the tears that would follow when I was safe in bed, tears for George and for me, and for daring to hope. 'Me too, George.'

He took my hand and shook it formally, though he was still smiling. 'I guess we're just not destined to be good people together.'

At the weekend, I found myself staring into Mum's sink. I wasn't sure how long I'd been there when Dad came up behind me and peered over my shoulder.

'What are we looking at?' he whispered.

I pointed my finger. 'The teabag.'

'Oops, let me get that,' he said, reaching in and pinching the teabag out, lifting it into the bin.

'You always do that, don't you?'

'Throw your mum's teabags away? Done it as long as we've been together, I suppose. I don't even think about it now.'

'But why do you do it? Doesn't it bother you?'

He laughed. 'If I didn't do it, who would? And no, it doesn't bother me. It's just part of living with her, I suppose. Part of the rich tapestry that makes up your mum.'

'Don't you find it. . . gross?'

'It's just a teabag, love.'

'I know. But it is a bit gross. To just leave a cold teabag in the sink.'

'I've noticed the apple hasn't fallen too far from the tree in that respect – I've seen plenty of teabags in your sink.'

'I know. I think I've just realised. . . why it would bother someone, though.'

'There are a lot worse things to do than that, love. Your mum and I – we've made a lot of compromises over the years. But I wouldn't change her for the world. Teabags or no.'

I kept staring at the tiny brown tea stain by the plug, until Dad turned the tap on and washed the whole thing away in a single moment.

At school, coursework demands were building up. My seven-hour day became a twelve-hour day, spent in the classrooms and Science office, and as I got home one night I realised that I hadn't even seen the sun that day. I yawned and stretched my arms high over my head, and said out loud, 'Ugh, I need a *holidaaayyy*.'

'You and me both, Zo.'

I jumped several inches off the floor, then winced at the muscle I'd pulled in my back.

'Jesus Christ, you scared me.'

Jack walked out of the bedroom. 'I didn't know I was supposed to wear a bell.'

'It was so quiet in here, I didn't think anyone was home.' I tried to stretch my back out. 'You're lucky I don't carry pepper spray.'

Jack chuckled. 'Sounds like you had a good day at school.'

'It was fine,' I said, tenderly feeling my pulled muscle. 'I just really would like to get away for a while.'

'No plans with your boyfriend?'

'Oh. No. That's. . . We've definitely finished that.'

'Oh. Right.' Jack turned away and busied himself with something in the kitchen hatch.

'No romantic holidays ahoy, sadly. But it if we're talking about this, can I ask – what happened with Jessica?'

He looked away. 'It. . . just didn't work out.'

'Can I ask why?'

'You can ask. I don't think I know, though. It was going and then it wasn't. What happened with you and that George guy?'

257

Now it was my turn to look away. 'Same. It just works or it doesn't, doesn't it?'

'Maybe next time,' Jack said. I couldn't look at his face.

'Yeah. Maybe next time,' I muttered.

THIRTY

One year earlier

Zoe was weeping with laughter, tears rolling down her cheeks, as she dabbed at her running nose. She was clutching the edge of the table, rocking back and forth, as Liz put her hand on Zoe's shoulder, in a similar condition herself.

'Don't – don't–' Zoe tried to shake her head.

'And the worst thing was – I didn't even know the guy who was in there! It was just some dude from the bus station!'

Zoe and Liz were both gasping, vaguely aware that others were watching them. Zoe couldn't breathe for a moment as she imagined the terrible, terrible situations that Liz somehow always managed to find herself in, in some form or other. She'd just about managed to calm herself down, hiccupping, when Liz muttered, 'As if *I'm* meant to carry bananas around the whole time, *just in case*,' and they were both off again, Zoe's mascara running down her face and her breath catching.

Eventually they calmed themselves, and Zoe's breathing had returned to normal, with the aid of a dose of cold water, when Liz asked, semi-casually, 'How's the wedding planning going? I know you love that question.'

Zoe quickly sobered up, pushing around the scraps of food left on her plate. 'I don't know. It seems like ages away. Do we need to do anything now? Isn't there some honeymoon period of being engaged where you don't have to actually do anything else yet?'

'And are we hoping that honeymoon period lasts around sixty to seventy years?'

'Maybe.' Zoe smiled. 'What would you do in this situation?'

'If I was engaged to someone I wanted to marry? I dunno – book a venue, buy a dress, get the drinks in?'

'It's not that I don't want to be *engaged* to Jack. . .'

'But it's the bit after that you don't fancy?' She cleared her throat. 'Look, let's think about it this way: if you imagine yourself in one, or three, or ten years' time, already married to Jack, how does that make you feel?'

Zoe clutched at her throat and started making choking noises. 'I feel. . . interesting?'

'Right. Perhaps I won't book that hen-weekend spa break just yet.'

Zoe slumped in her seat. 'But how do I tell him? "Sorry I said yes, Jack, I actually don't want to marry you and never will"?'

'But you do still love him?'

'Yes! Hugely! I want to be with him, and only him, for as long as I can possibly imagine. But I just don't want the wedding and the marriage and all that stuff. And we'd talked about it, we'd agreed that we weren't going to get married, that we were fine just as we were – that's what I can't get my head around. And he knows all about. . . the Chuck stuff. Well. Enough of it at least.'

'Blimey. Right, so you're not breaking up with him. Maybe try and talk to him about all of this then. And if it looks like he's freaking out, maybe just ask how he'd feel about a very, very, very long engagement. It's not cancelling the wedding, it's extending the pre-wedding.'

'Nice. Ok. You're right, this is crazy. I shouldn't be keeping something like this from him.' Zoe rolled Jack's engagement ring around her finger. 'I could live with an indefinite engagement. If that's what it took. A pre-wedding. I can do that.'

Somehow, she'd known something was wrong before her key had even reached the lock. Afterwards she'd wondered if the sound of Jack's voice had seeped through their front door into the shared hallway. Her heart was pounding by the time she was through, and she could see him, pacing in front of the sofa, almost shouting into the landline receiver in his hand: 'WELL FIND SOMEONE WHO DOES THEN.' As he saw her, he collapsed, banging his leg against the corner of the coffee table and lying crumpled in a grey heap against the sofa. Zoe gently took the phone from him. She heard the voice on the end, speaking in Spanish and broken English, talking in a gentle tone, gently but repetitively saying over and over, *un accidente* and *coche* and *tu madre*. It was the language and the tone that told her everything, just as it had told Jack before her, and they only needed a translator at the other end to confirm that their worst impression was, in fact, the correct one.

Somehow she found herself writing notes, listing the details of what they would need to take to Spain, the things they had to do, and then she was making Jack drink a strong, sugary tea, while she also looked up flights. Later, there was a howling from the bedroom – Jack howling, tears drowning his face. She pressed herself against him as though she was trying to get into his skin and carry all of this pain for him, because what use was anything if she couldn't help the person she loved most in the world, right at this moment? Then he was asleep, and it was dark, and

261

she called her parents because that was the only thing she could possibly do now, and they cried too, but in a way that made her feel better. Her mum said she'd be over in fifteen minutes, even if she had to jump every red light there was. When they'd hung up Zoe thought for a horrible moment, *Is that how Linda died? Jumping a red light?* And there was a horrible quarter of an hour where Zoe thought her mum would never arrive and they'd get another call, this time in English.

Eventually, she was there on her doorstep, holding Zoe and squeezing her. She knew they were both thinking, though neither of them could say it, that one day she wouldn't be here to squeeze Zoe like this, and this shared, silent thought made them both hold each other even tighter, until Jack woke again and Zoe's mum was in their bedroom, holding him like she'd held Zoe, as he howled into her shoulder. Zoe sat on the sofa, staring at the pattern on her socks until Jack was asleep again and her mum was next to her.

When she finally went to sleep that night, almost as the sun was coming up, she was glad that she hadn't said anything about pulling out of the wedding to anyone in the family. She decided that she'd never think about it again.

They flew out the next evening, with bags someone had packed. Her mum had offered to come too, and Zoe had wanted to say yes, but Jack had said, *No, thanks very much, but no.* That night, they slept in Linda's spare room. Neither of them could bring themselves to open Linda's bedroom door, but they were alive enough to wash and dress the next morning, taking a taxi to the crematorium. Everything felt hurried. Jack just wanted everything done. Here. Now. Graham wasn't coming – he was himself in hospital, having developed a touch of pneumonia. Zoe couldn't help but think that at any other time they would have worried themselves sick about him. But this time, there were other things to focus on.

It still seemed like a dream.

They'd spoken to Linda only a few days before. She'd teased Zoe about the wedding, and Zoe hadn't really minded, because it was *Linda*, wasn't it? How could they be standing here, doing this? Listening to these words she didn't really understand? She felt dizzy. Just an accident on the road, they'd explained, a dangerous corner, maybe an animal had scared her, maybe she'd just lost concentration, but that was all it took to switch from Linda Alive, teasing Zoe on the phone while Jack mouthed jokingly *I'm not here* in their kitchen, to Linda Dead, in a box, about to be burnt up, Zoe thought wildly.

She felt sick. She took Jack's arm, and he pulled her to him, holding her so she couldn't see the box going in, even though Zoe felt it should be her protecting him from such a monstrous sight. They both cried and Zoe could feel him shaking and shaking, every last part of him.

Afterwards, they emerged outside, the sunlight disconcertingly bright and warm on their skin, although both of them looked grey. Some other people followed them out – local friends of Linda's who had somehow heard of the funeral – but Jack just looked at Zoe, wanting to avoid conversation with the other mourners. He lifted her hand to his mouth, kissing her finger where her engagement ring was, and Zoe understood then that any wedding ceremony was purely a formality. She was married to Jack now, as far as it mattered.

Over the next few weeks and months, they didn't talk much about the wedding at all. Nothing had been settled by then anyway: whatever had been a point of discussion was now just understood, with details to be signed and sealed later on. Jack was deep in his grief, and Zoe just tried to focus on being there with him, carrying him through those moments where he wasn't at work, concentrating and nodding and smiling and reassuring his professional world that yeah, it was shit, but he was ok.

Every day he went to his shop like he was on autopilot. At home he would sit in silence, on the sofa or at their little table, no radio or TV on, just staring into space, with Zoe, Iffy or sometimes even Liz looking on. They'd make him warm drinks, encourage him to sip them, and have a slice of toast or some chopped fruit, which mostly he'd do, uncomplainingly but mindlessly taking what they gave him, chewing and swallowing without noticing what it was. Jack would sometimes come to her parents' house; the first time, Zoe's dad had hugged him, then all of her sisters had come and wrapped themselves around him too, and they'd stood like that for a long time. Zoe's mum made him meal after meal, meals that he'd thank her for but leave to cool and congeal on his plate. Her parents would turn up at the flat from time to time, separately, with yet more food, or a magazine, or a book, or some fresh fruit from the market.

Once, when Zoe came home from school, Jack was just standing at their window, staring out, wrapped in a duvet over his work clothes. She came to stand with him and he opened up the duvet to her, and they stood there for over an hour, until it was completely dark and she put him to bed.

A month after they had brought Linda's ashes back from Spain, Zoe met Ava to catch up over coffees and bagels at their favourite café. 'I just don't want him to ever feel that I'm waiting for him to get over it, to be. . . normal again,' she said, thoughtfully.

'Which you are,' Ava said.

Zoe sighed. 'I just want to stop him hurting, that's all. I

know he's grieving, and he's got to grieve, and it's right for him to grieve, but I want to be able to *do* something. To just have to watch and not be able to make him feel any better, ever. . . It's torture.'

'That's normal too, Zo. You love him, and you want to fix him.'

'But I know that I can't. That it's not something that can be fixed.'

But honestly, Zoe did want to fix him, and she was waiting for the day when life would return to some semblance of normality. She'd never admit it, never out loud, but there were tiny fragments of moments where she'd think, *Oh Jack, is this how it's going to be forever? If I could wave a magic wand with just one wish, I'd make all of this pain go away, set us all back to normal.*

She understood the theories of the importance of grief, but she also knew how much she missed Jack, *her* Jack, and how different everything felt in her life while he found a new way to live with his loss. She wanted to carry him through a time when he didn't even seem touchable. She wished things were how they used to be.

Then, one day, he started coming back. She woke up one morning and he was in the kitchen, making bacon-and-egg sandwiches for them, although she could see no external change in circumstance between that day and the day before. One day she got home and the lights were on in the flat, and Jack was humming a little as he ironed his shirts in front of the TV. They had sex again, which had seemed an impossible silence between them, she realised once it had been broken. He went to one of Iffy's dinners, and though he was quiet on the way home and went straight to bed, cocooned in the duvet, Zoe still knew that progress had been made. The progress wasn't linear – some nights he woke her, woke them both, crying in their bed, confused and lost and full of pain – but he was coming through something, a different shape, but coming back to her, each of them full of joy at being together again.

Then, one morning, over marmalade toast and a cafetière of brewing coffee, Jack pulled down the newspaper she was reading and with a huge smile of glowing joy, said, 'Shall we just get on with this? The wedding, I mean. Life's too short. Let's just get married.'

And Zoe had wondered what she'd wished for.

Iffy would be best man, of course, and Zoe, to save blood-shed between her sisters, asked Liz to be her maid of honour. Liz had never mentioned the conversation between them about cancelling or postponing the wedding; she'd seen Jack too, had understood that in the face of such pain, this wasn't about Zoe's relatively minor concerns. But she had given Zoe a look, and said, 'And are you ok with all of this? Are we happy with these plans?' Zoe had known exactly what she was talking about, but said, 'Yes! Yup! You're my only choice for maid of honour!' Liz hadn't pushed it any further, instead just squeezing her hand and saying 'Zo, you're my priority at this wedding, right? So whatever you need, I'll make sure you get it, ok?' Zoe knew again what she'd really meant, and knew too that despite the offer, Liz couldn't get her what she needed, which was either a decent backbone or a time machine.

Her mum and dad agreed to walk with Zoe down the aisle, and Esther said they could borrow little William, if they wanted, as some kind of flower-carrying, ring-bearing, token cute child in the wedding party. Before she knew it, the January date was decided, the register office was booked, and a venue with a late cancellation had been found.

'It's a sign!' Jack said, and Zoe had smiled and looked for a fire exit and tried to think about how happy Linda would have been about all of this. She didn't want to dwell on how Linda had spent her entire life in a marriage she didn't want to be in. And she certainly didn't want to think about how little life Linda had been given to enjoy the way she'd wanted.

So Zoe just watched Jack's face, as they designed invitations and chose food and paid deposits. And she decided that for the rest of their lives, his pure, shining happiness would just have to do for them both.

THIRTY-ONE

Now

As promised, Ava and Esther were waiting for me outside the bar when I arrived at 8.30 p.m.

'He in there?' I said, wrapping my arms around myself.

Ava nodded.

'And he looks so pleased with himself,' Esther added, pulling her coat tighter. She was wearing Kat's bright purple lipstick. 'Listen, it's freezing. Let's get on with it.'

'Hang on, hang on,' I said, grabbing her arm. 'Get on with what, exactly? What's the plan here?'

Ava and Esther looked at each other. 'Tell Kat the truth, I suppose. Tell her everything you told us about him. And ask what the hell is going on with her.'

I must have looked doubtful, as Ava said gently, 'She needs to hear it from you, Zo. We need to know we've done everything we can to keep her safe from him.' Ava put her hand on top of my hand on Esther's arm. 'She'll believe you.'

'If she sees how he reacts when you tell her the truth about it, she'll have to. It's better that he's there,' Esther added.

'We don't want him wriggling his way out of it when we're not around.'

I nodded at them both and we turned as one. I stepped into the bar first, and saw them straight away: Kat on a stool at the far end of the bar, Chuck leaning into her, a rich leer across his face, his hand twitching upwards behind her as it strained to make contact with her lower back.

I didn't even remember walking over there, but I was aware of grabbing his hand and jerking it away from her.

'What the fuck!' Chuck cried, and Kat turned around, her jaw dropping when she saw the three of us standing there.

'Er. . . small world?' Kat looked furious. 'What are you three doing here?' I released Chuck's hand.

Ava looked at Kat, at Chuck, and then at me, and said, 'You need to listen to Zo. You need to listen to how she knows Chuck.'

Chuck's face was turning purple. 'I *don't* know her, I've never had anything to do with her. This is a business meeting.'

Kat stepped back and crossed her arms. 'You *do* know her. She's your ex's best friend, remember?'

Chuck made a gesture of dismissal. 'Sure, whatever. I don't know what she's talking about, though.'

Esther stepped closer to Kat; our little sister towered over her in her heels, but Esther pulsated a kind of deep fury that made her the largest thing in the room. 'Sis, you *need* to listen to her.'

Kat's anger was almost equal to Chuck's. 'I don't know why you guys think this is ok, but I'm having a work meeting with my boss and this really isn't appropriate. We can talk about this at Mum and Dad's, but now *really* isn't the time.'

I hesitated a moment. *Had* we got this wrong? But then I remembered Chuck's words to me, and our removal – twice! – from their office. If there was nothing sinister going on

269

here, then I'd be willing to lay money on Ava making it as next year's *Ninja Warrior* champion.

'Kat. Listen. He's not Liz's ex. He's mine. He was my boyfriend when I was in sixth form.' Chuck made a scoffing noise. 'He's. . . he's not a good person, Kat. You don't want to get involved with him.' Kat looked dubious. 'He's controlling, Kat. Majorly controlling. He told me where I could go, who I could go with—'

'Excuse me, can we stop the tall tales now, please?' Chuck interrupted.

'He told me which uni to go to. He told me we were going to get married, gave me a ring that I wasn't allowed to wear.'

'You were engaged?' Kat said in a quiet voice.

'He – he made me sleep with him when I wasn't ready.' I gulped. 'Kat, please. Please don't give him any of your time.'

'This is one hundred per cent garbage. Aren't you embarrassed making this shit up?' Chuck said, shaking his head sadly at me. 'This is actual slander. Kat, can you control your sister?'

There was a long silence, where Kat's unconvinced look didn't change. Chuck made another noise, like a minor explosion, when Kat didn't ask me to leave, as he'd clearly hoped.

'You're crazy,' he blustered. '*Crazy*! I warned you to stay away from us—'

'Us?' Kat said quietly, dangerously.

'And I told you what would happen if you didn't.' The three of us drew closer together, closer to Kat. He turned to her, incredulous, then a snarl grew on his face. 'Sorry, kiddo, looks like your delusional sister just cost you your job.'

He knocked back his whisky and turned to storm from the bar with a triumphant look on his face, but his belt loop caught on the bar rail and he was jerked sharply. Esther snorted. Chuck unhooked himself, gave me a look of pure hatred, and walked slightly more carefully away from us and out of the door.

Kat's face showed quiet shock. She looked at her watch; I put my hands up to my face and started sobbing. I'd lost her her job, Chuck still insisted I was lying, and Kat didn't even believe me. Then I felt her arms go around me, and she pulled me into a tight hug. 'Shhh,' she whispered in my ear. 'Shhh, it's ok.' I was still sobbing as she put her hands on my face and lifted it to hers. 'Zo, it's ok.'

'But it's. . . all true. . . It's true, Kat, I didn't make any of it up—'

She smiled at me, wiped my tears away with her thumbs. 'Zo. I wish you hadn't done that.'

I cried harder. 'Please, please, don't trust him. . . please. . . please don't listen to him—'

She pulled me into a hug again and whispered in my ear. 'Zo, I'm sorry. I've got to go with him. But don't worry, ok?' She gave me a soft kiss on my forehead, pulled away, grabbed her coat and followed Chuck out of the door.

I felt myself shutting down. I had tried everything to save my little sister from a monster like Chuck, and she hadn't believed me. She hadn't stayed with us. She'd gone with him. I'd lost Jack, and now I'd lost her. Ava reached for me, but I couldn't feel her. I walked to the door, pulled it open with the last of my strength, and hailed a cab.

The next morning I was leaning on the kitchen counter, staring into space with a cold cup of coffee in my hand, wondering if I would ever see Kat again, when Jack came out of the bedroom dressed for work, and headed past me without a word. He grabbed his coat and went straight out of the front door, slamming it closed, then the main door outside after it. After a moment, I heard him heading back in, his key rattling in the locks.

'Right. Sorry, this is actually melting my fucking head. I thought I was ok but I'm not.' His fists were balled up. 'Why

271

did you do it? Why did you go ahead and marry me? I didn't put a gun to your head! I never forced you! Or did I? Did I somehow manipulate you into doing something major against your will? Please tell me exactly how I did that, Zoe, because I imagine that'll be really fucking useful in any difficult interactions I have for the rest of my *fucking life*.'

I didn't know how to start. 'Sorry, are we talking about this now? Just like that?'

Jack was speaking through gritted teeth. 'I know it's a lot to ask, but I do feel like I deserve even the most meagre of explanations, beyond, "I just don't really like marriage."'

I heard my breath shudder as I drew it in, trying to stay calm. 'You didn't *force* me. But you did. . . put me in a position where I couldn't say no, Jack.'

'By what? Holding your beloved pet hostage? How the fuck did I do that?'

'You knew I never wanted to get married! You knew that! We'd talked about it! We'd agreed! I thought we both felt exactly the same. Then your parents divorced—'

'Oh, I'm *so sorry* my parents split up, Zoe, at least you can be reassured that it won't happen again—'

'And you decided that apparently that was the perfect reason for us to get married – which, FYI, is *not* a romantic way to propose to someone—'

'Well, thanks for letting me know.'

'And then I'd wanted to call it off, once I'd said yes. I'd realised that it was a mistake, and we were better off just staying as we were, or having one of those endless engagements, then—'

'Then *what*? Oh my god.'

'Then—'

'Oh my god, you're going to do it, aren't you?'

'Do what?'

'You're going to blame your wrong decision to marry me on my mum dying. Aren't you?'

'Jack.'

'Aren't you? That's what you're going to say, isn't it? ISN'T IT, ZOE?'

I jumped, my heart pounding at his sudden shout. 'I'm not saying it's anyone's fault—'

'Thanks SO MUCH for that weight off my mind, Zo. I can't tell you how it's been preying on me that my mother's unexpected accidental death was in some way responsible for your forced marriage.'

'Jack, it was an awful time for you. For all of us. It was the worst thing that could have happened, in the worst possible way, and all I could think of was how to make you feel better. How to somehow make this unbelievably shitty and overwhelming situation into something fractionally less shitty and awful and nightmarish. And if that meant just sucking it up and going through with the marriage, if that's what you wanted, and what your mum would have wanted—'

'Don't even mention her. Don't you even say her name. You didn't know her. You swanned in and suddenly the two of you were best friends, while she's on the other side of Europe and you secretly don't even want to marry her son—'

'Jack, please.'

'What, don't remind you that you betrayed her? Don't remind you that you're saying this is all somehow her fault? What is it that I'm not supposed to do? Is it marry you? Because you had the chance to make that call and apparently never thought piping up would be at all useful or appropriate *before* we'd actually signed our marriage certificate.'

'Jack. Please.' He paused for a moment, hunched over in one corner, panting slightly. 'Please, Jack. You know that I don't want to hurt you. That I'd never want to hurt you or your mum.'

'No medals for thoughtfulness for you today, Zo. Sorry, we must be all fucking out.'

'Can't you even try to understand?' I begged. 'I loved you so much. All I wanted was to make you happy. But you asked me to do the one thing that we'd talked and talked and talked about, and both seemed to understand would definitely not make me happy. What was I supposed to do? You tell me. What was it I was supposed to do to not be the villain in that situation?'

'Oh, I'm sorry, Zoe, I was too busy grieving my parents' thirty-year marriage and then the death of my mother to be too concerned with your moral compass.'

I gave a low growl and smashed my cup onto the floor. 'Jack! I'm sorry about their divorce! I'm sorry about your mum! You know how sorry I am – I was with you! I was always with you! I loved her and I loved you and you cannot throw that back in my face anymore. But for fuck's sake, Jack, what was it I was supposed to do? It was an impossible situation you put me in, even before the car accident, and then I couldn't tell you how I really felt once I'd finally worked it out for myself, but I'm not the monster you're trying so hard to paint me as here!'

'*Loved*,' Jack said softly.

'What?'

'Nothing. So what, then? What's so awful about this marriage that you so desperately need to get out of it?'

'It just. . . is. It's not you, it's not me. It just doesn't work. This idea. The way we got into it. I don't want to be with you because you don't want to be like your parents. Or because I felt guilty about upsetting you when your mum died. I don't want us to be tied together in all the ways that made your parents so miserable for so long, or in all the ways that my parents aren't – and they've been so happy all their lives. I just never understood what was so bad about how we had it before.'

'Nothing was bad! But people do get married when they love one another!'

'But I didn't want to and you made me feel like I was wrong! Can't you understand how horrible that felt? That every single day was a reminder that no matter how much you said you loved me, we were living a life that *you* chose for us. In direct contradiction of everything *I* thought we'd agreed on.'

Jack stared at me, then dropped his eyes to the shattered cup on the floor. 'I didn't realise it was so horrible for you.'

I leant against the kitchen cabinet. 'No, you didn't. You never wanted to. You just wanted us to be this picture-perfect couple in our picture-perfect flat with our perfect jobs and friends and lives. You never once considered why I'd suddenly be saying yes to you when every conversation between us about marriage had always been me saying no.'

Jack dropped down, sliding his back against the cabinets until he was sitting on the kitchen floor, at my feet.

'I loved you so much, Jack.' I saw him wince, momentarily. 'But it was never fair to put that pressure on me. And we had talked about it! I just don't understand how you thought just asking me – in public! Down on one knee! – would make everything I'd decided, everything I'd wanted, all my principles, suddenly completely reverse. I just never understood how you could believe that worked.'

'I'd always felt the same way you did,' Jack said softly. 'Always. But then. . . this massive thing happened in my life that made me question everything, and so I thought. . . I thought that if I asked you, and we talked about it, and I could explain to you why I'd changed my mind, then maybe you would, or could, change your mind too. If I just asked you in the right way. . .' He put his head in his hands. 'I thought I could just do this to make sure one part of my life wouldn't fuck up. That I could hold onto one good thing without it. . . disintegrating.' He laughed bitterly. 'I never thought – not for one second – that you still felt like you had before. I would never have forced you – I would never

275

have wanted us to marry if I'd thought for one second that you didn't want it. Zoe, you must know that's true.'

I nodded, but I felt something creeping up my throat. 'I know. But you never asked. And I never said. And so we're both to blame for where we are now.'

Jack lifted his face and looked at me. 'But what's so bad about it? Really? Now we're married, what's so bad about actually being married to each other? We've done the hardest bit, haven't we? Why do we need to. . . What's this divorce stuff about?'

My hands balled into fists to match his. 'Besides me not ever wanting to get married?'

'Back *then*. Yes!'

'And you pitching it to me as a way to beat your parents' mistakes?'

'Yeah, I said that wrong, but—'

'And me feeling like it was something I had to do so you didn't feel extra bad about your mum's death?'

'Jesus, Zo—'

'And then me explaining all of this to you, right now, and explaining how I've felt trapped and betrayed every single day since our wedding, and I thought you might be able to understand, and then asking me *again* like we haven't *ever* discussed a *single* aspect of this, why I don't want to be in this marriage anymore? Besides all that?'

'Zo, I—'

'No. I think we've done enough talking. Now *I'm* going.' My face was burning, my muscles were screaming, and it was all I could do to just remember my wallet and keys and coat as I walked out, the edges of my vision sparkling with anger and hurt at the corner we'd found ourselves in. I didn't regret anything I'd said to Jack. I just regretted every moment of our lives since he'd decided to propose.

THIRTY-TWO

Benni called me into her office, looking carefully about to see that no one was following me as she closed the door.

'Are we being followed? Is the room bugged?' I whispered, pointing at the ceiling lights.

'I don't want anyone else getting any ideas. Listen, darling, are you ready for your Halloween half-term? Costume all ready?'

'Ten days and counting till last day of term, Benni. Between disastrous dating, my almost-former husband and worrying about my sister, this year I'll be going as one of the Walking Dead.'

'Great!' Benni exclaimed. I crossed my arms. 'So how would you feel about leaving the country?'

'Amazing.'

'Good. Because the deadline for the global teaching exchange programme is tomorrow. And I think you should apply.'

'Teaching exchange?'

She offered me a handful of print-outs. 'They do them every year, all over the world – obviously – and they'll get back to you fast if they want you. It's normally a year-long placement; they only tell you your new school about a month in advance, but they'll confirm whether you've been successful in time for you to hand in your notice before half-term. Ok?'

I was stunned. 'Benni? Are you trying to get rid of me?'

She sat at the edge of her desk. 'Darling, you know how bloody impossible it is to get Science teachers these days, particularly ones that I actually like. But they guarantee me a replacement teacher for the year – or two – that you'd be gone for, and they guarantee *you* a fresh new start, away from all of this stuff. And then, when you're ready, you can come back here and show me allllll the valuable skills you picked up in Beijing or Vancouver or Rome or New York or wherever.'

'Really?'

'Really. I've spoken to the Head, she's all for it. Says it'll raise our profile, attract more teachers to the school and so on. Or maybe she just can't wait to get rid of your miserable face too.' She tipped her head to one side. 'Just kidding, darling. So what do you think?'

I thought it was a brilliant idea. I spent my lunch hour filling in the paperwork, and was so engrossed in it that I didn't hear Miks coming into the Science office and sitting down in his cubby beside mine. There was a loud thunk as he dropped a pile of textbooks on his desk, which made me jump guiltily. He nodded at the forms.

'Teacher exchange?'

I half covered them with my arms, before realising how much I looked like a pupil caught out, then laughed. 'Yeah. Benni recommended it.'

'I mean this in the nicest way,' Miks said, 'but I think you need it.' I laughed again, but he carried on: 'Seriously. My sister got divorced last year. It's pretty shit. But she said the one thing that helped her the most was when someone said that sometimes, there's just no one to blame. That sometimes, it's just one of those things.' I stared, open-mouthed. He shrugged. 'I'm not saying that's the case with you – I'm just saying it might help.' Then he picked up a lab coat and a different pile of textbooks and headed out again.

Three days later, I was still wondering at Miks's unlikely pep talk. I wasn't sure what I was more stunned by – that, or the Head's swift sign-off of my application, and the subsequent acceptance form from the exchange programme which I now held in my hand.

By Halloween half-term, I'd handed in my formal notice to leave Walker High School in January for a minimum twelve-month stretch. And so I semi-severed another tie to the life I had thought would be mine for years to come.

Friday night blackjack at the pub, and Dad brought over three pints of cider to our table. Esther took a huge gulp of hers then slid mine over. I swallowed half of it in one go, needing some support against all the changes going on in my life right now. Kat still hadn't responded to anything I'd sent her. I wondered if we'd ever speak again.

'Ooh, cider really is the only thing to drink in this miserable weather,' Dad said, taking a gulp to rival mine while Esther shuffled a deck of cards.

'Right. Who's in?' We cleared our pints out of the way while Esther dealt, then each picked up.

'How's everything going at home, love?' Dad asked, while we moved our cards around in our hands.

'Besides Kat not responding to any of my texts? Pretty great.' I sighed and took another sip. 'Jack and I aren't speaking at all at the moment.'

'Good.' He looked at me. 'Isn't it?'

Esther raised an eyebrow. 'Better than their previous death by a thousand cuts, I suspect.'

'Thanks, Es.'

'It wasn't that bad, was it?' Dad looked worried.

'It's fine, now, honestly. Just have to get through these last couple of months, then we're off on our separate ways.'

I saw Dad look at Esther, then down at his hand. 'Alright, love. As long as you're ok. And Kat will be too, don't you worry. . .' He was getting distracted by his cards. 'You girls will all be alright.'

'It's just. . .' I took a swig of my cider. 'I don't know why we had to get married in the first place. I honestly don't know what we were thinking. You and Mum have got on fine all these years, not being married, and it's never mattered to you one way or another. Why do people care so much?'

I noticed Dad was sinking lower and lower into his cards. Esther put hers in her lap. 'Dad.'

'Yes, love?' he said, from the depths of his bunched hands.

'Dad,' Esther said again. 'There's a reason we play black-jack and not poker with you, you know.'

I gave him a hard stare. 'Dad, what is it?'

He was blushing a deep scarlet by now. 'Nothing serious, girls, nothing for you to worry about.'

'Dad.'

'It's only. . . last year, your mum and I got married.'

Esther and I screamed together, '*What?*'

'Calm down, it's not serious.'

'Not *serious?*' I gasped.

'Dad, you and Mum got married without telling us! You got married! And you didn't tell us!'

'That's pretty serious, Dad.'

'Now come on, girls, it really isn't. It was more for the paperwork. Sue at your mum's old work had just lost her partner, and it turns out it's a hell of a lot easier in the event of someone's death, with wills and inheritance and things—'

'You're not going to die, neither of you are ever going to die.'

'—if you're married. That's all it was. We didn't want to make a big song and dance about it, because we didn't think it was a big deal. Like I said, just paperwork. You didn't ask to come and see us sign our wills, did you? We talked about it, and thought it was best to just get on with it and not mention it.'

'But you did know we'd find out eventually, didn't you? Like, when you died, and we couldn't talk to you about it anymore?' Esther said.

'I thought I'd made it clear – neither of them are ever going to die,' I insisted. 'And seriously, what the hell is it with parents sneaking off and getting secretly married these days? Have they put something in the blood pressure medications?'

'Esther, love, we didn't think you girls would be so upset about this. We really did talk about it for a long time. We didn't kick up a fuss when you said you'd be moving abroad in January, did we, Zoe? We understand that it's your life, and we're all happy for you, however much of a surprise it was. And we thought we'd raised you all to not care whether a couple was married or not. To look a bit deeper than whether or not they'd signed some bit of paper. To understand that marriage – or not marriage – was purely between the couple themselves, and nothing to do with anyone outside that relationship. Didn't we raise you that way?'

Esther and I looked at each other, shamed. 'Sorry, Dad.'
'Sorry, Dad.'

'It's alright. We'll say no more about it.' We picked up our cards.

Then Esther put hers down again. 'Hang on a minute, Dad, that's bullshit. You absolutely know you should have told us.'

'I know, love, but it was worth a try, wasn't it?' He smiled sheepishly. 'Shall we get on with this game?'

* - * *

281

We didn't talk about it any more that night, except when we were all going our separate ways outside the pub; Esther squeezed my hand after we hugged, and just said, 'What the hell, right?' I nodded, wide eyed, and knew the four of us had to get in touch, as soon as possible, to discuss this, take it apart, and put it back together, united and consoled, so that we could face Mum and Dad without this confusion and slight betrayal we were feeling. That's if Kat would even speak to me.

I wondered if my feelings would be different to my sisters': Kat and Ava hadn't been married, and Esther, as far as I could tell, was happily hitched. It was only me who'd got sucked in and chewed out by the marriage myth, feeling that if my mother had been able to emigrate from her family and home, to later begin an interracial relationship, with four children born outside wedlock in the seventies and eighties, I was betraying them by going down the white frock and rings and legal certificate route.

How different would I have felt about these last months if I'd known Mum and Dad had secretly married, too? God, how differently would I have felt on my wedding day? I thought back to Dad's silences, his closed face, and I wondered if he hadn't wanted to tell me, if he hadn't recognised, or at least suspected, that the information might have some effect on me. That it might have made marriage seem something I could do, if I'd known they had done it too.

Getting home and checking my phone once I was safely in bed, I saw that the group chat between my sisters was already thirty-four messages long. I'd read them all in the morning, even if the chain was four times the size by then. And I knew at least two of my sisters would be at my door, bringing food to share between us all for the invariable summit to follow.

* * *

At 10 a.m., I poured a coffee for Es and herbal tea for Ava. I was amazed that the door had only buzzed at quarter to – I assumed there must have been some kind of bus strike to have prevented them from getting here before the sun was even up. Kat said she couldn't come – work commitments. On a Saturday. Since Ava had told me, I couldn't even bring myself to dig into the sourdough loaf Es had cooked as soon as she'd got home last night.

'Where's Jack?' Ava asked as we settled around the table.

'Didn't come home last night. I was up watching garbage until two, since I was on sofa shift last night. No sign of him by then, or now, for that matter.'

'Well then,' said Esther, carefully spreading butter onto her slice. 'This is pretty massive.'

Ava blew on her tea before taking a sip. 'I don't think it *has* to be,' she said thoughtfully.

'Have *you* spoken to Kat?' I asked her.

She shook her head. 'Just a text in reply to this, that's all. She's keeping us all in the dark, Zo.'

'Look at it this way,' Esther said. 'At least we didn't have to wear bridesmaids' dresses.' We were silent for a moment as we all considered the kind of thing Mum would have chosen for us.

'Mmm,' I said. 'Narrow escape.'

'Plus,' she went on, 'I've been thinking about what Dad said last night. I know he was only chancing it, to try and get us off his back, but it was also true. It isn't really our business.'

'They're our parents!' I said.

'Yeah, but they don't owe us every single piece of information about their lives. Would you want to know everything? *Everything*?'

'I think Es is right,' Ava said. 'They didn't forget to mention it – it sounds like a conscious choice to not tell us. It's been

283

a really big part of their identity for so long – the couple who didn't marry, in an age where that was basically like having horns on your head – that it must have been hard for Dad to tell you.'

I looked at Ava again. 'What did Kat actually say? Is she alright?' Ava put an arm around me. I sighed. 'It's all made me think. . . how much knowing about Mum and Dad might have made all this stuff between me and Jack go – or at least *feel* – differently.'

Ava stirred her tea with her free hand. 'Do you mean you don't think you'd be splitting up?'

'I don't know. I wouldn't put it that strongly. I think I've spent too long being brainwashed against marriage for it to turn things round entirely. On my wedding day I definitely felt like I was. . . letting Mum and Dad down by marrying.'

Esther shrugged. 'Marriage has been good for me.'

I sighed again. 'So I'm just the failure then.'

'I'm serious. We were all programmed to be so impressed with Mum and Dad's choices – they were brave, and I'm proud of them, it must have been really damn hard. But when I got together with Ethan, I knew immediately that I wanted us to be married. It didn't feel wrong because that was my choice, and I was happy with it. Maybe it's not about Mum and Dad not being married – maybe it's just as you thought. That marrying Jack wasn't right for you.'

'So you don't think I should have married Jack?'

'How the hell should I know? I always thought you seemed like a great couple. You made each other happy. You had a great time together.'

'We do! Or we did.'

'But I've also seen how miserable you've been since the day you got married. I don't know what that change was. Did you stop loving him?'

Ava stopped stirring her tea.

'No! Never. That's what's made this whole thing so fucking awful! I don't feel any differently about him – it was just the relationship we were in. It went from free-range to battery farmed. I'd never wanted it. And I thought he felt the same. Then his parents divorced, and his mum died, and now we're trapped in this flat, ricocheting from sofa to bed to kitchen, bickering and smashing bits off each other.'

'But none of that would be any different if you'd known Mum and Dad had got married, would it?' said Ava. 'You loved him then, you love him now, but you just don't love being married.' She blew on her tea again. 'Maybe divorce is the right thing to do.'

'It definitely looks that way. It's just so. . . miserable. I miss him so much. And I can't understand how everything that was so good – so *great* – got so broken. We were never like this before we got married. We disagreed, but this? It's. . . *ridiculous*.'

There was a thump in the bedroom, and we all leapt from our seats.

'What the HELL was that?' hissed Esther.

The door opened slowly and a sleepy Jack stepped out.

I stared at him. 'I thought you were out!'

'I got back really late.'

'But I've been into the bedroom this morning. There was just balled-up duvet at one end. You weren't in there!'

Jack ruffled his hair. 'I think I had a few too many last night. I think I climbed inside the duvet and fell asleep in it at the pillow end. Hey, everyone.'

My sisters gave him a shocked wave, all of us looking at each other. It had been a long time since they'd seen Jack.

He rubbed his beard, looked around the table and said, 'Sorry, I've only just woken up – my head's not in one piece yet. Does anyone want more coffee?'

The three of us must have been quieter than he'd ever

seen us before. My sisters left minutes later, Esther mouthing 'OMFG', Ava giving me hugs and telling me to call whenever.

Jack and I had been ignoring each other since our big argument, but his surprise appearance had kicked me completely off balance. Back in the kitchen, I said to Jack, as innocently as I could, 'How come you were so tired? It's not like you to sleep through me stomping through the bedroom.'

With his back to me, in the same anodyne tone we used for most conversation now, he said, 'Just a lot on at work. A few late nights. Didn't realise, you know, how tired you can get and not even notice. I think I fell asleep trying to read the paper at some point – check it out.' He turned and lifted his chin; along one side of his jaw was a huge smudge of black, and half a headline about Scotland. I smiled at him with genuine warmth and offered him some of the sourdough loaf.

'Esther's been baking? What emergency caused that, and the council meeting I interrupted?'

I told him about Mum and Dad.

'Seriously? Jesus.' He chuckled. 'We've clearly done it the wrong way round. Should've taken some tips from the experts. And why do our parents keep sneaking off for their weddings?'

I laughed a little. 'I know. I said the same when Dad told us. He didn't even want to tell us, you know. Could have been *years* before we found out.'

Jack was laughing too. 'People are crackers, aren't they? All of us. Just. . .' He paused and looked right at me. '*ridiculous.*'

Suddenly, neither of us was even smiling. I could feel my pulse pounding in my throat. I put my hand on the worktop, next to him. He turned to look at me, straight on.

286

Then his phone rang. Both of us jumped – too much excitement for a Saturday morning, I thought – but he saw who was calling, lifted it with an apologetic look at me, then took it into the bedroom, shutting the door again.

He came out ten minutes later, with a half-guilty, half-relieved expression on his face. 'It was Gillett.'

'Must be serious to be calling at the weekend.'

'They want to open another branch.' He looked at me.

'In London?'

'No. In New York.'

'Wow. That's amazing.'

'They want me to run it, Zo. And be a manager to the other store managers. It's a big step up.'

'Is that how it works? They just call you up and offer you a job in New York on a Saturday morning, out of the blue?'

'No. I've been interviewing for months. I had to write up a whole business plan, talk to the US staff. That's why I went there in May.'

'Oh.'

'I didn't know when the right time to talk to you about any of this stuff was. I didn't know how solid it all was, whether it would even happen. And, well, it's nearly the end of the year. I thought maybe you wouldn't care what I'd be doing.'

'Jack!'

'I can't make any claims on you anymore, can I? We're just ticking off the days until we can legally be free of each other, right? I mean. . . You know what I mean, Zo. That's where we are now, isn't it?'

I didn't say anything.

'Zoe? Isn't it?'

Eventually I nodded, grabbed my bag, and headed out.

* * *

287

I collected the orders and brought them back to our table, where Liz was sitting, looking fantastic. Even at 7 p.m., she was still wearing yesterday's make-up and a ratty old cardigan, not a hint of Henry's trophy wife about her anymore.

'Jesus, it's still so good to see you back again.' I slid her burger over, tipped the chips in between our two paper dishes, and covered them in salt and vinegar.

'Thanks very much.'

'Seriously, you're looking radiant.'

'I licked my finger and ran it under each eye this morning, just to get off the old mascara.'

'Must be that.' We each took a bite of our burgers, then swapped, to try each other's. 'Really though, you do look well.'

'It's contentment, that is. Being on my own. See? The theory works.' We swapped back. 'How's your stuff going? Still got to share a flat with Jack?'

'Not for much longer.' I took another bite. 'Hmmm mffoffan mo mmm mooor.'

'Nope. No idea what you said.'

I took a drink of beer. 'He's moving to New York.'

'Dear god, it never stops with you two, does it?'

'With work. They want him to man the new Manhattan store out there, and start overseeing management of some other branches. Alright for some, eh?'

'And you're. . .'

'Fine. It's fine. Better he moves out there than we're constantly tripping over each other round here. You know what London's like – you're always bumping into your exes when you've just nipped to Boots for a box of tampons.'

'Ok. I like this positive thinking.'

I took another mouthful of chips. 'I don't have to think positive. It's just the way it is. Anyway, with the teaching exchange all approved, I'll be off in the new year to who knows where. I won't have to worry about bumping into Jack at all from then on.'

Liz wouldn't come out for more drinks – she was heading off to a house party, she said, just to show her face to some old friends – so I headed home, where Jack had fallen asleep on the sofa. I didn't wake him, but just stood at the door and tried to imagine all of his stuff gone – life with him gone.

THIRTY-THREE

Heading into the Science office, I could hear the school choir getting stuck into their rehearsals for the Christmas concert next month, filling the corridor with festive joy I was in no way ready for.

'Zoe, darling, could I have a quick word?' Benni swung around the edge of her office doorway before disappearing back inside.

I followed her in, and watched her sit down behind her desk, with a folder in front of her bearing the logo of the teaching exchange programme.

'Well?' she said. 'Shall we open it?'

'Wait. Do you know what's inside?'

She shook her head. 'No. They don't email, just send this package over for you and me to go through and sign. I'll discover who I'm getting too, let's remember.'

We both leapt for the folder and tore it open, looking for the appropriate sections.

'Oh my god,' I gasped. 'Berlin!'

'Oh, darling, that's fantastic! Hasn't living there always been on your wish list?'

With Jack, I thought. *At least I didn't get New York.* I didn't know whether to laugh or cry.

I took a deep breath. 'This is amazing. Thanks, Benni.'

'You're welcome, Zoe. You deserve this. You better come back when your time's up though, or I will hunt you down and drag you screaming to afternoon detention.'

I grinned at her, and tried to imagine my life in two years' time. 'Well? Who did you get to cover me?'

Benni opened her folder, revealing a photograph of an elderly man with white fluffy hair and a thin grimace. 'Oh well,' she sighed. 'At least my wife has nothing to worry about.'

It was three days before Jack and I were home and awake at the same time.

'It's crazy, trying to get everything ready for New York in time for January. A month might be long enough to get myself ready, but I'm not sure about the store over there. I'm starting to worry that the clichés are true – Manhattan never sleeps.' He looked grey with fatigue.

'Are you still looking forward to it?'

He thought for a moment, then closed his mouth with a snap. 'Yeah. I'm sure it'll be fine, once I'm out there.'

I took out the details of my new school, lifted it up and vaguely waved it. 'Looks like it's the season for new jobs abroad.'

'Really? Where? Not New York!'

I looked at him for a second, wondering if he was feeling the same pull-push of emotions I'd had at that thought. 'No. . . Berlin.'

Jack whooped. 'No way! Zo, that's amazing! When do you start?' His delight at my news felt great; I remembered why he was always the first person I wanted to tell about anything. I told him about the paperwork I'd filled in back in October for a start in the new year, how I could have been placed at any international school in the world, how it felt like a great piece of luck to have been given the one place I'd most like to go.

He went in for a hug, but checked himself – we ended up in a clumsy high five, yeah, cool, high five. Of course: we didn't hug anymore. This was just sharing some good news with the person you most wanted to tell, with the person you wouldn't see again after a month or so. But no hugging.

'So we're both off,' I said. 'Both out of the country.'

'Yeah, I guess so.' He looked around the flat. 'Two continents. Wow. That really is divorcing, isn't it? I guess we'll need to get this place sorted, then. One way or another.' He rubbed his head, looking blank, distant, and said he really needed to get some sleep – the investors in Asia wanted a 5 a.m. call with him.

I made myself a cup of tea, and for the first time ever, feeling in an experimental mood, opened the bin straight away and put the teabag inside. Whoah. Jack was right. That really did take no time.

Pity he wouldn't be around for long enough to notice the difference.

THIRTY-FOUR

Liz had asked if I was free for a quick drink after work. At the bar, I saw her chatting to a familiar face.

'Well, hello, stranger.'

Adam, he of the house slippers and also, it seemed, Liz's heart, gave me a huge hug, then held me at arm's length to grin and say, 'Hello back at you.'

'It is really, incredibly nice to see you.'

Liz was beaming, shooting actual rays of happiness from each and every pore of her skin as she held his hand under the table. She could hardly stop smiling the whole evening. We sat at a booth and talked about our Christmas plans – even with Berlin only weeks away, mine felt flat and grey, so I encouraged them to talk about the cottage they were renting with Liz's mum for the Christmas week.

'And of course,' she said, looking serious, 'I've asked Adam to bring his slippers.'

He shrugged. 'Over time, she'll learn their importance. It's an understanding that comes only with many years' wisdom.' They both laughed, and I thought, *Yeah. Liz's theory really does work.*

When Adam was at the bar, Liz told me what had

happened: they'd both ended up at the same mutual friend's house party – the one she'd been heading to when I'd seen her for our burger date. She knew before they'd even spoken that she still had feelings for him, but decided to try and avoid him in case he didn't feel the same. She'd been hiding up in a bedroom for half an hour before she heard a noise at the bedroom door, and opened it to find a pair of slippers with a note inside, reading, 'It's cold out there. You might need these.' Adam was waiting around the corner, and they hadn't even spoken, just fallen into each other's arms (although Liz may have used slightly less romantic language). Since then, they'd been almost constantly together, and Liz confirmed that her theory had definitely worked – she had never, in any prior relationship, appreciated just how good it was to be with someone nice. And compared to Henry's sunglasses (I asked if he ever took them off, but Liz only looked at me with wide eyes; I said, Even in bed?, and Liz merely opened her eyes wider), Adam's slippers were comforting and acceptable – lovable, even.

'And,' Liz went on, 'I've remembered that the slipper thing wasn't even his worst habit! But Henry taught me that not only are Adam's habits pretty harmless, but that I'm hardly perfect either. I'm not!' she said, seeing my laughing, shocked expression. 'But I feel like my imperfections and Adam's imperfections fit together. For now.' She laughed as she watched Adam push his way through the crowds towards us. 'I'm really happy, Zo. I can't guarantee where this is going to go. But at least I can give it a fair run.'

On the way home that night, I had my first text from Kat since our encounter with Chuck at the bar. *Can you get the first three lessons off tomorrow? Emergency. Come to Chuck's office at 8.30. Ask for Damian xxx*

When I texted back to ask a handful of my million questions, I got no reply.

I only had one lesson before lunchtime, and when I explained that Kat had an emergency, Benni told me George could cover my lesson. She sent another message shortly after: *If you try to pull this kind of stunt again I'll have you transferred abroad o_o*

I then had two messages from Esther and Ava, who had apparently both received Kat's text too. *See you there?* I sent back.

The next morning, the three of us met up outside Kat's former offices, and I could see we were all remembering our last visit here together. But inside, at reception, there was no Miranda. A tall, curly-haired woman greeted us with a distracted air, although when I said we were here to see Damian, she gave us a small, private smile as she talked quietly into the phone.

A dark-skinned young man came through the frosted glass doors and held them open for us, smiling. He followed us through, then gestured for us to follow him down a corridor; he stopped at a large wooden door, which opened to reveal a huge meeting room, with chairs lined up in front of a TV screen that was showing the news on mute, and a table covered with breakfast food, coffee pots and tea urns.

'Help yourselves,' he said in a soft voice. 'It's just you guys in here, so make yourselves at home. And I'm to tell you to keep an eye on the TV.' He winked at us, then shut the door gently.

'What the *hell* is going on?' said Esther, piling almond croissants onto her plate.

Ava looked confused too, but poured herself a cup of tea and nibbled at a fruit bowl. I was too nervous to eat, and kept looking from the TV to Es and Ava. After a quarter of an hour, the TV popped and crackled: the channel was changing to a live link from another room, the volume being turned up by someone. It was a meeting room similar to this one, but with chairs arranged around a large table, instead of facing a TV screen. People were filling the seats, each of which had a glossy print-out in front of it on the table. Once almost all the chairs had been occupied with confident-looking suits, and the space behind by nervous-looking lesser staff, Chuck strode in with a headphone mic on. He greeted a few of the suits by name, glad-handing as he went around the table, then stopped near the white screen that had been set up at the end of the table and put his hands together.

'Namaste, everyone.' He bowed from the waist. 'Thank you all for coming today. It's a real honour to have a visit from KSTW, the largest digital agency in the US. It's so great that you guys could come and see our humble little office in real life.' Some of the staff behind the suits, Kat's former colleagues, started giving each other nervous glances.

'Ok, so. . .' Chuck clapped his hands together. 'What we're doing here today, is showing KSTW just how great a little agency we are, and how much we could offer them if they decided to take us under their umbrella. First of all – savings.' He chortled. 'We all know that any business wants to know they're getting a bargain, and I can reassure KSTW that they will be – there are plenty of savings to be made here when you consider scale costs, plenty of overlapping roles that can simply be cancelled out into financial savings for any buyer of our agency.' Kat's old colleagues were giving each other slightly more nervous looks; between some of them, glances were escalating into outright hostility as they realised Chuck was planning to get rid of most of his staff for a sale that would doubtless only benefit him. Those feelings seemed to grow as Chuck launched into his presentation: countless inspirational images – sunlit woodlands, wild waves, Muhammad Ali, Gandhi, people cresting mountains – and phrases on each one like 'visionary global influencers' and 'leveraging collective reach' and 'strategic networking partnerships' and 'sustained storyscaping synergy'. By the time his final slide came up, with an image of lightning splitting an oak tree and the phrase 'integral collaboration with dynamic disruption' written across it, the suits were smiling tightly at each other.

'Any questions?' Chuck said, adjusting his gait to stand even wider by the side of the screen.

'Yes,' said one of the women at the table, tapping her glossy print-outs into a square. 'I just wanted a few more details on your. . .' She paused, looked down at the print-outs. '. . ."impactful platforming"?'

Chuck hesitated. 'I think, to be fair, everything I need to say is in your documents there. I mean – if you want breakthroughs in your social conversations, I'm your man!' He stood back and rocked on his heels.

The woman looked almost pleased. 'And can you talk us through any of your figures for future projections? Any of the partners you've got lined up?'

Chuck rocked back on his heels again. 'I can show you – but I think it's better for our relationship if we all know what page we're on creatively, before we worry about the nuts and bolts of the whole thing. Right?' He smiled at them, his charm turned up to eleven. 'It's the vision that's going to make this relationship work, isn't it? Any chump with a calculator can tell you the numbers and show you a few spreadsheets.'

He looked around the meeting room.

'Ok? Great! Thanks again for coming in. Guys, can we give our visitors from KSTW a big hand for welcoming us into their family?' The staff around the edge of the room looked shell-shocked, and only one gave a slow clap.

The woman at the table murmured to her colleague beside her, then said, 'Sorry, Chuck, we've just got one more person to hear from.'

Chuck blinked, his face frozen with confusion, but when the door opened and Kat walked in, followed by Damian carrying another pile of glossy print-outs, his face began melting into something between nausea and fury.

'I'm so sorry,' he said through gritted teeth. 'There seems to be some kind of confusion. Ms Lewis is actually a former agency employee. I'll just call security to remove her and we can carry on.'

'Actually,' said the woman at the table, smiling, 'I've asked Ms Lewis to talk to us today. I think you might find her presentation. . . enlightening.'

Kat stood at the front of the meeting room, her beautiful braided mohawk adding to her height and giving her an air of calm authority.

'Thanks very much,' she smiled. 'Thanks, Damian,' she added, as he worked his way around the table, handing out documents. Kat pointed her controller at the projector, and clicked open a new slide: 'KSTW: Where we can take you'. Her presentation had fewer slides than Chuck's, but each one contained a simple idea: a business area to target with suggested companies and ways to improve their marketing; a new way of using social media with mocked-up samples; using her agency's British identity as a way to expand both further into the UK and into South American markets, with suggested companies to aim for. Each slide was followed by rough figures, comparing current and potential profits and consumers.

I felt a nudge from Esther, who was almost bouncing in her seat. 'Look at Chuck!' she whispered, and when I did I almost felt sorry for him. His face was purple, the same shade I remembered from the bar the other night with Kat; and his leg was jiggling angrily as he leant against the wall with poorly feigned apathy.

When Kat finished, both the KSTW employees and the

agency staff applauded. Chuck stepped forward, knocking a chair over in fury. 'Sorry, have I lost my mind? An ex-employee of mine comes in here, steals my ideas, and what, gets a big pat on the back for it? I'm calling security, and I'm going to get some kind of semblance of reality back into this meeting.' He reached for the intercom.

Damian went to hold him back, but Kat looked at a colleague standing at the edge of the room, who simply shook her head, and Damian sat down again.

'Reception?' said Chuck. 'Can I get security in meeting room two? Now? There's someone who needs escorting out.' He released the button and leant back against the wall, relaxing into his triumph.

The woman who had shaken her head at Kat raised her hand.

'What?' said Chuck, irritated again.

'Hi. Belinda? Head of HR.' Chuck shrugged at her. 'It's just. . . when you say *ex-employee*, I can't actually find any of the paperwork about her termination.'

'Fine, fine,' Chuck hissed. 'We'll sort this out later. It's *really* not the time.'

Belinda went on. 'Only – it seems this is quite a clear case of wrongful dismissal. And Ms Lewis has quite a good case against you for this.'

'Against me?' Chuck laughed. 'Against the agency, I think you'll find. This is your job, isn't it? You can sort this out.'

'Yes, it is my job. And I've been talking with the other people who do my job at KSTW, and it seems that if this buyout is going to happen, those people who do my job there. . . well, they want Ms Lewis *here*.'

Chuck's face began re-purpling. I was starting to wonder if I would ever grow tired of seeing that colour change.

'And,' Belinda continued, 'well, they don't want *you*.'

Gristle and co. burst in through the huge door.

Belinda pointed to Chuck. 'Please, Simon, if you would? Mr Johnson was just leaving.' Gristle looked surprised, but the other two looked at each other and gave small smiles. They stepped up to Chuck and took an arm each. Gristle held the door open as they started walking him out.

Chuck looked at Kat over his shoulder. 'I don't know how you've convinced everyone, but you're a liar, and you won't get away with this! You WON'T GET AWAY WITH IT!'

'Alright, Scooby-Doo,' I heard Kat say, which made many of her colleagues chuckle. The meeting room stayed silent to listen to Chuck's shouts and curses as he was carried out of the building; there was a beat of complete silence, and then everyone started clapping again, with shock and relief and embarrassment stirring even the KSTW suits to clap along. Eventually, the clapping subsided and people started drifting out of the room, chattering and still laughing. The suits began packing themselves up and the woman at the table walked to the front of the room, talked quietly to Kat, shook her hand, then gave her a hug. Kat smiled at her, watched everyone file out of the room, then turned towards the camera and gave us a huge thumbs up.

We heard her footsteps before we saw her – our own door flew open, and there she was, beaming and jumping up and down.

'Oh my god, we did it, we did it, we did it!' she was singing.

'What just happened? What did you do?' Esther was calling, but Ava was squeezing me from behind and rocking me back and forth.

After more singing and calling and rocking and hugging, Kat got us all to sit down again. 'I knew all along that he was a bastard, Zo. I'm sorry I didn't say anything. But I suspected for ages that he was up to more than simply trying to put his—'

300

'Yes, thank you,' said Esther. 'We all know where he was trying to put *his*. Carry on.'

'Exactly. But I didn't know precisely where his scumminess would end. He was so gross, and I couldn't work out how to get rid of him. It was really pissing me off for a long time: he'd schedule lots of evening meetings with me, one-to-one discussions that revealed quite how useless he was at his job. Christ knows how he got it. Then, a couple of months ago, he called me into his office for some "consultation", and he left his screen open on his email while he went to pour us some prosecco to "inspire us".'

'Ewww,' we said, simultaneously.

'I *know*. So on his screen was this whole email exchange with KSTW about them possibly buying us, and he was saying he could offer all these redundancies and this great package in exchange for a huge bonus and stock options for him.'

'Classic sleazeball,' Ava said.

'Right? But what he didn't realise was that a) almost everyone here, besides him, is good at their job and is an integral part of the business, and b) I now had the contact details of the KSTW partner who was in discussion about the whole thing. So. I made my own proposal instead.'

'Kat!' I gasped.

'Brilliant, yeah? And we had a lot of back and forth emailing, our KSTW partner and me and a few other staff here, and we decided that we'd let Chuck make his presentation before I made mine. I had to keep him sweet, not let him know we knew anything. That night at the bar, half the team were here pulling all the info we'd need for our presentation off the systems. I was terrified that Chuck would go back to the office and catch them at it. That's the only reason I was out with him. As if I would touch him with a ten-foot pole!'

We sat, agape, as we began to understand quite how brilliant our youngest sister was. 'You really can take care of yourself,' I said. Kat smiled cockily. 'But why couldn't you tell us? Why the hell would you let us worry, and let me think that he was going to hurt you like he'd hurt me?'

Kat stopped smiling. 'I'm sorry, sis. I'm really sorry for that. But I realised pretty much straight away that he wasn't Liz's ex – I do know you, remember – and I knew that if any of you knew what I was up to, and what was going to happen to him, there's no way – no offence, Zo – but there's no way you wouldn't give that away when you saw him. And your slightly nuts but touchingly overprotective behaviour was the perfect distraction; he would never guess I was up to something if my sisters were so worried that *he* was going to hurt *me*.' She laughed at an idea that seemed, to her, beyond absurd. 'I'm sorry, Zo. I'm sorry if I added to the stress of Jack and your moving and. . . I meant it when I said you could trust me. That I would be ok.'

'I know.'

'And you will be too, sis. Wherever you go in the world, you're going to be great. And wherever you are, I – we – will always be looking out for you. We'd never let you get hurt like that again. Ok?' She patted me on the head, filled our bags up with croissants and Danish pastries, then began herding us back outside to reception. 'Right. Haven't we all got jobs to go to?'

'Yes, boss,' Esther said, standing up on her tiptoes to kiss Kat.

I shook my head and marvelled.

Sheer sugar rush must have carried me to school, and I had absolutely no memory of the lessons I taught that afternoon. All I could think of was Kat's gift to me.

THIRTY-FIVE

With Christmas looming, it was beginning to feel like the season of joy was sponsored by Dignitas this year. It seemed ridiculous to get a tree when I was the only one who cared about it in the flat, but I couldn't bear the thought of three and a half more weeks in the Saddest Home In The World, bereft of decoration or Christmas furnishings. Jack was never a fan of the season – although in his defence, I didn't have to listen to looped Christmas songs every hour of my working day for six weeks before the day itself – but I'd convinced him over the years to add at least a wreath. In the end, I picked a three-foot-tall tree; I could put it on the table, by the window, and it wouldn't be in anyone's (Jack's) way. It was even just about possible to get on the bus with it.

Upstairs Jan caught up with me in the street and offered to help me inside with it: it had taken me thirty sweaty minutes and a tangled fumble in the doorway of Homebase – the only Christmas action I'd be getting this year – to get it this far already. In the shared hallway, I lowered the tree to the floor to adjust my grip, and noticed that our front door wasn't quite closed. I could hear voices from inside – Jack and Iffy.

303

'It's not leaving London. It's those guys, the people in the US offices. They work in such a different way to me, and the culture there is so different too. It's as if their sole aim is to be able to retire at forty, once they've pushed away all friends and family. Seriously, anyone who's married there just remarries once they've made their money, rebooting with a younger partner who can give them the kids they never had time for before. It's bloody grim.'

'So what's the alternative, you'll stay here forever?'

'That's not the worst thing in the world. People do seem to quite like London, you know. It has stuff going for it.'

'There's a mini Waitrose just round the corner.'

'Exactly. You wouldn't get that in New York.'

'It'd be all "pizza slices" and "cheesecake".'

'*Exactly*. But. . . they're offering me a great deal. I wanted to expand the shop. I wanted to take it to new places . . . If you'd told me ten years ago that I'd be in this situation, with a company offering me this money and this opportunity, I'd never have believed you, but now I've got this offer to work in New York. . . Iffy, this is amazing.'

'I know, man. And I also know the mini Waitrose isn't the *only* thing you'll miss about London.'

There was a heavy sigh. 'What am I supposed to do? Wait around here in case she changes her mind? She won't change her mind. I know her. I think. I mostly know her. I used to know her.'

'I don't think the alternative to waiting for your ex-wife to change her mind is "move to New York".'

'She's not my ex-wife.'

'Yet.'

I heard Jack sigh. 'Normally, no. But in this case it is the alternative. Would I necessarily choose this otherwise? Collaborating with people I don't want to work with? In a professional culture that's alien to everything I believe in?'

'Ok, ok, you've convinced me, this sounds amazing for you.'

Jack laughed. 'It's not amazing. But I think it's best for me. It'll take my mind off things. And in a few years, who knows? Maybe I'll move back and focus on the original shop. Maybe I'll even be able to open one in Europe.'

'Which is what you actually want to do?'

There was a silence. 'But this is the offer on the table right now, Iffy. If there's one thing this last year has taught me, you can't always get what you want.'

'Mick Jagger taught me that ages ago.'

'What?'

There was a moment's silence. 'Jack, please tell me you're joking. You do know that's a Rolling Stones song, don't you?'

'No. I don't really like the Stones. Oh yeah, and also, I'm not in my mid-fifties.'

Another silence, in which I could picture Iffy struggling for words. 'You don't need to like the Rolling Stones to know one of the most famous songs in pop culture.'

'Clearly I do.'

'Oh my Jesus Christ.'

Laughter floated through the open door, followed by the sound of Iffy throwing something at Jack and Jack throwing it back. In their noise and bustle I jumped when Upstairs Jan coughed softly behind me in the hallway, still half carrying the Christmas tree.

'Can I go now?'

I whispered my thanks to her, balanced the tree against the front door, then stepped outside so I could come noisily back in and Jack wouldn't know I'd heard anything.

I'd never thought that I was forcing him to leave. I thought he'd wanted to go. So now I was not only forcing him from his marriage and his house, but from his country too. Awesome. I couldn't wait to collect my humanitarian award.

I banged open the main door, then scraped the tree through our front door to announce my presence. But when I turned around, I saw that the flat was swathed with baubles and fairy lights, the windows were frosted with foamed snowflakes, and the mantelpiece had a huge evergreen display. Over it all sprouted an eight-foot tree, onto which Jack was hanging striped candy canes.

'Have I bumped my head somewhere?' I asked Iffy.

He laughed and disappeared into the kitchen, muttering loudly, 'Hi, Iffy. How are you? I'm great, thanks, Zoe, it's really good to see you too.'

'Sorry. Hi. Hello, Iffy!' I called. 'Jack, what is this? I thought you hated these Christmas festivities.'

He rubbed his head. 'I do. Well, not hate. I was just thinking how much effort you always used to put into Christmas—'

'I'm still alive, Jack.'

'Yes, the effort you always still put into Christmas. And I've never really appreciated it. And. . . I don't know when I'm going to get a British Christmas again, all puddings and shabby tinsel and choristers on Radio 4.' He gave a small gesture – half shrug, half displaying his hard work. 'So I thought I'd do this.'

'Is that. . . is that Bing Crosby playing right now?'

'In for a penny, I always say.'

'And are those mince pies I can smell?'

'Yup.'

'And you're sure I haven't had a head injury? I'm not actually freezing to death in a snow bank somewhere right now, and this is a hallucination in my final moments?' He gave a bigger shrug. 'Oh well. There are worse ways to go, I guess.'

Iffy brought out three steaming mugs of mulled wine a

306

moment later, and we stayed up until midnight drinking and rating various M&S Christmas snacks. I understood what Jack might miss when he moved to New York.

A few nights later I was blu-tacking the 400th snowflake onto Esther's windows when she appeared behind me, reflected in the glass, carrying a cardboard box with a bow on top. She'd invited me over after school for the annual test of her own mince pies, an offer I was never going to turn down. William was with his dad in the kitchen, doing some taste testing of his own from the sounds of it.

'Are you in the mood for an early Christmas present?' she asked.

I leapt down from the chair and held out my hands, then drew them back, hesitant. 'Wait. Is it just another Christmas-themed task to do somewhere around your house? I've fallen for that once already.'

She laughed and handed the gift-wrapped box over. 'This is from Kat and Ava too.'

Inside the box was a mass of white tissue paper that reminded me of the evening before the wedding. And beneath it all. . .

'What? How. . .'

Nestled in soft paper, chain gleaming, leather unmarked, undamaged, perfect: my bag.

'The three of us all chipped in to have it cleaned up and repaired. That's your main Christmas present though, so you might just get some socks or something from us on the big day. I just got it back today. And you get it now, because we all agreed you'd want it over Christmas. Don't forget to send a photo of your happy face to our sisters – they wanted to see your face too.'

'Es! This is amazing!' I hugged it to me, feeling the butter-soft leather against my face again, smelling its beautiful old smell.

'Some things are too good to throw away, you know. You have to do everything you can to fix them, if they were that good to begin with. If they matter that much to you.'

I gave her a hug.

'Thank you.'

She looked at me. 'You're alright, little sis. It's going to be ok, you know.'

I looked back at her and she gave me a wink before leaving the room. She was right, though – maybe good things did deserve looking after.

'Well, this looks festive!' the estate agent chortled as he came in, leather folder in hand.

I'd booked the estate agent after Benni had asked what was happening with the flat when Jack and I both went abroad. I'd pulled a face and started slowly shrugging, and Benni had squealed and said, 'Darling! You must get this sorted out now,' and then added gently, 'It's better if you start getting all this stuff between you organised, Zoe.'

Jack sat on the sofa while I showed Ian around: kitchen, bathroom, bedroom, lounge. Windows, doors, wifi, storage. It was impossible not to feel like the notes Ian was making were about us, as he went around the flat valuing what our home was worth. Awkward silence, terrible body language, sleeping in separate beds; tick, tick, tick. I took deep breaths as I watched him boiling down more than three years of living here into abbreviations and shorthand, ready for someone to take our place, to maybe do better here than we'd done.

'Of course, with both of you leaving the country so soon, it may be easier for you to let it for a while, create some income there, and you can always sell at a later date when the market. . . suits you.'

Our home, reduced to a monthly percentage for Ian. And

when the market suits you was clearly shorthand for *when the first of you finds someone else to shack up with*. I pictured Jack, picking up the phone to let me know he'd met someone new and needed the money from the old flat. Our final tie would be cut.

Ian wrote down our valuation figures, told us to drop off the keys whenever we liked and he would get the photos done and begin viewings immediately. He gave us one more look – Jack, slumped on the sofa; me, folded up in the armchair in the corner – and waved at us. 'Ok, folks, thanks very much. Give us a call when you're ready, ok? Happy Christmas.' He let himself out. I looked around at the lights and baubles and wondered when I'd ever be ready to make that call.

Jack lifted his feet onto the coffee table. 'I suppose that was as painless as it could be. Do you want to give him a call tomorrow?'

'Not particularly.'

'We'll both need to sign the contract.' He nudged the pile of paperwork Ian had left, and I thought of the other paperwork ahead of us, a decree nisi and a decree absolute, all the bonds between us being signed away.

I shrugged. 'I'll do it now, if you like. Best to just get on with it, I guess.' I'd be in Berlin in a month. I didn't need to worry about this flat. 'When can a tenant move in?'

Jack rubbed his beard with his hands. 'Gillett have given me a ticket for New Year's Eve. So I guess it just depends on when you're off.'

'I can stay at Mum and Dad's whenever. We might as well get someone in here sooner rather than later.'

He nodded. 'Makes sense.'

I called Ian and told him I'd drop off the keys and the forms that afternoon. I wasn't ready, but it had to be done.

*   *   *

It was already five minutes after I should have left to meet Benni, Gina and the twins, but I couldn't find my favourite top anywhere. I thought it was in the laundry and I could give it a quick steam in the bathroom, but I couldn't find it there, in the wardrobe, or in my drawers.

Jack looked up from his laptop. 'What's up?'

'Nothing – I just can't find my top. The blue one with the gold bits? I feel like I'm going mad.'

'Sorry, Zo, that's my fault – it's on the drying rack, on the hanger. I just did a load yesterday. It'll be dry by now.'

In the corner, on the rack, was yesterday's clean laundry; only I hadn't thought to check there because it wasn't my load of laundry. I stared at it.

'Is it ok? Oh Christ, did I wreck it?'

I slipped the t-shirt on over my vest top. 'No, that's great. Thanks. See you later!' I grabbed my coat and bag without looking at Jack again, and was out the door before either of us had a chance to say anything else.

A week before Christmas, I finally plucked up the courage to ask Jack what he was doing for the festive period. I hadn't wanted to give him the impression that he owed me that information, or to remind him of Christmases past, with my family.

'Oh, I don't know. I hadn't really thought about it.' I suppressed a squeak of dismay. 'I guess I'll probably go up to Dad's. He's having Christine's relatives over, but she reckons she can squeeze me in if needs be.' It was so exactly like Jack's dad and Christine that I couldn't even tease Jack about how terribly Tiny Tim he sounded. 'You?'

'Mum and Dad's. I think we're all going to be there this year.' *Almost all*, I thought. *You won't be.* 'Esther's convinced Mum to let her do the Christmas trifle. I reckon Mum will probably have a spare hidden, just in case.'

'Your dad does love your mum's trifle.'

'And no one wants to ruin Christmas for him, do they?' We were nearly laughing. 'So.'

'Yup. So I'll probably head off last thing on Christmas Eve. You?'

'Afternoon, I reckon. Mum'll want us to do the carol singing thing, although William's nearly old enough to take over from our caterwauling. Give him a year or so and it'll be tear-jerking renditions of "Away in a Manger" for everyone. And we'll be off the hook, thank god.'

'I don't know, I always thought you four enjoyed the carol singing. You all complained about it, but you sounded pretty good.'

We did complain, but of course we loved it. The four of us, singing together in harmony, bickering happily – of course we loved it. I'd forgotten that Jack would know that.

'Yeah. It's alright.'

'Well – I guess we'll see each other before then?' I laughed, and Jack smiled. We said goodnight and headed to bed, twelve feet away from each other, either side of our thin bedroom wall.

At the school's Saturday night staff Christmas party in the upstairs room of the Queen's Head, Miks had ended up on the decks, and was scratching away at The Waitresses' 'Christmas Wrapping'. *Merry Christmas, Merry Christmas, but I think I'll miss this one this year*, played over and over until Benni went up and took his headphones away from him. Maybe I will skip this one, I thought. Maybe I'll head to Berlin early, and sit in my new apartment eating bratwurst all on my own.

'You look like you're feeling sorry for yourself,' shouted Kat at my elbow, over the music. 'We've got a lot to celebrate, remember? We got Chuck-fired! You're moving to glamorous Europe!'

311

'I think I'm allowed to feel a little bit sorry for myself,' I shouted back. Given my mood, I decided it was best not to dwell on the sight of several couples slow dancing to Eartha Kitt on the dancefloor and Benni smooching her wife under the mistletoe. Added to which, I had my younger sister as my plus one. Liz had her work party tonight with Adam and I felt too pathetic to rope in anyone else. Besides, Kat was usually great fun at these events. But tonight, surrounded by romance and Christmas and songs about couples by the fireplace, and couples in the snow, and couples returning from war to be with one another, I just couldn't hack it. I wanted to be at home with a fleece-lined blanket and a cup of hot chocolate that was ten per cent marshmallows, ninety per cent Kahlúa.

'I know that face,' Kat shouted. 'It's your blanket-time face.'

'What are you talking about?' I shouted back.

'It's when you're having emotional feelings about your blanket and your sofa and your TV. I know you. I might be younger than you but I have sharper eyes.'

I rolled my eyes at her. 'Whatever.'

'Don't you whatever me, old lady. I'm here to give you a good time, and a good time is what we're going to have. Your year has sucked, sis, but let's not have Christmas go the same way, yeah? Don't forget: *I'm the boss now.*'

I tried to smile at her. 'I appreciate what you're saying,' I yelled over the music, 'but you don't have to face the jolly, goodwill prospect of' – the music stopped, leaving dead silence in the air just in time for me to continue bellowing – 'dying alone.' The whole room turned to look at me in horror. I looked at Kat. 'Oh good, Father Christmas did get my letter after all.'

Kat turned to a frozen waiter beside us and picked up two more drinks from his tray. 'Look. Christmas party. Like this?' she said, and knocked one of them back in a single gulp.

Who was I to refuse?

I was still home before midnight – at which time I was worried that I'd fully transform into a mince pie – and was surprised to find Jack still up, on the sofa, still in his coat and shoes.

'Hey.'

'Hello. How come you're up?'

He leant back against the sofa. 'It was Henderson's Christmas party tonight.'

'Snap. Ours ran out of canapés, though, so I thought I might as well come home.'

'Our Christmas tree caught fire.'

'No!'

'No. But I sort of wish it had.' He kicked off his shoes. 'It was pretty rubbish. Half the team are pissed off that I get to go to New York, the other half are angling for my job and trying to butter up the investors.' He looked almost pleased when he added, 'And Jessica doesn't talk to me anymore, which makes working together difficult to say the least.'

I tried not to feel happy about the last part. 'I'm sorry it was so bad.'

Jack rubbed his beard. 'It wasn't a disaster. I just realised I'd rather be here than there. And everyone was already so drunk they didn't notice me sneaking out. It was strangely liberating.'

I took off my coat and shoes and dumped my keys on the table. 'I know what you mean. It's nice to be home. At the end of a night out, I mean.'

'Mmm,' Jack agreed, his eyes closing. I sat down beside him on the sofa. He opened his eyes and took my hand. 'It is nice to be home.'

313

I stopped breathing – holding his hand felt just like coming home. Just as I was about to relax into it, Jack said, 'Nope, no, not helping,' stood up, walked into our bedroom and shut the door. 'Good night,' he called through the wall.

He's right, I thought, that wasn't helping at all.

'Right then.'

'Right. Happy Christmas for tomorrow. Say hi to your family from me.'

'Yeah. You too. Happy Christmas.'

I had my bags packed – a small bag for my stuff, and eight other bags full of gifts for my parents, sisters, and various children and tagalongs. Jack would pack later, then head up to his dad's place.

Jack bobbed his head at me as I made my way out the door, bags tugging me back and catching on everything. Eventually I got out, made it to the bus stop and crammed my way onto a bus. I thought I'd feel better about Christmas with my family – the food, the fun, the games, the company – but I felt flat. I felt sad for Jack, spending it with his distant dad and his pernickety stepmum, and I felt sad for our flat, so beautifully decorated and with no one to enjoy it on that day of all days. I tried to shrug it off, and by the time I got to the stop nearest my parents' house, at least it felt like my guts were no longer in my throat. This would be lovely. It was quality family time that I needed. Time to decompress, time to think about what was really important to me.

Some good old-fashioned family time.

THIRTY-SIX

By 4 p.m. on Christmas Day I was ready to fire myself into the white-hot heart of the sun. Mum was crying that no one would like her cooking – the same Christmas meal she cooked every year, which we invariably wolfed with swelling bellies for Christmas Day and the days after – Dad was tipsy in front of the Christmas tree, shouting out instructions to the board game Kat, Esther, Ethan and William were scrapping over. He may only have been little, but William already seemed to know that cunning and physical strength were what won a board game in the Lewis household. Ava was trying to calm everything, bouncing gently between kitchen and living room to try and rescue everyone. And everything felt like it had a Jack-shaped hole in.

I needed to escape, the unforgivable Christmas Day sin. But I figured, if ever there was a single year in my life where I might get away with doing that, it was probably this one. I couldn't face telling them, though, and the endless discussion and comforting and boxing up of food that would entail. Instead, I grabbed a Christmas card, bent it backwards, and wrote on the blank side, *Just going back to the flat for a bit, see you later xxx*. I tucked the card against the front door handle and pulled my coat, scarf, and hat from the pegs; then I was out the door and away.

The walk took less than an hour; the streets were almost deserted. It was turning dark, too late for families to be taking a Christmas stroll, so I walked in silence. I'd never seen London like this before. It felt like it was just for me. Even walking up our road made me feel better, and by the time I had the key in the lock, I realised that this was where I really wanted to be. At home, with peace and quiet: safe, warm, comfortable.

Opening the main door I could smell turkey – ah, lucky Upstairs Jan. But when I opened our front door, the smell was even stronger. Stepping in, I saw a single tray rotating in the microwave, and a single cardboard wrapper on the counter top. 'Luxury Individual Turkey Dinner'. I heard the toilet flush in our bathroom, saw Jack's slippers kicked beneath the coffee table, and realised who the dinner was for.

Without even thinking, I leapt behind the armchair in the corner of the room and crouched down. I'd wait here until he left the room again, or the flat, or went to bed. I didn't want him to know that I knew he was here, on his own. I heard him walk closer, hesitate, then continue on into the kitchen. The microwave pinged, he popped the door, then I heard him open the cutlery drawer, fish about, and bring it all back to the sofa.

'I've got two forks, if you want some.'

I jumped. Then slowly stood up from my back-breaking crouch, as casually as I could.

'Oh! Hi, Jack! Hey. Just. . .'

'Come and sit down.'

I did. He passed me a fork, and I took a mouthful of turkey, dark with gravy. 'How did you know I was there?' He reached up with his fork and tapped my antlers. 'Dammit.'

316

Jack got up and brought back a bag of bread, and we made dripping sandwiches and ate in silence for a while. 'What are you doing here?'

'I was about to ask you the same thing.'

'I just. . . You know I love my family, but I just. . . wanted to be here, I suppose. This is my home. Was my home.'

'It's still your home, Zo.'

'Not for long, though.' We ate in silence for a while. 'So what's your story?'

He shrugged. 'I never planned to go. I just didn't want you feeling sorry for me. I've always been curious to know what it's like to spend Christmas alone—'

'Oh, so you *are* Tiny Tim. Well, I've ruined that for you now.'

'Nah, it's actually been pretty shit.'

'Yeah. I can imagine.'

'Still. Christmas Day's not over yet. Baileys?'

'Don't mind if I do.'

He filled two glasses with ice then sloshed in the Baileys. We found a deck of cards in the drawer of the coffee table, and started up a game of Cheat. When the Baileys ran out, we switched to the sloe gin Kat had given me, that I'd known better than to leave unsupervised in a house with my family.

At some point, I got a text from Ava. *You ok? We calmed Mum down and she just wants to check you're not in a ditch somewhere. Love you sis xxxxxx*

I wrote back, surprised at how long it took me to type, suddenly, and how sneakily those letters were leaping about. *All fine, at the flat, Jack here too, safe and sound, see you soon, love you tooo xxxxx*

She sent me seventeen smiley faces in reply. I'd deal with that another time.

Right now, Jack was suggesting Monopoly. I laughed and said, 'How about Charades instead?' That led to us trying to make eggnog – five different versions, at least – then we were making tinsel headdresses, then we were telling cracker jokes. And then we were kissing.

It felt so different from the kiss in the summer. There was no holding back. There was no confusion. We kissed in the lounge, then in the doorway to our bedroom, then we gave up and kissed on the floor of the doorway, unbuttoning and unzipping and laughing and kissing again. It felt like every Christmas present I'd ever received, rolled into one and topped with a giant shiny bow. As I flung my bra away over one shoulder, Jack looked up at me and said, 'What would Father Christmas think?' before I stopped his mouth with a kiss and we didn't do much talking after that.

Seven a.m., and my mouth was dry. We were in bed; it was so warm, Jack's hand safe on my back, my feet pressed against his. My head was throbbing, but I didn't regret last night. It was good. Better than good. A final Christmas present to each other. That was the best way to think of it, wasn't it? But I didn't know if I could look Jack in the eye and tell him that. I didn't know how to say any of what I was feeling right now. I slid out of bed, trying not to wake Jack.

He looked so right, lying there. In my bed. In our bed. But the situation was what it was. Our paperwork was written up, my new job contract was signed, my plane ticket was waiting for me. I'd made my choices, and all I could do now was stick to them. We'd spent this year trying not to completely destroy one another and, for both of our sakes, I couldn't stay in this marriage, however I felt about him. I'd hurt him so much. Even if I'd finally had my relationship demons exorcised by my magical sister, it was time to set Jack free so he could start something good, something new, with someone else. Me leaving, with no fuss, no tears, just this good memory between us, felt like the best gift I could give him.

In the living room, I pulled my clothes on, then my hat, scarf and coat, and slipped out of the door.

The walk back to my parents' was miserable. Dawn-rising children were everywhere, playing with their new toys, while my pounding head was thumping harder and harder with each step. Terrible. I also knew I'd have to deal with Mum and Dad, which was even worse.

Kat, wrapped in Mum's fluffy purple dressing gown, let me in, gleefully hissing, 'You are in *so much trouble*.' I took the long walk to Mum's kitchen, where she was standing with a cup of tea in her hand, and a deep frown on her face.

But when she saw me, her face lit up. 'Ah, Zoe, you are back! My dear daughter, how was your Christmas Day with your husband? Your first one!'

I looked at Ava, who mouthed *Sorry* over Mum's shoulder. 'I don't. . .'

'Your father and I are just sorry we didn't think about this already – of course you would want to spend it with Jack, just the two of you. But you should have said! Of course we would not have minded that, after this year you have had, you would want to be together. Your father and I were the same, of course, when we first got married, we could not stop—'

'MUM!' Kat yelled. I winced and clutched my head.

'Mum, he's not my husband.'

'Silly girl, of course he is.'

'No, I mean, yes, he's my husband, but that wasn't why I went.'

'What are you talking about?'

'I didn't know he was going to be at the flat when I went there.'

319

'So you are not calling off all this ridiculous divorce nonsense?'

'Mum! I thought you supported the divorce!' I noticed too late Ava's wide eyes and Esther's frantic neck-slashing stop-now-and-save-yourself actions behind Mum. 'No. I don't know, Mum. I don't know what we're doing. I've got my new job, I'm leaving the country, and. . . and. . .' I burst into tears. I'd thought all my crying was done, but the combination of my hangover, Mum's misunderstanding that we were back together again – and how happy that misconception had made her – and my own confused feelings dissolved me into a teenager again, Mum on one side, Dad, coming down from upstairs, on the other. They stood with me like that for a long time, until my crying slowed and Dad said he'd best put the kettle on for another pot for us all.

Eventually, I was tucked up on the sofa under one of Mum's heavy blue blankets, and brought tea, Christmas pudding and a turkey sandwich like I was a sickly child. Ava came down and put on *The Sound of Music*. It was lovely. This was a hangover cure that should somehow be patented: copious weeping, hugs from my parents, the von Trapps and all the Christmas food you could imagine (and then a bit more, in case Mum suspected you weren't enjoying her cooking). But by the evening I knew that, soon, I had to face up to what I had to do.

Nothing had changed. Our Christmas Day had been great – maybe it was even my favourite Christmas Day, if you were still allowed to rank them at the age of thirty – but that couldn't wipe away the year we'd had. It couldn't undo our decision. We had to keep going forwards. Marriage hadn't worked for us, and although that fact might keep on breaking my heart until I died in my sleep in my nineties, it couldn't change the truth of it.

And my heart was still breaking, even under all the layers of turkey and cold roast potatoes and ginger jam roll and cheese and mince pies. It was breaking into pieces, until I was amazed the shards of it weren't poking through my skin.

Two days later, Dad sat next to me and, as gently as he could, reminded me that our flat would have tenants in a few days, and unless I wanted to lose everything in there, I'd probably need to do a bit of packing. 'It won't hurt you to get sorted, ready for Germany, too, love. You can give me a call when you're ready, and I'll come and give you a lift back here with everything.' I wasn't ready to face Jack, I didn't imagine I'd ever be, but he was due to fly out in only a few days and I knew I had to see him before he went, that both of us would need to sort through our things, divide them up, make claims on all that furniture and kitchenware and the books and films we thought we'd share for the rest of our lives.

So I finally left the comfort of my parents' house and headed back to the flat. The buses were running again, and in front of me was the same girl from the bus to Ava's, months before. She was with someone new, who was apparently trying to get his whole arm down her top. That's what happens, I thought. You move on, and keep moving on until you find someone compatible. Maybe this was her compatible one. Maybe this was the guy she'd stay with forever. I rang the bus bell and stepped to the door, and found myself smiling at the girl. She popped her bubble gum and smiled back, before smirking at her boyfriend's attempts at accessing her bra. By the time I was outside the bus, under the bus shelter, I could see that they were arguing. Not this one either then.

No turkey smells greeted me at the flat this time. It was cold and dark. I called out, but Jack didn't reply. He wasn't on the sofa, in the kitchen, in bed, or in the bathroom. Going back into the kitchen, I noticed the worktop: a full breakfast for two, laid out, stone cold and decaying. Croissants and coffee, bacon and eggs, juice that now had a few clumps of mould floating in it, clearly left over from my Boxing Day escape. To one side lay a parcel, bearing a huge luggage label with my name on. I didn't know what else to do but open it. The gnawing pit in my stomach became a terrible, guilty abyss.

Inside was a leather photo frame, a travel frame that folded up, with two photos facing each other. On the left was the picture of my grandma that had been wrecked, but this was in perfect condition, repaired and reprinted, mounted carefully, the leather of the frame matching her sweater perfectly, just like my original frame.

On the right was a photo I'd never seen before. It was of me, at a party when I was fifteen or so, long before I knew Jack. Mum or Dad must have given him this. I was in a green jumper and dark jeans, and in an almost identical pose to Grandma's. We looked like strange twins, separated by decades and by infinitely different lives. But we both looked so happy. We looked so loved.

But all I could think of was where Jack was now – what state was he in, the meticulous Jack, to leave his home in this condition?

I called Iffy to see if he knew anything. His tone was carefully neutral.

'I haven't seen him since yesterday, Zo. He wasn't in a good way, though.'

I looked around the flat again. 'I could have guessed as much.'

He sighed. 'What happened with you two?'

'. . . Nothing.'

'Oh, nothing like at my party?' I didn't say anything. 'You didn't honestly think I wouldn't know about that, did you?

I thought you'd have sorted everything out after that, but then I saw you the next morning, and Jack got together with that *awful* Jessica. . .'

Just then, I heard the scraping of a key in the lock. 'I think – he's here, I'll call you back, Iff.' I didn't wait to hear his reply, just rushed to Jack, who looked like I felt. 'What happened to you? Are you ok? Jack, are you hurt?'

He swung his head round to look at me, and left it hanging, gently weaving back and forth. I realised he was unbelievably, uncontrollably hammered. He tried to speak, but then settled on slowly shaking his head, and pursing his lips.

'Are you hurt anywhere, Jack?' I was speaking loudly and slowly, scared and angry and heartbroken to see him like this.

He squinted and gave me an A-ok sign, missing his thumb with his forefinger a few times before using the other hand to bring them together.

'Ok. Ok, let's get you into bed.' He slowly smirked at me, before blinking hard at the new action of his face. I got closer and smelled him. 'No, new plan, shower first. Come on.'

I took his arm and drew him into the bathroom, where I peeled off his clothes, gagging, and ran the shower. It was worse than the time I'd left fruit in the glove box of Dad's car one summer, and our old dog Sandy had eaten the subsequent maggots and been sick on baby Kat. I helped him step under the water, then I washed him, hair and face and body, wrapped him in my dressing gown and took him to bed.

By the time I'd got back from the kitchen with Lucozade, a banana and crisps, he was fast asleep, but I woke him to drink some water and take two paracetamol. Then I sat on the sofa, texted Iffy to let him know Jack was still alive, and waited to check whether that was actually true.

*   *   *

At 11 p.m. I heard a croaky voice calling my name. Jack was trying to sit up in bed, so I put pillows behind him and passed him the Lucozade. He drank thirstily, stopped, then took a few more sips. He was certainly more sober now, but he didn't seem any more able to communicate than before. He stared at the bottle in his hands.

'You feeling better?'

He hesitated a minute, gave a tiny shrug, and nodded.

'What happened?' I said, and he finally looked at me.

'What happened?' His voice had almost entirely disappeared, but I could still hear the pain in it. 'Are you seriously asking me that?' He swallowed, painfully.

'I mean, what happened to you these last few days? When I saw the flat and realised you hadn't been here, I was worried sick.'

Silence.

'You don't have to tell me. Sorry. You don't owe me anything. But I was worried. Jesus, I thought you'd vanished, Jack—'

He laughed, a harsh bark. '*I* vanished? I wake up after the best Christmas night I've ever had, and don't even get a goodbye from you? I waited for hours for you to come back. I thought you'd just gone out for some milk. Then I thought you'd just nipped to your parents'. By the end of the day, I was going to text you, but then it finally clicked. . . you weren't planning on coming back.' His voice was just a flat hiss. 'But *I'm* the one in trouble for vanishing? Why do you keep doing this? What do you think is going to happen here?'

'I'm really sorry. Jack. Please look at me.' I took his hand, but he gently pushed it away.

'No. Aren't you getting *tired* of this routine yet?' He folded himself further into the bed, tucking his hands away. His face looked grey again. 'How much do we need to keep *hurting* each other, Zo?'

'Jack. Please. I've fucked all this up so much. Please . . .' I couldn't say it. He didn't look at me. 'Please let me say sorry to you. You might not want to hear it now, but maybe one day you'll understand how sorry I am. I thought I was doing the right thing, for you, for both of us. Please, Jack.'

He shook his head slowly and turned over in bed. 'Just leave me alone. You really need to go now.'

So I did. I left him a note, saying I'd be back to pack all my stuff up before the tenants moved in, that he could take what he wanted, then I took the bus back to Mum and Dad's. And that was that.

I stayed on the sofa for another couple of days, sleeping there under a duvet Kat had brought down for me, not talking, not washing, not eating. On the morning of New Year's Eve, Mum finally got me to have a shower, then gave me her big purple dressing gown and tucked me into my own bed, pulling the Strawberry Shortcake duvet cover up over my stomach. She sat down beside me, on the edge of the bed, and took my hand.

'Zoe, there is something I must say to you.'

I pulled the duvet up higher, over my chest, up to my shoulders, squinting against the sun coming through the windows. 'Please can we do it another time? I'm just so exhausted.'

'No, Zoe, you must listen to me now.'

'Mum, I know you're disappointed about the divorce. I know that I've let you down, that you didn't want me to end up like this.'

Mum grabbed my other hand too, holding both, and shook them, hard. But her voice was gentle. 'My darling girl. I have loved you since the very moment I set eyes on you, when you were passed to me in that hospital room. In that moment, with just the two of us, you were the most beautiful, the most strong, the most smart girl I had ever seen, and I knew what greatness you had ahead of you. When you introduced us to Jack, I was so happy; someone to make my Zoe as happy as she deserved. I saw you, the two of you together – because he made you so happy, he made your father and me happy too. We loved him. But we loved him because you did. And when you told us that the two of you were getting divorced, I thought, I do not understand it. But that's ok. I do not need to. Because what matters is that you have the happiness you deserve, however that may be. I don't care if you have a hundred husbands or no husbands. You could join a convent, or be like – what is her name? With all of the husbands?'

'Elizabeth Taylor.'

'Yes, *puh*! Elizabeth Taylor. You could be like her and it would not matter to us one little bit, do you understand? What has always, always, always been important to us is that you are happy. Sometimes you will be happy on your own, and sometimes you will be blessed enough to find someone to share your happiness with.'

'But, Mum—'

'No, my girl, listen to your mother. If you really do not want to be with Jack' – she mimed throwing something over her shoulder – 'it is no problem. And you might find someone to be with for the rest of your life, someone who makes your life better, and who makes you better, or you might not. And if you don't, my darling, smart, strong, beautiful girl, if you don't, it will be ok, because you *are* a smart, strong, beautiful girl. The *most* smart, strong, beautiful girl. And if you spend your life only with yourself, you will live the most amazing life the world has ever seen. You need to know this. Do you understand me?'

And I did, even if I wasn't sure it was true, but I couldn't answer because I was crying so hard and she was hugging so tight, and I wondered if anything would be any different if Mum had said that before we'd got to the wedding.

Dad came in with three cups of tea and a plate of biscuits, and he sat on the bed with us, and Mum took turns telling me stories about their life together, to make me laugh. How they'd met; how Grandma had taken against Dad immediately, but had eventually come to call him her second son; how they'd moved in together, scandalising everyone, and decided to have children; what we were like as babies, as young kids; how they'd coped with family life, with each other. We laughed and laughed, and I had hiccups from laughing and crying, and sometimes I'd laugh so hard I'd be crying again, properly, but Mum or Dad or both would put an arm around me and I'd feel better. Then eventually I felt really calm, almost sleepy, and they kissed me and put the duvet back over me and went back to the kitchen. I wished I could stay here forever, thinking about what they'd faced, and how they'd done it together.

I thought about what Mum said, too. About how maybe I'd meet someone who would make me happy, who would make me a better person. Someone I would want to be with for the rest of my life.

I thought of someone who wouldn't do my laundry. Who wouldn't always see my friends. Who sabotaged my favourite handbag. I thought of someone who made me laugh. Who knew me inside and out. Who always saw the best in me. Who would always support me. And who I always wanted to support. Who I could always make laugh. Who I got, even when he baffled me. I thought about the rest of my life, and I thought about who I wanted to share it with.

I looked at the clock radio on my bedside table, still covered with scratch-and-sniff stickers from twenty years before.

And I realised that it was time for me to go.

327

THIRTY-SEVEN

Dad took one look at me when I came downstairs, and said, 'Car, love?'

Mum looked at me too. 'Jack's flying out today? Sandwich?' I nodded at all three questions, and in an impossibly short amount of time, Mum was at the front door with a tinfoil-wrapped chicken sandwich, while Dad gave a short toot on the horn outside. Mum kissed me. 'Good luck, my lovely girl.'

In the car, Dad and I didn't speak. He drove faster than I've ever seen him go, heading straight through ambers and even, once, not letting someone out from a junction. When we reached the flat, I kissed him on the cheek. 'Thanks, Dad.'

'No problem, love. Good luck. Give him a hug from us.'

I ran in the front door, pulse pounding, but the flat was empty – really empty, like when a heart has stopped and the spirit has left the body. Jack's stuff had gone, either off to the airport or packaged up in brown parcels, neatly labelled in one corner, behind the door. On the mirror was a spare print-out of Jack's tickets; he was due to take off within a couple of hours.

Right, airport it is, I said to myself, heading to the door to try and flag down Dad before he disappeared. I was just locking up, my hands shaking with adrenaline, when Upstairs Jan came out. I hurried faster, desperate not to get caught today.

'Hi Zoe! I've been meaning to ask —'

'Hey, I'm sorry about the noise, but I've got to run.'

'No no, it's not that,' she started.

'Ok, shall we grab a coffee and talk another time? It's just that I've got to catch someone.'

There was a momentary pause while we both heard my offer echoing down the years of no coffees, all the times I'd never wanted to talk to her.

'Um, no, that's – it's just—'

'I'm really sorry, I do have to go though, is it alright if we do this later?' I started backing away from her. I had to find Dad.

'It was only that I wanted to say I'm glad your bag is ok.' She indicated my bag, looped across my chest.

I stopped altogether. This might be the strangest small talk I'd ever been offered.

'My. . . bag?' I clutched it to me.

She nodded, embarrassed.

'We weren't watching you, or anything – we were just having dinner – but you'd come in quite late, and you were a little. . . well, we could hear you were a bit tipsy, and we looked out the window and you were in the garden, trying to smoke a cigarette in the rain or something, and you just dropped your lovely bag on the grass and went back inside. We tried to knock to let you know, but you didn't answer. . .'

'What?'

'When we knocked. I was a bit worried, but then we heard Jack get back later, and I thought if you needed anything, he'd be there. . .'

'*I* dropped my bag?'

'Yeah, I was banging on the window—'

'But it was definitely me?'

She gave me a look that said, *Yeah, I'm pretty sure I don't see too many drunken women falling over in your back garden*, before she remembered to swallow it. 'Definitely you.'

'And Jack wasn't out there?'

'He didn't get back until much later. Hours later, I reckon. Your poor bag just sat out there in the rain.'

'Oh god.'

'Did I. . . Was that not the right thing to say? Anyway, I'm glad it was ok. I kept meaning to ask, but you know what it's like, everyone's always rushing in and out. . .'

'Oh god. I've – shit, I really do have to go. Thank you! Really, thank you!'

I slammed out of the building before she could react and raced up the hill, running, running, lungs bursting. Up the hill to Dad's turn-off, where I could see him waiting, indicators blinking, back to his thoughtful, generous, three-miles-below-the-speed-limit driving, thank god. I thought for a moment I might have given him a heart attack when I slammed into the side of the car as he began to turn, but he just wound down the window and said, 'Airport?'

I jumped in and off he drove, back up to exactly the speed limit, the fastest he'd ever gone. Dad looked at my shaking hands, and said, 'Maybe it's time for that chicken sandwich now, eh, love?' It had got slightly squashed in my pocket, but we split it and ate in silence on the journey.

When we were nearly there, backed up in holiday airport traffic, I remembered something. 'Dad. On our wedding day, you said to me that I should get married, even if it seemed like the hard thing to do.'

Dad nearly stopped the car. 'I did no such thing!'

'We were in the pub? I was panicking on the way to the register office?'

He took his eyes away from the road to look at me for a moment, amazed. 'No, love. I said that you had to do what was right, even if you thought it was the hard thing to do.'

'What?'

'Zoe, I could see you were struggling with the idea. Your sister was completely different on her wedding day. I just wanted you to know that you could stop the whole thing, if you'd wanted to, and even if it seemed hard, we'd have been there for you. I just didn't want you to feel I was trying to push you one way or the other – particularly since your mum and I had got married a few months before.' He reached over and patted my hand.

I was stunned. He had understood. And he hadn't been telling me I should go through with it. If only I'd known.

Eventually, ten minutes before Jack's plane was due to take off, Dad pulled up in the drop-off zone and said, 'That was exciting, wasn't it, love? Now, off you go. Take some money for your journey home.' He pressed a folded ten-pound note into my hand.

I hadn't even considered the journey home. I couldn't. Not yet.

Inside the airport, there were people and luggage and trolleys everywhere – familiar chaos. Everything was chaos at an airport, and even more so today, on New Year's Eve, everyone rushing to get to where they could start their fresh new year. The optimistic part of me couldn't help thinking that planes were late all the time – he might still be on the ground! I could get through boarding somehow and reach him! I could do this. I could find him. It didn't *have* to be too late. My heart swelling with joy, I started running again, racing to the departure boards, sweating, shaking, and scanning back and forth across the times for Jack's plane. I looked, took a deep breath, and looked again. His plane was taking off in the next five minutes, and I suddenly realised that I wouldn't even make it to the security line in that time. I stared at the boards for at least another five minutes, as if that would make the departing plane de-board everyone and send them rushing back to the check-in desks. I scrubbed my face with my hands, hard, took another deep breath, and wondered what the hell I was going to do with myself.

I'd have to face the flat, bare of Jack. And I'd have to face living without him, forever, constantly replaying the last year over and over in my head, wondering what I could have done differently.

After a long time of staring with desolation at the departure boards, I heard my mother's voice in my head: *First things first. Food. Then thinking.*

At the burrito counter, the server winced a little as she looked at me – I hadn't thought what I'd looked like, having had no time to clean myself up after my crying jag back at my parents' house – but grabbed a soft tortilla. 'One with everything?' she said, and I nearly started weeping again. I didn't feel one with everything at all. I felt like I was the crumbling core of disaster, everything disappearing away from me only to hurtle back just to knock me down.

Instead I nodded, swallowed the sob, followed her round to the till point, paid, and grabbed my burrito and tortilla chips, ready to take any spare seat still left in the busy airport.

I scanned the chairs. There was one seat free.

I felt my mouth twitch. In this whole restaurant, in this whole airport, in this whole town, in this whole world, there was only one seat for me. I headed over, my mouth twitching harder. I put my food down at the table, pulled out the chair, and sat down.

'Excuse me. May I sit here?'

The man next to me looked up. He smiled. 'Did you follow me here?'

'I tried.'

'Did you do the dramatic chase to the airport?'

'Yup.'

'And when did you realise I'd decided not to get on the plane?'

I took a big bite of burrito and beamed at Jack.

'About now?'

He pulled the burrito from my hands and lifted me onto his lap.

'If you swallow that burrito, do you think we might kiss?'

'I think. . .' I paused to swallow, one finger in the air. 'I think I'd like that.' I wiped my mouth.

After a long, long time, I moved back to my chair, and kept going on my now-cold burrito.

'This burrito is nice, but it's no. . .' I put my face close to his, so we were eye to eye, *'beef wellington and chocolate mousse.'*

Jack grinned. 'How did you know about that?'

'I like to spend my evenings going through the bins. That looked like a nice meal.'

'It smelled like one too. Pity neither of us got to eat it.'

'Why didn't you *say* something?' I asked.

'I was trying to,' Jack said, smiling. 'And why didn't you?'

'Wait, I want to ask a different question: why didn't you get on the plane?'

'Because I knew you'd come running along begging me to change my mind and stay with you,' he said, as I tried not to smile. 'Ok, fine. That was my *dream*. But I *knew* that if I didn't have you, there was no point making myself extra

333

miserable with a job I hated too. They called me five times last night about a bonus scheme for the staff. Now you know I care about bonuses, but that's not the life I want. I want to be designing, hands-on, talking to customers, not in meetings and offices and management sessions. Yes, I want to work abroad, yes, I want to live abroad – I just had a revelation that actually, this time, I didn't have to go. I didn't want to go. And definitely not without you.'

'Can I ask another question? Why did you even think I might come running along begging you to change your mind and stay with me?'

'I said it was my dream, didn't I? Besides, there were hints.'

'Like what?'

'Like. . . you referring to this year of utter nightmarish hideousness as *interesting*. That's your code word for utter nightmarish hideousness. And I realised then that if you'd found it that bad, you probably still cared about me. Just a little.'

'Ha! Is that why you suddenly stormed out? I thought you'd lost your mind.'

'I spent the entire evening at Iffy's, raving that you still had feelings for me. I think he actually medicated me just to shut me up. Oh, and that time you stood outside my door shouting to your sisters how much you still loved me. That was nice.'

'I *knew* you weren't asleep! You bloody scoundrel. I wasn't shouting, anyway. And I really did think you'd gone out.' He smiled at me and we kissed again. I could get used to this. 'I saw Upstairs Jan as I was headed here. She told me what really happened to my bag. Why didn't you set me straight and tell me that it was nothing to do with you?'

Jack blushed. 'Honestly? You didn't really give me the chance. And we were in such a bad place, and I was missing you so much, and I could see it all falling apart. . . I just wanted there to be a reason for it to be going so wrong. It seemed easier to accept that everything was going to shit because I'd done something mean to you than to believe we couldn't stop our relationship crumbling even if we wanted to. I sort of thought I'd actually done it, after a while. Plus, I liked the idea that I had a crack team of trained squirrels to do my destructive bidding.'

'Upstairs Jan told me they'd seen the whole thing. I'm not saying they couldn't have fashioned some kind of rope out of torn-up sheets and shimmied down to rescue that priceless fashion artefact – but I am saying that you should have told me. That I was so wrong.'

'Zo—'

'Wait. No. Sorry. I meant to say. . .' I took a deep breath. 'I meant to say that it was my fault. I got drunk, I left it out there, I blamed you, I didn't listen when you tried to tell me, I stayed angry. . . It was one hundred per cent my fault. And I'm really, really sorry.' I took Jack's hand. 'I'm sorry for everything. I should never have agreed to marry you.'

'I'm sorry for everything too.' Jack looked at me for a moment, smiling sadly. 'I love you, Zo.'

'I love you too, Jack.'

'Really?'

I smiled at him. 'Really.'

'As much as before we got married?'

'Really, really, really – even more. I didn't appreciate how much I loved you then.'

'I agree. We've kind of fucked this up, haven't we?'

'We sure have.' But I was smiling more. 'If you still want me, though, there are options. . .'

'Are there now?' His fallen face brightened. He began smiling too. 'Still getting a divorce?' His hand was creeping up my thigh.

'Still getting a divorce.' I leant over towards him, my hand sliding up his thigh too. 'This marriage was never going to work.'

'I think you're right,' Jack said, smiling a little more. 'If there were ever two people who should never have got hitched. . .' He beamed at me.

'But do you know what?' I kissed Jack. 'I think we're going to be very happy.'

THIRTY-EIGHT

This morning I woke up with a huge buzz, feeling so happy I thought I might pop. It was bucketing down outside, but Jack brought an umbrella to protect my killer new frock between our front door and the taxi taking us to the pub.

All our friends and family were there, everyone we needed, warming themselves beside the sparking January pub fireplaces. Liz and Adam were talking to Iffy's new boyfriend, Ava was dancing with tiny William, and Mum was forcing more food on Jack's stepmum. Kat showed us a website on her phone – apparently Chuck had gone back to California and set himself up as a motivational speaker. His 'About' page was simply a slow slideshow of the incomprehensible presentation he'd made to KSTW.

Food, done. Drinks, flowing. Music, about to be dimmed so Jack and I could make our speech. We'd ummm-ed and ahhh-ed about how to do it, but ultimately we thought that at our anniversary party, we could at least get everything cleared up in one fell swoop – although most people were baffled as to why we were having this party at all, given the year we'd had.

The DJ turned the music off. Jack and I stood up, and I tapped a glass.

There were fewer tears, shouts or questions than we'd expected when we announced our upcoming divorce and plan to remain together regardless. We both looked so happy, Mum said, why would anyone do anything but join the unusual toast. So it looked like the party was going to be fine.

Right up until the point that Jack broke the news to our guests that his company had offered him a new design role in their lead Berlin store, and he'd be coming with me – straight from the party, in fact.

Then the celebrations really kicked off.

LOVED *SUNSHINE ON A RAINY DAY?*

Then you'll love these laugh-out-loud books
by Mhairi McFarlane.

Rachel and Ben. Ben and Rachel.
It was them against the world.
Until it all fell apart...

Hilarious, heartbreaking and everything in between, you'll be
hooked from their first 'hello'.

Get the number one bestselling novel from Mhairi McFarlane now.